Collected Short Stories

Collected
Short Stories

ROSE TREMAIN

SINCLAIR-STEVENSON

First published in Great Britain in 1996
by Sinclair-Stevenson
an imprint of Reed International Books Ltd
Michelin House, 81 Fulham Road, London SW3 6RB
and Auckland, Melbourne, Singapore and Toronto

The Colonel's Daughter and Other Stories
first published by Hamish Hamilton Ltd in 1984
© 1984 by Rose Tremain

The Garden of the Villa Mollini and Other Stories
first published by Hamish Hamilton Ltd in 1987
© 1987 by Rose Tremain

Evangelista's Fan and Other Stories
first published by Sinclair-Stevenson in 1994
© 1994 by Rose Tremain

Copyright this edition © 1996 by Rose Tremain

A CIP catalogue record for this book
is available at the British Library
ISBN 1 85619 547 3

Typeset by CentraCet Ltd, Cambridge
Printed and bound in Great Britain
by Clays Ltd, St Ives plc

For the Romantic Biographer, with love

Contents

Contents

The Colonel's Daughter

It is July. In Wengen, Colonel Browne is standing in the shallow end of the swimming pool of the Hotel Alpenrose, preparing himself for the moment of immersion on a late Friday afternoon. The sun, which has shone on the pool for most of the day, is grimacing now on the corner of the mountain. In moments, even before the Colonel has swum his slow and stately six lengths, the shadow of the mountain will fall splat across the water, will fall crash across the copy of *The Day of the Tortoise* by H. E. Bates that Lady Amelia Browne is peering at on her poolside chair. Lady Amelia Browne will look up from *The Day of the Tortoise* and call to Colonel Browne: 'The sun's gone in, Duffy!' The Colonel will hear her voice in the middle of his fifth length, but will make no reply. He will swim carefully on until he has made his final turn and his sixth length is bringing him in, bringing him back as life has always brought him in and brought him back to his wife Amelia holding his bath towel. Together, then, they will walk slowly into the Hotel Alpenrose, she with her book and the suncream for her white legs, he wrapped in the towel, shivering slightly so that his big belly feels cramped, carrying his airmail edition of the *Daily Telegraph* and his size ten leather sandals.

Ah, they will think, as they run a hot bath in their pink private bathroom and see their bedroom fill and fill with the coral light of the Swiss sky. 'Ah,' Amelia will sigh, as she takes the weak brandy and soda Duffy has made for her and lets herself subside onto her left-hand twin bed. 'Ah . . .' the Colonel will bellow into his sponge, as his white whale of a

1

body displaces the steaming bathwater. 'Cracking day, eh Amelia?'

At the very moment Colonel Browne finishes dinner, at the very moment Lady Amelia Browne smiles at him with fondness and remembers for no particular reason the war wound on his upper thigh which might have killed him but for a surgeon's skill, at this precise moment a green Citroën car enters the drive of one of the most beautiful houses in Buckinghamshire. On either side of the drive, great chestnut trees are in full candleburst. Multiple minute pink blossoms are squashed by the car as it comes on, fast, sidelights two glimmerings of yellow in the quiet grey dusk. No one sees the car. Garrod, the only person who might have seen it, had he been standing at the scullery window, might have heard it had he been walking the dog, Admiral, round the garden, doesn't hear it, doesn't see it because he is laid up with sciatica and dreaming a half-drugged dream of his days in the desert in his small sparse room at the top and back of the house. So the car comes on as if in silence, as if invisible, and stops soundlessly in front of the stone porch.

Out of the car gets Charlotte, carrying a suitcase – Friday visitor come from London as so many have come on summer evenings before, during and after the flowering of the magnolia on the south wall, getting out gratefully from their cars and smelling parkland, smelling cedar and chestnut blossom and aubretia and rock roses on the stones, then opening the heavy front door as Charlotte opens it now, standing on the polished scented parquet of the hall and thinking yes, this is how it always felt to be here: the portrait of the seventh Duke of Abercorn in momentous place at the foot of the staircase, luminous white face breathing a half-smile through the crust and dust of varnish and time; the stuffed blue marlin, caught by the Colonel near Mombasa, clamped fast to the wall above the massive fireplace, robbed of its body's dance and sheen – the trophies of lineage and leisure announcing to the tired Friday traveller that here, by a gracious permission only a few of us understand, is permanence, here at Sowby Manor beats one of England's last-remaining all-too-few unsullied hearts of oak. So welcome, if indeed you were invited. Garrod has lit a fire in the sitting room, drawn the curtains, turned down the beds. Come in.

Garrod sleeps. The dog, Admiral, older by human calculation than Garrod, barks feebly on his blanket-bed in the gunroom, gets up, turns a circle, sniffing his body warmth on the faded blanket, and lies down again in the circle he has made. Charlotte stands by the Duke of Abercorn, above whom she has switched on a bar of light, hears the distant barking and sets her suitcase down. Charlotte is tall. The Duke of Abercorn stares mournfully through time at her bony shoulders and small breasts, at the grey of her eyes, pale-fringed with sandy lashes the colour of her hair that has been pulled back and up into an untidy bundle, making the face stark, a chiselled face, a whitewood face but with a line of mouth as thinly sensual as the Duke's own, a replica, it seems, more moist than his, merely pinker and half open now in expectation, in wonder at her own presence there in the hall, in the summer-night dusk . . .

Move, says her voice, begin. So she, who like St Joan is obedient to her voices, begins to move out of the hall, opening a door to a dark panelled corridor. She hears Admiral whimper. So lonely and quivering is the existence of this dog in the stone gunroom, she can imagine, as she carefully removes her shoes, its smooth wiry body tensed to the tiny sound she has made by opening the door and which floods its dog's brain with the obedient question: who?

Garrod sleeps. The dog sniffs the door, sniffs the dust on the stone in the minute dark space under the door. Charlotte walks barefoot down the corridor, remembering the dog's name is Admiral; on its expensive collar hangs a brass engraved disc: 'Admiral', Sowby Manor, Bucks. The stone flags are cold under her long feet. The house felt cold the moment she entered it. Now, outside, light seeps away, dusk becomes near-dark, the white roses on the wall are luminous. Charlotte opens the door to the gunroom and the dog springs up. The dog's feet reach almost to her breasts and she pushes it away, careful to fondle its head, to let it remember her, the Friday visitor who once came often to the Manor – long ago, before Garrod was hired, before Admiral grew old – and took the dog for walks in the beechwoods. 'Good boy Admiral, good boy . . .'

Still holding the dog's head against her leg, her hands calm, she reaches up into the gunrack, takes down the 12-bore cleaned so perfectly by Garrod since it last popped off the scattering birds in the valleys and woods of Sowby, on the heatherblown moors of Scotland, and places it on a ship's chest, this too cleaned and polished with Brasso by Garrod. She releases the head of the dog. It returns whimpering, nuzzling at her crotch and she pushes it away: 'Good boy, Admiral . . .' The cartridge drawer is heavy. Charlotte takes out two cartridges only, drops them into the twin barrels, clicks the gun shut. Admiral barks suddenly. Charlotte's heart, so calm until this second, jolts under her skinny cotton sweater. She stares at the dog and at the gun. Dog-and-gun. She has seen them from childhood. Dog-and-gun and the red hands of the men going out into the frost: 'Hurry, Charlotte, if you want a place in the Land Rover, if you want to watch the first drive . . .'

She closes the gunroom door, closes her thought of dog-and-gun. She slips silently back down the panelled corridor to the hall, where the light is still on above the Duke of Abercorn. Garrod sleeps. She has never seen Garrod. 'I was before your time,' she might say, 'and, at the same time, long after it.' She knows the room, though. A man called Hughes slept there all through her childhood. He told stories of the war, stories of missions, crack units, lads with special training, heavily decorated lads, the ones who didn't die. Then Hughes died and somebody cocksure and young and unsatisfactory came and went with an Italian name and a pungent body odour, and then it was Garrod's turn, a meticulous man, she had been told, getting on, troubled by winter colds and sciatica, but thorough. And honest. You could leave the house in Garrod's care and be sure, on return, to find everything in its place, not so much as a sheet of writing paper missing from the bureau drawer.

Garrod sleeps. Charlotte, holding the gun, climbs the back

stairs to his high landing. In the hall, near the Duke of Abercorn, the grandfather clock chimes ten. At this precise hour, in Wengen, Colonel and Lady Amelia Browne are served coffee – excellent Viennese coffee – in the comfy lounge of the Hotel Alpenrose, and the Colonel, nodding at the waitress, reaches for his cigar case. In Garrod's dream, he is lying on a stone. The sky is empty and yellowish white with colossal heat. He tries to move the stone from under him, but the stone is grafted to the small of his back. Charlotte reaches his door. She listens. She can't hear the agony of his dreams. She hears only her own breaths, like sighed warnings, turn back, leave the gun by the front door, go out into the dark and fly. Garrod wakes to night-time and sciatica pains. He turns over, grumbling, tucks his head into the pillow. Sleeps. The door opens. Out of darkness and sleep come the command, the drumroll, the moment when, from nowhere, the wild animal leaps: 'Get up. Garrod!'

At ten o'clock on this warm night, scriptwriter Franklin Doyle, born Colorado, USA, 1936, is scratching his chin, trying to save a love affair and failing. Opposite him, across a white table in his rented London flat, a woman called Margaret, sullenly, whitely beautiful, is spilling guilt-corroded truths about her body's longings for a man called Michael that squeeze and bruise the chest of Franklin Doyle so that he has to gulp for air and begin this repetitious scratching of his face to keep himself from laying his greying head on the table and wailing.

'It wasn't,' says Margaret, 'the kind of thing I wanted to happen. I didn't invite it.'

'Yes, you did,' says Doyle pathetically, 'at Ilona's party you sat at the creep's feet.'

'There weren't any chairs. Ilona never provides chairs.'

'He was sitting on a chair.'

'On a sofa.'

'On a fucking sofa. Who cares? You sat and fawned and I brought you drinks. But you know you've gone mad, don't you? You know he'll leave you, don't you?'

'He says he loves me, Franklin.'

'And you believe the asshole?'

'You don't need to call him that.'

'Yes, I *need*. For me! Have you forgotten about *me*? You're screwing my life up – and yours – for an asshole!'

'I told you, I didn't want this to happen . . .'

'Why don't you go, Margaret?'

'What?'

'Now. Just go now.'

Margaret is silent, frightened. She's used to Franklin Doyle, his flat, his fruit press, his lumpy dressing gown, his electric typewriter.

'Why now?'

Doyle puts his hands round his head and scrapes his scalp. 'For my sake.'

Margaret feels homeless, adrift, afraid of night-time and cold weather and dreams.

'Can't I go tomorrow, Franklin, when I've had time to fix something up and pack . . .?'

'I'll pack for you,' says Doyle, throwing his body up and out of the heavy designer-designed chair, hurtling it breathlessly towards his bedroom where his clothes and Margaret's, thrown together, softly litter it. He picks up at random a brown bra, a pair of high-heeled sandals, a pink sweater, a copy of *Ten Days that Shook the World* (a gift from him, unread), a jewellery box and a white nightdress and throws them into a pile on the double bed. He drags a suitcase from the top of a louvered wardrobe and begins tossing things in, scrunching and crumpling them, magazines, boots, tights, shirts, scarves, Tampax, leotards, dresses . . .

Margaret, relieved of her confession, alive to the sudden consequence of that confession, starts to sob for what she has destroyed, starts to weep and weep as her possessions go tumbling in. She feels vandalised, spoiled.

'I've nowhere to go!' she says. Doyle stops snatching her belongings, slams the suitcase lid on the stuff he has collected,

6

zips it up and hurls it at her. 'Go to the creep! Go and bawl in his lap!'

So Margaret gathers up the case, remembering item by item all the things she is leaving behind, takes her pale jacket from a peg in the hall, turns, stares at Doyle, at his clenched hands, at his mouth, opens the door of the flat, turns again, sees Doyle through her shimmer of tears, goes out onto the landing lit by a brass chandelier and closes the door behind her. Slowly, and with sorrow she never expected, she walks down the stairs.

Doyle is at the sitting-room window. He pushes back the net curtains which smell mustily of dust and city rain, waits for the sound of the front door and the white figure of Margaret creeping out with her suitcase into the London night. He feels the failure and rage of forty-seven years lift his arm and bring it crashing down onto the window. Margaret slips from view. A cascade of glass fragments hurtles two storeys onto the pavement, startling a middle-aged Bavarian sculptress walking her dachshund on a tartan lead. '*Mein Gott!*' she exclaims and gazes up. She sees the light at Doyle's window. Nothing else. She walks on.

Near dawn, which comes early on their side of the mountain, Colonel Browne half wakes and mumbles across the space between him and his wife in her twin bed: 'Funny old Admiral didn't get his share of the meat.'

Lady Amelia sits up and stares at her husband's arm which is dangling onto the carpet. 'Duffy?' she says. 'What's this about meat?'

Colonel Browne opens a yellowed eye, notices his trailing arm and withdraws it into the safety of the Swiss-laundered duvet.

'All right, Amelia?' he asks.

She has put on her bedjacket.

'I was perfectly all right until you woke me up with some nonsense about Admiral and meat.'

'Meat?' The Colonel strokes a few strands of hair into place across his head. 'Got that damned pins and needles in my hand again. Must be the birds.'

'*Birds?*'

'Vultures or something. Dream, I suppose. Must've been. You put a carcass out on the lawn and all these birds came . . .'

'This is a holiday, Duffy dear,' says Amelia gently but firmly, 'No nightmares on holiday.'

Yet at dawn, in his Camden basement, Jim Reese is dreaming his habitual nightmare which no holiday has ever obliterated since he was a Brighton schoolboy and his mother's house stank of lodgers' tobacco and frying eggs. He dreams and redreams the day his room is given away to Mr John Ripley, a North Lancashire toys and novelties rep making a summer killing on the south coast, and his boy's bed is squashed into a suffocating space no bigger nor better than a cupboard, and all his *Eagle* cutouts are torn down and his drawer of fag cards emptied for Mr Ripley to lay his handkerchiefs and his metal hip flask in.

Jim Reese wakes and stares out at pale light on the area steps. He is sweaty, uncomfortable, suffocated by the dream. All his life, since the Brighton days, he has moved on – place to place, woman to woman – and yet he has always felt contained, fenced up. John Ripley's ghost and the ghost of his mother frying eggs have gawped at his efforts to understand himself. Now he feels emptied of understanding. Emptied of the will to understand. He has a set of drums. Playing these, he feels intelligent. He soars. He knows life is for living, learning, creating. He wanted to form a band or group. He knew a singer, Keith, getting small-fry gigs but confident, with a cracked black-sounding voice like the voice of Joe Cocker. Keith was interested in the group idea for a while, till he got a US recording contract and pissed off into the big time. Now Keith sings in Vegas and Jim Reese is where he is, looking out at the area wall. The drums are silent most days. Sometimes he polishes the chrome and wood, because if things get tougher than they are, he might be forced, just to hold himself together, to sell them. Two weaknesses have blighted his life and he knows them: he cannot sell himself and he cannot get angry. It isn't that he doesn't *feel* rage. He feels it all right, souring his blood, a poison. Yet he can't express it, just as he can't express himself (only through his hands on the drums). Like his person and his will, his anger is contained, walled up, silent.

Jim Reese gets up, lights a cigarette, looks at his watch. He can hear a blackbird in the cherry trees above his window. He begins listening for a car. He returns to the bed and sits on it, still smoking, still listening. High summer, yet his body is pale – kept underneath the road where soon trucks will thunder, kept uselessly out of sight. He is thirty-seven. Far too old, says his mother's fat-spattered ghost, to be a pop star. You should have put all that out of your mind.

Time passes. He makes tea, sits and waits. Sun glints on the rail of the rusty area steps. Saturday traffic starts to rumble. He feels knotted, anxious. Charlotte. He says her name, listens to the minute echo of her name that hangs for a second in the drab room. When she is with him, he feels breathless, hot. Her intelligence suffocates him. Now, without her, he feels the same breathlessness in his fear that she's deserted him, as he's sometimes wondered if, even hoped that, she would. Yet the flat is hers and everything in it except him and his drums. In place on the desk is her typewriter and in place beside it, half finished, is her latest article, *Eve and the Weapons of Eden*. She worked on the paper all the previous day, he remembers, until seven-thirty when she came and found him sitting by the drums with a tin of chrome-cleaner and a T-shirt rag, crouched on the floor beside him and told him: 'I'll be out most of the night. I'm driving to Buckinghamshire, to collect some things. I can't say what they are. I'll show you when I get back – probably very late, towards morning.' He took up the chrome-cleaner and the rag blotchy with stain and didn't look at her as she went out, carrying a suitcase. I don't own you, he said to her when she could no longer hear him, don't imagine it.

The tea is cold. The traffic is loud. The traffic reveals to him, day after day, his own stasis. His air is blasted with the lead fumes of other people's purpose; they fart their travelling ambitions into his face. He thinks of moving, as he has always moved, on. Somewhere quieter. Wales, even. Go to a mountain and hear the silly bla of sheep. Why not? Quit the notion that you can ever make anything of the city, or the city of you. Yet it is Charlotte who holds him, balanced on the edge of being there and not being there. She stands between him and his own disappearance. She feeds him tiny grains of her own purpose in the meals she makes and a little of herself creeps inside him.

Jim Reese will wait for another twenty-seven minutes before the green Citroën is parked near the gate to the basement and he sees Charlotte come slowly down the iron steps. In these twenty-seven minutes, a brilliant yellow sun rises on Wengen, flooding the balcony of Colonel and Lady Amelia Browne's room in the Hotel Alpenrose. Lady Amelia, wearing a blue robe de chambre, slips out onto the balcony without waking the Colonel, who has returned to his muddled dreaming, and begins her breathing exercises, gasping in the champagne air, dizzying herself with the cutting breath of the mountain. Into her mind, as her thin chest rises and falls, comes a delicious flowering of appreciation for the well-ordered world spread out like a gracefully laid table before her. Even, she notices, the arrangement of geraniums on the balcony itself is scrupulously wise, colours tossed into each other, growing, spreading, hanging, each bloom excellently placed. For Amelia Browne, order in all things has been an absolutely satisfying principle of sixty-eight years. In her valuable Victorian dolls' house, given to her when she was four, the little pipe-cleaner men and women she moved from room to room never – as occurred in the dolls' houses of her friends – stood on the beds nor lay down on the kitchen floor.

Charlotte is lying on the basement bed. The traffic is roaring now. Jim Reese finds her beautiful in the early morning light, with her tired eyes. He touches her with a tenderness he often feels yet can seldom express.

'Jim,' she says, pushing away his hand, 'this is the most important day of my life.'

Jim leaves her body, snatches up the cigarette packet. He stares at the crammed suitcase she has planted in the middle of the room. The explanation, he thinks suddenly, will be worse than what she has done. Because she is grave with achievement. She sits up, pushes wisps of hair out of her eyes.

'Open the suitcase,' she says.

Jim feels cross, weary. Revelations have always disturbed and irritated him. But Charlotte's eyes are pools of red. It's as if she's tracked for days and nights across some desert, living only on her will. Her hand shakes as she fingers her hair.

'Go on . . .'

Bored, resigned, he goes to the suitcase and opens it. As the lid springs back and the case falls with a thud onto his bare feet, bruising them with its extraordinary weight, Jim curses, tips the case, extracts his feet, kneels and rubs them.

Now he looks into the case for the first time and is motionless. Charlotte's red eyes stare at his crouching back and over his shoulder.

'Jesus Christ!'

'It's for you. Some of it for my work. But most of it for you. There are other things in the car – pictures and a clock . . .'

So he begins to scoop it all out now and pile it round himself: loops of pearls, diamonds stiffly jointed into necklaces and bracelets and inset with emeralds, gold chokers and chains and pendants, a moonstone tiara, rings, earrings, jewelled paper-weights and boxes, boxes of amber and onyx and lapis lazuli, an ivory fan, silver knives, forks, spoons, silver tea spoons and napkin rings and salt cellars, silver table birds, bronze statuettes of deer and dogs and naked women with fishes, gold snuff boxes and cigarette boxes, tortoiseshell card cases and combs and brushes . . .

So he is trapped, between this weight of devastating objects at his feet and Charlotte's burning at his back.

'We'll put you on the road now. Pay agents. Find someone to replace Keith . . .'

He looks dumbly down, stirs the treasures and they clink and clack. Minute lasers of light glance off the diamonds. 'Shit,' he says.

Charlotte stands up, crosses to him, crouches down.

'Jim, it's a simple conversion.'

Conversion? When he couldn't understand her, he hated her.

'It's so obvious, so right. We convert all this artifice into life.'

'Shit,' he says again.

'It's the most perfect thing I've done.'

But Jim stands up, kicks a pearl necklace away from him like a snake and it scudders under a chest of drawers. He can't look at Charlotte with her eyes like coal, so he turns away and leans his head against the wall. I want to break her, he thinks now. I want to break her for imagining this. For her vanity. She relegates me, miniaturises me: 'His life is so pitifully small, it can be transformed, reshaped by the selling of pearls and little boxes and ornaments.' But yes, for once in my life, I want to break someone. I can feel it start. Anger. Starts in my temple, but pushes out across my shoulders and down all the length of my arms and into my hands.

'I could kill you!'

His voice is a sob, weak, vanquished. But when he senses her moving to him, he is round like a whip and facing her. She reaches out to him, but he binds her arms to her side and shakes her, shakes her till she screams and pulls away, stumbles over the suitcase and almost falls. But no, he grabs her again and his hands cut deep into her arms, so hard does he grip, because he can feel her strength, equal to his and he must keep hold, keep hold and let it mount in him, the new anger so long buried in bone marrow and trapped, but now flooding muscle and sinew, pushing and bursting till it hurtles from him and he sees it arc and fall in Charlotte's body hurtling over into the air, then falling, falling as slowly as his long cry, her head crunching the grey metal of the typewriter and all her papers crushed and scattered as the body dives to the floor and is still.

Jim Reese gazes at the ribbon of blood threading her golden hair. And breathes.

A blue ambulance light turns. Four thousand miles from the ancient, restless mother he is dreaming of, Franklin Doyle is driven to hospital covered with a red blanket. All night, blood from his flayed arm flowed onto the vinyl floor of his kitchen, where he had stumbled in search of cloths with which to bind it, and where, as he began to wrap it round with a faded jubilee tea towel, a deep unconsciousness tipped him head-first into violent and useless dreaming. He lay with his head in the cat litter tray. The cat (a London stray who lent permanence to his long sojourn in the city) came and sniffed at his nostrils, sniffed at his blood, put a probing paw into it, licked the paw, then went to her milk saucer and drank, leaving a fleck of blood in the little saucer of milk. She urinated feebly near to Doyle's hair, then wandered to the sitting room, where she went to sleep on the sofa. Mrs Annipavroni, who made a tiny income cleaning the homes of exiles like herself, found Doyle at eight thirty and rang for an ambulance. By that time, he was near to death. This would be the first time in Mrs Annipavroni's life that she could claim to have saved a life – unless you included her children, whose lives she saved in her mind many times a day.

As Doyle is received by the hospital, sunlight falls into the gunroom, where the dog, Admiral, has begun a violent barking and tearing of the door, a yowling and whimpering which express its desolate confusion. Its bladder is full. It is yowling for the damp and earth and shiny leaves of the rose beds, yowling for Garrod, jailor and deliverer.

Garrod is lying in the hall. The yellow bar of light over the Duke of Abercorn's portrait is still on, though the sun is flooding in and glimmering on the dead scales of the stuffed marlin and the post has crashed into the wire basket fitted to the inside of the letter box. It is at this moment when, if Colonel Browne were at Sowby Manor, he would be relishing a substantial breakfast and Lady Amelia toying with an insubstantial one. Then they would separate, he to his study to write letters and orders concerning the estate, she to hers, where she would spend considerable time rearranging her snuffbox collection before settling down at her bureau to 'tidy up a few odds and ends'. But the thoughts of Colonel and Lady Amelia Browne are not with Sowby. They are certainly not with Garrod, lying under the light of the Duke of Abercorn in the thick pyjamas he's had for eleven years. Their thoughts are with the Swiss morning that has broken so exquisitely, with such purity of light, on the thirteenth day of their holiday.

'Lunch at that nice high-up place with the fat owner?' says the Colonel as he dresses.

'The Glockenspiel?'

'That's it. Fancy that, do you?'

Lady Amelia has put on a lilac dress and new lilac shoes. She feels weightless, young.

'So pretty, the Glockenspiel.'

'Cold lunch at the Tannenbaum, if you prefer?'

'No, no. The Glockenspiel would be lovely, Duffy. What a heavenly day!'

So they go out – the large man and the thin, meagre-breasted woman – into the 'heavenly day', while Admiral pees in zigzags onto the gunroom floor and Garrod's doleful breaths confirm the pattern of his life: through seventy years he has rendered service and found none in return.

But Mrs Annipavroni and Jim Reese are doing the ultimate service – saving lives. Charlotte's head is bound so thickly the brilliant hair is hidden to all but Jim who mourns it, knowing it will be shaved when the head is stitched. Like Doyle, Charlotte rides to hospital under a red blanket. Like Doyle's dreams, hers are of her mother. And it is through the same hospital doors that Doyle has been wheeled only moments ago that Charlotte now travels, along the same corridor, nurses pushing, hastening, flat, bright light tingeing her palor with green, Jim Reese, a frayed tweed jacket put on over the vest he has slept in, jogging and pushing with the nurses till green swing doors open and receive Charlotte on the trolley and close on Jim, while a surgeon holds his hands up for the sterile gloves, moistens his mouth before the mask is tied round it. Jim stares at the closed doors. Only then, as Charlotte is snatched from him, does he remember the diamonds, the silver spoons, the gold and onyx boxes that still littered the floor when the ambulance men arrived to take her away.

Just before mid-day on this Saturday which is warm in the Swiss Alps, warm in Buckinghamshire and stickily hot in London, the police arrive at Charlotte's flat. The door is unlocked and they walk in: Sergeant McCluskie and Police Constable Richards. A voice growls on McCluskie's intercom. He snatches it and speaks quietly to it, like a man calming a dog: 'Delta Romeo X-Ray two five McCluskie. Arrived Flat Nine, Five Zero Ballantine Road. Er. Valuables. Liberal quantity of. Pictures and gun in Citroën car. No sign of residents, over.'

By 12.10, Charlotte's hoard has been returned to the suitcase which is wrapped in a polythene sack like a corpse and placed with the gun and the paintings in the boot of McCluskie's Granada. Delivering the treasure into the surprised hands of Camden Police HQ, McCluskie is then ordered to find Jim Reese and bring him in for questioning. McCluskie sends PC Richards to buy him a cheese sandwich from Vincente's Sandwich Shop. Vincente Fallaci is a cousin by marriage of Mrs Annipavroni, who has recently saved the life of Franklin Doyle. But such is the fine mesh of the British judicial system that this extraordinary fact entirely escapes it, and the relatedness of Julietta Annipavroni and Vincente Fallaci swims away from detection like a tiny glimmering sardine.

McCluskie and Richards drive to the hospital. Charlotte Browne is in no danger, they are told. However, the head wound is more than superficial. She is weak. She is sleeping. She cannot talk to them, and no, Mr Reese, who accompanied her in the ambulance, has not returned. Nobody can remember seeing him leave, yet he isn't there. McCluskie says he will wait and parks his heavy, muscular body on a plastic chair which creaks under his buttocks. Richards is ordered back to 50 Ballantine Road, to 'clobber' Jim Reese if and when he returns there. Meanwhile, police at Camden are sifting the diamonds, the lapis lazuli boxes, the bronze statuettes of naked women with fishes and trying to trace their origin. Meanwhile, Charlotte and Garrod and Doyle lie in pools of light and dream of their loneliness.

It's lonely, lonely utters Charlotte child to her parents on a sand-dune, to be sliced as I have been sliced with Timothy Storey's metal spade, lonely, lonely to feel the blood of my buried leg flow into the sand as Timothy Storey runs away to his Nanny in a deck chair. I call out – to you, to Timothy Storey's Nanny with her crochet, to anyone – but no one comes to the bleeding leg in its tunnel of sand, no one comes because I am no longer here, I have slithered away in my own blood and the same tide that washes away the crochet pattern inadvertently dropped by Timothy Storey's Nanny will wash away the shiny crimson puddle that was once a girl, only child of a Colonel, a girl with hair the colour of the sand which now receives her life.

Far away on the dunes, the wind clutters through the pages of Colonel Browne's *Daily Telegraph*, slaps through Lady Amelia's copy of *The Day of the Tortoise* which she is reading for the first time. Above and below and round and inside the wind, all is silence.

Garrod has turned. He lies face up to the sun. The stone in his back has turned and grown in size and weight and sits on his white chest. Heat floods his head. His head drips with the pain of the boulder flattening his heart inside the light and brittle rib casing. His heart has become a moth, beating its wings in a glass bottle. Far away where the tanks are massing, where the lads cool their skulls on their ice-blue visions of Rommel's eyes, a dog called Admiral is yowling for the battles to come, and the dead.

In slatted light, blood drips and fills, drips and fills. The body of Franklin Doyle is returning, drip by drip, from the death gathered up in the wide arms of Julietta Annipavroni and exchanged by this exile for an exile's life. Doyle is enjoying his journey back to existence. The way is littered with hope. This hope takes the form of glittering stones and flints as dazzling as jewels. He picks his way among their sharp surfaces, treading softly, walking on, on to the beat of a muddled verse twanged out by an old man whose skin has the colour and texture of rust:

> 'Fuck the Lord and screw damnation,
>   Pappy's bought a gasoline station!'

Only the hand holding his is missing, the quiet hand of a girl called Margaret with shiny eyes and a fawn summer coat. She is hiding somewhere. She refuses to come out and introduce herself to the rusty man, his father, singing his rhyme. She is waiting, out of sight. Why waiting? Doyle doesn't know. But he walks on. Happy.

Colonel Browne leads his wife onto the cool terrace of the popular mountain restaurant, the Glockenspiel.

'It's so perfect,' sighs Amelia, 'don't you think?'

All, *all* that day is singing and yodelling with joy in the heart of Amelia Browne.

'They know how to do things up here,' smiles the Colonel.

Down below, in the basement of number fifty Ballantine Road, Constable Richards, alias Delta Romeo X-Ray two four Richards, picks up scattered papers, some torn, some stained with blood, and begins to read an article entitled *Eve and the Weapons of Eden* by Charlotte Browne. Constable Richards's A-level results enable him to understand that the article is talking to him about the oppression of women and their children, born and unborn, by the militaristic souls of the descendants of Adam. Constable Richards takes out a slice of Dentyne from his heavy blue pocket and chews on this anxiously, perplexed as he follows the jumpy words, the capital letters of which keep leaping up above the line, but which begin to reveal to him patterns, looping, diving, zigzagging, the mighty capitals standing over them like irregular trees, patterns of thought for which his A-levels, his obligatory studies of Marx and Mao, his months at the Police Academy have not satisfactorily prepared him. Into the hands of women, say these orchards of words, we commend the salvation of mankind. Constable Richards bites on the Dentyne, sighs, sets the papers down, rubs his eyes.

'Frightening muck!' he whispers to himself. But one sentence lurks in his mind. He has arranged this sentence into a rectangle which looks roughly like a door with no handle:

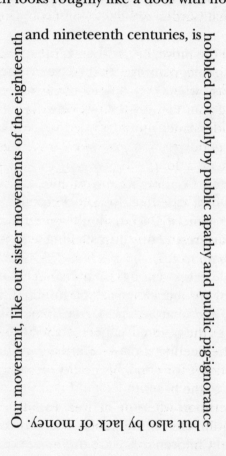

Our movement, like our sister movements of the eighteenth and nineteenth centuries, is hobbled not only by public apathy and public pig-ignorance but also by lack of money.

For several minutes he stares at the door, drawing and redrawing its lines in his head. Then he picks up the receiver of a green telephone that sits on Charlotte's desk near to her typewriter and makes an important call to Camden HQ.

Detective Inspector Pitt, CID, a smart, quiet stick of a man, offers Richards his curt congratulations.

And a clean blond waiter arrives. His hand is golden in the tableau of white cloth, crystal glass and green wine bottle that settles picturesquely into Amelia's mind. Beyond the high terrace, the sun is very hot. Blue butterflies flutter above a bank of euphorbia blooms.

'I think,' says Amelia, 'that these mountains simply must have been the original Garden of Eden. Don't you, Duffy darling?'

Jim Reese is on the move. As the train hurtles towards Brighton, he makes a simple plan for the recovery of himself. *Easy.* Everything's easy when you take control and stop the other fuckers shaping your life. Especially women. First his mother: 'I know you'll understand, Jimmy, I need the money and our Mr Ripley's a *very* good resident, so I see no alternative, now that it's a question of a long stay, to giving him your room...' Then, years later, Charlotte: conning him he could be something because of a caseful of stolen glittery shittery richness. The gall. The temerity! The dumb insensitivity! Jim Reese pummels the armrest of the British Rail seat. Strong women. How he has come to fear the smell and flesh and the souls of strong women. Never again will any woman matter to him. They will simply *be* matter: thighs, breasts, cunt. Dispensable. Uncherished. Sheer matter. And yet, perhaps not even that...

'Ticket!' snaps the train guard. Jim Reese returns to the stuffy carriage and the fleeting summer fields outside it. As he hands the guard his ticket for clipping, he decides that on arrival he will go straight to the beach.

It is late afternoon when he arrives. Families with rugs and towels and windbreaks on the pebbly sand are kindly lit by the deepening sun. Children make a bobbing and jumping line to the ice-cream van with its little jangle of Italian music. Posters advertise a costume exhibition from some TV Classic Series at the Pavilion. From the stately white houses at the east end of the front, dogs are harnessed for teatime walks by retired people in baggy clothes. Brighton. Jim stares. The sea rolls in, majestic but calm. He fills his lungs and begins to walk towards it.

The sunlight is slipping from the hall at Sowby Manor when Garrod leaves Rommel's desert at last, leaves his old comrades with their ice-cold visions of German eyes and wakes in the light of the Duke of Abercorn. He is lying with his head on the first stair. Inside his pyjamas, the pain is lessened. Slowly, tremblingly, he pulls a shaky old hand from under him and lets it knead his chest, exploring for pain and stones and weights. Under his hand, now, is his mothflutter of a heartbeat, irregular and thin. His hand sends no message of reassurance, only of confusion. His head lolls on the stair. Inside his head is, far away, the crying of an animal. He stares up. The Duke of Abercorn gazes above his head, out towards the fanlight of the front door and the tender sky beyond.

Garrod sucks his lips, removes his hand from his chest and presses it, palm down, to the cold wood floor. He pushes with this hand and arm till all the top half of his body is raised and leaning on the stair. His body feels empty and cavernous and dark. His heart flaps feebly like a bat inside this cave of flesh. He listens – to his heart, to the dog's yowling. He knows, yet cannot remember why he is alone in the house. Only the dog, perhaps, is in it somewhere, in a room too far away to find. The grandfather clock chimes six.

'M'lady,' he mumbles. Yet he knows she isn't there. He is merely inviting this cool, once beautiful woman to save him from the desert of his dreams. And there it is, about to form around him again: the terrible sun, the tanks like insects, a circling bird, higher than unimaginable height. So he fights it. He clings to the banister, holds fast to the shape and feel of the banister. The desert blurs, recedes, Garrod is panting, drenched with effort. Yet the banister is there, solid, real, a lighthouse, a mast . . . And the lifeboat is coming closer, closer. Onto the gravel of the drive bounds Detective Inspector Pitt's white Rover. Beside him, held tightly to herself by her inertia reel seatbelt is WPC Verna Willis.

'Beautiful house, Sir,' ventures WPC Willis.

'Yes,' snaps the dry Pitt.

And they come on.

Doyle is stitched, bandaged, replenished. He wakes and stares at the bottle of blood sending its drip drip of life into his arm. He does not yet know that Julietta Annipavroni saved his life, yet senses that hours ago, in a featureless darkness, it may have needed saving.

He is grateful. A young nurse is bending over him and he takes her smile into his head.

'Okay, Mr Doyle?'

The nurse has a fine, thin mouth and an olive complexion. She might belong rightfully to India or even to Italy. Doyle cannot yet say.

'My oh my!' he says. His mouth feels parched, like an old man's mouth. The nurse lifts him with ease, holds a drinking cup to his mouth. He sucks water, his head nudging the nurse's breast. He lies back on his pillow and tries a smile. The smile cracks him. He feels the need to apologise.

'Did I say anything about a gas station?' he asks.

The nurse smooths his sheet. Her arm is covered with a fluff of dark hairs.

'I didn't hear it.'

'Had a hell of a dream – 'bout my Dad. He died in '63.'

'I'm sorry.'

'Did I miss a day or anything?'

'Sorry?'

'What day is this?'

'Saturday.' And she examines the watch pinned to her starched apron. 'Six ten in the evening.'

It is then that Doyle remembers Margaret. Margaret is miles away on the other side of London, snoozing with her new lover, Michael, in her new lover's new double bed. These bodies are hot and gentle and drowsy, but down the corridor from the

21

room in which Doyle has just woken is the body of Charlotte Browne, cold and formidable under the shaven head, wide awake and angry. She plucks at her bandages. The wound burns like ice. A pink, floppy-breasted woman wearing lipstick is staring at her from the next-door bed. She smiles while readjusting the neckline of her pink nightie.

'Is there a telephone?' asks Charlotte.

'Yes,' smiles the pink woman, 'in the corridor, opposite the first of the men's wards.'

But then Charlotte remembers, she has no money, no handbag, no clothes. She opens her locker and looks inside. It's empty. Her anger with Jim Reese is infecting her wound and making her body ache.

'Was anyone here?' she asks the woman. 'A man?'

'Only the policeman. You were sleeping.'

'Policeman?'

'Yes.'

So the phone call is useless. She knows Jim has gone, gone heaven knows where, in spite of her will to give his life purpose and shape. Only her strength is left now and she senses that this has ebbed, like Samson's, with the shaving of her hair. She would like to kill Jim Reese, for the wounding, for his presumption that he could rob her of her will. She remembers triumphantly her drive in the dusk to the great manor smelling of polish and flowers; she remembers the pathetic whining of the old dog in the gunroom, then the feel and weight of the gun, the cottagey smell of the woollen balaclava with which she covered her face, and the scuttling obedience of the servile man, Garrod, going shivering before her down the cellar steps, opening the safe with the same timid hands that have worn gloves to preside at the gross and formal richness of Ascot dinners, Jubilee parties, election night suppers, standing to one side in his thick night attire, head sad and limp as her memory selects the items of greatest value and she arranges them unhurriedly in the big suitcase. She remembers her sorrow for Garrod as she sits him down on the polished parquet of the hall, gags him with a soft scarf and ropes him to the banisters with nylon sailcord. How long, she wonders, will he sit and mourn his failure to protect his employers' precious things? Before someone comes. A charwoman? A cleaning slave with a key? In her childhood, there were four living-in servants at Sowby. Time has passed. Sowby still stands, protected and protector, yet depleted. Charlotte drives fast away from it, away from the scent of catmint and childhood and trifling obedience to cruel ways. I, she says aloud as she flies down the chestnut avenue, have committed no crime. The fearful unkindnesses of genteel lives make wounds deeper than any I have inflicted. All I have done is to snatch the weapons of tomorrow – for use today. She feels then a rising in her of terrible excitement. She drives badly, blindly, fast, then she stops the car in a quiet lane, walks into the darkness and listens to the whispers of the momentous night. The past is dismembered, like a body, and inhabits only the space of a suitcase; the present is this warm, ripe darkness; the future is growing steadily in her and needs only the slow light of morning to begin.

Yet in the morning, the future changed. It was altered, as the future so very frequently is, by anger. The pink woman takes up some pink knitting. Charlotte senses that underneath the lump of bedclothes this woman is pregnant. She yawns at the terrible boredom of life's patterns. She curses the ebbing of strength. Jim Reese has beaten her, yet for what? For that drooling dog, pride? For that nameless stray, freedom? She sees his narrow white wrists on her bony shoulders, pressing her headful of understanding into his belly. Probably he loved no one, nor ever would, yet in her weakness, now, she begins to cry for the loss of him. She lies back on the clean pillows and lets her tears fall silently. The pink woman looks away. A ward sister appears at the door, unseen by Charlotte. The ward sister crosses to Charlotte's bed and, without speaking to her, draws the curtains round it. Charlotte stares at the flowery curtains and asks in a quiet voice to be left alone. The ward sister doesn't reply. She lifts Charlotte up and forward, plumps the pillows, sets her back on the plumped pillows and says coldly:

'All right, Miss Browne. A police sergeant is here. I shall now permit him to question you.'

Having woken so early on the 'heavenly day', Amelia Browne feels tired by the long walk down from the Glockenspiel. Her lilac dress is now a little crumpled and there are moist patches under her arms which she feels are 'most dreadfully common'.

'You have a swim, Duffy dear,' she says in the cool of the hotel foyer, 'I think I'm going to have a bit of a rest.'

Colonel Browne knows he can snooze pleasantly in the sun by the pool, so he changes into his bathing trunks, takes his bathing towel and his airmail copy of the *Telegraph,* leaving his wife to rest her papery body in the silence of their room.

Amelia Browne doesn't sleep, however. She lies still and examines her thoughts for the source of a minute trembling of anxiety that flutters round her stomach. She thinks of her Duffy, his heavy body on the pool lounger, his bald head shiny as a conker in the late afternoon sun. She knows Duffy is all right. His war wound has been mercifully quiet lately; there has been no recurrence, thank heavens, of the prostate trouble which threatened a year ago. He is healthy and jolly and she loves him for his health and jollity. No, it isn't Duffy causing the anxiety. So she searches. For a brief and uncomfortable space of time, she summons Charlotte to her mind. The anxiety is not lessened nor satisfied. Yet Amelia Browne feels glad that she has allowed herself, in this cool, pretty room, to confront this strange and vexing only child, to look at her as she must be now after seven years of absence and seven grim years of silence. She cannot distort or change her picture of the golden hair that scarcely darkened after childhood. She cannot believe that this has altered. But the face? The face will have aged a little, grown more severe no doubt, just as, from the little she ever hears, the life is of horrendous severity, unimaginable, alien, discomforting and cruel.

Amelia's emotional repertoire is 'not up to tragedy', as she once wittily said while eating profiteroles at Government House, Rhodesia. If it were, she might place herself in the role of Lear, more sinned against than sinning by the fierce daughter she has never allowed herself to understand. She has, of course, asked the genial Duffy several times: 'Where did we go wrong, Duffy sweet?' But the Colonel mistrusts all analysis, philosophical and psychological in particular, so cannot answer this bewildering question, except to state: 'We're not the ones who *went* wrong, Amelia. Blame the reds. Blame the Trotskyites or the Mao Tse Tungites or the heaven-knows-whatites. But don't blame us.' Yet Amelia is not comforted. Her memory returns very often to a windy day at Broadstairs – or was it Woolacombe? – when some loathsome little boy stuck a metal spade into her daughter's thigh, and the wind took the cries out to sea as she sat with Duffy in the dunes, and when they came at last to the child, the sand was crimson with her blood. She blamed the wind for taking the crying away into the ocean. She blamed the Nanny for allowing the boy to stray from her side. She did not blame herself. But now she suspects, though she doesn't mention it to Duffy, that other wounds may have been inflicted on Charlotte without her noticing them. Certainly Rhodesia seemed to wound her daughter, though nobody could understand why when it was such a paradise then. But when asking to be flown back to England, Charlotte had used peculiar words: 'I want you to release me,' she had said.

The sun nears the edge of the mountain that will extinguish it. The Colonel gets up, feeling chilly, and goes back into the hotel. Amelia Browne sleeps at last for a short while.

And on the beach at Brighton, the sun is getting lower. Canvas windbreaks are tugged up and folded away. The tops of thermoses are screwed on. Children are held and dried. Out in the deep middle distance, a well-fitted and elegant yacht makes headway in the evening offshore breeze. The captain and owner of this yacht is a ginger-haired bank manager called Owen Lasky. His wife, Jessica-Lee Lasky, is American by origin and still fond of cocktails. As Owen urges his boat towards the horizon, Jessica-Lee is hauling on ropes and thinking about manhattans.

Jim Reese is swimming. Brought up on the edge of that piece of ocean, sometime pale-limbed member of the Under Elevens Neptune Club, he swims well and strongly, enjoying the immensity of the water. Of water, of this sea, he wants to say: here is *my* element. He rolls onto his back and floats. The gentle swell is kinder to his head than any pillow or woman's breast because it moves him forward. Man breaks from the kind fluids of the womb and is dried and wrapped, tottering out his futile years on two dry legs. But the pain of those thousands of days of standing upright! The longings to lie down and be rocked by love or purpose or adulation! Earth. The wrong element. An evolutionary mistake. The root cause of all oppression and the abandonment of children in cupboard rooms smelling of damp laundry mangles and mothballs. WE ARE NOT PEOPLE OF DUST! He mouths this to the clear sky and the wind. A seagull shrieks. He sits up in the wonderful sea and it shows him the beach, grey-yellow, the white houses, the cliffs like crumbly coconut-ice. The people are not even blobs or dots. The people are not there.

So he lies back, comforted. Then he rolls over, holds the fathoms in his arms like a lover and each second the body he rides hurls him forward with its own changing shape. So begins the love affair of Jim Reese with the sea. As the sun sinks and the colours of the sun spread through the water, it grows more intense and harder to relinquish. From the stern of her husband's yacht, Jessica-Lee Lasky, holding an imaginary cocktail glass in her left hand, sees it for one piercing second: the flesh and dark head of Jim Reese embedded in the body of the ocean. She calls to Owen Lasky: 'Owen! I saw a man!' And Owen traipses to the jolting aft section of his boat and stares with his wife at the empty water. They stare and stare. Jessica-Lee Lasky forgets cocktails and starts to feel afraid. Owen pats her shoulder and says in his bank manager's voice: 'You must have imagined him, dear.' But no, Jessica-Lee feels certain that she saw him, this person holding fast to the water itself as if to a raft, and asks her husband to turn the boat round.

*

26

Detective Inspector Pitt and WPC Verna Willis have carried Garrod to a bedroom which he, yet not they, recognises as Colonel Browne's own bedroom. In this lofty bed, the old man is becoming for the second time in his life the returning war hero, the lad who showed courage and initiative, the lad who came through . . .

'Sailcord,' he says in a disdainful, tired voice, 'she tied me with sailcord. There's give in sailcord, you see, Sir.'

The ambulance has been called. WPC Willis, who did a year's nursing training before she joined the force, has taken Garrod's pulse and listened to his heart and both these manifestations of life are fluttery and feeble. She looks concerned as Pitt ploughs on with his questions.

'Did you recognise the woman?'

'No, Sir.'

'We have reason to believe the woman was Colonel Browne's daughter.'

'I never met the daughter. I came to this house in '76. She was on the television that year or the next. Some demonstration. She had red hair. But I never met her.'

'But this woman was about her age, was she?'

'I don't know, Inspector. Her face was covered. And the hair.'

'How had she got into the house?'

'Well. She walked in. There wasn't any noise.'

'So she had a key to the front door?'

'I reckon.'

'The door wasn't bolted?'

Garrod winces. Now the returning war hero remembers the unfastened safety catch on the rifle, the puncture in the spare tyre of the jeep . . . The circling bird begins its far-off turning and Garrod is silent.

'Mr Garrod? Was the front door not bolted?'

Garrod's head lolls. He whispers: 'Dunno how she could have known . . .'

'Known?'

'I've been ill, Sir. Laid up.'

'And you believe the woman knew this?'

'Or I would have remembered the door . . .'

'The bolt?'

'Yes. I would have remembered the bolt.'

Detective Inspector Pitt looks at WPC Willis, who has turned on a little green-shaded lamp in the darkening bedroom. Pitt has, in twenty-two years with the police, never felt comfortable with remorse. His look is a signal for Willis to take up the questioning.

'How long has Colonel Browne been away, Mr Garrod?'

'Oh. A fortnight. Thereabouts. They've gone for three weeks – to Switzerland.'

'And is it possible that Miss Browne was told about their holiday?'

'I don't think so. She wasn't told what they did.'

'Perhaps they go away every year at this time, do they?'

'Now abouts. Lady Amelia loves the Alps. In summer.'

And Garrod is right. Amelia Browne does love to gaze, as she gazes now, at the first stars peeping through their light years at her scented body on the hotel balcony and sense the now unseen presence of the mountains shouldering off the sky. She has dined well. At dinner, Duffy made a very un-Duffyish little speech about companionship and love, and his reassuring large presence at her side, coupled with these resonant words, have helped to quell the flutter of anxiety she had earlier struggled with. She has made no attempt, although it occurred to her to do so, to talk to Duffy about Charlotte. In spite of her protected life, Amelia Browne is like a patient birdwatcher of suffering. She detects it where others detect nothing. And in the spreading woods and rambly thickets of her husband's contented life she has often seen it, the camouflaged frail body of the bird, suffering. It has built nests in the once radiant part of him, in foliage the colour of her daughter's hair. But he isn't a wordy man. Duffy and words seem to be locked in a lifelong struggle – an iguana fighting with the Shorter Oxford English Dictionary. So he has never been able to say that Charlotte has

28

made him suffer, nor how, nor why. 'I just don't think about her, Amelia,' he once snapped into his glass of port. Then drained the glass like a bitter draught. And Amelia saw it: some cuckoobird quite alien to him, yet lodged there, and in certain seasons repetitively calling.

Now he lies in the hotel bed, reading a new book about the Falklands War and waiting for Amelia to come in off the balcony. Slightly over-fed, he is content and sleepy. He admires Amelia for admiring the stars. He is indifferent to stars. He is beginning, lazily, to wonder what gulfs of the spirit still separate him from Amelia when the telephone at his elbow jolts him into concerned wakefulness. He picks up the receiver. Amelia's face appears at the window and stares at him. From far away under the mountains, a dry English voice speaks in a tunnel of silence:

'Colonel Browne?'

'Yes.'

Amelia slips into the room. She presses a thin hand to her top lip.

'Detective Inspector Pitt, CID, here, Sir. I'm calling from Sowby.'

It is morning. Doyle has slept well. He congratulates himself on his refusal to dream about Margaret. He feels well in his new blood.

He hears nurses' voices whispering together over their dispensary trolley. He hears the words police . . . revolutionary . . . press . . . story . . . His scriptwriter's heart pauses in its pumping to let these words stream through him like plasma. He feigns sleep. The nurses' hands continue to measure out pills in little beakers. But over this measuring comes the almost inaudible conversation, patchy, like the shading of a face before the features are pencilled in:

'Someone . . . hospital . . . told the newspapers . . .'

'Sister Osborne . . . night duty . . .'

'The same policeman?'

'Yes.'

'. . . in Alexandra Ward . . .'

'Yes?'

'Charlotte Browne.'

Now they are at Doyle's bed.

'Mr Doyle . . .'

He opens his eyes and smiles at the nurses.

'Sleep well, Mr Doyle?'

'Yes. I didn't dream, thank heavens.'

A thermometer is stuck into his mouth. One of the nurses examines the chart at the end of his bed, looks at Doyle, looks back at the chart. Doyle, silenced by the thermometer, wants to compliment them on the quality of the new blood they have given him. He has been replenished with curiosity.

The thermometer is taken out, held, shaken, replaced in a glass of disinfectant. Doyle awaits pills in a red beaker, but he's given none and the nurses pass away from him, still whispering.

When they leave the ward, Doyle gets out of bed and stands up. In the bed next to his, a bald man who has dreams of tap-dancing is inserting his morning teeth. Doyle walks quietly over the lino to the swing doors of his ward, then out into the wide hygienic corridor where an Indian woman is polishing the floor.

'Alexandra Ward?' he asks.

The Indian woman, with a jewel-pierced nose, is a stooped and slow person. She examines Doyle's bandaged arm, his hospital nightshirt, his hirsute legs beneath.

'Left,' she says blankly.

Doyle nods, turns left into an identical corridor. No one sees him yet. He comes to a waiting area, where plastic chairs of the kind which creaked under the pelvis of Sergeant McCluskie are lined up in two rows. To his left, now, he sees a green and white sign saying Alexandra Ward, Princess Anne Ward, Edith Cavell Ward. He has come to the women's territory.

He hears footsteps approaching the reception area. Without hesitation, he opens the swing doors to Alexandra Ward and finds himself in a shadowy room, where the patients are still sleeping.

But at the far end of the room, he recognises her – the only

30

one awake and staring at the window. He knows the name, the voice, the profile. He has even read her book, with its preposterous title, *The Salvation of Man*. The minute he sees her, he feels excitement stir, shamefaced, under the ludicrous night garment. He moves gravely towards her. She is, he summarises, one of the stars of dissent.

Still no one discovers him. The pink woman sleeps with her cherub mouth wide and her knitting folded on her feet. All the other Alexandrine women sleep, rasping through the discomforts of the short night. Only Charlotte sees him now, ridiculous in his gown, unshaven, pale and wild. She isn't afraid. Charlotte is seldom afraid. She wants to laugh. He reminds her of a younger Jack Lemmon. Any minute, she knows, he will be carried off by the day-shift nurses beginning duty.

But the day-shift nurses allotted to Alexandra Ward are busy elsewhere. Burn victims of a tenement fire are being wheeled, screaming, into the hospital. Nurses are running, surgeons are hauled from sleep, lights are going on in anterooms and operating rooms, vents hiss and blow, in the sluice rooms water gushes. And so it is because of a fire, in which two people will have died, because of Sergeant McCluskie's need to open his bowels after his dreary, caffeinated night, that Franklin Doyle is able to walk out of his ward and into Charlotte's ward and sit on her bed for four minutes before McCluskie returns, sees him and hauls him away.

'You're Charlotte Browne . . .' he whispers lamely.

She nods, lazily. In this one, unfrightened gesture, she has accepted the stranger on her bed.

'Franklin Doyle,' he states hurriedly, 'scriptwriter, filmmaker, bum . . .'

She smiles. In the grey light, she is superb.

'I dare say that policeman will remove you.'

Doyle ignores this, hurries on: 'Why are the press interested this time?'

'Are they?'

'I heard the press are here.'

'They may be. They're always interested.'

31

'What have you done, Charlotte?'

'Something. So I'll do a stretch this time. Long.'

'Want to tell it to someone who gets it right?'

'To a bum?'

'Sure. Who better?'

'Then you find Jim Reese for me.'

'Jim Reese.'

'He might be in Brighton. Look there first. He's a drummer, or was. Thirty-seven. Dark. Very thin. Wearing a vest probably. I expect there's a warrant out. Try to find him first.'

'Okay. Sure . . . I . . . who is he to you?'

'No one any more. But if you find him, tell him love is probably stronger than springs.'

'*Springs?*'

'Yes.'

'Spring as in the season?'

'No. As in a coil of wire.'

'With what significance?'

'Just tell him – if you find him. And then,' she looks away from him at the day beginning at the window and yawns, 'you can tell everyone else the story, I suppose: I stole, but I stole nothing of true value. The true value of what I stole would have appeared in the currency I was going to convert it to. The owners of these so-called valuables are my parents. Neither of these people, my parents, have *ever* offered anything of themselves for the good of anyone but themselves. Even now, their selfishness is intact, so I've taken nothing from them. I carried a gun – my father's, used to kill game for sport – but I wounded no one. Only myself. My sense of obedience which I tried to extinguish long ago had refused to die utterly, until now. I think it's dead now. Yet its death wounds. Do you see? In a newly ordered world, I would be obedient to the law. I am, always have been, obedient to love. In a peaceful world, I would keep the peace.'

Charlotte pauses, looks away from Doyle, who is trembling.

'Do you expect to be understood?' he asks.

She smiles. The smile is gentle and sad. 'No.'

'By a few?'

'Do *you* understand?'

'Why did you need the gun? If it was your parents' house . . .?'

'There's a servant there. He wasn't harmed. He has the key to the safe.'

'And your headwound?'

'Nothing. I fell down some basement steps.'

'Did the servant try to defend the house?'

'No.'

'Did you act entirely by yourself?'

'Oh yes.'

'Jim Reese wasn't part of it?'

Charlotte turns away again and stares at the cracks of light in the blinds. The day will be hot again. A heatwave is coming. As Charlotte, child, she climbs to the orchard at Sowby. The ancient gardener with his black-creased hands lifts her high into a plum tree. The plum she chooses with her chubby hand is half eaten away by wasps.

'What organisation are you working for now, Charlotte?'

'Many.'

'Is Jim Reese part of an organisation?'

'No.'

'Jim Reese is not working with you?'

'No. He needed my help. I thought he did.'

'With what? With a political set-up?'

'No. He just used me as a shroud.'

'A *what?*'

'Over his past.'

Disturbed by the voices, the pink woman has woken. She is gawping with round scared eyes at Doyle and Charlotte and pressing her buzzer that will summon a nurse. Doyle feels dismay as acute as grief at the ending of this meeting.

'Charlotte. Can I come and see you in prison?'

'You won't be allowed.'

'If I find a way?'

She smiles again, touches his hand lightly. Then, with loathing, she whispers: 'It might be ten years.'

33

'No. No one was hurt. It won't be . . .'

It takes Sergeant McCluskie and Staff Nurse Beckett less than ten seconds to cross the ward and seize Doyle by his arms. In their zeal to remove him, they forget the deep wound in his right arm, and as they lead him back to his ward it begins to bleed afresh.

In brilliant early morning sunshine, the hired car takes Colonel and Lady Amelia Browne down and down the mountain to the waiting plane. Neither has slept for long. They wear their sunglasses and sit in silence behind the Swiss chauffeur who drives with ease and politeness, trying not to jolt his passengers from side to side on the sharp corners.

As they leave the mountains and the road straightens monotonously, Amelia brings out a little scented handkerchief, blows her nose and sighs: 'What an end, Duffy.'

Duffy coughs. His military mind had planned their holiday with the precision of a campaign. To sacrifice seven and a half days of that campaign has annoyed him deeply. And all night his mind has repeated the clipped utterances of Detective Inspector Pitt. Pitt – 'whoever this damn Pitt is!' – also annoys him deeply, because he, who prides himself on his knowledge of men, has marked Pitt for a dissembler. 'You see,' he explains now to Amelia, 'the British police are utterly bamboozled in ninety per cent of British robberies, Amelia. They have no more clue as to who did what than your average orang-utang, your average Maasai warrior. Less, in fact. But in this case, Pitt *knows*.'

'Knows what, Duffy?'

'He's trying to pretend he doesn't, but he does.'

'Does what?'

'He knows who broke into Sowby. He just isn't saying.'

'Why not?'

'That's precisely it, Amelia.'

'Well, I can't see that it matters much who did it. They say they've found the paintings and the jewellery, thank goodness.'

'So why is Pitt insisting that we cut short our holiday?'

'Well, poor Garrod. They want to stop this kind of thing happening again.

'Oh don't be silly, Amelia.'

'Well, how do I know, Duffy?'

'You mean you haven't been working it out?'

'Working what out?'

'Who robbed us.'

'How could I work it out? That's the job of Pitt, or whatever he's called. And I'm not even in England.'

'I've worked it out.'

'I can't imagine how.'

'It all fits: Pitt's lying, the summons home . . .'

'What fits?'

'It was Charlotte.'

Amelia is rigid in the car. Her mouth is a little scar of puckered lines. Duffy looks away from this petrified face. Yet he feels relief. She had to know. He, not the policeman, had to be the one to tell her.

Minutes pass. The car sways on. Lush fields flank the road. Amelia blinks and blinks behind her glasses. No, she promises herself, this can't be right. Because this would be it – the ending. The ending she has feared for years, the ending like a death, the death of all hope that the child she brought up in an English paradise would come home to thank her and save her. Save her from what?

'Ohh . . .' she wails. 'Ohh, Duffy . . .'

From guilt.

From her terrible neglect.

From the useless buying of bronze statuettes.

From the language of cliché and cruelty.

From flower arrangements and servants.

From indifference.

From her proud blood . . .

'Ohh . . . Duffy . . . I simply cannot believe that . . .'

Duffy puts a wide hand out to Amelia. He feels lumpen with dread, in need of comfort himself.

'I could be wrong, old thing,' he says in a choked voice.

35

So of course, in her agony, Amelia is cross: 'Then why on earth did you even suggest it? How could you imagine Charlotte doing a thing like this? She's not a criminal!'

Duffy sighs, removes the gift of his pink hand.

'In this society,' he says slowly, 'she is.'

Death. As she leaves the hospital in the police car, Charlotte has not imagined death. To Jim Reese, she had wanted to offer a birthright. This offered birthright would, she had decided, engender a birth: a birth of self-respect, a birth of energy and purpose. In other words, a new life. Because in the basement rooms Jim Reese was sinking, fading, disappearing. In his fingers, in his knuckles, rhythms of his onetime visibility were occasionally heard. But, parted from the drums, from the absolution of his own music, he was thinning, flaking, becoming opaque. How many people, Charlotte wonders, as the police car passes the Camden Plaza showing a black and white Italian film, are obscured by their own uselessness?

She hasn't 'saved' Jim Reese. Pride and anger prevented this. She is punished for her arrogance. And he, in the flood of his male violence, has rendered her useless to the women she has worked with, worked for, when to them too she planned to offer more, on this Buckinghamshire night, than an act of daring. They will come to her in prison, she knows. In their tattered layers of clothes, some with backpacked babies, some spiky and pale in their fierce lesbian love affairs, some weathered and worn into grannies, somebody's kindly nan in a woollen hat, holding a banner while the relations sneer and gasp at her picture on the nine o'clock news . . . They will circle outside the prison gates, sparrows of women, ravens of women, women with their dreams of peace. With the gold and the silver, they would have printed leaflets, bought newspaper space, funded crèches, financed a conference. Now, nothing is left for them from Charlotte, only her presence, soon, in the massive prison and the story of her crime, falling on them, asking them to stand responsible.

Charlotte is quiet as the car stops and starts in the dense

morning traffic. She sends away her sad thoughts of women and focuses instead on the stranger at the foot of her bed, the man Doyle with his wounded arm. Laughingly, she imagines him travelling to the south coast in search of Jim Reese, wearing his hospital nightie. He has become precious to her because he, in all the questioning to come, will be her only secret.

But secret deaths are occurring. Unplanned. Unexpected. Handcuffed to WPC Beckett, Charlotte walks up the steps of the police station. At the same moment, her solicitor, Mr Charles Ogden-Nichols, locks the driver's door of his BMW and prepares to walk into a limelight he has coveted for some years. At the same moment, Garrod dies.

Garrod dies. The struggle of his hands with a tangle of nylon sailcord is not unconnected with his death. While his hands struggled, his veteran's heart made a salient in death's lines. A few hours later, the salient became a bridgehead and his life goes teeming, streaming across the bridgehead, past and fast over the no man's land of imaginary desert and tanks like mice, racing to death as if his own spirit were death's batman. In the grounds of Sowby Manor, where a young constable called Arthur Williams is walking in Lady Amelia's rose garden with Admiral, the dog pricks up its ears and lets out a peculiar whine. PC Williams jerks at its lead. Lady Amelia's roses are funnelled by bees. A nurse comes running to the straight green line which is the technological death of Garrod. His desert is at last deserted.

Within hours, news of Garrod's death reaches Camden Police Station. Charles Ogden-Nichols looks grave in the manner of an idle poet as he privately notes that the charge will now be manslaughter. Charlotte is closed like a mollusc with her thoughts of prison-death. Months. Years. Prison-cancer. Release at fifty, old, obese, corrupted, idle, finished. And for what? It was fine, of course, the night of stars, the glint of flowers as she went in, the white face of the Duke of Abercorn watching her through time . . . And the Colonel is punished, her mother is punished at last – for their hearts empty of love and their heads full of silver knives and paperweights. Yet once more, because of them, she will be locked away. As a child, it was her head they imprisoned with sighings after royalty and debutante balls; now it is her body.

Charlotte sits. They allow her to sit. Already, Ogden-Nichols is composing the stirring sonnets of her case. He smiles at her, but she looks away. He and she are given cups of tea.

And at their Brighton mooring, Owen Lasky and his wife, Jessica-Lee, clamber out of their foam rubber bunks, twitch their elasticated curtains to let in a shaft of sun and put on their tin kettle to make coffee.

Until it was dark, they turned their boat in wider and wider circles, searching for the body of the man Jessica-Lee had seen for less than a second, lying with his mouth in the waves. Owen grumbled. What a stupid waste of time, this making of circles. But Jessica-Lee would not let them go back till they were dizzy and tired with their turning in the wind and all the lights had come on in the town. Then they limped in, moored the boat, took down the sails, went to their favourite pub to forget. Owen drank beer. Jessica-Lee drank gin fizzes. That night, they had dreams of Miami.

Jim Reese saw the boat. He saw it tack and turn, tack and turn. He knew that for the second time in twenty-four hours someone was trying to save him with clumsy, futile action. He laughed aloud in the gathering dusk, the laughter and the body that housed it still strong, still riding the water like a lover. He knew that the boat wouldn't find him. Darkness and his sea would cover and conceal him.

He remembered the exploding toys of John Ripley. One was a boat. You assembled it, piece by piece, deck by deck, around a central spring. You aimed amidships with your three-inch lead-painted torpedo. The boat burst into satisfactory fragments on the hearth rug. John Ripley laughed. Mother screamed a little scream. John Ripley said, don't worry lad, the whole point is you can't break it. You put it back together and then you have another go. Easy. Doddle! Like this, around the central spring . . .

The central spring . . .? The boat tacks, turns . . . Lights come on in it. The central spring will, if you aim too often and over and over again at the area of greatest weakness . . . yes, even there on the hearth rug in front of the brittle white tubes of the gas fire . . . right there, with Mother looking on, arms folded, hip slightly jutted to one side, makeup on, smelling of Blue Grass . . . there, where all had once seemed so exceptionally safe and familiar and comforting and eternal . . . *there*, the central spring will one day snap. Yet all continues to tack, to turn, to make its habitual movement, just as if nothing had occurred. No one but you perceives that the spring is broken. You reassemble the boat. The boat is whole, deck on deck. Merely, it will no longer explode when hit. And Mother takes up the tea cosy stained by her greasy hands, pops it over the brown pot, struts out into the hall and calls John Ripley down to tea. You leave the dead toy on the hearth rug. You sit at the table and watch their mouths, runny with egg, oily with bacon. They talk and laugh and gobble and suck their tea. You want to say to them, the central spring went. You take a breath, to begin. Before any words come out, Mother reprimands you with her eyes: you have ceased to matter.

When the boat gave up its useless search and returned to harbour, the great depths of the sea began to beat like music in the ears of Jim Reese. The music invaded him, commanding his hands, his arms, his legs, his pelvis to keep time. Water streamed off his forehead and into his hair. The cold of the ocean became, with its new rhythm, a fierce heat. Never had movement been so exquisite a thing. Never in the turning multicoloured lights and the screaming dreams of Vegas had body and music been one as they were now one. And Jim Reese knew that it would last forever. The sky would fill with stars and it would go on and on. Dawn would come and daybreak and autumn and sighing and sunset, and still it would play. Because it was his. His own.

Franklin Doyle discharges himself from hospital and goes home to his flat. On the mat is a note in Margaret's handwriting. He picks it up, almost without curiosity, and takes it to his desk, where he telephones a glazier and asks for someone to come and mend his window.

Mrs Annipavroni had cleaned out the cat litter tray and scrubbed with Flash and Vim at the bloodstains on the kitchen floor. The whole flat smells of Vim. But it is tidy and quiet. Doyle re-enters it with a feeling of gratefulness. He telephones a florist and orders carnations and cornflowers to be sent to Kilburn, to Julietta Annipavroni, whose address begins: 'Staircase B'. He feels grateful, too, that his own address doesn't begin with Staircase B. He imagines the Annipavroni family lugging their Italian life up and down dark concrete steps.

Doyle pours himself fresh orange juice and sits, stroking the cat. He ignores Margaret's note on the desk. His head is crammed with half-formed plans, jostling each other for place and meaning. His wound throbs. He is sweating slightly. He has a sudden longing to sleep. He imagines Charlotte's cold strong hands holding his head and laying it gently on her shoulder. She becomes the man, he the woman, content to lie safely at her side. He sleeps and offers himself. She is aloof in her hard body. She crushes him with her indifference, but his yearnings for her only increase.

The telephone wakes him. As he walks to the desk, he knows he has dreamed of Charlotte, yet the dream has left him. All he wants to hear, as he lifts the receiver, is Charlotte's voice. He is aware, in this instant, that he has fallen in love.

Margaret sounds close, as if she were calling from an adjoining room. She's been with Michael, she says. She thought she loved Michael, yet in his room, right there in his bed, she began to remember Doyle . . .

'Oh, Margaret . . .' Doyle's voice is weary, irritated, 'please don't bug me with this kind of thing.'

'But it happened, Franklin. I wasn't consciously thinking about you and I suddenly started to miss you and regret – '

'Regret what?'

'I don't think I can leave you.'

'You've left me. You left me!'

'I know. But it's all wrong.'

Doyle sighs. He looks at his wound. Yesterday, he might have died for Margaret. Now, already, he has replaced her.

'I think I need both of you, Franklin. Can you understand this? Franklin?'

'Oh bullshit.'

'What? I can't hear you, Franklin. Did you hear what I said about needing you both?'

He says nothing. His wound aches. He must buy painkillers. Then his dream comes back to him. He lies, arms and legs spread wide, and Charlotte's body is above him, moving gently, purposefully, yet almost invisibly in near darkness. Then she lowers her head and whispers to his mouth: 'This isn't love. I'm giving you blood, that's all.'

'Franklin? Are you there?'

'Yeah.'

'I know it's difficult for you. Can I come round and talk to you?'

Doyle isn't concentrating. The pain of Charlotte in him is as acute as the pain of his unhealed arm.

'I'm sorry . . .' he mumbles.

'Can't I come round?'

'I'm sorry, Margaret. Things have happened. I'm going to have to be away for a bit.'

'I could come round now, Franklin. We need to talk.'

'No. I'm sorry.'

'Why d'you keep saying you're sorry? I'm the one – '

'Yes, I know. I'll send on the things I didn't pack for you.'

He hangs up. He knows this is cowardly. He knows she will ring back. He goes quickly to the kitchen, opens a tin of food for the cat, then grabs a clean jacket from his wardrobe and a pad from the desk. His head is clearing now. He has set the visit to Brighton aside, because he doesn't want to go in search of Charlotte's lover: he needs Charlotte herself.

As he closes the flat door, he hears the telephone begin to ring. The sound follows him down the stairs. But moments later he has escaped it. He is out in the hot day. In the street, the air is warm and rich with the smell of privet. Sun gleams on the white fronts of houses and London is transformed into a kindly city. Doyle hails a taxi. His heart races with the engine as it whisks him towards the police station where, already, the reporters have begun to gather, and crews from the BBC and London Weekend Television are setting up cameras.

News is travelling in spirals and loops. Charlotte Browne, celebrity revolutionary, is for the third time in her life under arrest. The BBC's Home Affairs Correspondent, tanned from a holiday rather far from home, prepares to pass on to the nation facts known and unknown concerning the charges. Here, procrastination by the police is impeding the swift passage of information to the public at large, a public who, within a few hours, will know that Charlotte has robbed the house of her parents and been responsible for the death of an elderly servant. Reporters and camera crews shuffle and smoke and buy cheese sandwiches from Vincente's sandwich shop and wait in sprawled groups. Passers-by, sensing life altering here in a Camden street, hang around to marvel or condemn. They are joined by Doyle, who thrusts himself forward, holding high his bandaged arm like a white flag and pleads with the nervous-seeming constable on the door to be allowed to see Charlotte. His subterfuge – that he is Charlotte's fiancé – is merely smiled upon. Up and down the country, police are looking for Jim Reese. Even the PC at the station door knows that this middle-aged American is not Jim Reese. Doyle is turned away.

And then, in an hour, the news of the tumbling ashore of the drowned body of Jim Reese comes echoing down the telephone. The fact is as yet kept hidden from Doyle and the gathered reporters. The fact is as yet kept hidden from Detective Inspector Pitt who waits at Sowby for the afternoon arrival of Colonel and Lady Amelia Browne. It is given, however, to Detective Chief Superintendent Bowden, the man who, with the facts of Charlotte's case slowly accumulating, is now 'in charge'. Bowden is a lofty, remote man, with a thin moustache and flinty eyes. Articulate and bitter, he's known as a hardliner. His favourite meal is shepherd's pie. Whenever he eats this dish, he takes pleasure in the picture that he conjures of his wife sitting down all day to grind lamb through the mincer. Bowden dislikes women. He makes love to his wife no more than six or seven times a year. Women like Charlotte he would willingly see hanged. What repulses him most about her in particular is her dignity.

So now he walks to her cell, where she and Ogden-Nichols are for the moment sitting in silence. Ogden-Nichols's long poet's face is gloomy with certainty; for all his cleverness, for all the limelight that will spill onto his carpeted office in Queen Anne Street, he knows he will fail to alter the verdict of the trial to come.

Charlotte's cell is unlocked for Bowden. He stares icily at her, sitting straight and calm on the hard bed. Ogden-Nichols stands up as he comes in. Charlotte doesn't move. Bowden gestures to Ogden-Nichols to leave the cell. Charlotte, for the very first time since she drove to Buckinghamshire, feels a tremor of fear. Ogden-Nichols senses it too. Something has happened.

Bowden knows that Ogden-Nichols is entitled to stay. He knows also that he will leave. Now, he is alone with Charlotte, face to face. She puts her hands round her knees, calming her fear with this quiet rearrangement of her physical strength. She is like the leopard or the lioness, Bowden privately decides: she is savage.

He tugs out a packet of cigarettes and offers her one. She refuses. He puts the cigarettes back in his pocket, but doesn't sit down, as she expects him to. He stands, folds his arms, clears his throat, announces: 'Mr Reese has been found drowned at Brighton.'

Charlotte looks away from him, down at her hands. The knuckles are white, transparent she thinks, showing me the bone, the miraculous interior structure of me that will not decay when the flesh is gone. I must not allow myself to imagine the body of Jim on the sand. I must put the death aside and only fill my mind with this picture of hands – mine on his living body, touching, taking, soothing, his on my face and in my hair and on my breasts and at last in their ecstasy on the skin of the drums . . .

'We have positive identification of the body, and we are assuming suicide.'

Suicide. Of course, suicide.

Well, come to me, she thinks, the women who light their communal fires on perimeter railings, the hard and gentle women with their banners and their protestations, come and absolve me of my failure and my trust in a man. So she is quiet, imagining the gathering of this precious congregation. She still stares at her hands and doesn't even move her head to look up at Bowden. He stands and waits. He unfolds his arms, puts them behind his back. I have, he thinks, enjoyed every syllable inflicted here. But he is waiting for the physical show of shock and grief. He needs these. He won't be cheated of them. 'Come on, you cunt!' he wants to yell at her. 'Start crying!'

But still he waits and waits. Far away in Charlotte's mind, the bones of hundreds of women, still fleshed out and lit with life, begin to gather in clusters.

'Poems, Duffy. Do you remember, she used to send us poems from boarding school?'

'Did she?'

'They were all about quite sentimental kinds of things, like dead baby birds.'

'Don't think I read them.'

'Yes you did, Duffy.'

'Dead birds?'

'That kind of thing. A lot of death.'

'Trouble with my daughter, she's always considered herself clever.'

They are alone now. They are home. The bar of light glows over the white forehead of the Duke of Abercorn. Duffy has poured them strong drinks. It is the hour when Garrod would have entered the sitting room quietly, either to announce dinner or carrying their television suppers on identical trays.

At Amelia's feet, Admiral is sleeping. His flank trembles and twitches in his old dog's dreaming. Amelia stares down at the dog. He is ancient, she notices suddenly, and smelly and weak. Age creeps on invisible, until one day . . .

'I'd like to die, Duffy.'

She hasn't wept. She has held herself as cold and straight as an icicle. Her behaviour has won her the admiration of Pitt and of WPC Willis, whose cups of tea Amelia has stubbornly refused. But now she is alone. The truth of what has happened enters valves and arteries and begins to surge and stream through her. She gulps whisky, as if to dilute the truths inside her. Duffy stares at her: Amelia de Palfrey, great-niece of the seventh Duke of Abercorn, and what a slim beauty once, in her white gloves, smelling of pear blossom and gardenias . . .

'Don't talk bunkum like that, Amelia.'

'Though we ought to do something about flowers.'

'What flowers?'

'For Garrod. There should be a wreath. Something to lay on.'

'Don't worry about it, old thing.'

'You'll organise it.'

'Yes.'

'And one for me?'

'We can send one, Amelia, from us both.'

'I didn't say *from* me. I said *for* me.'

She dismays him now. Amelia de Palfrey. What an ideal wife she has made him over all the years. So good at choosing and arranging and reordering; she has furnished his entire existence. A simple man, he thinks, I am at heart a simple man and Amelia has perfectly understood me. Even at Christmas, in her choice of beige cashmere, she has never erred and in her peculiar love of mountains she has lifted me up.

'I think,' he says earnestly, 'we have to put all these tragedies out of our minds, Amelia, and try to go on as before.'

She doesn't answer. Her face looks slack, flattened almost, rearranged by some brutal palm.

'Amelia?'

'They were all about death.'

'What were?'

'Her poems. The deaths of one thing or another.'

'Stop it, Amelia! Got to keep a grip.'

The dog is woken by Duffy's voice. It gets to its feet and shakes itself. 'Siddown Admiral!' Duffy snaps.

Amelia pats the dog's head. It is, perhaps, the only thing left in need of her protection. Then she lifts her head and looks out. The evening is deep blue at the window and the room is getting dark. She remembers the day the rose garden was planted and a pedestal built for the sundial. How old was Charlotte then, she wonders. Four? Five? Too small to understand the symmetry of a rose garden. The child used to scrunch the perfect blooms in her fat little hand.

The sky is darkening, too, over Camden. The reporters have gone, notebooks and spools of film replete with facts released by the woman-loathing Bowden, too late for the nine o'clock news. In the morning, the popular dailies will lead with the story, in which they have already taken sides. Editors in search of imagery will invoke serpents' teeth and thankless children, the while aware of the gulf separating their readership from a work of literature Amelia Browne had only inadequately understood. Charlotte is friendless, alone with the suicide of Jim Reese. His death binds and binds her head, like her bandage. She refuses the supper brought to her. She can't eat while the body of her lover is unburied. Yet, like her mother silently taking leave of her senses in an armchair by an unlit fire, she doesn't weep. She has seen the challenge in Bowden's eyes. She will not cry. If she is alone with the drowned limbs of Jim Reese, so too is she alone with her strength. Jim has failed her. She will not fail herself. When, near dawn, she sleeps, she dreams of Sowby. Her parents, manacled together by the handles of their tennis rackets, go wading into the lily pond like adventurous boys. Goldfish and newts nose their legs, but they stand very still at the pond's centre, holding up their skirts and trousers with their free hands.

*

Margaret has telephoned Doyle twice since he returned to the flat, hungry and excited. He has answered neither call. Into his Answerphone she has stammered out messages of her confusion.

Doyle has visited an all-hours delicatessen, bought himself sesame bread, Russian salad, Italian salami and a bottle of wine and has eaten these watching the ten o'clock news, on which the first mention of Charlotte's crime appears, well supported with photographs and information about her involvement with pacifist and feminist groups and her previous convictions.

Doyle crosses the room and catches sight of himself in a gold-framed mirror. His beard is as long as the stubble growing through on Charlotte's head, his eyes are vast and bright, his cheeks are blotchy and feverish. Round his neck is the white sling which carries his arm. The ancient mariner slung with the albatross? The comparison slips into his mind and stays there while he stares at his altered image. The weariness in his limbs, the throbbing of his wound, the astonishing clarity of his eyes: all suggest some kind of journey. His rational self, the lazy, cautious Franklin Doyle, argues for sleep and rest. But he ignores the lazy, the rational. He simply removes himself from his own sight and goes almost hurriedly to his desk, where he sits down and begins to write. In no more than a few minutes, he covers a page with a minutely perceived description of Charlotte, focusing on the heaviness of her eyes, the seeming hard strength of her body, the wide spread of her hands. But then he sits back, gulps wine, slows his breathing, forces himself to think not of Charlotte but of himself. 'Exile (Voluntary. American),' he begins, 'Finds himself at centre of case which will shock this nation (in ways particular to this nation and its class system) more than far more terrible things, i.e. deaths in Lebanon. Or so I predict. Propose – yes, I do propose – to put myself in major role (for first time in life) in historic circumstance. Ways to go about this must include a) Visit to parents, b) Visit to parents of Jim Reese, if alive, c) Visit to all groups C. has worked or is working for, d) Access to press archives, e) Seeking legal ways to gain access to C. (NB phone Bob

Mandlebaum). Eventual aim must be saleable screenplay and/
or book like Mailer and Schiller's *Executioner's Song.*'

But here he stops writing. He knows why he feels like a
traveller, pain, excitement, fear, mingling in his blood. He
knows why he will stay awake till dawn, planning, constructing,
ignoring calls on his Answerphone, disdaining sleep: he has
entered on the most perfect love affair of his life. In Charlotte,
he has found both woman and livelihood, fortuitously joined.
Charlotte Browne is not only herself, but her story. Her story
will become his. He will make the two inseparable. It doesn't
concern Franklin Doyle on this long summer night that Charlotte the woman has, by giving him this story, put herself
beyond the reach of his body. Because his body, with its
disappointments of forty-seven years, is already anointed by the
brief touch of her in the hospital bed and he will not be denied
her. She will be locked away from him, but he will remake her.
To Charlotte, prisoner, he will offer the story of Charlotte; in
Charlotte, remade as fiction, will he spend his love.

The wine is gone. Doyle goes to the kitchen, hauls out an
opened bottle of cheap retsina. With this beginning to slide
through his excited blood, he returns to his description of
Charlotte. After a while, he abandons it again, continues his
note-making, then stops suddenly and looks up. He reminds
himself that all, *all* that is now taking place is taking place
because of the interception of Julietta Annipavroni, once
beautiful Italian girl, now struggling through middle age 'saving
the lives' of those rich enough to pay her two pounds an hour.
He smiles, remembering the flowers he has sent; Julietta
Annipavroni arranges them in a vast green vase, won at a
funfair. The blue of the cornflowers reminds her of the sky
above Naples. 'Don't touch them!' she yells at her children.

Like Charlotte, prisoner, Doyle sleeps at dawn. The sun
comes up on London. The same sounds of blackbirds trilling
in cherry trees, so lately heard by Jim Reese in a basement flat,
begin in the street, but Doyle is dreaming of fame and money
and does not hear them.

Wedding Night

At the time of my father's second wedding, we lived in Paris, in a house a little grander than we could afford. It was the kind of house, in the Avenue Foch, which is today divided up very profitably and let as luxury flats. It seems astonishing to me now that our family once owned the whole of it. The drawing room, I recall, was on the first floor. Two sets of French windows led out from it onto small balconies. On these extremely pretty balconies my mother had always placed stone pots of geraniums. Well, in summer she had, I suppose. Geraniums don't survive winters, do they? It was high summer when my father got married for the second time, and I know that, by then, there weren't any geraniums on the drawing-room balconies.

I have always remembered the details of things, especially of rooms where I've lived. My brother does this too: together, we can reconstruct places, object by object. I think this gift or skill of ours is not really a gift or skill at all, but merely a habit into which, as soon as we could talk, we were obliged to fall: because our father was blind. He was blind by the time we were born and he never saw us. He saw our mother for one year of their married life, and I must say that she honestly was, at that time, one of the most beautiful women I have ever seen. Well, according to the photographs she was. We, her sons, never recognised beauty (or what I now, as a man, think of as beauty) in her. We were too young, too close to her. We loved the smell of her, especially when she wore furs, but the fact that she was a beautiful woman entirely escaped our understanding. What we did understand, however, from the moment we could read

49

and converse and were taken travelling, was the difference between our mother's background and culture and our father's background and culture. Our father was French, the son of a colonel in the French army who was in turn the son of a colonel in the French army, and so on. His side of the family won so many medals, you could start a medal shop in the rue des Saints Pères with them. Anyway, we are descended from a line of brave men. (The ribbon attached to medals is of a quality that I find very pleasing to handle: ribbed, silken and heavy. My father's hands have the feel of medal ribbon, wrinkled and silky.)

Our mother was English. She was born Emily Tregowan, the daughter of a self-educated Cornishman who made a respectable name in publishing. Though she spent almost all her married life in France, she never, I think, immersed herself in it, so that you could always perceive her Englishness sticking out like a flower too tall for the arrangement it's set in. And we, sent to an English boarding school, taken on visits to our Cornish grandfather in blustery summers, spent our childhood trying to decide what we were. At our boarding school, we were known as the Frog Twins. In Paris, neighbours referred to us as 'les gosses Anglais'. We preferred Paris to boarding school, as any boy would, but we liked the wildness of Cornwall. We knew that our father and all his ancestors had been brave, but Cornwall seemed to tell us that our mother and all hers had been wild, and we were inclined to prefer wildness to bravery. We are twins. We are now forty-two and both of us have lived, married and worked in France only. We never visit England, except occasionally on business, so time, you might say, has decided what we are: we are French. Yet our mother, and Cornwall, and what we once recognised was wild in a world of tame things have never passed out of memory and never will.

I shall describe us, not as we are now, but as we were at the time when our mother died, and our father – five years younger than she was – decided very quickly to remarry. Our mother died on a January Sunday near to our fifteenth birthday. Our English headmaster summoned us to his smoky study to unfold this colossal tiding. He stood up behind his oak desk and stared at us over his pipe: sallow, dark-haired boys with a dusting of pimples, thin hands, legs thinner than the gym master would have liked, an identical tendency to glower. We glowered, however, out of eyes the colour of scabious flowers – an extraordinary feature in us that has conquered any number of women, and which, among the traits which made up her beauty, we inherited from our mother. The rest of us is, and was already at fifteen, recognisably our father's: his thick hair, his small limbs, his yellowy complexion.

The news, I suppose, travelled round the school in delicious whispers: 'The Frog Twins' mother just died!' Boys squirmed with horror and delight. But we were snatched away and put on trains and freezing steamers till we reached Paris and the house in the Avenue Foch and our blind father fumbling round it. Nobody wept. When told of the death, my brother had started to hiccup violently and he hiccuped for three or four days, waking and sleeping. I picked my spots and knew that I wasn't ready for what had happened; death was too adult for me. And our father? He tried to bear himself like the soldier he was. But he became clumsy: he spilt food down his expensive clothes, he dropped and broke things. He also began to burble bits of poetry to himself, a thing which was absolutely uncharacteristic of him. I don't know what poetry it was that he burbled (I was more familiar, at fifteen, with Keats and Shelley and Tennyson than with Victor Hugo or Rimbaud) but I had the impression that he was muddling one poem with another and getting lots of words wrong. It was a very peculiar time: the hiccuping and the poetry and my own unreadiness for grief.

My brother, whose name I should have told you is Paul (mine is Jacques, a name I couldn't stand at the English school because even the masters nicknamed me 'Frère Jacques', just as if this wretched song was the only bit of French anyone English could be expected to understand), quite often *tried* to cry. I suppose he recognised, as I did, that we had not merely lost our mother, but the whole half of us that was Cornish and Anglo-Saxon. We remembered her stately walk in galoshes over the sandworms of Constantine Bay, her fondness for the sound of the seagulls. 'We may never see or hear another seagull,' my brother whispered one night, in search of tears that refused to come. 'Imagine poor Grandpa banging the seagull tin and remembering his dead daughter . . .' We waited anxiously for the first sob to break through. (Mourning only needs one; the others follow obediently.) But he couldn't cry. He masturbated till he fell asleep, leaving me wide awake with the images of our mother he'd successfully summoned.

Grandpa's seagull tin was one that I have never forgotten. I can see my mother sitting on the wall at the end of his garden, smiling as Grandpa came out of the house. In an old washing bowl, Grandpa collected all the bread crusts and the leftover toast and stale cake. He came and stood in the middle of the lawn and banged loudly on the bottom of the tin with a wooden spoon. He'd done this twice a week for several years. Every seagull from Padstow to Trearnon seemed to know the signal. In seconds, even before he began to scatter the bread and cake, they'd come flapping in, hungry, unafraid, noisy with their cry which, even when it's near you, conjures distant oceans and faraway voyages. My mother sat on the wall and swang her legs and shrieked at them. Grandpa yelled, 'Go on! Go on!' as they came pecking and fighting. Paul and I ran up and down flapping our arms, as impressed by Grandpa as by a conjuror. We never knew Grandpa very well. Our father told us he was a reserved and self-disciplined man. But this is how I always remember him: surrounded by the seagulls, by the chaos he had caused.

We didn't go back to our English school after the funeral. We wondered if we would be sent back at all. Nobody said what was being planned for us. Our father stayed in his room, listening to the radio. Army friends called and the wives of army friends, who sometimes took him out for walks. He had an old manservant we called Blochot (I don't know whether Blochot was his real name, or just some family invention) who did for him all the things he couldn't do for himself. He seldom sent for us or wanted to be with us. In fact, he seemed to have forgotten us. We had one or two friends in the neighbourhood and we saw more of the parents of these friends than we did of our father. We spent weekends in the country with them. We went riding in the Bois. Now and again, we'd be taken to a meal in a restaurant.

The rest of the time we were in our room at the top of the house, reading the 'dirtiest' books you could get hold of at that time: *The Thousand and One Nights,* the *Rubaiyat of Omar Khayyam,* soothing colossal, inarticulate yearnings with solitary orgasms in crumpled handkerchiefs. As my life has gone on, it has occasionally hurt me – yes, *hurt* me – that I have known so little about my brother's sexuality. He has married two vain women in quick succession and kept his life with them secret from me. I remember the months in the room at the top of the house in the Avenue Foch, when every stirring of his penis and of mine was part of our shared grief, our shared confusion, our shared existence. And I remember of course the night of our father's second wedding, the night we decided to grow up. We parted soon after that. Now we meet for dinner and our wives bicker about the price of clothes. If I dared to ask Paul about his cock, he would get up and storm out of the restaurant.

It must have been in the spring that Pierrette arrived. She was a penniless person from a bourgeois family in Bourges. She had studied philosophy at the Sorbonne. She spoke a little very bad English. She didn't seem to know what to do with her philosophy degree except teach. She came to our house on a four-month contract to coach us until the end of the school year, at which time our father would decide what to do with us – send us back to our English school or to some new school in France. Nowadays, of course, an arrangement like this would never apply. In the event of the death of a parent, a child might expect a week off school and it would then be deemed 'in his best interests' to send him back to endure the gleeful pity of his friends. We were lucky, then, I dare say. We were allowed to stay in Paris – and at home. We forgot the cold English school.

Pierrette was twenty-three. Our father at that time must have been forty-two – the age we are now. Paul and I thought the name Pierrette was terrible. We couldn't imagine that anyone with a name like Pierrette could teach us anything at all. 'We'll teach her!' my brother crowed. 'We'll just speak English and confuse her and tell her the wrong meanings of words.'

She was a neat woman, very much a woman at twenty-three and not a girl. She spoke precisely and ate tidily. Her belongings were sparse and plain. She had a white, intelligent face and wispy, rather colourless hair. Her eyes were black and small and she had a black mole on her upper lip. Her hands were also white and neat and ringless. She wore tweed skirts and plain jerseys and her winter coat was ugly and unfashionable. 'Politeness!' growled our father from the depths of his favourite armchair. 'If you boys are not polite to this woman, there will be no summer for you!' No summer? Simultaneously, our minds flew to the seagulls and our mother on the wall. Of course there would be 'no summer', whether or not we decided to be polite. Summer as we had experienced it could no longer exist.

It never occurred to us, until we saw it happen, that Pierrette would fall in love with our father, and he, supposedly, with her. We thought Pierrette was just an episode in our lives, quickly gone and forgotten, like German measles. She was unsuitable as our teacher because she knew little Latin and her maths were second rate. She adored Pascal. She rubbed our noses in the *Pensées* of Pascal. All I can remember about Pierrette's lessons is Pascal: 'Jésus dans l'ennui . . .'

Her arrival coincided more or less with Blochot's illness. Blochot had glandular fever and though he struggled on, doing chores for our father, he was weak and silent and had to be encouraged to stay in bed. We tried to take his place, helping with tie-pins and bootlaces, searching for objects lost, tuning the radio, reading out wine labels, dialling telephone numbers. But I suppose we were clumsy and idle and impatient. Our father couldn't bear the way we did things. He used to push us away and whimper with frustration. And into the gap left by Blochot's glandular fever and our adolescent incompetence slipped Pierrette. Her careful hands and her quiet voice must have begun to press like a comforting little weight on Father's sightlessness, reassuring him that life and order still existed, reminding him that only one woman had died, not the whole of womankind.

I can say this now. I am able to understand, now, how people may recover from tragedy. At fifteen, I couldn't understand. From the day when I walked into the first-floor drawing-room and saw my father reach out fumblingly for Pierrette, gathering her head in one hand and pressing her bottom towards him with the other, I understood only one thing: betrayal. I stood and stared. Pierrette saw me, but didn't pull away. Her face was pink with embarrassment and excitement. Her upper lip with its blemish of a mole was quivering out my father's Christian name, his face was puckered, searching for those quivering lips. They kissed. My father's hand hitched up Pierrette's skirt and began scrabbling for the flesh above the stocking top. Pierrette turned to see if I was still there. I ran away.

Paul said he knew how to put an end to it. We lay in bed and planned how we would tell Father that Pierrette was cross-eyed and horse-toothed and that her stocking seams were always crooked. We would also remind him of his military name and reputation, of our mother's beautiful laughter . . . As the traffic ceased and we half slept, my brother murmured, 'Perhaps there's nothing serious in it. Perhaps he'll just fuck her and she'll leave.' But I had seen the frantic hands, the searching lips; these seemed betrayal enough. 'He's got no loyalty,' I whispered, 'for all that he's a military man.'

I stole Pierrette's leatherbound edition of Pascal. I took it to the Quai St Michel and sold it. With the few francs I got for it, I bought roses and a pewter vase and lugged these to my mother's grave. In this futile action, I found some relief from my own incomprehension. Pierrette began to fret about the lost Pascal and the more she fretted the more I felt triumphant. But from this time on, we knew that something irreversible was growing between Pierrette and our father. Not caring what we thought, he'd come tapping up to the top floor where we had our so-called lessons and ask her to come down to him, 'to help me answer some letters', or to continue the mighty task he had invented for her – the re-cataloguing of his military history library. She would set us an essay to write, or some research to do and not return to us that day.

We'd tiptoe to our father's study, carrying our shoes. Pierrette and my father would be talking in whispers. We'd press our ears to the door. Very often, they seemed only to be talking about books. We'd stay hunched by the door till our feet grew numb, and they would simply talk on and on, quietly, intimately, like people who have loved each other for years.

One night, we saw Pierrette go to our father's room. We crept to his door, but all we could hear was laughter. Paul hated this. He went very white and led me away. 'I'm going to put a turd in her bed,' he announced, as we crept along the passage. I felt frightened: frightened by change which is final and irrevocable, frightened by the whiteness of my brother's face. We went to the bathroom. I sat on the bath edge and rocked to and fro to calm my fear and Paul sat on the lavatory, straining to produce the offensive offering he would stick between Pierrette's sheets. But my fear wouldn't go and Paul's bowels wouldn't move. *Status quo* . . . I repeated over and over, *status quo.*

One part of me wanted to be back at school. At least in England, in that jungle of rule and counter-rule, we would be away from what was happening. We could grieve for our mother in her own country and have no part in this hothouse betrayal. But we knew we wouldn't be sent back until the autumn. Easter came, and Pierrette went home to her family in Bourges. We cheered up. Blochot recovered and started work again. We were given money for spring clothes. Our father resumed his walks with the army wives. Pierrette was not mentioned. We were invited to an uncle's house in the Loire valley. We left Paris with relief and our father stayed behind. When we returned, Pierrette was back.

We had never done any of the things we'd planned. We'd never tried to pretend to the blind man that Pierrette had flat feet or buck teeth. I had sold her *Pensées*, but she never knew it was me. At lessons, we were sulky and uncooperative and made snobby remarks about the bourgeois of Bourges, but to our father we were polite in a cold kind of way. He didn't seem to notice any change in us.

It was an extraordinary spring in Paris. The railings outside our house were warm; the magnolia tree pushed out its showy blooms into an air of utter stillness. We strode around in our new clothes and thought of the long summer. At the end of May, we were summoned to the drawing room and told by our father that he was going to marry Pierrette. Pierrette wasn't there. He had granted us this courtesy; he knew we would require an explanation. 'Never doubt,' he said, 'my love for your mother. She was a remarkable woman and I trust that you may be so fortunate as to have inherited some of her qualities. But when you grow up and become men, you will, I hope, understand that a man of my years cannot content himself with a celibate life. It is not in a man's nature. And Pierrette and I have found in each other an affinity I never thought I would be lucky enough to feel. I may as well admit to you that, much as I admired your mother, we were never sexually compatible and our marriage was not successful from this point of view.'

Tears began to stream down Paul's face. I remembered, grimly, how hard he had tried to cry after our mother's death. I pinched his arm. I didn't think this was a moment for weakness.

'May we go now, Father?' I asked.

'Go? Aren't you going to offer me your congratulations?'

Paul made a choking sound. I tugged him towards the door. My father's head jerked up.

'Is one of you crying?'

'No,' I stammered, 'Paul's got a cold. Congratulations, Father.'

I got Paul up to our room, where he lay on the bed and sobbed and shook. I stole a bottle of brandy from Blochot's pantry, took this upstairs and tried to dribble some into Paul's runny mouth. In the end, he gulped quite a lot of brandy down,

I covered him with my eiderdown and he went to sleep, still shuddering.

We were fifteen by then, not obviously tall or strong or handsome, yet, being twins, we enjoyed attention from people which, singly, neither of us would have earned. It was as if the two of us equalled one very striking person. We are not identical, yet have a strong resemblance. At forty-two, I know that I look older than Paul. At fifteen, our experience of life had been in every way identical and neither we, nor people we met, could separate us out. And over the question of Father's marriage, we acted of course as one. We offered Pierrette glacial felicitations; we told our snobby Parisian friends that Father was marrying 'an ugly bourgeoise from Bourges'; we fuelled Blochot's sense of something done too hastily by reminding him constantly of all the years we had been 'one family', with our mother, nostrils flared as if breathing the air of the sea, in her place at the helm. We did everything we could, in fact, to wreck the coming marriage, by insinuation, by sulking, by discourtesy, and by downright lies. Yet we knew it would happen. One morning we'd wake up and that would be the day, and after it what? After it, *what?* We asked each other that question very often: what happens when it's over?

It was a July wedding, held in Paris and not in Bourges in deference to our father's blindness and Pierrette's sense of grandeur. The reception took place in the drawing room of our house. Pierrette wore a white coat and skirt and an ugly white velvet hat which made her look like a rich American child. The Bourges relations clearly envied her her new life and wondered (but did not ask) how a philosophy degree had won her a soldier. My father pinned his medals onto his dress uniform. His blind person's gestures were already the gestures of an old man, yet on that day Blochot had helped him to look resplendent and brave, which, in his way, he was.

Paul and I had been bought identical grey suits. All suits, in those days, seemed to be grey and we wore them obediently, not proudly. The buttonhole carnations we had been given we decided not to pin on. At one time, Paul had wanted to make us black armbands, but these, I calculated, would have been more shocking and insulting in their way than any of the punishments we had thought up. So I suggested instead that we simply get drunk and try to pretend that nothing mattered – life, death, blindness, war, bereavement, marriage, crooked stocking seams – nothing signified. We had seen it all.

The honeymoon was to be in a house on the Côte d'Azur, lent by some uncle or rich godfather. But our father knew he would find the reception tiring, so it was decided that he and Pierrette would take the Paris-to-Nice sleeper the following evening. The wedding night would be spent in our house.

By eight or nine, all the reception guests, there since two, had trickled away into the stifling evening. My father stood on one of the balconies, jerking his head in the direction of the sun tumbling straight down behind the Avenue de la Grande Armée, his hand clasping his new bride to him, his body in its dress uniform very straight and proud. We, lolling on sofas, slightly bilious from the quantity of champagne we had drunk, stared at their backs in silent contempt. 'It's as if,' Paul whispered, 'Mother had never existed.' Pierrette turned and stared at us, her skin blotchy with excitement and alcohol. 'I suggest,' she said, in a voice of new authority, 'that you boys get yourselves some supper and go to bed.'

Father didn't move. We were dismissed. We slipped sullenly away, carrying our jackets and ties that we had taken off. We climbed the stairs to our room. We didn't speak. What had invaded us, at precisely the same moment, was a boredom so colossal, so heavy and unyielding that neither of us could utter. Life wasn't tragic after all; it was dull. In the south of England, an old man banged a washing bowl and greedy gulls began to circle, but there was no magic in it, only boring reflex and tearing, ugly beaks. All was predictable and ignoble and stupid. The roses in the pewter vase had long ago wilted and turned brown. Some old scavenging woman with her savings in a shoebox had stolen the vase, just as the leatherbound copy of Pascal had been stolen. Nothing signified – no gesture or act or artefact or idea. Jésus dans l'ennui . . . No one had redeemed man from his eternal mediocrity.

We lay in silence for several hours, sprawled on our beds, dozing now and then. Darkness came. In the dark, the sounds of the street below seemed to grow louder. Cars roared. Lights came glimmering on.

'I'm going down,' Paul announced suddenly, 'to buy us a woman.'

We stared at each other. In that instant, boredom had disappeared, belief in magic returned. To find it, we only had to reach out and dip into the darkness.

'It's expensive,' I said nonchalantly.

'We'll get a cheap one.'

'How would one tell . . .?'

'Which are the cheap ones? The old ones.'

'Let's not get an old one.'

'How much have you got?'

The thought slipped into my mind, if I hadn't bought the pewter vase . . . I banished it. 'About three thousand francs,' I said.

'I've got more than that,' said Paul. 'We should be all right. We can probably afford one who looks young in the dark.'

'What about the room?' I said.

'The room ?'

'Well, look at it. She'll be able to tell it's just a boys' room.'

'Yes. Well, let's tidy it at least.'

Urgently then we bundled away the litter of clothes into the wardrobes, put the *Thousand and One Nights* back into its *Jock of the Bushveld* dustjacket, and, silently as we could, moved the two beds together and covered them with the satin eiderdowns. Finally, Paul hunted in his chest of drawers for a red paisley silk scarf – a present from our English grandfather – which he draped round the central parchment lampshade. The room was transformed by the light, reddened, ready.

'Well . . .' I said.

'Why don't you go down?' said Paul.

'Me?'

'Yes. You're taller.'

'No, I'm not. We're the same.'

'You look older.'

So it was that around midnight I found myself with seven thousand francs in my pocket, carrying my shoes, creeping silently down past our father's room where the lights were turned out, past the drawing room where the one hundred guests had eaten salmon, down into the hall which had been filled with flowers and out at last into the street.

The night was colder than I had expected. I was glad I'd done up my tie and put my jacket on. I was nervous, yet I felt light with my own extraordinary purpose. My whole life shadowed me as I walked; the shadow was obedient and vast.

We knew where the whores congregated. The Avenue Foch was the rather verdant beat of a cavalcade of spiky-eyed women. In gateways and on corners, they stood and waited. Cars drew up. They got in, in ones and twos. Hunched up men steered them away down side streets. I had often passed these furtive stoppings, noted the quick exchange of words, the clacking heels being hurried over the cobbles, little wisps of laughter or anger trailing off into the night.

I felt tiny. The city hummed, like a dome, round me. I walked very slowly, hearing each footstep. The night was superb. I pitied my father who would never see it – the Arc de Triomphe on its hill of light, the glistening foliage of gardens and entrances, a cluster of stars above the tall-shouldered houses ... I thought of Paul, waiting on the satin eiderdowns and grinned. I have never admired my brother as ardently as I did that night. I admired him firstly for his daring and secondly for the cowardice which had tempered it and which allowed me to be here in the street. I truly loved him.

The two women I stopped at, hesitating, my hand clutching the money in my pocket, looked at me first with the disdain of giraffes, then, seeing me planted in front of them, speechless but earnest, they smiled and made almost identical movements of their hips, shifting weight from one long leg to the other. The thought whizzed through me: will women always be taller than me? I cleared my throat. 'I didn't know . . .' I began, 'whether one of you might like to . . . come along to my house. I mean, just for half an hour or something . . .'

The women looked at each other and grinned, looked back at me, grinned again.

'Which one of us did you have in mind?'

I remembered Paul's knowing statement: the oldest are the cheapest. Neither of these women seemed particularly old, nor particularly young. I couldn't have told whether they were twenty-five or forty. They were just women – available women. I stared up at them, trying to guess which of them might be the cheapest, but I simply couldn't tell. Nor, I realised, did I want to offend either of them by choosing one and rejecting the other.

'I don't really mind,' I said, 'I mean, I don't mind at all. The thing is that I've got seven thousand francs . . .'

Again, they looked at each other and grinned. One of them pulled a silky shawl round her shoulders, touched my chin lightly and tenderly and began to walk away. I watched her go with a feeling of dismay. She suddenly seemed perfect: long, dark hair, swinging as she walked, a fleshy bottom encased in a tight skirt that shimmered. I wanted to call her back, but I felt a gentle hand on my arm and forced myself to look more closely at the woman who was to be ours. She had red hair and a wide smile. She wore a lacy blouse over bunched-up, milky breasts. On her upper lip was the dark blotch of a mole.

'Somebody like flowers in this house?' she said, seeing the banked arrangements that filled the hall.

'Ssh,' I whispered, 'my father's in bed. He had his wedding today.'

She began to laugh, put a fist up to stifle it. From the fist hung a little ornate velvet purse with an amber clasp. Soon, all my savings and Paul's would be inside this purse.

A light was on under my father's door now as we passed it. I imagined him hearing our footsteps, feeling his way to the door and opening it – and seeing nothing of course. To live with a blind man is to have the power of invisibility. We hurried on up, me leading, not daring to look behind me. Was the red-haired woman old? How would she seem to Paul in the paisley lamplight? Would he mind the mole on her lip? Old women don't have red hair or high breasts, do they? I felt absolutely responsible to Paul for my choice. My own daring had only been in recognition of his. We had a perfect sense, in those days, of what each of us owed to the other. Over the years, this sense has clouded, disappeared.

'Here we are,' I said, quietly opening the door to our room. Paul, who had been sitting on the edge of the bed, trying not to crumple the eiderdown, stood up stiffly.

'Oh, good evening . . .' he said.

I put my hand on the woman's arm and led her forward. The skin of her arm was freckled and soft. Her hair, I saw now, was a marvellous colour and very clean.

'This is my twin brother, Paul,' I said apologetically. 'I wonder if you could tell us your name?'

'Oh yes. Bettina. All nations can pronounce "Bettina".'

'Oh. All nations, eh?'

'I think it's a terrific name,' said Paul.

Bettina was smiling. I felt relieved. I hadn't dared to tell her there would be two of us. She crossed to the bed, sat down and looked up at us.

'Money first,' she said, opening the velvet purse. 'Five thousand each. I like to get this part of it over. Then we can enjoy ourselves, eh?'

I produced the seven thousand. 'This is really all we've got . . .' I began, but Paul, without any hesitation, had tugged out the gold cufflinks given to him that very morning by our father and Pierrette (an identical pair to me) to mark their wedding day.

'I'd be honoured,' he said in a speechy voice, 'if you would accept these. They are worth considerably more than the three thousand owing to you.'

Bettina took them, inspected them for the gold hallmark, dropped them and the crumpled notes I had given her into the purse. She laid the purse down, kicked off her shoes and began to unroll her stockings.

I sat down. I was shaking, not with sexual excitement, but with a sense of absolute strangeness. I thought, the walk out into the night, everything from that moment is a dream and I shall wake up in the morning and life will be precisely as it was, with only the *Thousand and One Nights* within my reach. There will have been no scarf on the lampshade, no act of daring and maturity ... I blinked, rubbed my eyes, felt thirsty, stared at Paul, who was unbuttoning his trousers. I longed for a cool drink of milk or lemonade, but I had the notion that time was sliding away from me immeasurably fast; yes, life itself was slipping, altering, as Paul stepped out of his trousers, nervously fingering his penis, already erect, and I had to stay and be part of it, or miss it for ever.

I sat on the bed and watched as Bettina arrayed for us on the satin eiderdowns a body of such white voluptuousness its form has stayed huddled in memory all my life and through all my loving. Flesh has never again seemed in itself so magnificent a thing, so utterly and uncontrollably inviting. All strangeness, all fear vanished. Paul parted Bettina's legs, and we glimpsed for the first time in our lives the glistening dark channel that puerile imagination never imagines perfectly enough, the deep and private walls of ripeness, where the boy deluges his fountain of dreams.

I don't remember taking off my clothes, yet I was naked on the bed, my hand on Paul's buttocks. The motions his body made were tender, unembarrassed, as touching as an animal. His body shone. I was choked by his achievement, his beauty. My head on Bettina's scented hair, I pressed myself to the one body that hers and Paul's had become, rocked as they rocked, felt myself move as Paul moved through waves of mounting ecstasy. 'It's superb!' Paul trumpeted as he moved and I moved faster and faster, 'it's superb, Jacques!'

I don't know whether it was my father's decision or Pierrette's to separate Paul's life from mine, but this, at the end of the summer, was what happened. We were taken away from our English school for good and sent to different boarding schools in France. I have never been able to understand the reasoning behind this decision and can only guess at it: if we missed each other enough, we would cease to miss our mother, and thus to talk of her.

The odd thing is that ever since that time, I have, all my life, missed them both. Paul's life has taken such a different course from my own that I have long ago lost him as a brother. The man he is, the man I meet at restaurants with our wives, is at best an acquaintance – an acquaintance I don't even like very much.

During periods of anxiety or depression, and only then, do these two ghosts visit me as once they were: Paul making first love to Bettina under the paisley light; my mother sitting on a wall in Cornwall and yelling at the gulls.

My Wife is a White Russian

I'm a financier. I have financial assets, world-wide. I'm in nickel and pig-iron and gold and diamonds. I like the sound of all these words. They have an edge, I think. The glitter of saying them sometimes gives me an erection.

I'm saying them now, in this French restaurant, where the tablecloths and the table napkins are blue linen, where they serve sea-food on platters of seaweed and crushed ice. It's noisy at lunchtime. It's May and the sun shines in London, through the open restaurant windows. Opposite me, the two young Australians blink as they wait (so damned courteous, and she has freckles like a child) for me to stutter out my hard-word list, to manipulate tongue and memory so that the sound inside me forms just behind my lips and explodes with extraordinary force above my oysters.

Diamonds!

But then I feel a soft, perfumed dabbing at my face. I turn away from the Australians and there she is. My wife. She is smiling as she wipes me. Her gold bracelets rattle. She is smiling at me. Her lips are astonishing, the colour of claret. I've been wanting to ask her for some time: 'Why are your lips this terrible dark colour these days? Is it a lipstick you put on?'

Still smiling at me, she's talking to the Australians with her odd accent: 'He's able to enjoy the pleasures of life once more, thank God. For a long time afterwards, I couldn't take him out. Terrible. We couldn't do one single thing, you know. But now . . . He enjoys his wine again.'

The dabbing stops. To the nurse I tried to say when I felt a movement begin: 'Teach me how to wipe my arse. I cannot let my wife do this because she doesn't love me. If she loved me, she probably wouldn't mind wiping my arse and I wouldn't mind her wiping my arse. But she doesn't love me.'

The Australian man is talking now. I let my hand go up and take hold of my big-bowled wine glass into which a waiter has poured the expensive Chablis my wife likes to drink when she eats fish. Slowly, I guide the glass across the deadweight distance between the table and my mouth. I say 'deadweight' because the spaces between all my limbs and the surfaces of tangible things have become mighty. To walk is to wade in waist-high water. And to lift this wine glass . . . 'Help me,' I want to say to her, 'just this once. Just this once.'

'Heck,' says the Australian man, 'we honestly thought he'd made a pretty positive recovery.' His wife, with blue eyes the colour of the napkins, is watching my struggles with the glass. She licks her fine line of a mouth, sensing, I suppose, my longing to taste the wine. The nurse used to stand behind me, guiding the feeding cup in my hand. I never explained to her that the weight of gravity had mysteriously increased. Yet often, as I drank from the feeding cup, I used to imagine myself prancing on the moon.

'Oh this is a very positive recovery,' says my wife. 'There's very little he can't do now. He enjoys the ballet, you know, and the opera. People at Covent Garden and the better kind of place are very considerate. We don't go to the cinema because there you have a very inconsiderate type of person. Don't you agree? So riff-raffy? Don't you agree?'

The Australian wife hasn't listened to a word. The Australian wife puts out a lean freckled arm and I watch it come towards me, astounded as usual these days by the speed with which other people can move parts of their bodies. But the arm, six inches from my hand holding the glass, suddenly stops. 'Don't help him!' snaps my wife. The napkin-blue eyes are lowered. The arm is folded away.

Heads turn in the restaurant. I suppose her voice has carried its inevitable echo round the room where we sit: 'Don't help him! Don't help him!' But now that I have an audience, the glass begins to jolt, the wine splashing up and down the sides of the bowl. I smile. My smile widens as I watch the Chablis begin to slop onto the starched blue cloth. *Waste!* She of all people understands the exquisite luxury of waste. Yet she snatches the glass out of my hand and sets it down by her own. She snaps her fingers and a young beanstick of a waiter arrives. He spreads out a fresh blue napkin where I have spilt my wine. My wife smiles her claret smile. She sucks an oyster into her dark mouth.

The Australian man is, I was told, the manager of the Toomin Valley Nickel Consortium. The Australian man is here to discuss expansion, supposedly with me, unaware until he met me this lunchtime that, despite the pleasing cadences of the words, I'm unable to say 'Toomin Valley Nickel Consortium'. I can say 'nickel'. My tongue lashes around in my throat to form the click that comes in the middle of the word. Then out it spills. Nickel! In my mind, oddly enough, the word 'nickel' is the exact greyish-white colour of an oyster. But 'consortium' is too difficult for me. I know my limitations.

My wife is talking again: 'I've always loved the ballet, you see. This is my only happy memory of Russia – the wonderful classical ballet. A little magic. Don't you think? I would never want to be without this kind of magic, would you? Do you have the first-rate ballet companies in Australia? You do? Well, that's good. *Giselle* of course. That's the best one. Don't you think? The dead girl. Don't you think? Wonderful.'

We met on a pavement. I believe it was in the Avenue Matignon but it could have been in the Avenue Montaigne. I often get these muddled. It was in Paris, anyway. Early summer, as it is now. Chestnut candle blooms blown along the gutters. I waited to get into the taxi she was leaving. But I didn't get into it. I followed her. In a bar, she told me she was very poor. Her father drove the taxi I had almost hired. She spoke no English then, only French with a heavy Russian accent. I was just starting to be a financier at that time, but already I was quite rich, rich by her standards – she who had been used to life in post-war Russia. My hotel room was rather grand. She said in her odd French: 'I'll fuck for money.'

I gave her fifty francs. I suppose it wasn't much, not as much as she'd hoped for, a poor rate of exchange for the white, white body that rode astride me, head thrown back, breasts bouncing. She sat at the dressing table in the hotel room. She smoked my American cigarettes. More than anything, I wanted to brush her gold hair, brush it smooth and hold it against my face. But I didn't ask her if I could do this. I believe I was afraid she would say: 'You can do it for money.'

The thin waiter is clearing away our oyster platters. I've eaten only three of my oysters, yet I let my plate go. She pretends not to notice how slow I've been with the oysters. And my glass of wine still stands by hers, untasted. Yet she's drinking quite fast. I hear her order a second bottle. The Australian man says: 'First-rate choice, if I may say. We like Chably.' I raise my left arm and touch her elbow, nodding at the wine. Without looking at me, she puts my glass down in front of me. The Australian wife stares at it. Neither she nor I dare to touch it.

My wife is explaining to the Australians what they are about to eat, as if they were children: 'I think you will like the turbot very much. *Turbot poché hollandaise.* They cook it very finely. And the hollandaise sauce, you know this of course? Very difficult to achieve, lightness of this sauce. But here they do it very well. And the scallops in saffron. Again a very light sauce. Excellent texture. Just a little cream added. And fresh scallops naturally. We never go to any restaurant where the food is frozen. So I think you will like these dishes you have chosen very much . . .'

We have separate rooms. Long before my illness, when I began to look (yet hardly to feel) old, she demanded her privacy. This was how she put it: she wanted to be private. The bedroom we used to share and which is now hers is very large. The walls are silk. She said: 'There's no sense in being rich and then cooped up together in one room.' Obediently, I moved out. She wouldn't let me have the guest room, which is also big. I have what we call 'the little room', which I always used to think of as a child's room. In her 'privacy' I expect she smiles: 'The child's room is completely right for him. He's a helpless baby!' Yet she's not a private person. She likes to go out four or five nights a week, returning at two or three in the morning, sometimes with friends, sitting and drinking brandy. Sometimes they play music. Elton John. She has a lover (I don't know his name) who sends her lilies.

I'm trying to remember the Toomin Valley. I believe it's an immense desert of a place, inhabited by no one and nothing except the mining machinery and the Nickel Consortium employees, whose clusters of houses I ordered to be white-washed to hide the cheap grey building blocks. The windows of the houses are small, to keep out the sun. In the back yards are spindly eucalyptus trees, blown by the scorching winds. I want to ask the Australian wife: 'Did you have freckles before you went to live in the Toomin Valley, and does some wandering prima ballerina dance *Giselle* on the gritty escarpment above the mine?'

My scallops arrive, saffron yellow and orange in the blue and white dish – the colours of a childhood summer. The flesh of a scallop is firm yet soft, the texture of a woman's thigh (when she is young, of course; before the skin hardens and the flesh bags out). A forkful of scallop is immeasurably easier to lift than the glass of wine, and the Australian wife (why don't I know either of their names?) smiles at me approvingly as I lift the succulent parcel of food to my mouth and chew it without dribbling. My wife, too, is watching, ready with the little scented handkerchief, yet talking as she eats, talking of Australia as the second bottle of Chablis arrives and she tastes it hurriedly, with a curt nod to the thin waiter. I exist only in the corner of her eye, at its inmost edge, where the vulnerable triangle of red flesh is startling.

'Of course I've often tried to tell Hubert' (she pronounces my name 'Eieu-bert', trying and failing with what she recognises as the upper class 'h') 'that it's very unfair to expect people like you to live in some out-of-the-way place. I was brought up in a village, you see, and I know that an out-of-the-way village is

70

so dead. No culture. The same in Toomin, no? Absolutely no culture at all. Everybody dead.'

The Australian wife looks – seemingly for the first time – straight at my wife. 'We're outdoor people,' she says.

I remember now. A river used to flow through the Toomin Valley. Torrential in the rainy season, they said. It dried up in the early forties. One or two sparse willows remain, grey testimony to the long-ago existence of water-rich soil. I imagine the young Australian couple, brown as chestnuts, swimming in the Toomin River, resting on its gentle banks with their fingers touching, a little loving nest of bone. There is no river. Yet when they look at each other, almost furtively under my vacant gaze, I recognise the look. The look says: 'These moments with strangers are nothing. Into our private moments together – only there – is crammed all that we ask of a life.'

'Yes, we're outdoor folk.' The Australian man is smiling. 'You can play tennis most of the year round at Toomin. I'm President of the Tennis Club. And we have our own pool now.'

I don't remember these things: tennis courts and swimming pools.

'Well, of course you have the climate for this.' My wife is signalling our waiter to bring her Perrier water. 'And it's something to do, isn't it? Perhaps, when the new expansions of the company are made, a concert hall could be built for you, or a theatre?'

'A theatre!' The Australian wife's mouth opens to reveal perfect, freshly peeled teeth and a laugh escapes. She blushes. My wife's dark lips are puckered into a sneer. But the Australian man is laughing too – a rich laugh you might easily remember on the other side of the world – and slapping his thigh. 'A theatre! What about that, ay!'

She wanted, she said as she smoked my American cigarettes, to see *Don Giovanni*. Since leaving Russia with her French mother and her Russian father, no one had ever taken her to the opera. She had seen the posters advertising *Don Giovanni* and asked her father to buy her a ticket. He had shouted at her: 'Remember whose child you are! Do you imagine taxi drivers can afford seats at the Opéra?'

'Take me to see *Don Giovanni*,' she said, 'and then I will fuck for nothing.'

I've never really appreciated the opera. The Don was fat. It was difficult imagining so many women wanting to lie with this fat man. Yet afterwards, she leant over and put her head on my shoulder and wept. Nothing, she told me, had ever moved her so much, nothing in her life had touched the core of her being as this had done, this production of *Don Giovanni*. 'If only,' she said, 'I had money as you have money, then I would go to hear music all the time and see the classical ballet and learn from these what is life.'

The scallops are good. She never learned what is life. I feel emboldened by the food. I put my hand to my glass, heavier than ever now because the waiter has filled it up. The sun shines on my wine and on my hand blotched (splattered, it seems) with the oddly repulsive stains of old age. For a second, I see my hand and the wine glass as a still-life. But then I lift the glass. The Australian wife lowers her eyes. My wife for a moment is silent. I drink. I smile at the Australian wife because I know she wants to applaud.

I'm talking. The words are like stones, weighing down my lower jaw. Nickel. I'm trying to tell the Australian man that I dream about the nickel mine. In my dreams, the Australian miners drag carts loaded with threepenny bits. I run my hands through the coins as through a sack of wheat, and the touch of them is pleasurable and perfect. I also want to say to the Australian man: 'I hope you're happy in your work. When I was in control, I visited all my mines and all my subsidiaries at least once a year. Even in South Africa, I made sure a living wage was paid. I said to the men underground, I hope you're happy in your work.'

But now I have a manager, a head manager to manage all the other managers, including this one from the Toomin Valley. I am trundled out in my chair to meet them when they come here to discuss redundancy or expansion. My wife and I give them lunch in a restaurant. They remind me that I still have an empire to rule, if I was capable, if my heart had not faltered, if indeed my life had been different since the night of *Don Giovanni.*

When I stopped paying her to sleep with me, her father came to see me. He held his cap in his hands. 'We're hoping for a marriage,' he said. And what more could I have given – what *less* to the body I had begun to need so terribly? The white and gold of her, I thought, will ornament my life.

Yet now I never touch her. The white and the gold of her lies only in the lilies they send, the unknown lovers she finds in the night, while I lie in the child's room and dream of the nickel mines. My heart is scorched dry like the dry hills of the Toomin Valley. I am punished for my need of her while her life stalks my silence: the white of her, the gold of her – the white of Dior, the gold of Cartier. Why did she never love me? In my dreams, too, the answer comes from deep underground: it's the hardness of my words.

Dinner for One

He said: 'I'll take you out. We'll go to Partridge's, have something special.' She took off her glasses and looked at him doubtfully.

'I don't know, Henry. I don't know that we want to make a fuss about it.'

'Well, it's up to you.'

'Why is it?'

'Why is it what?'

'Up to me?'

She bewildered him. For years she had bewildered him. 'It's your choice, Lal; that's all I meant. It's your choice – whether we go out or not.'

She sighed. 'I just thought . . .'

'What?'

'I just thought it might be better simply to treat it like any other day.'

'It's not "any other day".'

'No.'

'But it's your decision. You're the one who makes these decisions. So you let me know if you want to go and I'll ring up and book a table.'

He walked away from her, sat down in his worn red armchair, fumbled for his glasses, found them and took up *The Times* crossword. She watched him, still holding her glasses in her hand. It's funny, she thought, that whenever we talk to each other, we take our glasses off. We blur each other out. I suppose we're afraid that if we see each other clearly – too clearly – communication between us will cease.

'Six across . . .' he murmured from the faded comfort of his chair, 'two words, four and three: "Facts of severing the line".'

'Anagram,' she whispered, 'I should think.'

Henry and Lal weren't what anyone expected. Separate from her, he seemed to belong. He belongs; she doesn't, was what people thought. You could pull old Henry's leg and raise that boisterous laugh of his, but with her you didn't know where you were. Quite ordinary remarks – things that everyone laughed at – seemed to worry her. But she never told you why: she just closed her eyes.

There had been so many friends at the beginning. Henry and Lal had belonged then. 'Isn't my wife the belle of the ball?' he used to say. And there were so many balls, once, to be belle of. The changes had stolen gradually into her; the changes had begun after Henry came home from the War, so that people often said: 'It was the War that changed her,' and even to her face: 'It was the War that changed you, Lal, wasn't it?'

But she didn't agree with them. 'The War changed everyone,' was all she'd say.

'It always seems . . .'

Henry looked up from the crossword. He was surprised Lal was still in the room. 'What, Lal?'

'Such a waste.'

'What does?'

'Going out. All that eating.'

'We can afford it, darling.'

'Oh, it isn't that.'

Henry took off his glasses. 'Well, I'm damned if I – '

'Look at our stomachs! Look at yours. So crammed with food you couldn't push any more in. And mine, a dreadful bulge.'

'Oh, Lal, for heaven's sake.'

'It's horrible to eat and eat. What's it for? Just to make us heavier and heavier till we die with all this weight.'

'You're not fat, Lal. I'm fat! I'm not ashamed of it.'

'Why?'

'Why what?'

'Why aren't you ashamed?'

'Because it's *my* life. I can be any shape I choose.'

No, she thought, that's wrong. I am haunted by the wrongness of things.

'Henry,' she said, 'I hate it – '

'What?'

'I hate it when – '

Larry Partridge was a popular man. 'We're so lucky,' ran the county's favourite saying, 'to have you so near us!' They didn't mean Larry himself (though they liked his silver-haired politeness), they meant his restaurant which, every night of the week except Tuesdays when it was closed, was packed with them.

'This part of the world was a culinary desert before you came, Larry,' they told him, 'but now we really are lucky. Partridge's is as good as anything in London and so much more reasonable.'

Of course they had been cautious – caution before ecstasy – because, glancing through the windows of the old run-down pub he had bought, they had noted that the old run-down walls were becoming resplendent in indigos and fruit-fool pinks and this had made them nudge each other: 'Well, you can tell what *he* is, duckie!'

Now Larry's tightly clad buttocks circled their contented after-dinner smiles. He extended to each table a limp-handed greeting and waited for the superlatives to flood his ears like warm water. 'You're so imaginative with food, Larry!'

'The sauce on the quenelles was out of this world, Larry.'

'We've had a superb meal, Larry, really superb.'

Larry's parents still lived in Romford. He had moved them from their council flat to a detached house. However, Larry's father still called him Lawrence. Lawrence: to say the name to himself was to remind Larry of his father, was to make him shudder as if the thin shadow of the man – neat in his dark green suit and white shirt, ready for work, working all his life, never giving up his dull and hopeless work till one day he would die at it – passed between him and the sun.

For Larry, Lawrence was dead, buried hideously down in the greasy kitchens of the catering school. Lawrence, born in poverty, reared in repression, was the detritus from which Larry, in all his colourful glory, had sprung. He had sprung in 1964, the year he had met Edwin, and each year since then he had bloomed a little more.

'What can I say about Edwin?' Larry had asked his mother at the time. 'Except that I love him.'

Oh, but they were not prepared for this kind of love, she told him. They had never thought that their own Lawrence, so popular with all the local girls . . . No, it had not once entered their minds and she really did think he should have given them some warning, some indication that he wasn't what they thought . . .

Larry left his parents' flat in Romford and moved into Edwin's flat in Fulham. Edwin found him a job in a local restaurant. Lawrence in Edwin's careful drawing room became Larry, became lover and loved.

All the past, like a dirty old bandage no longer needed, began to unwind and fall off; Larry was healed.

Edwin's money purchased the pub in 1972. One end of the large building was converted into a flat and the move from Fulham was made. A year later, Partridge's opened, each of its walls a reflection of Edwin's taste, Edwin's imaginative eye.

Larry moved with perfect ease and happiness about his steel kitchen, liking his own little kingdom the better because just outside it was a rich land that he shared with Edwin.

'I do it with love,' Larry sometimes said of his cooking. But the great golden weight of his love for Edwin he seldom talked of. It hung inside him, a burdensome treasure that he knew would never leave him.

Visitors to Partridge's never saw Edwin. Larry's nightly ritual of passing from table to table to receive his cupful of praise did not include him. He was glimpsed occasionally; there was talk of him, even questions to Larry.

'But it's all yours,' Edwin had said to Larry when the

restaurant opened. 'My bit's done. Don't involve me any more. Then the success and the glory will really belong to you.'

And even the invitations that came – to the lunches and the county cocktail parties – Edwin would never accept. 'You're their celebrity, Larry. Why muddle them?'

Edwin was never jealous. 'I am quite free of it,' he once said to Larry. 'I simply do not feel it. Jealousy is the vainest – in all senses – of the emotions. You must learn to rid yourself of that before it works its decay.'

But Larry had known no human relationship in which jealousy had not been present – sometimes screamed out, sometimes unspoken, but always there to stain and spoil.

And he knew that his love for Edwin was a jealous, greedy love. He thought to himself: 'Edwin is my life. How can I not be jealous of my own life?' Whenever Edwin went away, the weight inside him became a dead weight, immovable, full of pain.

When Edwin returned, he often wanted to run to him, discovering in his body a sudden miraculous lightness.

Daily, Larry watched Edwin for any sign of discontent. Three years younger than Larry his hair was still fair and thick. With an impatient gesture of his hand, he would push back the flopping hair several times in an hour.

Whenever he was angry or agitated, he would push back the hair almost constantly.

Larry dreaded his anger. Its occasional appearance in a man as contained and rational as Edwin was unsightly. Larry couldn't look at him. He would turn away, trembling inside.

But in the hundreds of times he had turned away like this over the years, there was not one time that he had not dreaded to turn round again, afraid suddenly that all the hubbub of Edwin's anger was nothing but an echo and that, unnoticed, Edwin had quietly slipped away and left him.

Edwin did little with his time. He gave to unimportant things the careful attention of his hands. He grew roses. He did occasional pen and ink drawings of old houses, which Larry collected and had framed.

He made an elegant coffee table out of glass and wood. He wrote a little poetry, always laughing at what he had written and throwing it away.

Money had bought Edwin a studied indolence. 'I'm really a rocking-chair man,' he once said to Larry. 'The little motions I can make are enough.'

Certainly, they were enough for Larry. He was quite content for Edwin to be just as he was – as long as he was always there.

Lal said: 'I've worked out that anagram.' Several moments had passed in silence. Henry had filled in two more clues in *The Times* crossword. Lal had walked to the study window and looked out at the bird table she festooned in winter with strings of nuts and pieces of coconut. The nuts were eaten, the coconut pecked dry: it was springtime.

Henry looked up. 'What was that you said, Lal?'

'Two words, four and three, "Facts of severing the line".'

'I've got that one, haven't I?'

'I don't know. It's "cast off" – anagram of "facts of".'

'Let me see, "cast off"? You're right, Lal. Good for you.'

Henry filled it in. Then he looked up at Lal standing by the window. 'Made up your mind yet, darling?'

Lal knew that he meant the dinner, knew that she had made up her mind. She didn't want to go out with Henry on that day.

A reward, she thought – a more fitting one for fifty years of marriage – should be to spend that evening alone, without him.

For the clear lines with which she encircled the petty wrongnesses of her life became each time like the lines drawn by aeroplanes in a blue sky: they fuzzed and were dissipated and the spaces where they had been were filled up, so that only a moment later you couldn't see that they had been there. Life went on in the old way.

In the mass of years she kept drawing and redrawing lines, kept believing that things might change one day and she would rediscover something lost.

'I have made up my mind,' Lal said. 'I think we should go out as you suggested. It would be nice to go to Partridge's, don't you think?'

'Well, I do.'

'Only . . .'

'What?'

'It's a Tuesday. Larry shuts on a Tuesday.'

'Damn me! Never mind, we'll make it the Monday. Why not? We can toast the midnight. As they used to say in the army, always better to have the feast before the battle; you might not live to enjoy it afterwards.'

Lal turned and stared at Henry. 'It has been a battle. The battle's going on . . .'

'Oh come on, Lal, not one of your frettings.'

'We never were really suited. Henry – only at first when we used to want each other all the time. We should have parted when that cooled off. We'd had the best of each other: we'd had all the wonderful things.'

'What rubbish you do talk, Lal. As couples go, we've been among the lucky ones. You name me the day when we've had arguments. I could count them on the fingers of one hand.'

'Not arguments, Henry, but a battle going on inside . . .'

'The trouble with you, Lal, is you think too much. We're old now, God bless us, so why not give your mind a bit of a rest?'

Lal turned back to the window. 'You'll book the table, then, Henry? I do think that if we are going to Partridge's, it would be safer to book.'

Spring arrived on the Saturday in the shape of a deep blue sky and a softening of the breeze. Larry never opened the restaurant for lunch. 'It simply is not fair on Edwin,' he said. Instead, he usually prepared a light lunch for the two of them and they sat by themselves in the restaurant, enjoying its peace.

Edwin always washed up. He did the job so carefully that their few plates and dishes sometimes took him half an hour, a half-hour usually spent by Larry, a cigarette in his curling mouth, in blissful contemplation of his friend. He took as much care over these lunches as he did over his evening menus.

After all, he said to himself, this is our home. Edwin has a right to my time. And to cook for Edwin was pure pleasure. Often, just before sleep, his mind would turn up some little dish that he would make for Edwin as a treat the following day.

Early on the Saturday morning, wandering out onto the patio (laid in intricate patterning of stone and brick by Edwin) Larry felt the warmth of the sun and decided he would lay a table for them outside, make them a cold lunch and serve it with a bottle of hock. He imagined this meal and others like it that they would share during the coming summer, and his imaginings laid on him a hand of such pleasurable gentleness that he didn't want to move.

Indeed was poor suffering Lawrence dead! He was dead without trace and only Larry, head crammed with joy, existed now.

'Larry!'

Edwin called him from an upstairs window. Larry looked up and saw that Edwin, whom he had left sleeping, was dressed.

'I'm going out,' Edwin called.

'Where?'

'Just out.'

'Oh.'

Larry knew that he shouldn't question him. This was what Edwin hated most.

'Will you be back for lunch?' he asked.

'Yes.'

He was relieved. They would still have their lunch on the patio and now, if Edwin was going out, he could spend the whole morning in the kitchen, do some preparation for the inevitably busy Saturday evening as well.

Larry waved to Edwin, saw him nod and then disappear from the window. He made himself stay where he was till he heard Edwin's Alfa Romeo roar out of the gate. Then he wandered into the kitchen and tied on his apron.

Larry made an iced tomato and mint soup, a cold curry sauce

for a roasted chicken and a watercress salad. He spread a pink cloth with matching napkins on the wooden patio table and set two careful places, each headed by a tall stemmed hock glass. He then went back into the kitchen, checked the contents of his huge fridge and larder against the evening menus for Saturday and Sunday, made a shopping list, took a basket and got into his car.

By the time I get back from shopping, he thought to himself, Edwin will be back; then I can open the hock.

When Lal woke on the Monday morning she experienced that bleakest of sorrows – the realisation that a dream had tricked her with a few seconds' happiness and was now gone.

She had dreamed herself young. She had dreamed a bedroom in someone's country house and a corridor outside it which creaked under Henry's footstep as in the dark he fumbled his way towards her room.

She had laughed a secretive laugh full of joy as she lay under the clean linen sheet and waited for him. Their wedding was in a few weeks' time. Then there would be no more creeping down corridors: she would be Mrs Henry Barkworth and the strong white body under the silk dressing gown that now shuffled towards her, moving slowly, prudently, but running, running like a hare in its desire for her, would lie in a big bed beside her – hers. Yes, Lal remembered, there had been a great feasting of love between her and Henry. Sex had never frightened her as it seemed to frighten some women of her sheltered generation. To touch and be touched became, after Henry's rough taking of her, all. All life, save this, paled and receded into insignificance.

For days together she would not let Henry go to his office, but kept him with her in their wide, comfortable bed.

'We fit so well!' she laughed. 'How could anything be more perfect?'

Then came the War. Lal's children were both conceived during Henry's brief periods of leave and born when he was away. When the War was over and he came home, he made love to Lal like a weary stranger. She wept for what they had lost.

Lal sat up, rubbed her eyes with a white hand. It was strange that she could dream a desire she had long since ceased to feel. Life was so stale now.

We smell bad, Henry and I, she thought bitterly. We're blemished and fat and no good to anyone. Why do we go on and on?

The day was interminable. Lal felt bilious, as if the meal they would gobble up at Partridge's was already inside her. She felt like crying. But I've shed so many tears for myself, she thought wearily, why shed more? So the evening crept towards her.

She thought as she dressed for it of the wine Henry would order: a heavy claret that they would both enjoy but which, soon afterwards, would give her indigestion and a headache. Fifty years! We've had fifty years together, so now we celebrate, but the unremarkableness of all that time, the waste of it all . . .

'Cheer up, darling.'

Henry was breezy, tugging on his braces, smelling of after-shave, his bald head gleaming.

'Oh, was I . . .?'

'You've been miles away all day, Lal. Something wrong? Not feeling up to it?'

'What? The meal?'

'No! Not just the meal – the occasion!'

'In a way not. We don't need to make any fuss, do we?'

'No, no fuss. But a bottle of fizz at least, don't you think? I asked Larry to put one on ice for us.'

'Yes.'

Lal dabbed her face with powder. She had decided to wear a black dress – the one concession to her real feelings. Pinned to the dress would be the diamond and sapphire brooch Henry had given her on their wedding day.

There was a small bar just off the dining room in Partridge's; it was too small really for all the diners who congregated there, but was pretty and restful, done up by Edwin in two shades of green. A fine tapestry drape hung down one wall and now Lal leaned back against this, her head almost touching a huntsman's knee behind her.

One of Larry's lady helpers (he had two, both about forty-five and confusingly called Myra and Moira) had brought Henry the champagne he had ordered and he was pouring it excitedly like a thirsty schoolboy might a longed-for Coke.

'This is the stuff, darling!'

Lal smiled and nodded. She often thought that the reason for Henry's pinkness of face and head was that he did simple things with such relish.

'So,' he exclaimed, holding up his own glass, 'this is it then, Lal! Happy anniversary, darling.'

Lal only nodded at Henry, then took a tiny sip of her champagne. 'It's a long time,' she said, 'since we had this.'

The restaurant was seldom full on a Monday night. The little bar was completely empty except for Henry and Lal, so that to make some accompaniment to their sipping of the champagne Lal needed to talk.

'Larry's not around, is he? He usually pops into the bar, doesn't he, with his apron on?'

'I expect he's hard at work. We wouldn't want Larry doing anything but concentrating on our dinner, would we?' Henry said jovially.

'I like Larry,' she said.

'He's a clever cook.'

'I think he's quite shy underneath all that flippety talk and showing off his bottom.'

'Lal!'

'Well, he does. Henry. He shows it off all the time. Haven't you noticed the way he ties his apron so carefully, so that the bow just bounces up and down on his behind when he walks?'

'No, I haven't noticed.'

'I mean, a less shy person wouldn't need the bow, would he?'

'Haven't a clue, Lal.'

'Oh, they wouldn't definitely. You can tell that Larry's very dependent.'

'On what?'

'Not on what – on Edward or whatever his name is: his friend. He loves that friend and depends on him. Edward's more cultured than Larry is.'

Myra (Henry addressed her as Myra; but Lal nudged him, fearing it might be Moira) came to take their order. Lal ordered champignons à la viennoise, followed by stuffed pork tenderloin with cherry and Madeira sauce; Henry ordered a venison terrine, followed by veal cordon bleu.

Henry then chose a bottle of fine claret and sat back, one hand on his stomach, the other holding his champagne glass. It's not hard, he thought, to find one's little pleasures – just as long as one isn't poor. He smiled at Lal.

His work done for the evening, Larry took off his apron and hung it up. Only two tables had been occupied – not unusually for a Monday evening – and he hoped those few customers would leave early so that he could tidy up and go to bed. He sat down on one of his kitchen stools and took a gulp of the large whisky he had poured himself. But the whisky did nothing to lessen the pain Larry was feeling. The pain squatted there inside him, an undreamed-of but undeniable parasite.

Even his hands which usually moved so lightly and quickly were slowed by the pain, so that he had kept his few customers waiting for their meal, waiting and growing impatient. I must go out, he thought wearily, and apologise. Not do my little round to hear any praise tonight, but just go out and apologise for the delay, for the gluey quality of the Madeira sauce, for cooking the veal too long . . .

Larry sighed. He had said nothing to Myra or Moira. For three evenings he had kept going almost as if nothing had happened, so humbled and grieved by the turn his life had taken that he didn't wish to find a word, not one, to express it, but rather held it in – held it so tightly inside him that no one could suspect how changed he was, how absolutely changed.

If I can keep it in, he said to himself, then my body will assimilate it; it will become diluted and one day – perhaps? – it won't be there any more. It will have passed through me – only the vaguest memory – and gone.

'Bill for table four, Mr Partridge.' Myra, carrying four empty wine glasses, came into the kitchen.

Larry got off his stool and, taking his drink, shuffled over to the pine desk Edwin had provided for him at one end of the kitchen. He wrote out and added up the bill for a party of four – young people he had never seen before – and handed it to Myra.

If they're leaving now, Larry thought, then I don't have to go, not to the strangers. I'll wait till they've paid and gone and then I'll go and have a word with the Barkworths.

Larry liked Lal Barkworth. She looked at the world out of fierce brown eyes. Neither the eyes nor the body were still for long: only when something or someone managed to hold her elusive attention did she stop pacing and watching. Larry sensed that she tolerated him – as she seemed not to tolerate most people she met.

But remembering her staring eyes, now he felt afraid of facing her – knowing that she of all people would see at once that something had happened, that his gestures were awkward, his mind slow.

He refilled his whisky glass and sat motionless on the stool, waiting to hear the door close on the party of young people.

When he heard them leave and Myra came back into the kitchen with their money on a saucer, Larry got off the stool and, without looking in the mirror Edwin had hung above his desk to see if his hair was tidy, wandered out into the dining room.

Lal was sitting alone, smoking a cigarette. Forgetting for a moment that he had cooked two dinners, Larry wondered if she had come alone and had sat there all evening in silence. This sudden feeling of pity for her made him forget his pain just for an instant and smile at her. Lal smiled back.

Larry noticed that her brown eyes seemed bereft of some of their sharpness, almost filmed over. So it's all right then, he thought. She's drunk quite a lot; she's not seeing clearly, not into my mind – she won't guess.

'Hello, Larry dear.'

'Mrs Barkworth.' Larry held out a limp, hot hand and Lal touched it lightly.

'I expect we're keeping you up,' she said.

Larry looked round at the empty restaurant. 'Monday night – no one at the feast! Washday doesn't give one an appetite, I daresay.'

'We had a good meal.'

'Did you? Not one of my best, any of it. We all have our off nights, don't we?'

'Mine was very nice, Larry. I couldn't eat it all, I'm afraid. I never seem to be able to, not when it's something special. I used to eat well when I was young. Will you sit down, Larry? Henry's gone to the loo, he won't be long.'

'Oh, yes, I see. Well . . .' Larry felt confused.

He wanted to say: 'I thought you'd come alone', then realised that he'd cooked the veal for Henry Barkworth and here on the table of course were two wine glasses, two coffee cups.

He sat, gulping his whisky. Over the rim of his glass he was aware of Lal watching him.

'It isn't the same!' Larry blurted out.

There was a moment's silence; then Lal said: 'What isn't?'

'Oh . . . you know . . .' Larry couldn't finish the sentence.

To Lal's amazement, he had begun to weep, making no effort to disguise or cover his crying, his face awash with tears.

'Oh, Larry . . .'

Larry took another drink from the whisky glass, then stammered: 'I haven't told anyone. I thought I could keep it . . . inside . . . I thought no one would need to know.'

'Yes,' said Lal, quietly, 'yes.'

'But . . .' Larry put a fist up to his eyes now. 'I can't. It just isn't possible . . . when something like that . . .'

'Is it something to do with Edward?'

'Edwin. *Edwin.* That's his name. Not Edward. He was never like an Edward. Only like himself, like Edwin. And we were so happy. We were just as happy – happier – than some people married. I thought we were. I thought I knew. And I never would have left him, never in my life, so how could he . . .?'

Larry's voice was choked with his sobbing. Facing him across the table, Lal's body felt freezing cold. She reached out a hand and laid it on his arm. She was glad of the warmth of his arm under her cold hand. 'If . . .' she began.

Larry looked up. 'What?'

'If . . . he had just gone for a while perhaps, for a kind of holiday, a break from routine, well then – '

'No.'

'But why then, Larry? Why should he leave you?'

Larry pulled out a purple handkerchief and wiped his eyes. 'He . . .' Larry stopped, sucked at the whisky. 'It was on Saturday. I had thought . . . because of the sunny day, we would have lunch out on the patio. I made us the lunch. Edwin was out. I didn't know where because he didn't tell me. So I made this nice lunch for us and waited for him.

'But when he came back he said he didn't want any lunch and I said: "Edwin, I made this for you and I opened a bottle of hock and thought we could sit out in the sunshine . . ."

'He got into one of his rages. He wanted to get into a rage. He wanted me to do something silly like sulking over the meal so that he could rage at me and leave there and then. He tried to make me the excuse. He said he couldn't bear it the way I always spoiled him and did things for him and then sulked if he didn't like them, but I said: "Edwin, okay, I do that; I do that because I want you to like things and be happy with me, but that isn't enough! You couldn't leave, not for that."

'So then he had to admit – he had to admit that wasn't it. He was drunk – got himself drunk on vodkas so that he could tell me. It's someone called Dean, nineteen or something, no more than a kid. Edwin's been sleeping with him. Whenever he goes out, that's where he's gone, to sleep with him. He says he can't be . . . He says he's obsessed with him . . . He says he can't be without him.'

Larry stopped talking. His sobs were only shudders now. Lal kneaded his arm. 'Oh, Larry . . .'

'I'm sorry,' he blurted. 'I'm sorry to burden you.'

'No, Larry, I'm the one who's sorry, so sad, because I knew

you had this – this precious kind of love. You see, I can't do any more for anyone now, but I was once very strong because I loved. I was so strong! I'm too old now. I just turn away. That's all I can do, isn't it, when everything's so ugly – just turn away. But you, Larry, you must fight to get him back, to get your love back. Life is so hideous without love, Larry; it makes you want to die.'

'Evening, Larry!'

Henry, jovially wined and full, staggered to the table. 'How's tricks, then?' he said.

Lal lay still. The meal lay in her stomach like a stone. Henry lay next to her, sweating a little as he snored.

As quietly as she could, not wanting to wake Henry, Lal got out of bed and crept to the bathroom. She made up one of her indigestion powders and sat on the edge of the bath, watching the powder dissolve.

When she had drunk it down, she belched and a little of the pain left her stomach, as if the stone had been blanketed by snow.

'There won't be another fifty, thank God,' she whispered, staring at her empty glass; but even though she smiled at this thought, she found that a tear had slid down her cheek on to her lip. Lal sighed. 'Oh, well,' she whispered, 'at least for once I'm not weeping for myself. I'm weeping for Larry.'

Current Account

'*Bronze?* I'm not as rich as I was.'

The Princesse de Villemorin crossed her still estimable legs and glared at the sunset now faded to a luminous mauve that almost matched her high-heeled sandals.

'People seem to think I'm immune from inflation. But no one is immune. Take just the servants. I'm paying them fifty per cent more than I was five years ago. So you see . . .'

The princess turned and reached out a caressing hand. Discreet turquoise bangles gently clinked as the hand came to rest on Guy's naked shoulder. The hand journeyed upwards, fingering the warm back of the neck, then tugging at the roots of hair so marvellously blond she privately compared it to the gold spun from flax in a fairytale she had long forgotten.

'Please don't be cross, darling.'

'I need the bronze, Penelope.'

'I know you do, but have you any idea what bronze in that kind of quantity costs now?'

'You can afford it.'

'Couldn't you work in lead or metal or something? You hear of terribly successful sculptors making things out of old prams these days and showing them at the Tate.'

'Not me.'

'You don't hear of anyone – except perhaps Henry Moore – working in bronze.'

'Bronze is the only substance I can relate to.'

'Substance? You make it sound like putty.'

The princess's hand tumbled as Guy rose and walked to the edge of the terrace. Beneath him, the garden lay in shadow, puffing its exotic breath at the encroaching dusk. He was aware, as he sighed, of Penelope on her chair, her body in its floating dress, her eyes watching, possessing, her thought: *without my money he can't work.* Anger welled up, familiar yet absurd. *One day, I will leave her.*

'Of course,' came her silky voice, 'you can have the bronze. Guy? Listen to me, darling. You can have the bronze. I'll ring my stockbroker in the morning and arrange the money. It's only that sometimes . . .'

'What?'

'I wish you'd be more grateful.'

Guy was silent, smelling the white flowers shaped like stars that climbed the terrace wall. His mind charged to her morning ceremonial, she exquisitely in place on her satin sheets, her body massaged and tremulous with its invitation, her eyes lidded with silver, sparkler-fizzing for the first touch of him. And the weight she demanded, the strength that had to clutch and devour so that her face lay buried in his neck, his dragon-panting fanning her hair, his sweat sucking his belly to hers, her deep and buried sigh of triumph as she used him up.

I wish you'd be more grateful.

She is fifty-five. She is twenty-three years older than me. She could have borne me.

The thought followed Guy from her bed to his studio. On entering the high room, he'd perch on a stool and will the thought to settle in the plaster dust, become obliterated in his work. Because here – only here – was he safe from her. This was Bluebeard's room, the one the Princesse de Villemorin couldn't enter. Once it had been a laundry. Far into the twentieth century, women had slapped and pummelled the soiled linen of the châtelaine on stones worn to glimmering. Now it held the quiet of his inspiration. Nothing moved in it but Guy and the straining forms imprisoned first in clay, then finally in bronze.

As the sculptor worked, he chose to forget, if he could, the presence of the Princesse de Villemorin embarked upon the journey of each sumptuous day, little chiselled heels clacking over sunlight on her polished floors, voice dealing faultless instructions to the sallow-faced people she called *les domestiques*, pointed fingers rearranging a bowl of roses, fluttering from the roses to the rosewood bureau to gather the telephone, to pick up a gold pen and begin to notate in ruled columns, ankles crossed now, the body at peace with its arithmetic. *I wish you'd be more grateful* . . .

She disturbs me. In every sense of this word, she is a disturbing woman. If she was French, she would disturb me less; it's the Englishness staring out of her French name – the Princesse Penelope de Villemorin – that gives her away to me and makes me loathe where (I have vowed to my art) I must try to love. Yet she says she belongs to France now. When she snoozes in the afternoons, she has nightmares of the old prince her husband and the line of noble cousins, nephews (yet not children) dangling from his limbs to weigh him down with magisterial expectations and with a voice bleating sorrow for the gravest of his failures, his bitter marriage. Mon dieu, mon dieu, an English divorcée and a Protestant, snickered the ancient trussed-up de Villemorin aunts. What a blow for the *famille*! What a muddying of the line! 'I was married to him for eight years,' said Penelope, 'and that family taught me nothing except how to hate them.'

Oh but they taught you how to value money! That was the legacy of the marriage, the one you used against them after the prince left you. Poor old prince, with his exquisite nails. He wanted to tear your flesh with his nails for squandering all that he gave you, for wasting it all, wasting his love. Yet he put on a clean silk shirt, tied his paisley tie from Simpson's of Piccadilly, clicked his heels at eight years of marriage and walked out without touching you or seeing you again. And you squawked like a macaw for the best lawyers. You scented a fortune and it hung like a whiff of tar in solicitors' rooms, crouched just out of sight in the creases of solicitors' smiles. You knew you should get half. But the family fought you. All with their filbert nails and perfected manners, they fought you like cockerels. So you settled for a lump sum. You stopped sniffing the tar smell of 'half'. The lump sum was more than enough.

Or so you thought then, when it was you alone, Penelope – no longer a princess, but still calling yourself one – and moved in alone to your pretty château 'with its own historical laundry and stabling for five cars'. But the years picked at it. Your own tastes became richer: the aloneness of you sought compensation. And the menopausal Penelope mourned the dying out of beauty. You touched the crevices of your body and remembered the gaudy kisses of the young. One night, you started going to the town in your Mercedes, drinking a crème de menthe in one of the bars and driving home with a young man's head in your lap. For a while, the young men were cheap. And then, in the same bar, in the same way, I met you.

The butler, Maurice, announced dinner.

Penelope adjusted the thin heelstrap of a mauve shoe and stood up. 'Come on, Guy darling. Stop pouting and put your shirt on. I've told you, we'll arrange for the shipment of bronze. I was only teasing about the old prams.'

She held out her arm, waiting for his hand to steer her inside to the candlelit dining room, but he was fussing with his shirt, his face turned away from her.

'Hurry up, darling. I want to talk to you over dinner, about Lorna.'

'What about Lorna?'

'I've got a letter from her, full of all her dull goings on in Australia. But it seems she's coming to Europe and wants to see me.'

'Why does she want to see you?'

'Money, I suppose. Why else do stubborn daughters creep back to mothers they affect to despise? But God knows, on a teacher's salary, how she can afford the airfare.'

Guy tucked his shirt inside the pale blue trousers the princess had bought for him in Paris. There were moments, and this was one of them, when Penelope de Villemorin felt impaled by her own yearnings. *Sainte Marie, let him never leave me.*

'Come along, Guy. Anita has made a soufflé and it will spoil.'

So they sat close to each other in the pretty dining room and were served. Guy noticed, in between forkfuls of the soufflé, that Penelope had begun to economise on her wines: the Pouilly-Montrachet he had learned to expect had been replaced by a cheap local Loire wine. He longed to ask her suddenly precisely how rich she was. Tell me *precisely*, he wanted to say, how much money and what assets you own. But certain questions breed for a lifetime and are never uttered. He would ask her instead about the gallery.

'The gallery?'

'Yes.' Guy wondered why she sounded surprised.

'Well, what can I tell you? You know it all already. Our policy is sound in my view. We search for young painters and help them on their way. We create fashions.'

'And your stake was half?' The word never lost its particular meaning for the princess.

'I believe it's an excellent investment – and a lovely excuse to go to Paris more often! Of course, one could wish that returns were higher. It seems not enough collectors are prepared to take the financial risks on new artists.'

'Art isn't a commodity, Penelope.'

'Oh no! I didn't mean to imply that. But as you yourself know, it's a very costly business. Art would simply not exist without the rich.'

'Of course it would exist!'

'Well exist, yes, but no one could live by it. Anyway darling, let's not argue. There's no earthly reason we couldn't give you an autumn show at the gallery.'

'And you take sixty per cent of everything I sell!'

Penelope smiled. She noticed, fleetingly, that the prawns in the soufflé echoed perfectly the colour of the dining-room walls.

'I expect,' she said, 'we could make an exception in your case.'

*

94

The princess couldn't sleep. She went to the rosewood bureau. She re-read Lorna's letter, written in large writing she had always considered plain and lacking in character. The letter told her that Lorna (now twenty-eight by Penelope's calculations) would 'take advantage, this year, of a European summer vacation'. The visit to the château was planned for August.

Memories of her daughter ('always clever, Penelope. Lorna was always clever...') made her fidget with guilt and irritation. She tugged at a piece of stiff writing paper and began: 'My dear Lorna, I'm so very sorry to say that an August visit won't be possible as I shall be travelling...' but quickly crumpled it. The clever girl would find some way to see her. The clever girl's eyes would ferret among the telltale creases of fifty-five years and decide with satisfaction, Mother's power is waning. Oh it was cruel, miserable! Why ever had this teacher daughter decided to poke and pry after eight blissful years of separation and silence?

She pulled out her portfolio (how it had dwindled!) of stocks and shares. How utterly miserable to be selling off yet more. But the bronze, though. She must find a way to purchase this wretched bronze for Guy. The princess rubbed her eyes, puffy from snatched sleep. *Money is power.* So whispered the de Villemorin aunts, clucking over each her own fortune. They died in their bonnets and were buried unmourned. The money was shared among the cousins who squandered it, so complained the prince, on American luxuries, not forgetting American women...

The sun came up beyond the steep apple orchards. The house began to murmur with the tiptoeing of servants. It was the hour when the princess usually rose and washed her body, before presenting it, creamed and scented, to Guy. *Obliterate me*, said this scented yearning body. But this morning, immobile at her desk, the princess felt too tired.

The bronze and Lorna arrived the same day, 10 August. Guy stood in the laundry, fingering the blackish lumps, beautiful as yet only by their incredible weight.

A stubbornly hot fortnight and the death of the one stock-broker she trusted had ravaged the poise of the princess. She had enraged Guy by drinking more wine than she could hold and wailing in her little-girl's voice that she had never been loved. As he touched the bronze, the sun falling on his wide hand, he tried not to measure the price he was paying for this precious metal.

He stayed in the laundry studio all day, working in clay. When the sun dipped from the high windows, he came out into the hot evening. He was tired. He longed to lie down in a cool bed, alone.

He showered and changed (this much I can do for Penelope's daughter) and went to find the two women. Penelope looked glittering. As a defence against Lorna's arrival, she had had her hair re-tinted, she had draped her body in a white, off-the-shoulder dress. She fingered the pearl choker clenched at her neck. 'This is Lorna. Lorna, this is Guy who . . . has the old laundry house as his studio. He's a very, very talented sculptor, aren't you darling?'

Lorna got up. The flamboyant introduction had seemed to demand movement of some kind. Guy saw a thin, bony girl with clever brown eyes and thick hair cut very short. She wore an Indian dress, skimpy and creased. Her breasts, covered by this whisper of material, seemed oddly plump, the only part of her body that betrayed any blood tie with her mother. Her smile suggested a knowingness that must surely irritate Penelope.

'My mother didn't say you were here.'

Australia. Yes, he could see it now, the woman-stayed-girl at twenty-eight. Freckled. Nourished by enormous skies.

Guy held out his hand, tried to stare past the smile.

'You've come a long way.'

'Yes. But then it's years since I saw Mother. I expect she told you.'

'Lorna loves the house, Guy.'

Penelope had never attempted to quell the enjoyment she got from showing other people her riches. Why bother with

Aubusson carpets if no one ever admires them? And Lorna had clearly been astonished by the château and its treasures. She had remembered her mother was rich, yet seemed to have forgotten that riches can gleam at you from surfaces you can touch and smell.

'And she's going to stay for ten days, which is wonderful for me. So much to catch up on, haven't we Lorna?'

Oh yes, thought the Australian girl. But surely you understand that that's precisely why I came over, to get a full account of a life I've only allowed myself to guess at since you left my father and married the stiff and straight prince and became wealthy. And of course you never told me about the sculptor, young enough to be my brother. You left me to imagine you getting old by yourself. I thought at last time had punished you.

Guy sat down. Penelope reached for the champagne in its brimming bucket and poured him a glass. The sun on the terrace was still warm. He took the glass from Penelope and turned to the daughter. Her eyes were lowered, seeming to contemplate her slim, dusty feet in flat sandals.

'To Lorna!' said Guy.

The nights are extraordinary, thought Lorna. So perfectly peaceful. Mother has created an 'island'. In it, everything breathes as ordained by her, and the world outside, the world I know of cramped rooms and pushing your body into the little corner of sun left on your balcony after four o'clock in the blistering Sydney summers, exists beyond. Useless to tell her of that other world. In it, for her, exists only terror, and she doesn't want to look. Sufficient that the stockbroker died. That was terror enough! She still talks of it: 'With my kind of money, you have to be careful, you see, Lorna. Because people can milk you. I'm being milked by everyone. By the servants, by accountants and even by the gallery in Paris. I honestly don't believe I'm getting my due on my investment. And this spring, I was forced to sell the one mingy tiara given to me by belle-mère de Villemorin. Luckily I know Arnaud Clerc of the Bijouterie Clerc in Paris, or even that could have gone for next to nothing . . .'

97

Oh Mother, what deafening complaint clanks across the acres of quiet, so carefully tended! I can hear your mind stoking its engines of dissatisfaction, even as you sit on your terrace, so poised, reaching for the bottle in the ice bucket, reaching for the sculptor's smile. Fears group and regroup in you. Your white dress, at dinner, was splashed with some reddish sauce or other. You looked to the sculptor for help, but he turned away. He turned to me with his smile, yet all I could do was stare. Because what does an artist do to himself if he locks himself inside Mother's island? What are you doing? Working you say, but working in an old laundry where women were paid a pittance to plunge their red arms into the stained, suddy water of the unassailably rich. How has Mother stained you? Guy, the sculptor. Why do you smile at me when, even this minute perhaps, Mother opens her arms and receives you like a gift of amber, spreads you on her like an ointment – your youth to heal her age.

Yet there is something. Not in you, Guy, as much as in me. Some feeling that made me turn away, made me gabble about myself, telling jokes about my Head of Department to see if you laughed and showing off my clever self ('Lorna is so unlike you, Penelope dear,' said long-ago friends) to let you know there was substance inside the shorn head, inside the cheap Indian dress so marvellously wrong for Mother's dining room. And you listened. You watched. Mother buys you. She buys you afresh each day. But a look in you – and in me – lets me believe I could have you free.

'Promise me,' whispered Penelope, 'that you won't.'

Half asleep, deliciously comfortable in the enfolding satin, Guy mumbled ambiguous assent, let the princess caress the side of his face, then slipped with perfect ease into a dream of Lorna. He was bathing in a river. Lorna waded in from a rock, still wearing the skinny dress which, once wetted, clung to her. He gazed at her eyes, lashes flecked with water like minuscule diamonds. When he kissed her, her tongue was long and gentle.

The princess wanted to pull him back from sleep. It was as if, sleeping, Guy deserted her. She said his name. He lay still and golden beside her, barely covered. Look at him, she wanted to wail to the ghost of the prince walled up in some mausoleum near Tours, look at my lover!

The princess had never known such terrible days. Ten in all, she reminded herself. After ten days, she will be gone. She belongs in the history classroom. She belongs in some ugly suburb. Only Guy and I belong here, with my treasures that keep us safe, with each our own role to play.

'I hate having my role confused, darling.'

'Your role?'

'Yes. Lorna confuses my role, Guy.'

The laugh was mocking, ungentle. The princess looked up sharply. 'Guy, you did promise me, didn't you?'

'Promise you?'

'That you wouldn't. You wouldn't ever, would you?'

'I already have.'

Not merely in his dreams. He and Lorna had gone walking early on the fourth morning of the ten. The princess sat in bed with her silver breakfast tray, calling Paris, calling London, too preoccupied with the telephone to imagine they could be gone all morning, gone still at lunchtime, eating joyously in a little café with memories of their morning bright in their eyes. Yet what made him admit it? What made him decide not to lie, when lying was so easy? *You believe what you want to believe.*

'Oh Guy . . .' Penelope's hands were rammed against her mouth. Guy stared, horrified. For a second, he imagined that neither words nor tears would come gushing out from between the fingers, but blood.

'Penelope . . .'

'Don't speak! I can't listen to anything!'

'It was terribly innocent, Penelope.'

'Innocent! Don't Guy! *Don't!* You make me want to be sick. You make me want to die!'

The act innocent because so joyful, he thought, yet the

inspiration cruel: two people who approach each other, aware of the invisible onlooker, whose torment drives them on. As they enfold each other, there she is in the touch and push of their bodies, there she is tangled in their moist hair, there she is in their breaths. And afterwards – the glorious knowledge that together they had conquered her, where each had failed to conquer alone. As they walk back, they hear it, the click-clack of Penelope's high heels, the clink and trinkle of Mother's bracelets. Perfect, thinks Guy. Perfect, thinks Lorna.

The Princesse de Villemorin sat alone by the first fire of September. The London accountant had been and gone, the Paris gallery owner had been and gone. She was left with their sums and her misery.

Maurice announced himself. Penelope sipped at her whisky and didn't turn. A reminder, Madame, says Maurice, only a *reminder* that no one in the château has received any *salaire* this month . . .

She waved him away. Let them all desert her. Nothing mattered any more. Only the plans she made in the golden whisky haze: she would buy bronze in quantities no mortal could dream of owning, she would fill the laundry with bronze, she would lay her head on the vast, unmoving lumps of bronze and let her tears flow onto its darkness.

I know him, she whispers to the spent fire, I know he will trade his Sydney teacher (firm though her breasts are, clever though her damned head has always been) for his own statues. The artist in him will win and without money the artist in him will pine. The mouldering de Villemorin jewels will go. They must all go. And Maurice must realise that no one can be paid now, not till I have wedged that studio with what he calls his 'substance'. Life drowns and gurgles in the sea of the whisky glass. Life sleeps. I am Sleeping Beauty ('What a joke, at your age, Mother!') and I refuse to wake up till the prince has picked his way through the briars and roses of my daughter's mind and comes crashing down here, his weight as potent as the weight of bronze, to crush me and still me with life.

Guy stayed with Lorna till his money and the summer ran out, then made his way south to the Princesse de Villemorin's château.

On her long flight home to Sydney, Lorna ate none of the food offered her and stayed absolutely still in her seat, talking to no one. Around her parting from Guy, a man who, had she found him before he strayed into a bar one night and met her mother, she believed she might have loved, she concocted an essay subject for her sixth-form students: 'What is the function of the creative artist in our materialistic society?' She saw the blackboard where she would write up the title. She saw the thirty or so faces staring at it with anxious frowns. One of the girls raised her hand. 'Please, miss, I don't understand.'

Words with Marigold

I don't know why me. I don't know why you want to talk to me.
I'm no different from anyone. I mean, there are hundreds –
thousands – of girls like me, aren't there? Perhaps you're going
to talk to us all, are you? Lost Generation, or whatever it is they
call us. I've always wondered how they do surveys. I bet they
take a tiny sample of people and call it a silent majority. I mean,
I bet they can't be bothered to go round asking hundreds of
people the same stupid questions. Except I met one on a train
once. A survey person. She tried to make me answer things like
'How frequently do you travel on this train?' I said, that's my
business, *dearie,* I said I don't own much, but I own what I do
and why I do it. She went puce. I followed her down into First
Class and she got this group of men in business suits and they
invited her to sit down. I suppose it was a great day for them. I
suppose they'd been longing for years for someone to ask them
what they were doing on that train! They were drinking
whiskies an' that. They travelled on that train every day.

I'm not extraordinary though. I suppose it's considered
extraordinary to have a termination at sixteen, but I can tell
you it isn't, if that's what you're thinking. I mean, it's no more
extraordinary than having a fuck. In fact, that's all it is, if you
think about it. A screw. With consequences. No one worries
about anyone having a screw, less they're real actual kids or
something. But try getting a termination at sixteen. I mean the
stuff you have to put up with. Fine till they suss your age. I
mean, perfectly okay an' that, but then they start on at you.
They start implying your whole life could be fucked, like you've
screwed your whole personality and your whole chances and

you're psychologically damaged. They want to make you start believing these things or they wouldn't just act like that, would they? And the stuff about your parents. They imply your mum's to blame or something because you're too young to think for yourself. They say things like, 'Was your mother aware of your relationship?' So I said, no love, my mum's not aware of any sodding thing these days. She's out of her mind most of the time on Special Brew. And her eyes are going as well – disappearing inside her flesh. She's put on three stone since last year.

But actually that is when things started to get bad. I'd have said I was quite all right, like you know, quite happy till that all began. I was working for my O-levels. Biology was my best subject. Biology and Art, but they said you can't take Art. I was okay at Maths. Not fantastic, you know, but okay. I could have got something like a C or something. Eddie used to help me with Maths. I mean quite a lot. Not just five minutes to get you through your homework, but he'd sit down with me when Mum was getting tea and he used to say, Marigold, you've got this tendency to think in straight lines and what I've got to do is to help you think in circles or spirals. He had a name for this kind of thinking. He was very interesting about it and it really started to help me because I'd tended to think there was always one way of doing something and this was the *meant* way. Because at school they never noticed things like how you were thinking, I mean they didn't have time, did they, but Eddie said he'd make time and he did.

I really enjoyed Maths homework after Eddie started to help me. I'd bring extra work home and you could just hear the teachers thinking God, Marigold Rickards taking extra Maths to do at home! But my results got better. It was terrific seeing the results get good. I mean, let's not exaggerate. I'd never be a mathematician or anything, like I could be a painter probably if I could get into art school and get my technique better. I still think I could be a painter. I mean I haven't lost hope, have I, and I know about one of the medical aspects of people in depressions is they lose hope. They just look into the future and see black or brown or something, just some dark colour and nothing in it. But I don't. I mean, I even write letters to people asking them for money to help me get through art college. I don't get any money back, but I keep writing, don't I, so that must be a good sign. I wrote to Lady Falkender. Someone told me she was a patron of the arts or whatever. Do you think she'll write back or send me something? I mean, I don't know. I can't really imagine how Lady Falkender lives, can you? I don't know if she'd write to someone like me.

I've thought of writing to Eddie, except neither of us – my mum nor me – know his address. And I bet it wouldn't do any good to write. But it did all start then, when I think about it. Till Eddie left our house I think we were all right. They'd have rows, Eddie and my mum, but not terrible ones. He never hit her. I mean, don't get me wrong, he wasn't at all a violent person. He liked jokes. He'd make jokes the minute he woke up. Sometimes his jokes got on my wick, but other times I'd think, he kind of keeps us all going and if he weren't here or something we'd probably have nothing to laugh at and we'd just go quiet like I suppose we must have been before. I suppose when I think about it, I dreaded the idea of Eddie leaving us. I mean I knew my mum would just go to bits, because you could tell what he was to her. There was nothing she wouldn't do for him. He got the works. Best food she could afford, terrific ironing, thermos washed up, cufflinks and stuff at Christmas . . .

It was the age difference, I think. They were about the same age about, but she looked older. I don't blame him. He was with us for seven years and that's quite long, isn't it? I mean, I was nine or nearly nine when he came. And he never said, I don't think he said Marigold's a fucking nuisance and got me palmed off with neighbours. He just accepted me and treated me like his own kid. I mean, better than some fathers are to their kids. Quite a bit better. Like helping me with my Maths I told you about. And other things. They used to go on outings to London and he'd always say, let's take Marigold, she should have the chance to see the big city an' that. His favourite thing in London was the Science Museum. He knew masses about some of the old compasses and chronometers. There was this man who invented a type of chronometer and he was a kind of hero for Eddie. Harrison. I don't know which century he was. Before Nelson, probably.

My mum wasn't too interested in chronometers, actually. But I don't think it was that. I mean, you wouldn't leave someone because they weren't interested in something, would you? I think it was definitely the other girl he met. She was some sort of secretary at the engineering works where he worked. I only saw her once, but I think she was quite kind of posh an' spoke all terrific an' wore skirts with linings in them. Know the type I mean? She wasn't specially pretty or anything. Not that I could see. But she was lots younger than my mum. I'd say she was twenty-eight or nine. And I think she hypnotised Eddie by being this different kind of person and he'd come home and start correcting my mum's grammar. And my mum got scared. I mean, this was the pitiful thing. She got frightened she'd say things wrong. She *wanted* her grammar to be better, to please Eddie. And food. He bought my mum a book called *French Cooking Explained.* She tried to do things from it for a bit till she sussed the flippin' insult in all that. Then she put the book in the oven and the oven caught fire and that was the first time I ever saw Eddie really angry with her. I heard him yelling at her and I came down and the kitchen was covered with white stuff from the fire extinguisher, and then my mum rushed past me and up to the toilet and sicked up. I think she knew that was the end with Eddie. I don't think she'd heard about the girl at work by then. But she knew it was all over for her. I mean, you do, I think. Don't you think? One minute you don't know and then another one minute passes and that's the crucial one, like going into a ghost train, know what I mean? Like this one minute is much longer than even longer, darker things like ghost trains. D'you get it? I got it there and then. I could see that was the crucial minute and our lives wouldn't go on like they were.

My mum blames Eddie. She thinks she's finished now. She's only forty-four. Eddie left some socks and things behind and she burned these in the yard. I started going off her when she did this. Up till then, I'd felt really sorry for her. I'd hear her crying through the wall. I used to make a tray of tea and go and sit on her bed. Waste of time though. She'd just snivel about 'getting even' and I went off her when she'd start on this. 'Cos it's Eddie's life as well as hers, isn't it? Like in my case it's Alan's life as well as mine. Least, that's what I've had to tell myself. No one's got control. You can be a king of somewhere or the head of a billion-pound corporation or whatever and still get clobbered. Only thing is you've got money if you're a king or something or the head of a billion-pound whatsit. So you can go to art college. Providing they'll take you. You don't have to write begging letters to people. And you've got O-levels.

My Maths got terrible. I'd relied on Eddie, hadn't I? I couldn't get myself to think in spirals or whatever. I lost the knack. So I knew I wouldn't get Maths O. Not even a C or something. I could have got biology because my drawings were good, I mean they looked professional and the drawings are half of it with biology: cross-section of the broad bean, mucor heads, habitat of the brown water beetle . . . I don't know about Eng Lit. I might have got it. *As You Like It* we did. Alan told me *As You Like It* is quite an important play, but I kept thinking, I don't know what they're doing exactly.

I think I'm attracted to people who want to help me. Or they're attracted to me. Alan wanted to help me. I went to get my mum out of the pub one night, 'cos she couldn't move. She was sitting in a corner, sweating. She used to dribble when she got to this state. Dribble and burp and sometimes sick up. Now I can't stand to see a person drunk. Specially her. I run a mile. I can't go near them or touch them. Alan helped me out with her. I got her to bed and Alan stayed. I don't mean he forced himself on me. I mean, what I did was talk. Like I'm talking to you, but better, because I was deeply attracted to Alan. I mean I'd had some boys, Badger Reid from school and Billy Tansley who thought he was Don Juan 'cos he'd got a second-hand Suzuki! But they were for laughs. Rubbish! Alan was older, see. I mean he was a mature man.

He had this cottage. It's called Green End. It's down a track, miles from anything. He thinks the world of it. He says if he lived in town, he'd wind up killing someone. I don't think he likes people. He likes women. He's a very attractive man.

He didn't seduce me or anything. It was five or something in the morning when I shut up talking and he just lay me down where we were in front of the fire in the front room. I was wearing my school skirt and he came all over it so as not to come inside me. He said coming on my skirt was the most exciting sexual experience he'd ever had. Men say these things, don't they? They say things to make you feel special. I mean, I know that now, but I didn't exactly know it then. So I've learned something haven't I? Means it wasn't all just a waste.

Alan had this handmade kiln in his garden. He'd built it himself, brick by brick. It was fate he was in the pub that one night, because he didn't go out hardly ever. He stayed at Green End and did his pottery. He let me make a pot once, but it was rubbish. He had a university degree from Oxbridge. I knew Oxbridge was two places by the time I met Alan, but I used to think they were one place. I don't think my mum even knows what Oxbridge is! If you said, what's Oxbridge, Mum? she'd say something like stock cubes. Eddie once told me she was ignorant. Eddie said it was sad when young people got older not knowing anything. He tried to make me promise I'd go on to A-levels and get to university if I could. He said qualifications were everything these days.

My mum got ill that night after Alan came. I had to stay home from school and try to stop her drinking, the doctor said. What a laugh, eh? I had to stop her going out to buy beer. Fat chance. She was down the off-licence soon as she could stand up, then down the pub. She looked like death. Like a suet roly-poly. She wasn't cared, though, was she? An' she never give me a thought, what I'd done for her. I mean, the day Eddie left, she lost interest in me.

Billy Tansley gave me a lift on his bike to Alan's place. Charged me a quid for the ride, greedy little bugger. Nothing's for nothing, he said. Wanted to charge me another quid for promising not to tell where I was, but I wasn't playing. You tell the whole effing street, if you want to, Billy, I said.

Alan got really excited when he saw me arrive. I mean, to have me coming to him and asking him to help me just gave him a gigantic hard-on. I'd put my uniform on again and I'd washed and ironed the skirt and he just grabbed me by the shoulders the minute he saw me and took me into his kitchen and fucked me against his fridge. You could hear bottles or something falling over inside the fridge 'cos we jogged it so hard. And I thought, God, this guy's the most fantastic person. I mean passionate. I mean, I got him really hyped up, you know, like a desperate animal.

He loved cooking, Alan. He made this terrific vegetarian thing for me the first evening I was there. He said I had beautiful breasts. He wanted me to eat his meal with my tits showing. He told me he had dreams of girls like me when he was married. He said they got in the way of normal marital relations. He said actually these dreams had destroyed his marriage.

His bed was really good, not like normal beds. He had Indian hangings on it and the sheets smelled like he'd been waving joss-sticks over them. I really liked that bed. The nights I spent in it were the best of my life. I used to come all the time. I mean, he knew what to do. He'd been married. He wasn't like Billy Tansley or Badger Reid, those babies. And he came masses. After the first times, he didn't bother getting out when he came. He said to come inside me was the realisation of ten years of dreaming.

I don't know why I go on about him, I mean how wonderful he was and everything. I don't know why I'm telling you all these private sexual things. I mean, I should have forgotten him, that's what everyone says. I shouldn't keep letting myself remember. But it's not exactly remembering. I mean, all those things I had with Alan are just *there*, they're still in me if you know what I mean? I still wake up and think, it can't have happened, what did happen. I still sometimes think I'm in that bed and then we'll have this day in front of us, the kind of day when Alan works at his pottery and I'm just there adoring him, like I was his wife or something . . .

It was a long way to school from Green End. I used to bike it on Alan's bike when I felt like it. But I'd gone right off work and off the other girls. I mean, they used to say crap like 'Billy Tansley told us you got a sugar-daddy, Marigold.' And you should have seen the rubbish they were going with! Those schoolboys couldn't make anyone feel like a woman. They couldn't make a *woman* feel like a woman! They were wankers. Didn't know a thing about passion. So I felt superior. Who wouldn't? Only thing I got better at at school was Eng Lit. Alan knew masses about Shakespeare. He knew what everything meant. He explained *As You Like It* to me from beginning to end. No, I got bloody cheesed off with school, though. Bossy teachers. Girls boasting about their spotty blokes. I was ready to give it up, except Alan kept saying just what Eddie had said – got to stick it out at school till you get the exams. And I think they were right. I regret it now that I had to pack it in.

My mum turned up one day. She looked a bit better, but she wasn't. She's on the booze now an' that's it. I thought, go on, Ma, do the mother bit. Tell your daughter she's filth. Tell her she's sweet sixteen and chucking her life away on a man of thirty-eight. I was wrong, though. She'd just come for a look. Alan made her a cup of tea and I could tell she was watching her grammar. He impressed her all right. She'd never met anyone like him. I think maybe she even fancied him, 'cos she started on about herself, telling him what a beauty she'd been before she got fat. But she disgusted him. He'd seen her that night in the pub. He thought she was awful, the pits. He pushed her out after we'd had the tea and she looked really hurt like as if she wanted to be invited to stay.

I never thought I'd wind up back with her. You bloody learn though, don't you? You think you've got something made. I did. I mean, I had in a way. If I'd been older and known more about everything and if I'd laid off a bit and not been the kind of slave I was to Alan, then he might have, well, you know, fallen in love with me. I don't say he would. I mean, when I think about it, I realise I'm not clever enough for a man like that, and they want more than sex after a while, they want you to know things and recognise famous paintings and understand Shakespeare and decide how you're going to vote and things like that. He liked my drawings, though. He said I could be a good artist if I got a better understanding of why I drew things the way I do. I never thought that aspect was important in drawing, but perhaps it is. If I went to art school, they'd help me with this, wouldn't they? I dunno. Don't suppose I'll ever get there, anyway. You've got to have A-level for art school, haven't you? It's not just a question of the money.

I thought of telling Lady Falkender about the baby. I think I need to talk to someone in a letter or something because quite often I feel clobbered by all that and I start to go down like I am now and not wash or eat or take care of myself. I don't cry. I just think about it and then I get this drained feeling, like being numb and losing touch with gravity or something. I hardly told anyone at the time. I mean, I told Alan because I told him I don't mind having it if it's yours and mine, in fact I'd love to have a little baby and care for it. But he didn't want it. He didn't even want to hear about it and he gave me this long lecture about his wife who spent nine years trying to have a baby and how she came almost to full term twice and then had miscarriages and how she suffered. It was like he hated me for wanting the baby his wife had wanted. He'd gone off me a bit after my mum came, but now he went off me really. I'd hang around him, hoping we could make love and he'd be like he'd been at the beginning, all hot an' that. I'd put my uniform on and go and kiss him on the mouth and push myself against him. Sometimes we'd fuck, but he didn't kiss me or hold me afterwards. He'd fuck with his eyes shut, like he'd get turned off if he looked at me.

He arranged everything. He got me an appointment with some Pregnancy Advice Group. He said, don't worry, Marigold, I'll see you through the actual abortion. But it was finished by then. He despised me. He thought I was stupid to have got pregnant. He said it was the fault of my upbringing. He said the working classes were still miles behind, specially the women, just stupid and ignorant.

His wife's back with him now. I biked out to see him just the one time when the thing was over, the termination I mean. I suppose I thought, if I can't have his baby, perhaps I can still have him. I don't know what made me think this. You're naive at sixteen, I guess. You hope for things you'll never get, I mean probably never get in your whole lifetime. But I thought, I've done what he wanted, got rid of the baby, so he owes me something. But there was this woman there. Someone about his age or a bit younger. She was ever so slim and she walked like she'd once been a dancer. I hadn't a clue who she was. She just came out and stared at me and said, 'I'm Alan's wife. What do you want?' I could have told her, couldn't I? I mean I could have just given it to her, the nights I'd been there and the baby and those dreams of schoolgirls he'd confessed. I could have let her have it all. But it wouldn't have changed anything. It was like when Eddie left our home. You couldn't have made him change his mind.

And I know I've got to get on now. Look at me. I look terrible, don't I? My mum says there's a job going at the turkey place where she works an' I ought to try to get it. I hate turkeys and meat of any kind. It's probably gone by now, anyway, the job. And I get depressed about not getting my O-levels. I mean, there was a time when I could have got Maths even, and I can imagine Eddie being ever so pleased and taking us out for a celebration at the Wimpey. I don't feel rancour, though. I mean, like I said, it's Eddie's life, isn't it, and Alan's life and you've got to make the best of what's left. Otherwise you just go down. And I don't want to go down, but I wish Lady Falkender would write to me. I mean, I've got hopes of that 'cos I think she's the kind of person who might understand. I could be wrong though. I've been wrong about a lot of things.

Autumn in Florida

'Special security passes,' said the travel agent to George, 'are needed for anyone staying at Palmetto Village. I shall require a passport-sized photograph of both you and your wife. These will be forwarded to Palmetto, together with your reservation documents, photostats of the first five pages of your passports – to include, of course, your US visa – and a signed statement by a professional person – doctor, solicitor or JP, say, – vouching both for the likeness of the photographs and for your suitability as a Palmetto resident.'

It was July in Ipswich and stifling in the travel agent's stuffy premises. George loosened his tie and prepared to comment that this seemed like a lot of unnecessary fuss and paraphernalia and red tape and smacked, furthermore, of the CIA, but sighed instead and nodded and thought, the central purpose of this holiday is recovery – recovery from mediocrity, recovery from my everyday self – so I must make absolutely certain that all the arrangements go smoothly and that nothing upsets me. 'Fine,' he snapped.

While the travel agent's fingers began a repetitive waltz with his computer, George picked up the Palmetto brochure. He'd owned an identical one since January and knew the pictures in it by heart: palm-fringed pale and empty beach, palm-fringed yachts jostling for space at a clean and sparkling marina, palm-fringed 18-hole golf course, 'exclusive to Palmetto residents', palm-fringed riverside nightclub hung with orange mandarin lamps, palm-fringed Palmetto Village itself, clusters of pale pink Mexican-style apartments, white umbrellas on roofs and balconies, oleander and hibiscus and Cana lilies framing the buildings not only with bright pink and orange, but also, in George's mind, with certainty. This was no mock-up, no deception: this was the tropical land limb where presidents sipped at brief idleness. While the driving October rains brought down the oak leaves and flooded the Suffolk ditches, here would George be, renewing himself.

George's wife, Beryl, had said at Christmas, it's been a bad year. What you mean, offered George, is you haven't got used to Jennifer being married and not here any more. No, said Beryl, I haven't, but it's not only that.

George understood. He sat in his office at the Wakelin All Saints branch of the Mercantile and General Bank, sipped the weak coffee he had taught his secretary to make and decided, Beryl knows I've been passed over. There's no fooling Beryl. She's heard me murmur about the managership and even though I haven't told her they'll bring a younger man in, she knows they will, a younger man from Head Office probably, cutting his razor-sharp teeth on the Wakelin All Saints branch.

The Wakelin All Saints branch of the Mercantile and General Bank occupied a low, Tudor building that had once been two workers' cottages. Rescued from years of decay in the sixties by a hairdresser called Maurice, they had given brief but unlikely houseroom to backwash basins, driers, mirror tables, infra-red lamps and black imitation leather chairs. But Wakelin All Saints was, as Maurice was forced eventually to point out, 'a far cry from Upper Brook Street'. His dream of combining his hair-dressing skill with his yearning for silence and home-grown mange-tout peas collapsed in 1971 and Mercantile and General snapped up his premises. Maurice moved to Billericay, George was installed at Wakelin All Saints as assistant manager. Maurice was thirty-five and a sadder man; George was then forty-nine and optimistic.

Optimism was an essential ingredient of George's nature. Without it, he believed he might have suffered, particularly as he aged, the kind of despair that had driven his mother to hurl herself out of a flying fairground car at Clacton to a grossly foreseen death on a knitting of steel girders. He hadn't seen her die, but his imagination supplied every terrible detail of the body's fall, its breaking and bursting. Though forever afterwards afraid of heights, George knew that he was more afraid of the mind's plummet to darkness, fearing that here was a phenomenon that might overcome him as easily, as seductively as his occasional cravings for young women. Sometimes, he imagined it in the form of a tornado hurling him upwards into a lonely twist of sky and from whose eternity there was no escape but the plunge down towards the faraway houses and the little ribbons of roads, dead, just as his mother had been, long before he heard the shouting and screaming of the watching crowds. George saw friends of his begin to exhibit the mannerisms of despair. He pitied and feared. He examined himself in his dressing-room mirror. He beamed. He thought of Jennifer's wedding. He offered an imaginary Jennifer his arm. He remembered his mother's flying body. He thought about Beryl's birthday party. He drank imaginary champagne. He saw his office at the bank. He moved his imaginary body next door and placed it at the manager's desk. He beamed at an imaginary customer. The imaginary customer was respectful and awed and anxious. He put him at his ease. He looked back at the mirror. His beaming smile had left him.

So yes, he'd been forced to agree with Beryl, it hadn't been a very promising year. The question of the gone-forever managership interrupted both his sleep and his continuing cheerfulness. The dingyness of his room at the bank began to irritate him. He filled in a request slip for a red desk lamp. When, after two subsequent requests, it didn't arrive, he went to Ipswich and bought himself one. And it was while he was in Ipswich that he confronted the poster ('confronted' is precisely what George did: he stood absolutely still and stared at a photograph of sand, palm and gentle surf). 'Florida,' it said. 'Seven heavens under one sky.'

'Seven heavens?' Beryl had commented, disbelievingly. 'Seven *figures* more likely.'

Beryl's pessimism, afflicting her more noticeably after the

menopause, served as an almost constant irritant to George's struggle with his own sanity. His desire to be loved by twenty-year-old women had perhaps less to do with sexual excitement than with his faith in the buoyancy of youth. Like safe, wide rivers, his love affairs kept his spirit afloat. He would never, as long as he kept company with firm flesh, be tempted off the roaring roller-coaster. In this way, he absolved himself of all his betrayals.

The shiny new golf clubs in their heavy white and red leather bag were, for George, the most perfect expression of an intention: a recently matured insurance policy, begun in 1962, would buy him and Beryl a Florida October. They would stay not in some anonymous Holiday Inn, but at the unique Palmetto Village Complex between Boca Raton and Boca West. Here, a short drive from Miami Beach, George planned to 'tee off for the experience of a lifetime', a phrase he coined the day he brought home the Palmetto brochure and which he used constantly in the months preceding the departure, finding that it captured perfectly both his hopes and the envy of his listeners (this last a necessity when he reflected that he had actually been saving for this trip for twenty years). The travel agent promised temperatures in the 80s. Onto the brochure picture of a couple eating breakfast under a parasol he had, in his mind, superimposed his own face. (A sense of loyalty made him try to superimpose Beryl's face opposite his own, but the woman under the parasol merely lost her identity, so that she was no longer the woman in the photograph, nor yet Beryl, but someone else, someone he could not actually put a face to.) He fondled the glinting golfing irons, felt their weight, putted balls across his sitting-room carpet, replaced them carefully and resisted any temptation to use them at the Woodbridge Golf Club. These were Florida irons. These were the tools of twenty years' grind. With these he would swing four thousand miles away, while England crept to winter under her soggy burden of leaves. With these he would decide whether he was ever coming back.

*

A black security guard, wearing a stetson and barricaded into a wooden booth examined the photographs of George and Beryl. He looked from the photographs to the back of the Chevrolet cab where they sat. 'Get out please, Sir,' he snapped.

The guard looked from George to the photograph and back to George. He saw a freckled, stocky man – the colouring of a Scot, the craggy build, perhaps, of a Welshman. Once powerfully blue and considered his best feature, George's eyes had faded, strangely, with time. His hair, once red, had faded too, not yet to white, but to an odd mixture of chestnut and grey, the colour of a certain breed of horse the name of which he always forgot. He was quite proud of his hair because it was still thick. He loved women to touch it.

'Can your wife get out please.'

Massively unsmiling, the guard astonished George. His bulk, his blackness, his hat, his abrupt commands: all were astonishing.

'He wants you to get out, Beryl.'

'Do we have to sign something, or something?'

'Dunno, dear. Careful of the clubs as you get out.'

The guard picked up Beryl's photograph. It showed a woman in a cardigan, hair newly set in a style resembling as nearly as possible the Queen's. (In his limited experience of English tourists, the security guard had noticed that a great number of women adopted this identical royal old-fashioned fashion.) Now, in a summer frock, Beryl's flesh looked very pale, almost blue-white at her ankles. In the blinding sunshine, she manoeuvred herself cautiously round the car and lined herself up beside George. The guard stared at them.

'Know the rules, Sir, Ma'am?'

'Sorry?' said George.

'No one gets in or out of the village without the security passes or a phone-in ID from a Palmetto resident. Day or evening guests are exempted, *pro*-viding they're with you, okay?'

'I don't think we'll be having guests . . .' began Beryl. 'We don't know anyone.'

'Pass expires last day of October,' the guard said with finality.

116

'What if we want to renew?' inquired George.

'Re-new?'

'Yes. If we decide . . .'

'Take minimum two IDs to the PVC Office . . .'

'PVC?'

'Palmetto Village Complex Office, 3125 Oranto Boulevard, Boca Raton. Two IDs minimum, plus apartment rereservation documentation.'

It was all a bit of a jumble to me, said Beryl ten minutes later, as she slowly took in the details of the apartment, her home-to-be for a month of her life. But George wasn't listening. He was standing at a sliding window, gazing with awe at two smiling men in check trousers and white short-sleeved shirts embarking for the tenth hole on their motorised golf cart. George was open-jawed. No one had told him that the golf course would be spread out, like the Garden of Eden, in front of his veritable window.

'What about this, Beryl!' he exploded.

'I like the bathroom, George. Do come and see the bathroom . . .'

'Twenty-four hour round the clock bloody paradise!'

'What, dear?'

'It's right *here*. Right in front of our balcony!'

'What? The golf course?'

'Yes.'

'Do you think we're members automatically, being Palmetto residents?'

'Of course we are. It's one of the privileges. Golf and the swimming pool. Free to all Palmetto inmates.'

Beryl crossed the soft-carpeted room and stood next to George, looking out. As the two golfers drove off, a sudden wind frayed the inert palms and sang through the mosquito meshing. Beryl blew her nose. 'I don't expect those little carts are free,' she said.

George woke with a feeling of joy he couldn't remember experiencing since he was twelve and sent one summer from a morbidly quiet home to a seaside scout camp in Cornwall.

He lay and admired the room. He sensed the different ways in which it had been designed with the privileged in mind: heavy drapes at the window, letting in no hint of the colossal day beginning outside them, wall-to-wall white louvered cupboards with heavy gold-plated knobs, built-in dressing alcove, complete with lace-covered tissue dispenser, additional makeup mirror and gilded ring tree (on which Beryl had hung her only ring, a faded bit of Victorian turquoise), heavy glass table burdened with heavy magazines and a piece of modern sculpture which George's unpractised eye had privately christened 'Man Copulating With Hoop', chandelier-style ceiling light, high pile white carpet, a framed bullfight poster, a set of eighteenth-century French prints, showing wigged aristocrats engaged in what seemed to be flirtation. It was worth it, George whispered to himself, worth every penny just to have got this far.

His clock, re-set to US time, told him it was 7.10 a.m. Beryl slept her habitual hunched-up sleep, unvarying it seemed in any time zone. George crept to the bathroom, peed as quietly as he could (Florida lavatories seemed to echo less than English ones) and dressed quickly in brand-new lightweight trousers, holiday shirt and new canvas shoes. Picking up the apartment key, monumentally tagged to stop anyone pocketing it, he tiptoed out, pausing only to stare breathlessly at the quality of the light coming into the sitting room from across the golf course.

The Palmetto apartment buildings, though near to each other, were each arranged around their own careful garden. The grass was constantly watered and very green; in sculptured stone basins, shaded by palms, apologetic fountains sent feeble jets of water onto ferns and lilies. Planted among the oleander trees in each central courtyard was a marble map of the village. Gold lettering informed George YOU ARE HERE. Thanking the Palmetto planners for their foresight and helpfulness, George began to follow the memorised marble path to the circle marked GOLF COURSE ENTRY.

I am walking, he thought, with springy step. I slept a free

sleep, uncluttered by any hint of nightmare. It's seven in the morning of my first day and already I've shaken England off like jumble sale clothes, just chucked it away, the better to breathe, the better to relax my shoulders, the better to tap a miraculous new energy located if I'm not wrong, or rather, beginning, at my groin and going through me like spring sap. And I am, extraordinarily, alone. It's as if, on this entire peninsula, no one is moving yet, unless it's the security guard, housed up in his booth, gun at the ready to protect me and all those asleep including Beryl from marauders and rapists and felons. A light wind is making me wish I'd brought along my pale blue C & A poloneck, but this is no doubt a dawn wind, very likely to die down as the sun hots up. Someone, I can now hear, is vacuuming the swimming pool. I dare say this is done regularly every morning to leave it jewel-bright for my pre-breakfast swim. If I was wise, I would pop into the pool complex to ascertain the temperature of the water . . .

A wagon, not unlike an enlarged version of the little golf carts, was parked at the entrance to the swimming pool. On its immaculate sides was written PALMETTO GARDENING and George now noticed that the vehicle was stocked with every variety of garden implement, including heavy yellow hoses. Nothing looked dirty. He recalled the rusting rural slum of his own garden shed and marvelled. Hardly any rain, of course, he remembered, that would explain the absence of rust, but not the astonishing appearance of newness. A hoe looked as bright as his No. 2 iron.

Beside the wooden doorway to the pool was another marble map, again informing George, YOU ARE HERE. Wondering whether any resident of Palmetto had ever been lost anywhere in the village, he pushed open the door. The pool, roman-ended, was forty feet by eighteen. Gently moving the vacuum pole around its shallow end was a girl with long, colourless hair. She looked up immediately and stared at George. George stared. The girl was twenty. She wore skimpy, faded shorts and,

119

above these, what looked to George like a home-stitched vest over ostentatiously milky breasts, damp nippled.

'Hi,' she said.

Beryl woke with astonishment and with the immediate certainty that she had a cold. Her throat was sore and her head ached. She called in the direction of the bathroom, 'George, are you up?' She waited. The only sound she could hear was a distant whooshing noise, perpetual, the Florida wind blowing in off the sea. Drawing back the heavy curtains, she blinked at the startling blue and green. The clarity of the morning made her wish that her own head would clear. She blamed this misfortune of a cold on altitude and climatic change.

'GOOD MORNING, PALMETTO RESIDENT!' said a plastic notice screwed to the kitchen wall. 'You are reminded that we do not serve breakfast as part of our four-star Palmetto Hospitality Agenda, but we hope you will make the fullest use of your kitchen facility. Your PALMETTO SHOP is located on Square 3 and will be delighted to sell you hot French bread, butter, jelly, tea, coffee, chocolate, milk, and of course Florida oranges. Meat for your griddle may also be obtained from your PALMETTO SHOP, should you prefer a substantial morning meal. The SHOP is open Monday through Sunday, eight to eight. Have a nice day.'

Beryl opened the fridge to see whether the previous Palmetto tenant had kindly left her anything in the way of breakfast materials, but the fridge was completely empty except for a cellophane-wrapped half bottle of Veuve Cliquot champagne, given free with every reservation of a week or longer. 'Drat it,' she commented, and, crossing back to the bedroom to dress for shopping, was startled by an unexpected and quite unfamiliar noise. The telephone was ringing.

Deciding that it must be George, and marvelling that he, who forgot important things with such regularity, had somehow memorised this number, she picked it up and said: 'George? What are you doing?'

'Beryl?' said a near sounding English voice. 'Brewer here. Brewer Smythe.'

Beryl thought, I've been astonished by every single thing since we got here and now here's Brewer Smythe astonishing me even more by ringing me when it was months ago that George wrote to Brewer and Monica, and as far as I know there's never been any reply from them.

'Heavens!' said Beryl.

'Surprised you, eh?'

'Well, to be honest, Brewer, I was just saying yesterday when we arrived that we didn't know anybody in Florida. And how wrong I was. I mean, I'd just forgotten about you. Isn't that terrible?'

'Oh, don't worry about trivial things like that, Beryl. How are you, anyway? And how's the old man?'

'Fine. We're fine. A bit jet-lagged, I mean I think I am because I seem to have got a cold, which I'm sure isn't usual. George has just popped out to . . . survey the golf course.'

'Well, listen. What about a plunge in at the deep end on your first day, eh?'

'Plunge in, Brewer?'

'Yes. Mr Weissmann wants me to take him up to River Kingdom for lunch. That's the best seafood place between here and Miami, and I've got you and George invited on the boat. Set off at 10.30-ish. Have cocktails on board. Get to River Kingdom at 12.30. George'll love it, Beryl.'

'Well, I don't know if I'm up to it, Brewer. I mean, with this cold . . .'

'Course you are. Best thing. Blow the cobwebs away.'

'Well, are you sure Mr Weissmann doesn't mind?'

'Absolutely! Told him George was not only an old friend, but a banker. He has the greatest respect for bankers.'

'It's very kind of you, Brewer . . .'

'Monica's coming. She's really looking forward to seeing you.'

'How is she?'

'Monica? Well, you wait till you see her! I tell you, Beryl, she's a changed woman since we moved here. If you say Woodbridge to Monica now, she can hardly remember what you're talking about!'

'Really?'

'Changed woman! But how are you and George finding it? Paradise, eh? Good first impressions, eh?'

Beryl hesitated. She realised the hesitation made her sound somehow ungrateful.

'I think it's all ... extraordinary, Brewer. It'll take a bit of getting used to, but I'm sure once we do ...'

'You'll never want to go home! Guarantee it, Beryl. Only to pack and get back here as fast as you can. You wait and see. But hats off to George for getting you here, anyway. So look, I'll be round to fetch you at 10.15. Oh, and Beryl, lunch is on us.'

Beryl sat down in the foodless kitchen. It's the kind of day, she thought, when I'm going to find it quite hard to believe anything that's happening.

'I'm new,' George had said to the girl.

'Yeah?'

She moved the pool vac with a steady, practised motion. George watched her. Her feet were bare. Her legs were long and tanned, the hairs on them golden and flat and unshaven.

'This is my first morning.'

'Yeah?'

'Yes. I was just doing a little, you know, recce.'

'Pool's okay. I prefer the ocean, though.'

The ocean. The thundering little word struck chords of magnificence in George's willing mind. He saw the girl walking bravely into breast-high surf, hair flying and wet, mouth parted on gleaming teeth. America, he thought. She is vigorous America. He wanted to scoop her and the ocean into his lap.

'You've got the lot here, I'd say.'

'Pardon me?'

'Here. Climate, beaches, comfort, golf, ocean ...'

'Yeah, it's okay. I miss the city, though.'

'The *city*? Do you?'

'Kind of. People want to learn in the city. Here, they're just all hipped on forgetting.'

George began to walk round the pool. Trying not to stare at the girl, he concentrated on its tiled blue depths.

'I suppose you do gardening as well? I saw your truck. If I may say so, I think the Palmetto gardens are most attractive.'

He heard her laugh. The young laughter made him feel suddenly old, and he stood still.

'I'm a qualified landscape architect,' said the girl. 'I got fired when I had my baby. Gardener was all I could get.'

'Um,' said George, uneasily, 'there's a lot of that happening.'

'Pardon me?'

'Well, that kind of thing. People over-qualified for the jobs they're doing.'

The girl didn't comment. George allowed himself to look up at her arm, slim but seemingly strong, moving the pool vac. The vigorous brown hair she chose to display in her armpit gave him a feeling both of excitement and of disquiet. Everything, he thought, in this country is utterly unfamiliar to me. I will go home an altered man.

'So you've got a baby?'

'Yeah. She's three months now.'

'A daughter? I have a daughter, Jennifer. She got married this year.'

'So you miss her, uhn?'

'Yes. In a way. My wife does.'

'Your wife with you out here?'

'Yes.'

'Great. Well have a nice stay.'

George recognised this as a dismissal. He began to walk slowly towards the pool exit, disappointed that the encounter had had a dull shape. Without identifying what, he knew that the minute he saw the girl he had hoped for something more. He stood, hands in his stiff new pockets, and stared at the roman end of the pool.

'Bet no one much gets up this early,' he said.

'No. We do, the gardeners and cleaners.'

'If I'm not being rude,' George began, 'I'd very much, I mean very much like to know – '

'Know what?'

'Your name.'

The girl held the pool vac still and stared accusingly at George.

'Want to fly me, or something?'

'What did you say?'

'Never mind. I don't give my name, though. Not to strangers.'

'The telephone went,' said a brightly dressed Beryl, who had decided bravely that she wouldn't mention her cold to George. 'It was Brewer.'

'Brewer?'

'Yes, Brewer. We're invited onto Mr Weissmann's boat for the day.'

'Which day?'

'Today. Now please let me have the key, George, and I'll go and buy us some bread and what they call jelly for breakfast.'

'How was Brewer?'

'Very cock-a-hoop. He said Monica was a changed woman.'

'Did you agree?'

'I haven't seen her yet, dear, so how could I agree or disagree?'

'No. To go on the boat.'

'Yes. It's very kind of Mr Weissmann.'

'It's our first day, Beryl.'

'Well, I know, but Brewer said there's a trip to some fish restaurant and I know you'd like that.'

'Suppose we can get in a game of golf this evening.'

'If we feel like it. I mean, after cocktails and lunch and all that, we may want a little sleep.'

'Oh I won't. We've only got a month, Beryl. We shouldn't waste a second.'

'Well, we'll see. I'll go and get the breakfast on Square 3, wherever that is.'

'Easy, dear. Just follow the map.'

When Beryl had gone, George opened the sliding window and sat down on the balcony under the white parasol. Here I am, he thought, like the man in the brochure. In the picture, though, there didn't seem to be any wind. Everything seemed hotter and calmer and much safer than it feels. Slightly breathless from what had been a long walk, he noticed in himself a mildly disturbing sense of unease, a feeling of fright. He slowed his breathing, took gulps of warm air. Careful never to lie to himself about his states of mind, he asked himself, was it the girl, her presence by the pool, her misunderstanding of an innocent, yes innocent question? Had the girl got in the way of contentment? He'd tried to forget her as he'd trod the lush turf of the Palmetto Golf Course, saying to himself she doesn't belong, she's a fugitive from the city, that's it, the Fugitive Kind, giving birth on Greyhound buses, breastfeeding on the freeway, in the subway, no matter where, never belonging with her provoking underarm hair, belonging nowhere, particularly not here, in a guarded village where no one passes without a pass, where the marble maps reassure you every few yards, YOU ARE HERE. Yet he hadn't been able to forget her. The girl and the great wind blowing from the east, they buffeted him and made him feel small.

George got up, crossed to the louvered bedroom cupboards and dragged out the leather bag of golf clubs. He carried them to the balcony and sat for a moment with his arms around them.

Brewer Smythe drove a Cadillac. George and Beryl sat beside him in the wide front seat, both wondering but not asking whether the car was Brewer's or Weissmann's.

Brewer was immensely fatter than when last glimpsed, trailing fatigue and failure around his Woodbridge boatyard. But he wore his new flesh proudly, like he might have worn a new suit, set it off with the whiteness of his naval shirt, topped it with a grinning, ruddy face and a naval-style cap gold-inscribed *Nadar III*. Body and uniform said, I've prospered. Freckles had formed on his arms so densely, they merged into a blotchy, chestnut coloured tan. On his wrist, an oversized platinum digital watch seemed put there as a reminder that here was a man to whom time had behaved kindly. Fifty-five now, this was Brewer's fourth year in Florida, working for the rich boat-owners of the most expensive waterways in the world, transforming years of worthless nautical knowledge into a sudden bonanza.

'Well, Monica's falling over herself!' said Brewer, simultaneously pressing a knob marked 'window lock' and another marked 'air'. 'Faces from Suffolk in our very own Boca Raton! It's hard to believe, honestly it is.'

'You look ever so well, Brewer,' said Beryl.

'Me? I'm in the pink. Never happier. Honestly. Best years of my life out here. You wait and see.'

'What's this Weissmann like?' asked George.

Brewer drew effortlessly into the fast lane of the freeway and accelerated.

'He's rich, George. I'd never seen wealth like his till I came out here. You wait till you see *Nadar*. And his house. Jesus! I'm not fooling when I say he's got a Picasso in his hallway.'

'Good to work for, is he?'

'Man of the world. Married three times. Knows how to treat people. We'd be nowhere, Mon and me, without someone like him.'

'What do you do for him exactly, Brewer?' asked Beryl. 'I mean, I know you're his kind of captain, but is all you do is look after his boat?'

'I provide a service, Beryl,' announced Brewer. 'I think today will give you a fair impression of the service I provide. Men like Weissmann, people in the art and business field, don't have the time or the knowledge for practicalities; they want leisure to run smoothly, you understand what I mean? So he relies on me. Total trust. Absolute round-the-clock responsibility. And that's what I'm paid for.'

Off the freeway after a few miles, the Cadillac was ambling now along a series of identical avenues of houses, low, detached and white, or built of sandstone blocks, each with a sloping front garden, tarmac driveway and wrought-iron gates leading to patios and swimming pools. Palms dwarfed the houses everywhere. 'You can travel,' Brewer informed George and Beryl, 'from your back garden to the ocean through the Florida canals. Unique in the world, and we've done it in *Nadar III*. Extraordinary, eh?'

'Cracking,' said George.

Their arrival at *Nadar*'s mooring was awkward. Monica, in slacks and shocking-pink silk shirt and rattling with charm bracelets, mouthed an enthusiastic silent welcome to George and Beryl, while Weissmann, perched like a beady little penguin at the forward controls of the bulky boat, stared at them sullenly. Near to the thrice-married, sixty-year-old Weissmann was a fat, huge-eyed boy of ten, who also stared, sucking gum, with the brazen stare of the uniquely pampered.

Beryl looked up cautiously and smiled at Weissmann. His face remained impassive. Beryl turned to Brewer for help. Brewer, dwarfed by the boat, seemed momentarily to have lost both bulk and bounce.

'Mr Weissmann,' he said politely, 'may I present my good friends from England, Mr and Mrs Dawes – George and Beryl.'

'Welcome aboard,' said Weissmann, flatly. His accent was pure Germanic, almost unmixed with Yankee. He put a hirsute arm on the boy's rounded shoulder and announced, still unsmiling: 'This is my son, Daren. You see my boat is named *Nadar*. Daren is one half of *Nadar*. Daren is Dar. The *Na* piece of it comes from my wife's name. Nadia. Unfortunately, Nadia is in Paris, so Daren is stuck with his old Daddy, aren't you, Choots?'

'Choots' didn't reply at once, but continued to gaze blankly at George and Beryl.

'It's very kind of you, Mr Weissmann,' began Beryl.

'No, no,' said Weissmann, 'friends of Brewer's from England, this is the least we can do, eh Choots?'

'Daddy,' said Choots, 'are you going to pay for their lunch?'

*

'Do you want to handle her today, Mr Weissmann?' called Brewer from the aft controls, as he swung the boat out into the wide canal.

From the front cabin, where George and Beryl waited silently with Monica, you could just glimpse the enormous metal and plastic chair on the upper deck where Weissmann sat, a complex control panel laid out in front of him. Choots stood disconsolately beside him.

Monica whispered, 'Brewer has to be ever so careful. It's a new boat, you see, and Mr Weissmann hasn't quite got the hang.'

'I'll handle her,' Weissmann called back to Brewer, 'then when we get to River Kingdom, you take her in.'

'Okay, Sir. She's all yours, then. I'll do the cocktails.'

'Good. No cocktail for Choots today,' and here began a tremor of a smile in Weissmann's voice, 'he's too young.'

Brewer turned to George and Beryl who were now both looking at Monica. Monica was indeed a changed person. Like Brewer, she seemed to have undergone a colour metamorphosis. They remembered a faded, brown-shod woman with greying hair and an illusive, apologetic smile. What now confronted them was a blonde with shiny, tanned face, wearing Italian white sandals and azure eye shadow. The smile had broadened, found confidence. The voice, when she eventually began to talk to them, had taken on enough American vowel-richness to alter it greatly. It was, in fact, difficult to believe that this was Monica. Brewer put his arm round his wife and offered her proudly for inspection. 'Looking neat, eh? Looking terrific, isn't she?'

'I wouldn't have recognised you, Monica,' said Beryl.

Monica beamed, let Brewer smack a kiss on her blonde head.

'What can I say?' she said. 'That's what Florida does.'

'You look great, Mon,' said George.

'Thanks, George. Well, it's great to see you, isn't it, Brewer? And on your first day. You just wait till you've been here a week. You'll never want to go home.'

'So Brewer says,' said George.

'What's it to be?' asked Brewer, opening a polished drinks cabinet. 'Bloody marys, whisky sours . . .?'

'Heavens,' said Beryl, 'we don't normally drink this early, do we George?'

'That's the whole point of it, Beryl,' said Brewer, 'to start doing what you don't usually do. We've learned that, haven't we, Monica? Only then will you get in tune with Florida life.'

'I'll have my usual,' said Monica.

'Oh, what's your usual?' asked Beryl.

'Make one for Beryl, Brewer,' said Monica, 'then she'll see.'

Every room and compartment on *Nadar III* appeared to have been designed to accommodate what George had heard was called Cocktail Hour. Little veneered glass holders were clamped to chair arms, recessed into walls, bolted even to the lavatory tiles. You could not move on *Nadar* without finding a convenient place to set down your drink. Noting this, George thought, being rich is the art of forethought. I am too random a person, despite my ability with figures, to predict accurately where I or my guests might want to set down their cocktails. Everything on this boat is in precisely the right place with regard to its function, but I have none of the skills I recognise in this kind of planning. He stared up at Weissmann's seat of power, wondered what it would be like to stare at it almost every day, as Brewer did, and to know that all one possessed emanated from there, from a German art dealer who was fond of bankers. He looked at Brewer, expertly shaking and mixing cocktails. He's grown fat, he thought suddenly, to protect himself. But then George berated himself for this idiotic tendency he'd failed to leave behind in England – his tendency to analyse and question and seek the comfort of certainties. It impedes, he thought, my positive response to whatever happens, and the only important thing, here, is to enjoy myself.

River Kingdom, a flat-roofed, blue-painted building with its own substantial mooring, was, George decided, rather like a fish theatre. Models of lobsters and crayfish and crabs and blue-fin sharks busked up the walls and across the ceiling, netting hung down in carefully arranged loops, tanks of living eels were spotlit, menus were like programmes: Act One, shrimp-crab-mussel-prawn-clam-oyster, Act Two, brill-striped bass-eel-mullet-lobster-shark fin and so on through a dramatis personae of water meat George had never in his life encountered. Waitresses in usherette black brought unasked-for salads as an overture to the meal. Outside the sun went in, as if the house lights had suddenly been turned down.

George was seated between Weissmann and Monica. Daren sat between his father and Brewer, which left the two women next to each other. But Weissmann, who had arranged the seating, had deliberately placed Beryl and Monica in seats where he wouldn't have to talk to them. Duty called on him to tolerate his captain and his friend as lunch guests, but not their wives. The elaborate courtesies he reserved for the women of his own elite weren't available for the likes of Beryl: patronage went only so far.

Beryl and Monica talked about England and Suffolk in particular and Woodbridge and Wakelin All Saints. At one moment, George heard Monica say, 'I've forgotten to ask him, I suppose George is manager by now?' and cast an anxious look at Beryl, who seemed defeated both by her gigantic shark steak and by the question. He looked away.

'So,' said Weissmann, turning an indifferent eye upon George, 'you like America.'

This was neither question nor statement, but something in between. George looked at Brewer, who was grinning encouragingly, then coughed.

'It's our first time,' he said. 'We flew from Gatwick yesterday. I'm quite surprised by everything I've seen.'

'Surprised? In what way surprised?'

'Oh, I don't know,' said George, 'it's very hard to pinpoint precisely where the differences occur. Everything seems unlike England in a way I can't yet explain. I thought it might just be a question of size and climate, but it isn't.'

'Well,' said Weissmann, portentously, 'this is the United States.'

'Right, Sir!' said Brewer. 'I've been saying to George, now that he's here, he'll never want to go back. We haven't. We've never had a moment's regret.'

'You like Europe?' asked Weissmann, blackly. And George felt an irritating panic rise in him. Europe. The images conjured by Weissmann's use of the word, the images to which he was expected to respond, were all, all as alien to George as words like quattrocento and surréaliste and schadenfreude and Auschwitz. Weissmann, American, Jew, *knew* 'Europe'; George, Englishman and part of Europe, did not.

'I'm fond of the country,' said George, taking up the wine one of the usherettes had poured for him.

'Which country?' said Weissmann.

'The countryside,' stammered George, 'the countryside of England.'

'But Brewer said you were a banker.'

'Yes. I am. I'm with Mercantile and General.'

'In the City, no?'

'What, London? Oh no, I'm not in London.'

'So you're not a real banker, then.'

George was saved from having to comment on his own reality by the nagging of Choots who, with the underwater world spread out for his delectation, had ordered cold roast beef and pickles.

'This isn't nice, Daddy,' said Choots.

'No?' said Weissmann.

'No.'

'Why did you choose it, then?'

'I didn't choose it. Brewer chose it for me.'

Brewer smiled. 'It's what he asked for, Sir.'

'Don't eat it,' Weissmann said, 'give it to Brewer.'

Choots went off to the serve-yourself sweet table and helped himself to a wedge of chocolate gateau. Brewer good-naturedly crammed the thick slices of red beef onto his lobster plateau and proceeded to eat both simultaneously.

Weissmann smiled.

'He's a good man, Brewer, your friend,' he said to George, 'he does what I ask, eh Brewer?'

'Yes, Sir!'

'I spoil my son, you are thinking. In Europe, children are not spoiled. I was not spoiled. I was kicked and bullied. Now, I'm the one with the boots, you see? But not for my son. He will have what he wants because I am too old to be a good father and this is punishment enough. So you're not really a banker?'

George found Weissmann's twists and turns of thought vexing; he invited you to enter a conversation, then left you no room to participate in it.

'I've been in banking all my life,' said George quietly.

'You know money?'

This was like the Europe question. It reverberated cavernously with meaning inaccessible to the likes of George. He sighed. This was the first sigh he had heard himself breathe since landing at Miami airport. To his own astonishment, he heard himself say angrily, 'I know, Mr Weissmann, what this holiday is costing me.'

Monica's special cocktail hadn't agreed with Beryl's stomach. Back at Palmetto, she was lying in the large bed (lying, she realised, rather stiff and straight so as not to rumple the sheets an unseen maid had so carefully smoothed) feeling pale and drowsy. George, perched by the Man Copulating With Hoop, stared anxiously at his wife.

'Why don't you go off and have a game of golf, George?' Beryl suggested.

George smiled. 'I can't play with myself, Beryl.'

Beryl placed her two hands comfortingly on her stomach and tried to breathe deeply. A novice at the Wakelin All Saints Yoga for Beginners, she had learned that pain can be relieved by mind control allied to correct breathing.

'I'm terribly sorry, George. I don't know whether it was the shark or Monica's cocktail, or just simply me. I didn't take to that Weissmann, did you?'

'Just rest, Beryl.'

132

'I'm all right to talk. I wouldn't want to be Brewer, would you?'

'He's changed.'

'I wouldn't want to be at the beck and call of a spoilt person like that.'

'Brewer doesn't seem to mind. And anyway, we don't know him, Beryl. I expect art connoisseurs are a difficult lot.'

'Do go and play golf, dear. I'm sure you'll find someone to give you a game.'

George got up and crossed to the bed. 'Going to have a bit of a sleep, then, are you?'

'I think I will.'

'Good boat, wasn't it? Imagine owning that.'

'Too powerful for me. Too built up.'

'Built up?'

'Well, it was just one deck put on top of another, put on top of another, wasn't it? No line.'

George looked fondly at Beryl. There were moments – not very many – when his abiding sense of his wife as a humdrum woman suddenly parted like the Red Sea and another (sensitive, sharp-witted) Beryl came striding through. This was one such moment.

'Rest, love,' he said gently, and touched her forehead with his finger, as if offering her a benediction.

Beryl closed her eyes and seemed, in that instant, asleep. George tiptoed out of the room and quietly closed the door. He walked to the balcony window of the sitting room and stared longingly at the golf course. Above it, behind the palms, the sky was flat and grey – a peculiarly English sky – and the wind was blowing hard. The sun hadn't been seen after they'd sat down to lunch at River Kingdom, and the journey home through choppy water had been disagreeable. Weissmann had left the boat with only a nod to George and Beryl, saying anxiously to Brewer, 'There may be a storm. Make sure the mooring is very safe.'

George had no sense of any impending storm, but the golf course was clearly deserted. Palmetto people only played golf in the sunshine. Or else they knew that a storm was coming, they read signs that George was unable to decipher, bought their evening griddle steaks and drew their heavy curtains.

It was warm in the room. George opened the sliding balcony window. The parasol had been closed and only the fringe moved slightly with the wind. George sat down at the table and rubbed his eyes. Too much has happened, he thought, in the space of time I had reserved only for an arrival. The extraordinary early morning joy, the girl with her damp breasts and her disdain, the ride in the Cadillac, the boat trip, lunch, Choots, tiny glimpses into worlds and lives he would never know; he was left with a feeling of stifling confusion. 'I need time,' he said aloud, 'I need more time.'

He began to soothe himself with the comfort of the coming days and weeks. Hot, quiet days spent with Beryl on the golf course, lunches at the pool, shopping for gifts for Jennifer in the famous shopping malls, a day trip to Miami beach . . .

George sat back, folded his arms. He was tired, he now recognised. The time change had suddenly hit him. He closed his eyes, heard the wind fill his head. Why had no one mentioned the presence of the wind? Then, on the edge of sleep, he heard his own voice announce with sudden and absolute certainty: 'They're gone.' His eyes snapped open. He stared down, tracing each concrete foot of the balcony on which he sat. He felt nauseous, drained. He ran a moist hand through his thick hair. 'They're gone.'

He got up. The maid had moved them, had she? She had put them back in the louvered cupboard or propped them up by the door? He crossed the sitting room, entered the kitchen. They weren't by the door, they weren't in the kitchen. He was sweating now, drenched in sweat. He would have to wake Beryl or risk waking her by opening the wardrobes. He opened the bedroom door quietly. Beryl was asleep, nose gasping at the ceiling. George moved stealthily to the cupboards, pulled them wide open, gazed at his lightweight clothes, Beryl's cotton dresses, their mingled pile of new shoes, recognising that what he was feeling was fear, a drenching of fear such as he couldn't remember since, as a timid boy, the secret mouldering apple store in his toy cupboard had been crushed to pulp by his mother's suicidal rage, dinky cars and lead soldiers, cigarette cards and painted matchboxes lying ruined and stained in brown rot.

'Beryl . . .' he said tightly.

Beryl moved but slept on, snoring gravely.

'Beryl . . .' George heard the choke in his voice and knew it for a suppressed scream. 'Someone has stolen my golf clubs.'

Beryl didn't move, but opened a bleary eye and looked at her husband. 'George,' she said, alarmed, 'are you crying?'

The black security guard shifted his massive frame on the high backed chair and turned towards the chain-locked side door of his booth on which George had tremblingly knocked.

'Come round to the window!' yelled the guard. He touched his gun with a wide finger, let a signal for dangerous and immediate action ripple through his chest and arms. George's rowan head appeared at the booth glass.

'Can I see your pass, Sir?'

George fumbled for his wallet, into which he had carefully put his pass and Beryl's.

'I've come to report a theft . . .' began George.

'Security pass, please,' snapped the guard.

George laid the pass on the little counter, wanted to comment that the guard had seen him not one hour ago as Brewer drove them home in the Cadillac, but refrained from saying this and waited patiently while the guard examined his (by now familiar, surely?) photograph inside its piece of transparent plastic.

'Theft, you said?'

'Yes.' George cleared his throat. 'I left my golf clubs on my balcony . . .'

'We don't get theft at Palmetto. You better have another search.'

'I have searched. The golf clubs are not in my apartment.'

'You got insurance?'

'Yes. I have a policy with Norwich Union . . .'

'Okay, this is one for the PVC Office. Take minimum two IDs down to 3125 Oranto Boulevard and state the exact nature and time of the theft. All unsecured property, however, is dis-claimed for responsibility purposes by Palmetto Village Security and balcony property is deemed unsecured for this purpose.'

'What?' said George.

'All unsecured, that is open or balcony property is *dis*-claimed for responsibility purposes by PV Security.'

'You mean Palmetto is not responsible?'

'You got it.'

'Then I don't see the point of these passes and all the security regulations. If you can just let a thief walk in and steal my golf clubs . . .'

'You tell the PVC Office, Sir.'

'And what will they do?'

'You got two IDs?'

'Yes. What will the Palmetto Office do?'

'Question you, Sir.'

'Question *me*! Look, I was out all day. I returned at four thirty p.m. to find my clubs missing. That's all I can tell them. But I am not exaggerating when I say that those clubs cost me almost a month's salary. I want them found and the thief caught!'

George realised that he was shouting. Fatigue, he thought, and fear have made me deaf to my own voice. The guard was staring at him with interest, the stare of a man watching a zoo-caged animal. He avoided the stare and turned to walk away.

Behind him the PALMETTO GARDENING van had appeared like an apparition, soundless and unseen. George stopped and stared at it. His hand, still clutching his wallet, was shaking. The girl tugged on the hand brake, unfolded her willowy body from the cart and strode to the booth. In the strong wind, her hair was whipped around her face, hiding it from George. 'Everything conspires,' he heard himself whisper, not knowing precisely what he meant. He watched without moving as the girl waved her security pass at the guard, heard the guard say, 'Hi, Cindy. Get home before the storm, uhn?'

George's eyes moved to the skimpy vest. He saw that her nipples were dry.

'Hello,' he said quietly.

The girl turned. The wind caught her hair, lifting it back from her face. She reached up and held the hair and looked down at George. He noticed for the first time how very tall she was.

'Oh . . .' she said.

George clutched his wallet, willed his body to stop shaking. I'm ill, he thought, and the girl began it. He tried to smile at her. Rested, refreshed and at peace with himself – on some other day – he could have said, 'Don't misunderstand the kind of man I am. I only asked your name because I prefer everything to be known and unambiguous. Although I find you extraordinary and might allow myself the luxury of erotic fantasising around your milky breasts and your eyes as grey as the sky, I would never presume, that is I would never be so vain as to suppose you would give me anything of yourself . . .' Instead, he said nothing at all, saw the girl glance anxiously from him to the cart full of tools to the guard who was smiling at her, his massive presence transfigured by the smile.

'Not many takers,' mumbled George.

'Pardon me?' said the girl quickly.

'For the pool,' said George, indicating the dense cloud above them.

'Oh,' said the girl, 'I guess not.'

And she was gone, springing back into the cart, waving at the guard, who waved back, and driving off down the clean grey road that led to the freeway.

The storm came rolling in on a sky blacker than dusk. Beryl made tea. The pains in her stomach came and went.

George sat on the sofa and listened to the vast, moving sheets of rain exploding against the sliding windows, felt the building shudder in the body of the wind.

Two thoughts chased each other round his brain which felt squeezed and bruised: Weissmann's boat is adrift and sinking in the storm; the girl stole my golf clubs, stowed them and hid them among her shiny garden tools, and will sell them to buy things for her baby . . .

Beryl came in and looked at George. 'Change your mind and have some tea, George,' she said.

But no, he didn't want tea. 'I'm beginning to think, Beryl,' he said, 'that we never should have come.'

A sudden spasm of pain rose in Beryl's stomach and she sat down on the sofa beside George with an ungainly bump.

'Don't be silly, dear,' she said with as much energy as her voice could muster, 'you're usually the optimist.'

'It was one of the gardeners,' said George.

'One of the gardeners what?'

'Stole my golf clubs.'

'I haven't seen any gardeners.'

'I have. Women.'

'Well,' said Beryl, placatingly, 'as soon as the storm's over – tomorrow morning – we'll go down to the Palmetto Office and get it all sorted out.'

She understands nothing, thought George, nothing, *nothing*. Things cannot now be 'sorted out' because they are irrevocably altered. I have, in no more than twenty-four hours, encountered worlds that I do not understand. The girl is one world, the girl and her crime and the guard who is not interested that a crime has been committed against me. The other world is Weissmann, whose voice challenged me, yes challenged me at the entrance to some cave or echoey place and in that cave were all the songs and sufferings of a continent and the rich, rich owners of the wealth of that continent that I do not, nor will ever possess nor understand. I have, in a trice, simply understood my own profound and unchangeable insignificance.

Answering voices placated, denied: you said you wanted 'recovery from mediocrity'. You cannot 'recover from mediocrity' unless you understand the nature of that mediocrity. You have now begun to understand. At sixty, it's not too late to make a start, just as autumn is not merely a dying off, but as the leaves fly, hard new buds form already and wait for April . . .

'I suppose,' said Beryl suddenly, 'we should have bought steak or something for the griddle. You'll be hungry later on.'

But they weren't hungry and didn't eat. The wind howled and screamed in the mosquito wire. On the balcony, the table fell over and the parasol went flying off into the night like a javelin. The pain in Beryl lessened and she got out the cards. George agreed blankly to play Gin Rummy and silently won every round till the lights went out and Beryl gave a little scream. Almost simultaneously, the telephone rang and George fumbled his slow and terrified way to the kitchen to answer it. Beryl found a table lighter, which clicked up a minute yellow flame. Holding this, she came and stood by George's side.

The voice on the line sounded far away. Jennifer, thought George, it's Jennifer. Something's happened in England.

'Jen?'

'What?' said the voice.

'Is that you, Jen? This is Dad.'

'George? It's Monica.'

'Oh, Monica . . .'

'Brewer thought we ought to ring, just to make sure you're okay. It's quite a bad storm. Have your lights gone?'

'Yes. They just went.'

'We're still okay in Boca Raton. Poor you. What a welcome to Florida! Would you like Brewer to come over and get you in the car?'

'No, no,' said George, 'we're fine. But what about the boat?'

'The boat?'

'Weissmann's boat. It'll be adrift, won't it?'

'Well, I don't think so, George. Why should it be?'

'In the storm . . .'

'Brewer will have taken care of it.'

'I think it's gone, Monica. I think it's drifting and breaking . . .'

There was a long silence at Monica's end of the telephone. George was aware that he was breathing petrified shallow breaths. Beryl's face, lit by the tiny lighter flame, stared at him aghast. She reached out and gently took the telephone receiver from him.

'Monica,' she said, 'this is Beryl.'

'Oh, Beryl,' said Monica, relieved, 'what's the matter with George? Is he afraid of the storm?'

'No,' said Beryl, 'I don't think it's that.'

'What's happened, Beryl?'

'Well, he's just a bit upset because his golf clubs have been stolen.'

'*Stolen?* At Palmetto? It's not possible, Beryl. Palmetto's like Fort Knox.'

'Well, I know, but there you are. He left them on the balcony and they're gone. They were brand new.'

'Is he certain, Beryl? Has he looked everywhere?'

'Oh yes. Everywhere.'

'Well, I'm amazed. I never heard of anyone stealing anything at Palmetto . . .'

'No. Well, I dare say there's always a first time.'

'Anyway, tell him not to worry. He can have Brewer's. Brewer hardly plays any more. No, honestly, he's too busy with Weissmann's empire. I'll bring them round in the morning.'

With Brewer's golf clubs, scarcely less new and shiny than his own, and with the passing of the storm, the month began to settle down. The parasol lost in the storm was replaced, and religiously every morning George and Beryl breakfasted under it, like the people in the Palmetto brochure.

They were never again invited aboard Weissmann's boat, nor did they glimpse the Picasso in his hallway. But they spent some time in the bungalow Brewer and Monica had recently bought at Boca Raton, struggling to find the superlatives with which to admire Brewer's Seafarer Cocktail Cabinet, fitted out with mock compasses and other nautical pieces of brass entirely unfamiliar to them, and Monica's polystyrene rock, dyed green and brown (like army camouflage, George noted privately) over which a recycled waterfall trickled continuously into a tiny circular swimming pool.

'Doesn't it all make you want to stay for ever?' said Monica one morning to Beryl, as they wandered the expensive shopping malls in search of presents for Jennifer and her new husband. Beryl caught a glimpse of herself in the shop window they were passing; her skin was lightly tanned, her hair had been reshaped by Monica's pet hairdresser, Giani, obliterating all its former resemblance to the Queen's.

'Well, I think I've changed,' said Beryl, 'and that's probably a good thing. I think at our time in life you need a little jolt like this – something different – to put everything in perspective. But George and I are happiest where we are. I don't think Florida is quite right for us, not like it's been right for you and Brewer.'

'But Wakelin All Saints, Beryl, it's such a backward little place.'

'Yes, it is. Oh, I know that.'

'And you said George won't even get to be manager. Now, I'm sure Mr Weissmann has strings enough out here to fix George up with something. I mean, money isn't a dirty word out here like it is in England. And if you're in money, Beryl, as George is . . .'

'Oh, he's not "in" it, Monica. I think to be "in" money, you've got to have some, and George has never had any, only his salary.'

'Well, he knows money.'

'No. I don't think he "knows" it, either. He just went into the bank because he thought it would be safe.'

'Safe? Safe from what?'

'Oh, you know, Monica. Sort of from the world.'

The world spins faster here, George decided. Storms and hurricanes arrive in moments; flowers on the Palmetto squares come out and die in a day; by the pool, my towel is dry and stiff in half an hour. And people disappear. The girl. Weissmann. I look for the girl every day. I've seen her little cart dozens of times, but she's never in it or near it. One morning, I woke early and thought I was lying on her, my mouth on her milky breasts, my hand holding fast to her hair, like a rope. I got up and went to look for her. But I found a young man vacuuming the pool and she was nowhere. Probably she's run away, knowing she committed a crime.

And Weissmann? Brewer has a photograph of the man shaking hands with President Reagan. Brewer sees Weissmann every day. Choots is dumped on Monica, who makes him apple pie. But Choots never addresses one word to me. We had our audience on the first day and now we're forgotten, dismissed. We hire a dumpy cruiser one afternoon and pass *Nadar III*. Brewer waves. Weissmann, from his perched-up control panel, stares at us like complete strangers.

Jennifer wrote from England: 'I don't believe we've had such a glorious autumn in Suffolk since 1976. We've been mushrooming before breakfast three or four times, and the misty, sunny early mornings are superb. No rain for a couple of weeks now and an incredible blackberry crop. Shame you're missing it, but trust the Florida sun compensates ...'

So the month drifted to its end. Beryl sorted and wrapped the presents she had bought and acquired a lightweight canvas bag in which to carry them home. George took photographs hastily, badly, a last-minute snapping of palm and balcony and pool and river bungalow, then a final indoor sequence with Beryl moving obediently from room to room.

'We should have thought about pictures earlier on, George,' said Beryl, 'I mean, pictures are half of it, aren't they?'

'Half of what, dear?'

'It. The experience. So you don't forget it.'

'Don't worry, Beryl. I won't forget it.'

Beryl was seated on the velvet pile couch, tanned legs crossed, hair newly set (Giani had cut the front into a rigid fringe, which made Beryl look more severe – and more intelligent – than she was), and George was backing nearer and nearer to a line of bookshelves crammed with unread, leatherbound volumes inscribed 'Weatherburns Classic Series'.

'Watch out for the books,' said Beryl.

'I want to get you in, and just a suggestion of the balcony view ...'

George's bottom rammed the bookcase. Beryl's mouth, composed primly for the photograph, fell open as she saw George and the books behind him begin to turn and revolve and finally disappear almost out of sight into a dark hole in the wall.

'George!' she yelped.

George tipped. The camera was jolted out of his hand and fell to the ground. He clutched at the books, recovered his balance, found himself inside a clean cupboard, smelling of airwick, completely empty except for one bulky, familiar object, propped up in a corner, safe, intact and still radiating its extraordinary newness – his bag of golf clubs.

Beryl was now at George's side. 'My God, George,' she said, 'you looked like a person on the Paul Daniels Magic Show!'

'Look,' said George, 'just look.'

George picked up the camera and handed it to Beryl. He reached out for the leather strap of the golfing bag, hauled the bag out into the room, and let the false cupboard door revolve back into place behind him. Beryl said nothing, just watched as George touched the clubs in disbelief, examining each one, brushing a thin film of dust from the bag.

'My God!' he said.

'Well . . .' said Beryl.

Then George sighed, let the bag fall, walked very slowly to the balcony window and stared out. There was no wind on this day. The palm leaves hung limp and dry, the fringe of the parasol wasn't moving. Gentle, tropical air filled the room with warmth, the sun dappled it with sprigs of bright light. In two days, George thought, we will be in Suffolk and the calendar on my office wall will say November.

'At least we found them,' said Beryl.

'Yes,' said George quietly.

'Now we can go back with everything we came with.'

'Yes,' said George, but smiled a wide, astonished smile that Beryl never saw. She's wrong, he thought. We won't go back to England with all that we carried with us to America. There's a part of me which has been replaced.

The Stately
Roller Coaster

I always say to the press, if you want me to blab, send me a pretty woman. You'll do. How old are you? Twenty-eight? You're not more than thirty, are you? Got a family, have you? Figure like Eleanor Roosevelt when she was thirty. Nice breasts. But too tall. How tall are you? Five ten? If more women had good breasts, they wouldn't need brassières. Can't stand to see the things curdling round their waists! One in seventeen of you get breast cancer. Know that, did you? I read it somewhere. P'raps you wrote it in your newspaper. One in seventeen.

That's it. You sit there. Lady Bressingham used to like that chair. My wife. She used to perch there and pat the dogs. Potty about those dogs! Let them clamber all over her, kiss their faces. She prefered them to our daughter. Women! Mothers, the lot of you. But my wife wanted to be mother to the spaniels. Let them into her bed. Turfed me out. Shooed me out into the dressing room and called to the dogs: Chuppy, Bimsie, Mac! Mac was short for Macassar. Lady Bressingham had an experience in Macassar, so she called the bloody dog after it.

Nice view from that chair. Think so? Used to be a bowl of flowers in front of the window, on that marquetry table. You could look out beyond the flowers if you wanted, or just look *at* the flowers. Lady Bressingham always looked *at* the flowers. Quite often she'd get up in the middle of a sentence and go and fiddle about with the flowers, rearranging them. But if I ever sit there, I look out of the window.

See the cedars? Planted by Gordon of Khartoum when he stayed here. Odd fellow, Gordon, they say. Mad as a hatter! The East does that – and the heat. If Lady Bressingham had stayed in Macassar, she'd have gone potty. But the cedars are jolly good. I like them. That was where it was going to begin – just beyond the cedars, just far enough so you couldn't see it if you sat in that chair. Can't remember the layout exactly, but I know the funfair was going to start there. Want to see the plans? Got them somewhere. Somebody called Curry did them: landscape man. Said he was 'in' with the county council. Said there'd be no fiddle-faddle. Formality, he said, just a formality. But he was wrong. Had to go m'self, in the end, to see the council people. Half of them women. First meeting we had I was told the toilet provision was inadequate.

Like a glass of sherry? Bloody cold, these winters. Told Mrs Baxter to light the fire early today, but she didn't. Chuck another log on, will you? Pull the chair nearer, if you like. Lovely smile, you've got. Always thought newspaper people were a humourless lot. Lovely smile and breasts. Tell at a glance you're a hit with the chaps. Children, have you? Husband? Did I ask you that? Can't remember a damn thing these days. Lucky man whoever he is. Sherry's behind you. Help yourself.

Tell you a bit about the place, shall I? Built 1612. High Jacobean. Been in my family since 1789. Passed to the Bressinghams from the Villiers via the female line. Called Villiers Hall till 1901. Name changed by my father after the death of the Queen. Bressingham suits it better: stronger word. Lived here most of my life. Got to know it as a boy. Knew every inch of it then. Every birdsnest. No wireless. No TV then. You made your own life up. We had cricket out there on the lawn. And a camp in the spinney. Made a tree house with my cousins. Called it The Flat.

Curry wanted to chop down part of the spinney, stick the aviary there. I said no. I said, put the aviary where Lady Bressingham's rose garden used to be and stick the bloody toilets behind it. Then you'd have had a walkway straight from the aviary to the funfair. It made sense. You can let a spinney go wild and it's still a spinney, but rose gardens won't do unless they're tidy. Hate rose gardens, anyway! Tea roses! Disgusting fatty blobs. Don't like them, do you? Well, it's all overgrown anyway. Covered in convolvulus. Not worth saving. I'd have liked to hear parakeets there. Much better idea. So I convinced Curry. And I told poor old Flannery, my head gardener, just forget about Lady Bressingham's rose garden, Flannery, let it go, let the weeds get it, because that's where the aviary's going to be. He's older than me, Flannery. Live long, the Irish, if they don't kill each other. But he's getting like the house now: corners falling off him!

Blabbing enough for you, am I? Saying the right things? Tell you the best thing I thought up with Curry – the lion pit! We were going to have lions anyway, but I said, why not a pit? Get a lion-tamer – someone who'll make the brutes go docile – dress him in an anorak, give him a folding pushchair to hold, make him look like a one-parent family, then throw him in. Gladiator of the Week, we'd call it – every Sunday, sharp at three. Curry wasn't keen. Said we'd be contravening some Protection of the Public Act, but I said, Curry, I know a good idea when I smell one. Take feeding time at any zoo across the country; it's the danger element people are dribbling for: the man going into the cage with the raw meat. And the trick was, they wouldn't know he was a lion tamer. I love tricks. They'd think the man was a social worker.

Never liked the winter. Gets dark too early. Sherry keeps me going. Top me up, will you? Nice ankles you've got, too. Remind me a bit of Daphne. Got a son have you? Daphne had a son. Can't remember the boy's name. Derek or Daren or something. Shouldn't be talking about any of that anyway. Often think Lady Bressingham's listening in from the Quinta San José – if she's still alive. We don't communicate, you see. She's there in the Quinta San José near Lisboa as she calls it. And I'm here. Dreadful name, Daphne. Don't you agree? Terribly common name. Daff, I called her. Make me a naughty boy, Daff! Lock the bloody door and get hold of me quickly! Sixty-two I was when Daphne came here, and randy as a trick cyclist. God, I was randy! Hadn't had sex for years with Lady Bressingham, but when Daff arrived I couldn't control myself. Like a sixteen-year-old, I was. Called it charvering when I was young. Odd bloody word for it. Day and night I'd dream of it – in my Bentley, down at the spinney, on the floor behind this bloody desk – charvering Daff. Don't print it, will you? Not meant to blab about any of that, but my God, it's lonely here. That's why I was all for the funfair. And the lions, and the aviary. Bring a bit of life in. Friends of mine said, don't do it, old man. Ruin Bressingham, you will, destroy its character. But I said what the bloody good's character when the place is crumbling? I'll show you round when we've had the sherry. You can see for yourself what needs doing. Hasn't been touched, any of it, since Lady Bressingham left for Portugal. No money. Sold off a hundred acres to buy Lady Bressingham the Quinta San José. I heard she grows oranges. Mac must be dead by now. But I'd know if my wife was dead, I dare say. Some letter in Portugoose. Have solicitors out there, don't they? Lady Bressingham's name was Fidelity Belcher, before I got her. I seem to choose women with disagreeable names.

Like it on your newspaper, do you? Interesting life? On the road a lot, chasing scandals and people with breast cancer? They loathe a scandal in these parts. Want life to run flat, like a motorway. But I don't agree. I've always liked ups and downs. Look like a stick-in-the-mud, I know that, but I was the one who thought up the lion pit. It's the council who won't play. Curry said point nought nought fiddle-faddle, but what do we get in the end? Vetoes. You write that down, young woman. You put, 'Lord Bressingham, 75, owner of Bressingham Hall, is being denied his chance to confront the world of today.'

My daughter would have approved. I thought of writing to her, to get her to come and talk some sense into the county council, but I don't know where she lives. The last I heard she was in Hackney. I grew up thinking all the poor of the nation lived in Hackney. Too bloody poor to breathe the sooty air! In the war, they sent evacuees out from Hackney, but we never took any in. Lady Bressingham disliked children. If they'd evacuated dogs, we'd have been over-run! We'd have had open house! Funny woman, Fidelity Belcher. Often hoped she'd tell me what happened in Macassar. Something damned odd.

Something she never forgot. She's probably going round her orange trees in her sunhat, this very afternoon, remembering Macassar. Imagine that! My daughter could be with her, but I doubt it. She didn't like us much, either one of us. Left us the minute she could. Lived with an Indian in Hackney. I said okay, good for you, no harm done, forgive and forget. I'm a tolerant man for a Peer. House of Lords is jam-packed with intolerant men, but I'm not among them. I said, bring Simon to Bressingham. He was called Simon, this Indian chap, not Vindaloo or Biriani, as you might expect. Simon. So I said, you bring him down and we'll kill the fatted calf! Forgot calves are sacred! Put my foot right in it there, eh? No harm intended. But she never forgave me. Worse than that, she tried to punish me.

Ever had children? Didn't ask you before, did I? Daff had a son. I wrote to Daff when this funfair scheme got going, took the liberty of reminding her of certain afternoons in my Bentley, asked her to come and see me and see Curry's plans. But I never heard a word. Shame, really. Beautiful buttocks, Daff had. Marvellous little fanny. Don't mind me talking like this, do you? Open-minded girl, are you? I'd have married Daff but for Lady Bressingham's Catholicism. Daphne was willing. I was a very potent man at sixty-two. She used to scream and tear at me. *Women!* My wife in bed with the dogs; Daff yelling her head off in the back of the Bentley! I thought my life had gone potty. No, I did. She was thirty-four. Not much older than you. Marriage hadn't worked. Left landed with her son. Came to me as a secretary. Had me going the minute I clapped eyes on her. I was well endowed then. I banged her all the time, better than an undergraduate. And she wanted me to marry her. She pleaded. So I thought, why not? What a wife to get at sixty-two! My God, I thought, my life's going to be a bloody miracle. So I went to Lady Bressingham. She was in bed with Bimsie and Mac, tickling their tummies. I sat on her bed and said, I'm in love with Daphne and Daphne's in love with me and I want a divorce. She was in her nightie. She said, pass me my bedjacket. So I gave her the bedjacket and she said, *never.*

There was a stink in the village, I can tell you. Lady

Bressingham told them all – all the servants, all our friends, even the tradesmen and shopkeepers – my husband is unfaithful to me: my husband is betraying his name and mine. And poor Daff just couldn't take it. Those lovely screams of hers turned to hysteria. I did my level best to comfort her. I said, Daff, I may not be able to marry you, but I'll leave Bressingham and live with you in a flat. But no, she wanted marriage and that was that. She told me she was pregnant. What a to-do! Thought Bressingham would fall down round my ears! Never heard parakeets screech like Lady Bressingham screeched then. She began to break things, too. China ornaments. Vases. Hundreds of pounds she must have smashed. Terrifying! Then she went away. To Lisboa as she calls it.

Just by the by though, all that. The filling in life's pie – the colourful part. Most people hide those bits. But I'm quite fond of colour. I said to Curry, if we've got to provide toilets, let's do them orange and red striped like circus tents, let's make a feature of them. And if we're going to have a funfair, let's for heavens' sake have a good one, with fast machinery and all the thrills. I think I overdid it. Got carried away. But don't tell me people wouldn't have liked it. And the lion pit. Cracking idea. Better than anything Bath has at Longleat. Outdo 'em all!

Lovely view from that chair, don't you think? Like it, do you? I agree. But if it all goes on crumbling and sinking, you won't be able to sit there any more. They'll have to pull the old house down. Stick me in some geriatric establishment. Breaks my heart. A flat with Daff I wouldn't have minded. Far from it. But I dislike institutions. People fart a lot in institutions. Top me up, will you? Plenty more sherry in the cellar. Never run short of that. Don't suppose you could track my daughter down, could you? Wrote to that Hackney address, but my letter came back. My daughter could have a go at the council. She's a strong character. Told you she tried to punish me, did I? She wrote to Flannery and Mrs Baxter and all the staff, telling them what I should be paying them, telling them I was robbing them blind. Flannery showed me his letter. I was paying him half what my daughter told him he should be getting. So of course,

149

he's never been happy since. I upped his wages a few pounds, but that didn't do. He threatened to leave. Leave, I told him. You leave, Flannery! You're too bloody old to work, anyway. But he never will. He eats practically free. He's got his cottage. He'll die there, or in the spinney poaching pheasants.

Wouldn't do that to your father, would you? Turn his own people against him? Dead is he? Oh. Expect I should be dead, by rights. That dog, Mac, must be dead by now. And those other fleabags, Chuppy and Whatisname. Only thing my wife could pronounce properly in Spanish as far as I know was Narcisco Yepes. Know him? *Narthithco Yepeth!* So how the hell does she manage in Portugoose? Eh? Just wanders about in her sunhat, pointing, I dare say. *Watero las orangerias gracias. Portare immediatementi il breakfastino!* Beats me how you can make a life out of that twaddle! Perhaps she hasn't got a life. She never writes to me. I send her a Christmas card each year, for old time's sake. Sent her an out-of-date printed one last year by mistake: 'With Best Wishes for Christmas and the New Year from Lord and Lady Bressingham', it said! My God, that will have made her break a few ornaments! Fidelity Belcher. I'll wonder to my dying day what happened to her in Macassar.

Show you round the house now. Got a scarf or something? Got any gloves? When I was a boy, there'd be twenty or thirty staying for Christmas. Everybody going in and out of each other's bedrooms in secret! We children used to spy on the night flitters; called them the Somnambulists. Always had a fascination for sex, but Roman Catholics want to take all the fun out of it. Can't imagine why I married one. Didn't suit me at all. I should have had a string of young wives with tearing fingers, like Daff.

Oh, I like your scarf. I like striped things. I told Curry, we're going to build a roller coaster bigger than Battersea! Paint all the structure green, shape the little cars like wasps and bees and let the people yell their heads off, flying above the cedars like insects. Imagine looking out of that window and seeing that – people whizzing over the trees! I'd have loved it. I'd have kept it going round the year. But I expect that's where I went wrong with the council: too keen. Phlegmatic lot! Don't seem to care a jot that Bressingham's sinking into the moat. I told them, give me permission for the funfair and the lion pit and the aviary and I'll put Bressingham on its feet again within a year. I was only asking for *permission*. Not for money. But they refused me. Story of my life: people reaching for their bloody bedjackets and saying, never.

Off we go, then. Always put a macintosh on when I do the tour of the house; protects me from the damp. Dry rot, wet rot, mould, fungus – we've got it all here now. The Somnambulists would turn in their graves! There used to be fires in all the bedrooms and furs on the four-posters. The room Gordon allegedly slept in had a tiger skin as a hearth rug. Can't remember what we did with it. It got the moth, I wouldn't wonder. Or perhaps I sold it off when I bought Lady Bressingham the Quinta San José. I can't remember. Rooms are practically empty, though, now. Don't expect finery, will you? Just a lot of cold, empty rooms now. Nothing much to look at. Terrible legacy, a house like this in an age like this. Glad I haven't got a son to leave it to. Daff's pregnancy was phantom. Did I tell you that? Your gloves match that scarf. Very nice. You're a very bright, lovely woman. If I was younger, you wouldn't be safe with me. Dunno how that phantom got into Daff. Through the air conditioning in the Bentley perhaps! Don't understand women. Never will now, will I? My daughter. Daff. My wife. All potty in one way or another. People are. That's why I wanted to give them a funfair – to let them have a good scream.

A Shooting Season

'You're writing a *what?*'

'A novel.'

Looking away from him, nervously touching her hair, Anna remembered, the last time I saw him my hair wasn't grey.

'Why the hell are you writing a novel?'

Grey hairs had sprouted at forty-one. Now, at forty-five, she sometimes thought, my scalp is exhausted, that's all, like poor soil.

'I've wanted to write a novel ever since I was thirty. Long before, even . . .'

'You never told me.'

'No. Of course not.'

'Why "of course not"?'

'You would have laughed, as you're laughing now.'

Anna had always been enchanted by his laugh. It was a boy's giggle (you climbed a cold dormitory stairway and heard it bubble and burst behind a drab door!), yet their son didn't have it: at sixteen, he had the laugh of a rowdy man.

'I don't approve.'

'No.'

'It's an act of postponed jealousy.'

Well, if so, then long postponed. Six years since their separation; four since the divorce and his remarriage to Susan, the pert blonde girl who typed his poems. And it wasn't jealousy, surely? In learning to live without him, she had taught herself to forget him utterly. If she heard him talk on the radio, she found herself thinking, his cadences are echoing Dylan Thomas these days; he's remembered how useful it is, if you happen to be a poet, also to be Welsh. Three years older than her, he had come to resemble a Welsh hillside – craggy outcrop of a man, unbuttoned to weather and fortune, hair wiry as gorse. Marcus. Fame clung to his untidy look. No doubt, she thought, he's as unfaithful to Susan as he was to me.

'How did it start?'

The novel-writing, he meant, but he had a way, still, of sending fine ripples through the water of ordinary questions which invited her to admit: I was in love with him for such a long time that parting from him was like a drowning. When I was washed ashore, the sediment of him still clogged me.

'I found there were things I wanted to say.'

'Oh, there always were!'

'Yes, but stronger now. Before I get old and start forgetting.'

'But a *novel*?'

'Why not?'

'You were never ambitious.'

No. Not when she was his: Mrs Marcus Ridley, wife of the poet. Not while she bore his children and made rugs while he wrote and they slept.

'Do your pockets still have bits of sand in them?'

He laughed, took her strong wrist and held her hand to his face. 'I don't know. No one empties them for me.'

Anna had been at the rented cottage for three weeks. A sluggish river flowed a few yards from it: mallard and moorhen were the companions of her silence, the light of early morning was silver. In this temporary isolation, she had moved contentedly in her summer sandals, setting up a work table in the sunshine, another indoors by the open fire. Her novel crept to a beginning, then began to flow quietly like the river. She celebrated each day's work with two glasses, sometimes more, of the home-made wine she had remembered to bring with her. She slept well with the window wide open on the Norfolk sky. She dreamed of her book finished and bound. Then one morning Margaret, her partner in her craft business, tele-phoned. The sound of the telephone ringing was so unfamiliar that it frightened her. She remembered her children left on their own in London; she raced to answer the unforeseen but now obvious emergency. But no, said Margaret, no emergency, only Marcus.

'Marcus?'

'Yes. Drunk and full of his songs. Said he needed to see you.'

'And you told him where I was?'

'Yes. He said if I didn't, he'd pee on the pottery shelf.'

'Marcus.'

The rough feel of his face was very familiar; she might have touched it yesterday. She thought suddenly, for all his puerile needs, he's a man of absolute mystery; I never understood him. Yet they had been together for ten years. The Decade of the Poet she called it, wanting to bury him with formality and distance. And yet he surfaced in her: she seldom read a book without wondering, how would Marcus have judged that? And then feeling irritated by the question. On such occasions, she would always remind herself: he doesn't even bother to see the children, let alone me. He's got a new family (Evan 4, Lucy 3) and they, now, take all his love – the little there ever was in him to give.

'You look so healthy, Anna. Healthy and strong. I suppose you always were strong.'

'Big-boned, my mother called it.'

'How is your mother?'

'Dead.'

'You never let me know.'

'No. There was no point.'

'I could have come with you – to the funeral or whatever.'

'Oh, Marcus . . .'

'Funerals are ghastly. I could have helped you through.'

'Why don't you see the children?'

He let her hand drop. He turned to the window, wide open on the now familiar prospect of reed and river. Anna noticed that the faded corduroy jacket he was wearing was stretched tight over his back. He seemed to have outgrown it.

'Marcus . . .?'

He turned back to her, hands in his pockets.

'No accusations. No bloody accusations!'

Oh yes, she noticed, there's the pattern: I ask a question, Marcus says it's inadmissible, I feel guilty and ashamed . . .

'It's a perfectly reasonable question.'

'Reasonable? It's a guilt-inducing, jealous, mean-minded question. You know perfectly well why I don't see the children: because I have two newer, younger and infinitely more affectionate children, and these newer, younger and infinitely more affectionate children are bitterly resented by the aforementioned older, infinitely less affectionate children. And because I am a coward.'

He should be hit, she thought, then noticed that she was smiling.

'I brought some of my home-made wine,' she said, 'it's a disgusting looking yellow, but it tastes rather good. Shall we have some?'

'Home-made wine? I thought you were a business*person*. When the hell do you get time to make wine?'

'Oh Marcus, I have plenty of time.'

Anna went to the cold, tile-floored little room she had decided to think of as 'the pantry'. Its shelves were absolutely deserted except for five empty Nescafé jars, a dusty goldfish bowl (the debris of another family's Norfolk summer) and her own bottles of wine. It was thirty-five years since she had lived in a house large enough to have a pantry, but now, in this cupboard of a place, she could summon memories of Hodgson, her grandfather's butler, uncorking Stones ginger beer for her and her brother on timeless summer evenings – the most exquisite moments of all the summer holidays. Then, one summer, she found herself there alone. Hodgson had left. Her brother Charles had been killed at school by a cricket ball.

Anna opened a bottle of wine and took it and two glasses out to her table in the garden, where Marcus had installed himself. He was looking critically at her typewriter and at the unfinished pages of her book lying beside it.

'You don't mean to say you're typing it?'

She put the wine and the glasses on the table. She noticed that the heavy flint she used as a paperweight had been moved.

'Please don't let the pages blow away, Marcus.'

'I'm sure it's a mistake to type thoughts directly onto paper. Writing words by hand is part of the process.'

'Your process.'

'I don't know any writers who type directly.'

'You know me. Please put the stone back, Marcus.'

He replaced the pages he had taken up, put the flint down gently and spread his wide hand over it. He was looking at her face.

'Don't write about me, Anna, will you?'

She poured the wine. The sun touched her neck and she remembered its warmth with pleasure.

'Don't make me the villain.'

'There is no villain.'

She handed him his glass of wine. Out in the sunshine, he looked pale beside her. A miraculous three weeks of fine weather had tanned her face, neck and arms, whereas he . . . how did he spend his days now? She didn't know. He looked as if he'd been locked up. Yet he lived in the country with his new brood. She it was – and their children – who had stayed on in the London flat.

'How's Susan?'

No. She didn't want to ask. Shouldn't have asked. She'd only asked in order to get it over with: to sweep Susan and his domestic life to the back of her mind, so that she could let herself be nice to him, let herself enjoy him.

'Why ask?'

'To get it over with!'

He smiled. She thought she sensed his boyish laughter about to surface.

'Susan's got a lover.'

Oh damn him! Damn Marcus! Feeling hurt, feeling cheated, he thought I'd be easy consolation. No wonder the novel annoys him; he sees the ground shifting under him, sees a time when he's not the adored, successful granite he always thought he was.

'Damn the lover.'

'What?'

He'd looked up at her, startled. What he remembered most vividly about her was her permanence. The splash of bright homespun colour that was Anna: he had only to turn his head, open a door, to find her there. No other wife or mistress had been like her; these had often been absent when he'd searched for them hardest. But Anna: Anna had always *wanted* to be there.

'I'm not very interested in Susan's lover.'

'No. He isn't interesting. He's a chartered surveyor.'

'Ah. Well, reliable probably.'

'D'you think so? Reliable, are they, as a breed? He looks pitiful enough to be it. Perhaps that's what she wants.'

'And you?'

'Me?'

'What do you want, Marcus? Did you come here just to tell me your wife had a lover?'

'Accusations again. All the bloody little peeves!'

'I want to know why you came here.'

'So do I.'

'What?'

'So do I want to know. All I know is that I wanted to see you. If that's not good enough for you, I'll go away.'

Further along the river, she could hear the mallard quacking. Some evenings at sunset, she had walked through the reeds to find them (two pairs, one pair with young) and throw in scraps for them. Standing alone, the willows in front of her in perfect silhouette, she envied the ducks their sociability. No one comes near them, she thought, only me standing still. Yet they have everything – everyone – they need.

'I love it here.'

She had wanted to sit down opposite Marcus with her glass of wine, but he had taken the only chair. She squatted, lifting her face to the sun. She knew he was watching her.

'Do you want me to go away?'

She felt the intermittent river breeze on her face, heard the pages of her novel flap under the stone. She examined his question, knew that it confused her, and set it aside.

'The novel's going to be about Charlie.'

'Charlie?'

'My brother Charles. Who died at school. I'm imagining that he lived on, but not as him, as a girl.'

'Why as a girl?'

'I thought I would understand him better as a girl.'

'Will it work?'

'The novel?'

'Giving Charlie tits.'

'Yes, I think so. It also means she doesn't have to play cricket and risk being killed.'

'I'd forgotten Charlie.'

'You never knew him.'

'I knew him as a boy – through your memories. He of Hodgson's ginger beer larder!'

'Pantry.'

She's got stronger, Marcus decided. She's gone grey and it suits her. And she's still wearing her bright colours. Probably makes not just her own clothes now, but ponchos and smocks and bits of batik to sell in her shops. And of course her son's friends fall in love with her. She's perfect for a boy: bony, maternal and sexy. Probably her son's in love with her too.

'Can I stay for dinner?'

Anna put her glass to her lips and drained it. He always, she thought, made requests sound like offers.

Anna scrutinised the contents of the small fridge: milk, butter, a bunch of weary radishes, eggs. Alone, she would have made do with the radishes and an omelette, but Marcus had a lion's appetite. His most potent memory of a poetry-reading fortnight in America was ordering steak for breakfast. He had returned looking ruddy, like the meat.

Anna sighed. The novel had been going well that morning.

Charlie, renamed Charlotte, was perched high now above her cloistered schooldays on the windswept catwalk of a new university. Little gusts of middle-class guilt had begun to pick at her well-made clothes and at her heart. She was ready for change.

'Charlotte can wait,' Marcus told Anna, after her one feeble attempt to send him away. 'She'll be there tomorrow and I'll be gone. And anyway, we owe it to each other – one dinner.'

I owe nothing, Anna thought. No one (especially not pretty Susan with her tumbling fair hair and her flirtatious eyes) could have given herself – her time, her energy, her love – more completely to one man than she to Marcus. For ten years he had been the landscape that held her whole existence – one scarlet poppy on the hills and crags of him, sharing his sky.

'One dinner!'

She took the car into Wroxham, bought good dark fillet, two bottles of Beaujolais, new potatoes, a salad and cheese.

While she was gone, he sat at the table in the sunshine, getting accustomed to the gently scented taste of her home-made wine and, despite a promise not to, reading her novel. Her writing bored him after a very few pages; he needed her presence, not her thoughts.

I've cried for you, he wanted to tell her. There have been times when – yes, several of them – times when I haven't felt comfortable with the finality of our separation, times when I've thought, there's more yet, I need more. And why couldn't you be part of my life again, on its edge? I would honestly feel troubled less – by Susan's chartered surveyor, by the coming of my forty-ninth birthday – yes, much less, if you were there in your hessian or whatever it is you wear and I could touch you. Because ten years is, after all, a large chunk of our lives, and though I never admit it, I now believe that my best poems were written during those ten and what followed has been mainly repetition. And I wanted to ask you, where are those rugs you made while I worked? Did you chuck them out? Why was the silent making of your rugs so intimately connected to my perfect arrangement of words?

'So here we are . . .'

The evening promised to be so warm that Anna had put a cloth on the table outside and laid it for supper. Marcus had helped her prepare the food and now they sat facing the sunset, watching the colour go first from the river, then from the willows and poplars behind it.

'Remember Yugoslavia?'

'Yes, Marcus.'

'Montenegro.'

'Yes.'

'Those blue thistles.'

'Umm.'

'Our picnic suppers!'

'Stale bread.'

'What?'

'The bread in Yugoslavia always tasted stale.'

'We used to make love in a sleeping bag.'

'Yes.'

Anna thought, it will soon be so dark, I won't be able to see him clearly, just as, in my mind, I have only the most indistinct perception of how he *is* in that hard skin, if I ever knew. For a moment she considered going indoors to get a candle, but decided it would be a waste of time; the breeze would blow it out. And the darkness suits us, suits this odd meeting, she thought. In it, we're insubstantial; we're each imagining the other one, that's all.

'I read the novel, as far as you've gone.'

'Yes. I thought you probably would.'

'I never pictured you writing.'

'No. Well, I never pictured you arriving here. Margaret told me you said you "needed" me. What on earth did you mean?'

'I think about you – often.'

'Since Susan found her surveyor?'

'That's not fair.'

'Yes, it's fair. You could have come to see me – and the children – any time you wanted.'

'I wanted . . .'

'What?'

'Not the children. You.'

For a moment, Anna allowed herself to remember: 'You, in the valley of my arms,/ my quaint companion on the mountain./ How wisely did I gather you,/ my crimson bride . . .' Then she took a sip of Beaujolais and began:

'I've tried.'

'What?'

'To love other people. Other men, I mean.'

'And?'

'The feelings don't seem to last. Or perhaps I've just been unlucky.'

'Yes. You deserve someone.'

'I don't want anyone, Marcus. This is what I've at last understood. I have the children and the craft shops and one or two men friends to go out with, and now I have the novel . . .'

'I miss you, Anna.'

She rested her chin on folded hands and looked at him. Mighty is a perfect word, she thought. To me, he has always seemed mighty. And when he left me, every room, every place I went to was full of empty space. Only recently had I got used to it, decided finally to stop trying to fill it up. And now there he is again, his enormous shadow, darker, nearer than the darkness.

'You see, I'm not a poet any more.'

'Yes, you are, Marcus. I read your new volume . . .'

'No I'm not. I won't write anything more of value.'

'Why?'

'Because I'm floundering, Anna. I don't know what I expect of myself any more, as a poet or as a man. Susan's destroying me.'

'Oh rot! Susan was exactly the woman you dreamed of.'

'And now I have dreams of you.'

Anna sighed and let Marcus hear the sigh. She got up and

walked the few yards to the river and watched it shine at her feet. For the first time that day, the breeze made her shiver.

Light came early. Anna woke astonished and afraid. Marcus lay on his stomach, head turned away from her, his right arm resting down the length of her body.

A noise had woken her, she knew, yet there was nothing: only the sleeper's breath next to her and the birds tuning up, like a tiny hidden orchestra, for their full-throated day. Then she heard them: two shots, then a third and a fourth. Marcus turned over, opened his eyes and looked at her. She was sitting up and staring blankly at the open window. The thin curtains moved on a sunless morning.

'Anna . . .'

The strong hand on her arm wanted to tug her gently down, but she resisted its pressure, stayed still, chin against her knees.

'Someone's shooting.'

'Come back to sleep.'

'No, I can't. Why would someone be shooting?'

'The whole world's shooting!'

'I must go and see.'

Marcus lay still and watched Anna get up. As she pulled on a faded, familiar gown, both had the same thought: it was always like this, Anna getting up first, Marcus in bed half asleep, yet often watching Anna.

'What are you going to do?'

'I don't know. But I have to see.'

The morning air was chilly. It was sunless, Anna realised, only because the sun had not yet risen. A mist squatted above the river; the landscape was flattened and obscured in dull white. Anna stared. The dawn has extraordinary purpose, she thought, everything contained, everything shrouded by the light but emerging minute by minute into brightness and shape, so that while I stand still it all changes. She began to walk along the river. The ground under her sandals was damp and the leather soon became slippery. Nothing moved. The familiar breeze had almost died in the darkness, the willow leaves hung limp and wet. Anna stopped, rubbed her eyes.

'Where are you?'

She waited, peering into the mist. The mist was yellowing, sunlight slowly climbing. A dog barked, far off.

'Where are you?'

Senseless question. Where are you? Where are you? Anna walked on. The surface of the water, so near her slippery feet, was absolutely smooth. The sun was climbing fast now and the mist was tumbling, separating, making way for colour and contour. Where *are* you! The three words came echoing down the years. Anna closed her eyes. They came and shot the ducks, she told herself calmly. That's all. Men came with guns and had a duck shoot and the mallard are gone. When I come down here with my scraps, I won't find them. But that's all. The river flows on. Everything else is just as it was yesterday and the day before and the day before that. I am still Anna. Birds don't matter. I have a book to write. And the sun's coming up . . .

She was weeping. Clutching her arms inside the sleeves of the faded gown, she walks from room to room in the empty flat. Where are you! London dawn at the grimed net curtains . . . fruit still in the bowl from which, as he finally went, he stole an orange . . . nothing changes and yet everything . . . his smell still on her body . . . And where am I? Snivelling round the debris of you in all the familiar rooms, touching surfaces you touched, taking an orange from the bowl . . . Where am I? Weeping. The ducks don't matter. Do they? Keeping hold on what is, on what exists *after* the shot has echoed and gone, this is all that's important, yes, keeping hold on what I have forced myself to become, with all the sanding and polishing of my heart's hardness, keeping hold of my life alone that nothing – surely not the wounds of one night's loving? – can destroy. So just let me wipe my face on the same washed-out corner of a sleeve. And forget. A stranger carries the dead mallard home, dead smeared heads, bound together with twine. But the sun comes up on the same stretch of river where, only yesterday, they had life . . .

*

Marcus held Anna. They stood by his car. It was still morning, yet they sensed the tiredness in each other, as if neither had slept at all.

'I'll be going then, old thing. Sorry I was such a miserable bugger. Selfish of me to disturb you with my little problems.'

'Oh, you weren't disturbing me.'

'Yes, I was. Typical of me: Marcus Ridley's Lament for Things as They Are.'

'I don't mind. And last night – '

'Lovely, Anna. Perhaps I'll stop dreaming about you now.'

'Yes.'

He kissed her cheek and got quickly into the car.

'Good luck with the novel.'

'Oh yes. Thank you, Marcus.'

'I'll picture you working by your river.'

'Come and see the children, Marcus. Please come and see the children.'

'Yes. All right. No promises. Are you going to work on the book today?'

'No, I don't think I can. Not today.'

'Poor Anna. I've tired you. Never mind. There's always tomorrow.'

'Yes, Marcus,' and very gently she reached out and touched his face, 'there's always tomorrow.'

My Love Affair with James I

Exercise 4, Week 4 of the Eric Neasdale 'Make Money by Writing' course: Describe with honesty and, if possible, humour, a recent major event in your life.

William Nichols – or 'Will', as I think of him – is an actor I'd never actually met. It's odd I'd never met him because a) he's filthily famous and b) his pic is on the same page as mine in *Spotlight*. Actually, my pic is above his as I'm fractionally superior to him alphabetwise, but our page goes: Stephen Nias (me), William Nichols (Will), Bob Nickolls (spelt with a k and two l's and pullulating with his resemblance to Alain Delon), and Ken Nightingale (the less said the better; cast as the eternal traffic warden; should never have had his pic in 'Leading').

You may think the question of the *Spotlight* pics is a bit of a waffle (this writing course is tediously keen on the word relevance), but I don't think it is. You see, my pic was actually taken in '79 (hair darker, bags minimal, *you* know . . .) and in it I look so absolutely dead right for the part of the Duke of Buckingham that I was offered it sight unseen, or virtually. I did have lunch with the producer, Alfie Morton, before contracts went out, but Alfie likes to lunch at The Rasputin, an utterly excruciating Russian restaurant he thinks is de rigueur for the famous, and luckily the bloody Rasputin is so dark – and I mean *pitch* – that you honestly can't tell whether the cav in your blinis is red or black. So you see, in those conditions I could still make thirty-five; Alfie stares at me like an icon over our red-glassed candle and his only worry is, is my voice, which viewers hear almost nightly extolling the nutrient virtues of a catfood called Tiggo, too domesticated a tool for the cadences of the haughty duke? He decides no, and he's right. The reason I got the Tiggo VO is that my voice is – and I say this without vanity – my greatest asset as an actor. I'm not a deep person; I know my failings. Life's a bit of a game to me, a bit of a tap-dance. But my voice is redolent with depth. It's as if it was engendered in one of those *grottes* the green Michelin guides keep encouraging you to visit. It reverbs. It has texture. I'd be dead on for Son et Lumière. I'm wasted on frigging catfood – but that's television for you, and my bank manager isn't complaining. So I have no difficulty convincing Alfie Morton that he and old 'Eyelids' Mordecai, our illustrious director, have made the right choice.

By the time we get to coffee, Alfie's making his 'Welcome Aboard' speech and I know I've got the duke. I actually begin to rattle with excitement: a four-month shoot, one month of which will be in Greece. And Will Nichols playing King James. With Will's name on the picture, it's certainly going to get coverage. It's a major movie all right: Jon Markworthy on script, Billy Nettlefold on cameras, the Morton/Mordecai clout with distributors, Will in his first screen role for over two years, and me. After lunch with Alfie (I put my shades on the minute we get anywhere near natural light) I brisk along to Dougie, my agent, and to my utter amazement he produces a bottle of Taylor's port from a filing cabinet marked 'Clients SS'. I'm much too surprised by the Taylor's gesture to ask Dougie what 'SS' stands for.

When I got home, I took my trousers off and examined my legs. My bathroom's all mirrors, so I shot little glances at them from every angle. They're okay. I'm five eleven. But they're not the exquisite legs the Duke displays in that picture of him in the Portrait Gallery. Those legs look as if they begin at his armpits, and my thighs seem positively neanderthal by comparison. But then I remembered that Will Nichols is a short man – sturdy and stubby – so that compared to his legs, I thought mine would have a touch of the gazelle about them. Heaven knows why I was so worried about legs. There were far more excruciating things to worry about, had I known it at the time (as the lion said to the unicorn), but I was all breezy innocence and excitement! I got out a pair of ancient bermudas and stuffed them out with a couple of cushions to make them look like hose. Protruding from these, my legs looked plain ridiculous. It's at times like these, with cushions puffing out my bum, that I'm thankful I live alone. At least, after everything that happened, I haven't lost my sense of humour!

Reading this, I see that there are two exclamation marks in my last para. The writing course says 'use these sparingly'. May have to cross them out in my rewrite. And the joke about the unicorn: 'Avoid doubtful and distasteful humour' says the bloody course. Never mind. I'll leave it in for now.

There was one fact which, from the start of this film, I found slightly odd, but which no one else remarked on: namely, Will Nichols, about to play the most Scottish king since Macbeth, was Welsh. I'd long ago seen Will Nichols grapple with a Scots accent in one of those thunderous war movies that are all about detonating bridges over the Rhine, and he'd done dismally. His voice has what I'd call gusto, but it's unmistakable Welsh gusto. He can do a passable English baronet, but not (well, I don't think he can) a Scots king. I felt like saying to Morton: you might as well cast an American, love, and have done with it. But by the time I was offered Buckingham (the juiciest film part I've ever had) Will Nichols's name was on the project and there it would stick. Over the Taylor's, Dougie told me that at least Will was off the booze.

I'll tell you what I knew about Will at that time. (You'll know most of it already. His life is pretty well public knowledge.) He'd crawled onto a stage bent double from his deprived childhood in a Welsh mine, straightened up enough to do a memorable Hamlet aged twenty, married a then star of the English stage called Myrtle Bridehead, years his senior and opposite whom he played a rather chunky Romeo. (Myrtle Bridehead as Juliet, nudging thirty-seven, was one of the finest embarrassments of my protected youth.) He'd then been whisked off to America. In Hollywood, he began to make a string of romantic movies and by the age of thirty he was a flash name and a millionaire. He should have died then. Or am I being unfair? He's done one or two respectable things since then – he's now forty-seven, looks older – but his fame has bred on itself, rather than on additions to itself, if you get my drift. He dumped Myrtle the minute LA swam into vision through the smog and only played a bit-part at her suicide two months later. Rumour has it that since Myrtle, the last scales of Welsh conformism have fallen from his eyes and that from that time he has tangled off-screen only with men and boys. His most faithful companion of recent years has been the whisky bottle. His Welsh lungs have begun to sound as if they're filling up with coal. Despite all this, he's still a bankable star.

As to me (virtually unknown Steve Nias), I tried to prepare myself meticulously for Buckingham, and I don't just mean staring at my legs. Jon Markworthy's script suggested a relationship between Buckingham and King James which, if it wasn't a love affair in the understood sense, was as least as passionate as one. Now I loathe ambiguity. So I spent hours in Chelsea Public Library trying to decide for myself precisely what the nature of this friendship was – and failing. History itself is ambiguous on the subject, as I might have guessed. So all I had to go on were Markworthy's scenes. In one of these, I am summoned in the middle of the night from the bed of my wife, Katherine, to the bedchamber of the King. I arrive breathless, and no wonder. The King stammers on about his role as 'nurturer of peace in this land'. I, wearing a night robe (which turned out to resemble and to be as heavy as a forty-foot drape), start to mutter ominously about the need to take England to war. A verbal scuffle ensues. The King starts to weep. I hold him and he kisses me. *Lorks!* In the run-up to my first meeting with Will Nichols, I phoned Dougie and asked for a meeting with Markworthy and Eyelids re the persistent ambiguity of this and other scenes. Dougie simply laughed and told me to stop jittering.

*

I can't leave *lorks* in. But this one word conveys precisely what I felt every time I read this scene. One of the commandments of the Eric Neasdale Writing Course is 'Avoid ejaculations where possible.' *Lorks* is an undoubted ejaculation. Oh well. Perhaps something else will come to me in the middle of the night, as they say. NB I must take this piece of work seriously. I would seriously like to become a writer. But writing about 'real events' seems to have its little problems.

Before I plunge in to the main thrust of my story (this last is a shitty sentence and must go), I think I ought to say a word or two about my life – as it was before I met Will Nichols, and as it is becoming again.

I came to acting from dancing. The love of dance hasn't entirely left me and I sometimes do little dance routines on the flat roof of my Fulham top-floor flat, among my plants. I grow cucumbers on this roof in the summer and shrubs and herbs and roses all the year round, in big tubs and old baths and sinks. I never grow tomatoes because I'm allergic to them. This allergy makes some dinners problematical: you find tomato in almost everything from *daube* to *douglère*, from Bolognese to braised oxtail, and the unsightly neck rashes I then have to endure are one of the penances of an otherwise quietly agreeable and civilised life.

I live alone, as I said, but I'm seldom actually lonely. I lived with someone called David for a year and with someone called Donovan for about nine months. Otherwise, I've always lived alone since I left school and home. My mother is an elderly person and safely put away in a home for elderly persons near Swindon. My father, who disapproved of me and all my works till his dying day, mercifully reached his dying day in 1976, and since then I've felt guilty about nothing and fairly positive about most things.

The money I make from Tiggo and other VOs I do for ITV have brought me a high standard of living, even though I don't get as much acting work as I'd like. Between you and me, I'm not that fantastic an actor. I've got my following because, as you've guessed from the Buckingham thing, I'm still fairly morbidly handsome. Sexually, I'm what they call alert and I honestly don't have any difficulty in that *département*. My West Indian cleaner, Mrs Baali (I call her Pearl Barley. That's the kind of joke that's typical me) is allowed to tease me about my boyfriends, but I keep them low profile. 'Sex = love' is pure romanticism, pure bunkum, in my view. Jon Markworthy at least understood this in his famous script, if nothing else. I'm a very meticulous person, day to day. I like clean things. Lately, I've been a slut, though. I've had weekends when I didn't wash or shave or go out or wash up. Pearl Barley's been dying to comment. She's like a huge, wobbling brown fruit, my Pearl Barley, and comment on my sluttishness has been on the brink of bursting out of her for several weeks, I can tell. But she hasn't cracked yet. She's a loyal woman. I'm not all that loyal myself, but I value it in others.

Well, that's me. Enough said. On to the main thrust, as they say: my love affair.

I was forty-one the day I met Will Nichols for the first time face to face. An odd coincidence that this project should kick off on my birthday, 6 May. In fact, it had kicked off months before of course, but old Eyelids actually sat down with his lead actors on 6 May in what appeared to be the boardroom of his Wardour Street offices, flanked by Markworthy and Morton and Nettlefold and legions of PAs, and over a rather troppo minceur lunch of smoked salmon mould he began to talk about 'my great new royal baby, King James I'.

'Eyelids' Mordecai is seventy-eight years old. My allergy to tomatoes (uncomfortable enough, God knows) is but a shade compared to the ghostly army of allergies haunting Mordecai. Mordecai rightly belongs in a Swiss sanitorium, muffled to the neck in polyanimide, breathing cloudless air. Here, he would die calmly, snow would settle on his globally famous eyelids and that would be that. As it is, his quaking body is carried on and off aeroplanes, wheeled around scorching Spanish locations in the modern equivalent of a Bath chair. Some days, even his voice has a quake to it and his brain has patches of blank, like sunspots, and all his instructions fall out of his drooling mouth in slow motion, like elephants' feet. It makes you wonder, when you consider what Mordecai earns per annum, about the film business.

The first thing Will told me about Mordecai – on that first day we met, my birthday – was 'Don't expect him to direct.' I stared at Will. Our bedroom scenes were still some weeks distant, but prior to them I had been banking on a little 'guidance' from Eyelids. Will then related how, in 1975, Eyelids had cast him as Ulrick Voss in a film he proposed to make of Patrick White's justly famous (but in my view dead difficult) novel, *Voss.* Will invoked his education-deprived childhood to explain his confusion with this man (the casting was moronic, of course. Will Nichols is far too gross a person to play Voss, even in a weightless after-life) and went grovelling to Mordecai for a bit of direction. Mordecai was having one of his quivering and quaking days. They were in southern Australia in temps of 100° fahrenheit (I can't do this centigrade thing; I'm much too old to learn) and Mordecai's brain was blank white. He told poor old Will to read the book five more times (448pp. in my King Penguin edition and Will had one week), went off to have his morning enema and would not brook the subject again. Luckily – or perhaps in consequence of this sad scene – the film was so excruciatingly bad and so catastrophically over-budget, it was put into turnaround half way through and never re-started. Will caught sunstroke that year and in his fever believed he was getting nearer to understanding the hauntings of Ulrick Voss. Will's life is full of little such ironies.

I'm a bit off track, I see. The course says: 'Imagine your subject as a Roman Road (*sic* caps). Its foundation must be your understanding and, except where absolutely necessary, you must try not to veer from it.' I don't know if information about Will and Mordecai is 'absolutely necessary', but I think it might be. (I hate the word 'veer'. There was a boy at school called Vere Pickersgill, whom I loathed.) Pearl Barley's just arrived to do me out. She says all this writing I'm closeted with is making me deadly pale. Better phone Dougie and see if there's a little role-ette for me in a hot clime.

I had expected to dislike Will Nichols. The fame and success of other actors can bring on neck rashes as badly as the virulent tomato. And who was Steve Nias compared to Golden Will, the lad from the Rhonda turned superstar? A nothing. An 'SS' in Dougie's vocab. (I'll explain 'SS' later.) But then – and this is the key to the events which followed – who was George Villiers, later Duke of Buckingham, compared to the King himself? A bit of trumped-up gentry with elongated calves. A hitherto also-ran at the court. Until, that is, the King singled him out. Until the King made him his confidant, his favourite, his own St John. With his stubborn Scottish hand, King James parted the sea of court bathers and gave Buckingham the Navy. Hence-forth he was dressed, metaphorically anyway, in sapphires.

At the end of that first afternoon in Mordecai's boardroom, just as I was about to sally home to water my cucumbers, Welsh Will invited me to tea. Mumbling something about needing to get to know each other better 'before the schedules start to bite', he shepherded me into his chauffeur-driven Jag and I was whisked off to Claridge's. (Will is a tax exile now and has no home in England other than Claridge's, which he treats exactly as if he owned it all.)

In his sumptuous suite, decorated in remarkably subtle shades of pale lemon and oyster grey, he ordered iced tea (a Californian fad I utterly loathe; it reminds me of my two years at Ipswich rep), then sent his secretary and other minions away and began to talk. He talked about exile. My eye wandered to an Indian rug which totally complemented the shades of the room, adding blue and a hint of white. I sort of waded in the lovely symmetries of the rug's pattern while Will's coal-silted voice rasped on about the loneliness of LA and Monaco. I was dying to ask Will where he'd found the rug (grey and yellow with blue and white are dead unusual colours in Indian wool work) but he was embarked on a monologue and I couldn't get my question in.

Gradually, over the field of the rug, Will's talking began to
hang like a nearing thunderstorm. I stared up at him, sensing
in his gaelic heart gigantic rain clouds. And lo, over the cragged
hillsides of his cheeks, rivulets of tears began to beat down! I
felt *livid.* Honestly, I did. Used. Acted upon in more ways than
one. 'God,' I felt like saying, 'if you understood the sacrifices
us lesser mortals have to make for our so-called art (and the
frigging Tiggo VOs aren't the only ones) you wouldn't be
blubbing about fame's adverbial negatives and qualifying
clauses. You'd be admiring the management's superlative
flower arrangements and saying to yourself, fortunate me! Life
had me marked out for rickets and TB and all I got was success.'
But I'm a soft-hearted person. I poured Will a brandy and
said: 'I'm terribly relieved you're such a sensitive thing, Will.
James I was a terribly sensitive man. And you know what he said
about privilege? "The taller be the trees, the harder doth the
wind blow on them."'
Then I left. It was a hot day and my bloody birthday and I
wasn't going to waste it all on Will.
We were shooting the interiors at Pinewood. Designer, Geoff
Hamm, had done a great job on the Theobalds sets and on Day
One old Eyelids' pearly veins were rippling with expectation.
Dougie's assistant, an intelligent, pretty person called Victoria,
had sent flowers to my dressing room. I'd never had the flower
treatment before and they put me in a lovely mood. Jon
Markworthy, reputedly sulking in his tent like Achilles over
script changes commanded by Eyelids, turned out not to be
sulking at all and had done a nice new scene between me and
Jimmie Henraes, the very dear actor playing Charles (later
Charles I), the King's son. So all seemed set fair. I was feeling
just the right amount of mingled fear and excitement. Makeup
did a super job on my bags and this and my black wig took five
years off me, or more. Ready, steady, go, I thought. But then
Will appeared. Eyes like fried eggs, capillaries popping like a
coral forest, tongue like old pipes. Terror and self-pity had led
him back to demon drink, the whole process begun, I later
learned, by the single brandy I had poured him at the Claridge.

Mordecai's voice grew guttural with suppressed rage. Will threw up into one of Geoff Hamm's supposedly Jacobean fireplaces and was laid to rest in his dressing room with Vichy water and Aludrox. The entire first day's schedule was changed and I spent the day mainly unused, just feeling ancient inside my wig.

Will slept through most of the day, then woke up and ordered a bottle of claret, which was evidently brought him because at five, when he asked to see me, he'd already drunk half of it and was looking better.

He apologised to me. At least he had the grace to do this. He also apologised for crying in Claridge's. Then he said, quite utterly out of the blue: 'There's only two who are going to funk it on this picture, Steve, and that's you and me.'

I poured myself a glass of his Château Something and sat myself down in his idiotic rocking chair. (Will Nichols has this sentimental stick of furniture flown and carted to every dressing room and every caravan he's ever worked from. It's his 'trademark'. You could have gone on a world cruise with the travelling money that rocking chair has consumed.) I said something reasonably lame about not intending to 'funk it', but he cut me off. 'I,' he said majestorily, 'shall fail because I no longer have the courage or the voice a talent like mine requires, and you, Steve, will fail because this part has come to you ten years too late.'

I don't know, but I think I'm in my stride a bit now. I think my writing's got a bit better as this story's gone on. That's because I'm worrying less about Neasdale's rules and just trying to remember what happened and put it down. There are still words I'll have to alter, though, like 'frigging'. Dougie phoned. The VO Clinic (as I call it) want me to do Buffi-pads nappy liners. Have I reached my nadir, prostitutionwise?

For as long as we were in England, I was able to steer clear of Will, except actually on set. The schedule (and the script) were redrafted to enable Will to 'get into' King James rather better than he appeared to be doing before the big key emotional scenes were asked of him. In Mordecai's age-yellowed eyes, you could visibly see thoughts about replacing him doing battle with dollar signs. Cut his losses now and re-start the movie in a year's time with a new star? Keep Will on, stay more or less inside budget, take the risk he'd pull something out in the big scenes? Some mornings Eyelids would look used up, poor old thing, as if he'd died in the night, but then out would come some quavery instruction and the hopeless day would start.

Will was dead right about him not directing. I came to rely on Markworthy (and thank God he was around) to help me step by step through Buckingham. Markworthy is a very plain (I don't mean ugly) and honest and kind man – a far cry indeed from the petulant Marxists masquerading as dramaturges I've had the misfortune to meet at play rehearsals in condemned warehouses. Markworthy seems to handle success as if it were Health Food. It's made him extremely calm and sensible and you sense that his bowel movements are exquisite. I rather envy him. And we've stayed in touch. He and his wife, Jane, grow cucumbers in Barnes (a great bond, the growing of things) and I've entertained them on my rooftop.

But on. Markworthy didn't come with us to Greece. (Let me just mention that the bit of the film we were to make in Greece was, in the script, meant to be made in Spain. Now, in most filmscripts, if the writer has been foolish enough to suggest Africa, India, Australia, Ceylon, Mexico, or anywhere parched-seeming, these bits are invariably made in Spain. In our case, we had a bonafide reason for shooting in Spain – namely that Buckingham and Prince Charles did actually go to Spain to woo the Infanta Donna Maria and are visited there (in the film, but *not* in the history books) by the King. But such is the pachydermic stupidity of this business that we lugged ourselves and our hardware an extra thousand miles, to dress one country up as another far closer to home. Perhaps we were getting money from the Greek Film Foundation, or whatever. I honestly have no idea. I didn't even feel it was worth mentioning to

Dougie, let alone to Alfie or Eyelids. Play the part, Nias, and shut up.)

I'm having a lot of trouble with my brackets. The problem is, quite a portion of my life seems to lie within this particular form of punctuation. Neasdale doesn't seem to have a rule here.

So, no, Jon Markworthy couldn't come with us to Greece, which was a blow for me. He was off on a talking tour of seventeen American cities, and we were flown to an arid bit of Olympian hinterland we immediately christened Poxos. Poxos had one verdant edge – palms and cypress and yuccas and hibiscus and the sound of a bird or two, and hidden in the verdure a sublimely beautiful seventeenth-century palazzo, undergoing conversion to a 5-star hotel. It was called the Palladium Hotel, which gave rise to a series of panto gags among our irreverent group, brought on not merely by the name, but also by the fact that we weren't actually *staying* at the Palladium; the Palladium was our location – the King of Spain's alleged summer palace, the setting for our scenes with the infanta. (According to history, all these scenes took place in Madrid itself. Someone suggested Eyelids would pass on if forced to consume the oily paellas of that city.)

We were billeted – and this included our star, Will and his rocking chair – in a modern motel called the Eleusis, upon whose low-fashioned concrete walls the summer *meltimi* wind remorselessly blew, from six in the morning till dusk. At dusk, having boiled your mind to leaden grey meat all day, it died. You began to hear the birds and the crickets. You relaxed. The terrace of your favourite taverna would be bathed in last light. You began to drink.

Jimmie Henraes drank to forget Mary Powell (the actress playing Katherine, who wasn't in the Spanisho-Greek sequences) and with whom he had fallen in love that day in Eyelids' boardroom. (A love consummated so many times during the Pinewood days, poor old Jimmie could hardly stagger through a scene without having a lie-down.) Morton and Mordecai drank with some rotund Greek businessmen who had appeared in suits on Day One. Nettlefold and the crew drank Greek beer and spent a lot of time scorching the sparse local flora with untreated urine. Geoff Hamm developed piles and drank in solitary pain. And I, well I drank because I was there and because, by that time, I had fallen under the spell of Will Nichols.

I was so balanced, I thought. I knew what Will Nichols was – a failed genius, a lush, an egomaniac. But what he still had, and this I suppose was why he was still a star, was a terrible and irresistible charm. I say terrible because honestly I thought at forty-one I was immune to anything so *peripheral* as charm. I'm a wicked flirt, but I'm jolly hard to ensnare. I actually think my ensnarement stemmed from what Will had said about the two of us funking our roles. I'd become determined to prove him wrong – not only as far as I was concerned, but also as far as *he* was concerned. Can you understand this? I wanted to be a marvellous Buckingham, but I knew I could only do this if I helped Will (yes, *helped* him) to be a marvellous King James. And he sensed this in me. He sensed, right after the tea in Claridge's, that I wanted to help him, to nanny him, to love him through it, if you like. And don't forget, he was a lonely, exiled man, terrified out of his skull. He knew he'd get sweet nothing from Mordecai. He didn't get on with Jon Markworthy, as I did. So he plonked himself on me. James's obsessive need of Buckingham somehow became utterly mixed and mingled with Will's need of me. Will's psyche was just as plagued by imaginary enemies as the King's. He saw enemies all around him. He had dreams of terrible persecutions and woundings. He needed a shrink, I suppose, and instead he found a soft heart – yours truly, Steve.

Pearl Barley has an amazing son, who calls himself T-Bone Jack. He wants to be a rock star, she says with a groan. He just arrived to collect her in a borrowed Cortina. Pearl B. insisted on showing him my roof garden, so I went up with them. T-

Bone Jack has the hardest eyes and the tightest buttocks I've ever seen on any man, ethnic or no. Yet, surprisingly, his handshake was rather soft and moist. NB Must remember to expunge all random jottings (i.e. about T-Bone's buttocks) when I commit this piece to my stone-age Olympia portable.

On the fifth day at Poxos, we reached one of our key scenes. Finding Buckingham's absence from England unbearable, King James has crossed the treacherous water and arrives in Spain. Paying scant respect to the King of Spain (an excellent Mexican actor, Leoncio Iagos – known of course to us as 'Iago') or to the infanta (an American actress, Jane Bellamy, doing ineffectual battle with Spanish consonants), he strides in to Buckingham's lavish suite of rooms and tells him he 'cares not a jot for England, nor for any man on this earth' if he is to be deprived of his 'Sweet Steenie's presence'. ('Steenie', as you probably know, was James's pet name for George Villiers, Duke of Buckingham, derived from the angelic St Stephen. The fact that my name is Steve seems to have been, in Will Nichols's confused subconscious, additional vindication of his need of me.) An exceedingly emotional duet is then played out: Steenie refuses to return to England until he's nabbed the infanta for Prince Charles; James says he will die if he returns alone. Cut, meanwhile, to a posse of wily Spaniards, who start to mumble into their ruffs in the following vein: 'Willst you not remark, my dear assembled lords, that James of England hath, by his untimely passage, vouchsafed to us a timely royal hostage?' (This entire scene is historical bunkum. As I have previously noted, I learned in Chelsea Library that James never went to Spain. However, it thickens the plot nicely and gives to Will and me another challenging scene.)

I was dreading these scenes. I'd begun to have dreams of London and soothing wet weather. The *meltimi* and the retsina and Will's talk of his infancy and the dust of Poxos were starting to get up my nostrils. I still wanted to help Will, but fear of my big scenes with him wasn't allayed by his ongoing drink

situation (as I heard Alfie Morton describe Will's attachment to
the flagellating local wine).

But then Will pulls it off, as they say. On the first take, there
he is, line-perfect, his Welsh-cum-Scottish voice at last singing
with absolutely convincing pain, his hands pawing me in
perfectly convincing Jamesian little futile gestures, his eyes
starting to brim with the jewel in the brave actor's crown – on-
camera tears. The floor is hushed. Mordecai signals to Nettlefold to keep turning over. And as Will at last pulls me to him
and breaks down, sobbing out his months of loneliness and
fear, I feel my heart start to pound with the thrill, the utter
euphoria of being in the arms of a great actor.

Well, I'm not that young, as I've told you (my bags were
brutal that day, what with the wind and the early starts), but I
am a very over-sensitive man. There's a lot of the child in me.
I've never quite got over my love of excitement and fame. And
although you'll be thinking I should have known better at my
age, I can only tell you that then and there, in the fly-blown
Palladium, with a battery of 2Ks masquerading as sunlight and
Eyelids Mordecai staring at me like an anorexic iguana, in the
mingled smells of the Robin starch on Will's ruff and his Pour
la Vie aftershave on his bearded neck, I was caught with my rib
cage down and my unprotected heart fell suddenly and hopelessly in love.

I went back to Wardrobe quaking and shaking from the
triumph of our scene. It's all turned, I thought. From now on,
the film will start to work. In fact it will be a good movie. And
the high spots will be my scenes with Will. I longed for the rest
of these scenes now. Playing opposite Will, I knew I could be
superb. There might even be a 'Best Supporting' Oscar in it, or
at least a BAFTA nomination, who could say? I took off my
costume with trembling hands, felt my lips quiver as my wig was
hung on its friendly buff wigstand. So, out into the night, I
thought! Have a shower, then on with the white seersucker
blouson and down to the taverna to start the hot night's revels
with Will!

Well, I sat in the taverna for two hours. I toyed with the

goatsmeat kebabs, swished down a couple of carafes of red. Jimmie Henraes came and sat with me and we talked about England and Mary Powell. The *meltimi* dropped and the lovely evening quiet came on. At the next table, Nettlefold and some of the crew were talking excitedly (for a camera squad) about the day. But Will didn't show. At ten thirty, I went back to the Eleusis. Will was in his room, but his light was out. Someone said he'd gone to bed straight after we'd finished shooting. I went to my room and tried to sleep. I tried to stop it, but under the thin covers, I knew my whole body was shaking.

One of the instructions in the Eric Neasdale Writing Course is 'Always write about what you know. Unless you actually are a blind philatelist, do not try to write about this.' Well I disagree on two counts with this instruction. Firstly, I think, if you're going to bother to be a writer, which isn't exactly a laugh-a-minute kind of life, you might as well also bother to see how far your putrid imagination can travel – even (sorry, E.N.) into blindness or philately or both, because why not? Secondly, the question of what one *knows* is much more complex than what is suggested here. I think so, anyway. For instance, do I, through my recent experience, actually *know* a jot more about the following: James I, George Villiers, Will Nichols, the psyche of actors, the price of success, seventeenth-century English civil-isation, twentieth-century Greek civilisation, love, infatuation, envy, childhood, Welsh miners and so on? I'm not sure. But all these are vital ingredients in the *knowing* of something I can only fully understand by writing about it. (This last sentence is very confused. I know what I mean, however!)

Will had complained, since arriving in Greece, that his Moga-don had stopped working and that sleep was a fiasco, hardly worth bothering with. On previous nights, he'd kept me up till two or three, talking and talking, yet on this night – when I felt we at last had something to say to each other – he'd gone to sleep at eight and stuck his ne déranger svp sign on his door. I felt, and I admit this is childish, cheated. I mean, willingly that night would I have stayed carousing with Will. I can be terribly charming when I want and I felt pretty sure of my terrain that extraordinary evening. Instead, I went miserably to bed and shivered and shook till I heard the bloody wind get up, and in the mournfulness of the *meltimi* cried myself to brief sleep.

Because by then I'd understood. It's not complex. I'd read all the signs right and a more intelligent man than me would have understood right away, but it took me most of the night. In the run up to his first big scene (with me, as it happened, but this is neither here nor there) Will had used me, as I've already explained, to help him conquer fear. And today? When the first big scene was safely over? Well, quite simply, I'd done too good a job. I'd played nurse to Will's terror for five weeks and, through me, he had managed to stumble through self-loathing, alcoholic fog and sheer funk out into a mood reminiscent of his younger self, when he was sober, energetic, imaginative and as an actor extremely fine. Today, as he'd held me against his hot, tear-stained face, he knew he'd done it. The King is himself again! Let the resurrection of Will Nichols begin! Really, it's terribly simple. I'm just the ninny who didn't see what was happening till it was too late. ('Write about what you *know*', says Neasdale. If only I'd *known* what Will was doing to me!)

I expect I sound dreadfully self-pitying, don't I? I mustn't whinge, because life goes on, as they say, and actually, now that I'm getting over all my feelings about Will and settling back into what I call 'my little Fulham routine' – my plants, the odd dance to Berlioz on the roof, civilised meals with old friends, visits to the NT and the Barbican (Jimmie Henraes, who married Mary Powell, is currently doing a lovely Benedick in *Much Ado*) and of course sessions at the VO Clinic to pay the housekeeping, etc. – now that I'm becoming myself again (I've decided I *will* do Buffi-pads), I can at least laugh about my own gullibility, and I know this is a sign there's been no permanent damage.

The bloody old film, now entitled *The Wisest Fool*, comes out next spring and there's rumour of a Royal Gala Performance.

If forced to go (and Dougie will force me, because I'm one of his 'SS' clients, the *senza soldi* boys, the ones who haven't quite got there and who need to be 'seen' therefore), I think I'll dress my Pearl Barley up in quivering sequins and take her along on my arm. She, at least, will know where to stick such a piece of artifice.

Will and Lou's Boy

This was an average dawn in the early summer of 1948, the year I got to be eighteen.

'Eat your fishcake, Dougie,' said Lou.

They were barracouta fishcakes. Awful. They tasted like it was the fish's seaweedy liver you were eating.

'Yes, eat your fishcake, Doug,' said Will.

Will and Lou. I thought of them as one: *Willou.* I was their son, Douglas. I was their only child.

Chief in our household was Lou's obsession to win the Queen Mary Gardening Cup. In 1947, we'd entered for the Princess Royal Gardening Cup, but we hadn't won it and Lou had turned her disappointment into rage. Until then, she'd been a moderately contented woman. Now, she was raging and cooking barracouta. Poor Will. Poor me. The world was funny those years.

We had a pre-fab. They'd built the row we were on in about one day. Only pre-fab dwellers were allowed to enter for the gardening cups. Rain had knocked down a lot of Lou's gladioli the night before Cup Day. It hadn't rained in Wandsworth, where the winner lived, and this was one among lots of things that didn't seem fair to Lou. 'Soddin' Wandsworth!' she'd say. She never normally swore much. She'd learnt 'soddin' from my Aunt If, who'd learnt it from my Uncle Pepino who sold ice-cream and illegal nylons meant for export. My Uncle Pepino was Italian, but pretended not to be during the war. 'Call me Pep,' he'd ask. 'Yes, call him Peppy,' said Aunt If, who, at the age of sixteen, had rebaptised herself Iphigenia. Her old name, which my father still used sometimes, was Gladys. She could get as angry about being called Gladys as Lou could get about Wandsworth. The men in our family, including me, seem to be calmer people than the women. Peppy was arrested that year, but he stayed calm.

The best thing about dawn in that pre-fab was knowing you'd be out of it all day. We were all out, even Lou, who worked in a rayon factory. Will was a wireless assembler. He had the same reverence for wirelesses as some people have for God. He relied on the Home Service to tell him who or what he was. He'd polish our wireless, this fount of understanding, with Min Cream and old stockings. Lou said a man like him ought to have a secure future. And she'd look at me. Sometimes, this sideways look of hers made me think she was thinking I didn't have a future of any kind, let alone secure. Lou and Will. Will and Lou. *Willou.*

I was a park attendant. My wage was four pound ten a week, not bad for then. Bits of my park had been ploughed up and sown with barley. This barley spoilt the atmosphere of the park, made it somehow noisier. Also, the kids used the barley to piss in. I'd see the heads of the girls, squatted down. But despite or notwithstanding the barley, I loved that park. That year, all the benches were getting painted and the fishpond was restocked with goldfish. We had a new Head of Parks called Mr Dowdswell, who wasn't like a clerk, but more like a visionary. The day they ploughed up his lawns for cereal, he developed the habit of tugging out hanks of his hair.

For my eighteenth birthday, Lou said, 'You ask a friend, Dougie.' I didn't have any friends really, as Lou perfectly well knew, so I asked Knacky Mick, who sold matches and empty boxes and tins of bootblack on the corner by my park gates. Knacky Mick was a Wicklow son, blue-pale in that way only the Irish are in winter. He must have been fifty. 'I'm an orphan, you know, Doug,' he often said. I liked him. When he heard I had an uncle getting black market stuff, he began to take an interest in me and sneak me matches for Lou, 'For the gas fire, like.' We didn't have a gas fire in the pre-fab. We didn't have a fire at all, but a paraffin heater Lou christened Old Smoky. But

Lou liked getting matches. She grew to expect it. Free anything, in those peculiar days, was appreciated – a rubber band, a safety pin, a half yard of knicker elastic . . . and one afternoon, Lou won second prize in a raffle, one solitary brown egg. The first prize was three bananas. Lou didn't complain. She scrambled the egg with a lot of milk and we shared it on toast. She dreamt about the bananas, though. She dreamt someone gave us a banana tree for the pre-fab garden.

Two things were coming: the party for my eighteenth birthday and the day of judgement in the Queen Mary Gardening Cup. There was a long heatwave. The barley in my park started to ripen. Courting couples began the habit of lying down in it and I was supposed to shoo them away. 'I'm sorry, Sir, I'm afraid you're spoiling our crop,' Mr Dowdswell told me to say. One day, I said by mistake, 'I'm sorry, Sir, I'm afraid you're *soiling* our crop,' and I was so miserable at getting the wrong word, I left the couples alone after that, and the barley, which had once been a kids' lavatory, now became a field of iniquity.

The most iniquitous person in our family was my cousin, Patricia, daughter of Aunt If and Peppy the Italian. In the war, she'd fallen in love with a G.I. called Wedderburn C. Wicklens, a Southern, beefy man, raised with his gut full of corn pone and his brain full of cotton. He was from Louisiana State. Patricia could just imagine the kind of wooden house she'd own on the New Orleans delta, and when Wicklens left her in '46, she cried herself almost into the grave. Now, two years later, Wedderburn C. Wicklens was back and cousin Pat was made a bride. Peppy's son-in-law was exactly one foot and four inches taller than him, as witnessed to this day by the wedding photograph. In this picture, everyone's grinning except me. I'm standing to attention. 'God!' Lou sometimes used to say, staring at the photo on Aunt If's tiled mantelpiece, 'just look at that nincompoop!'

Preparing our garden for the Cup and preparing for this grand meal we'd have when I was eighteen took a lot of resourcefulness. We nicked bricks from the bomb site on Weatherby Road to make a garden 'wall' that never got higher than two feet. I nicked bedding antirrhinums and nemesia from the park and stakes for the gladioli, over which Lou was taking no chances. I would have got the sack if Mr Dowdswell had caught me, but Mr Dowdswell was a man who saw vistas of things, not small transactions. Uncle Peppy, not yet in prison, figured big in our planning, so did Wicklens, whom we now addressed as 'Wed'. 'In more than one sense Wed,' I said. But no one laughed. 'Shame Dougie was too young to see Combat,' I heard Wed say to Lou one evening. 'Yes,' she said, 'it might have been the saving of him.'

They thought being eighteen might be the saving of me. If we could just scrimp together enough ration cards, if Peppy could just do a nylons deal with the butcher, if Wed could just get whisky and chocolate powder and margarine from the PX, if If could just run me up a new tweed jacket. If, if, if. . . . 'You'll feel better when you're eighteen, Dougie,' Lou lullabyed as she tucked me in. 'You'll feel more like a man.' So I lay and thought about this. I didn't think I'd grow up like Will – to be good. I knew I wouldn't grow up like Peppy – to be smart. When I imagined my future, it was exactly the same as my present. The only thing that changed wasn't me but the park. They harvested the dirty barley. They ploughed in the stubble and back into the soil went the sweet papers and the used johnnies and the hairpins, and the land was resown with grass and everything in the park became orderly again. Mr Dowd-swell's hair grew back. We were allocated some new shears. The thing I wanted to say to Lou was, 'I'm not unhappy.'

Then we heard about the housing lottery.

The coming of the news about the housing lottery was like the coming of malaria. Lou began to sweat. It was like the jungle had suddenly surrounded her. She'd fan the air with her knitting patterns. 'You can't breathe in this place,' she'd say, making our barracouta cakes. 'Help your mother,' Will would say accusingly. So I'd set the table and get out the tea strainer and stare at Lou's arms, white and moist above the greasy pan. Love for Lou has always been something I've suffered from. Even in my imagined future, I still suffered from it. 'I don't mind the pre-fab,' I'd say to Lou's arms preparing our seaweed meal. Without looking up at me, she'd say, 'Don't be silly, Douglas.'

It was me they sent to get our lottery number. The Housing Office had women queuing right down the stairs and into the street. I missed an entire afternoon's work standing in that queue, risking my job for Lou's malaria. 'You're not eligible if you've got a pre-fab, love,' someone told me, but I hung on. There must have been a thousand people there, not counting babies, two thousand upper and lower jaws all wagging about hardship and eligibility and fairness. Our number was 879. Aunt If said this was auspicious because 879 was a close-together group of numbers. I thought of the number as representing our family. I was the thin 7 in the middle, with Lou and Will leaning over me. Even now – and they're both long dead, actually – I still sometimes think of Lou as 8 and Will as 9. 'Dear God, please take care of the immortal souls of 8 and 9,' I sometimes pray. And I feel them at my side, Will watching me, Lou with her profile turned.

A lot happened the following day. Mr Dowdswell gave me a Severe Reprimand, Knacky Mick was taken to hospital, and Uncle Pepino was arrested for illegal trading. Aunt If, who is something of a gypsy to look at, read catastrophe in the stars, pawned her sewing machine to raise Peppy's bail, and cried on Lou's shoulder. 'At least,' said Lou to her sister-in-law, 'you've still got your own house.' I left them and got a bus to the hospital. Our lottery ticket was stuck up on the mantelpiece behind a glass unicorn. Knacky Mick, when I found him, was Irish-blue under his stubble and dosed to his skull. 'Suppressing me, they are,' he muttered. In his locker were his matchboxes and his tins of shoeblack, piled up. 'Come to a party,' I said, 'I'd like to invite you to my eighteenth birthday party.'

'Very good,' he said.

I didn't mind the hospital. I sat by Knacky Mick for quite a while. A drip was hitched up to his vein. Other patients winked at me, the ones on their own without visitors. Knacky Mick slept a drugged sleep. The room was high and light and full of people whispering. It wouldn't be bad, I thought, working here. This was the first time I ever imagined having a job quite far away from Will and Lou. It gave me an odd feeling, as if I'd made myself an orphan.

Now, four things were coming: the Gardening Cup, my eighteenth birthday party, Pepino's trial and the housing lottery. No wonder Lou couldn't breathe. These things were like weights on her chest. My ideal future was one in which there was nothing to fear and nothing to hope for. I didn't mind if we got chocolate powder for my party or not. I didn't care if we went to live in a new flat with a refrigerator or not. 'The trouble with Dougie,' said my cousin Pat, dreaming still of her Louisiana clapboard house, 'is he's got no imagination.' Well, I didn't care if I had imagination or not either. The thing that was awful was that Lou had started to care so much about everything, she seemed deranged. And I cared about that. I wanted her to be like she'd been when she'd won the solitary egg – contented.

Our pre-fab garden looked neat on Cup Day. We'd stuck in the shearings from a conifer hedge in my park, to look like a new little conifer hedge. We took down our washing line. Mr Dowdswell let me borrow the edging shears to straighten up the grass. It wasn't bad. The adjudicator smiled at Lou's new home perm and said, 'Very nice. Congratulations.' Under the perm, her malaria was still raging away. 'It means a lot to us,' she said, in a choked voice. And the adjudicator took off his look of admiration and put on a look of pity and I knew we hadn't won.

'We haven't won, Louie,' I told her.

'You know nothing about anything, Douglas,' she told me back. Which, in a way, was true.

Wedderburn Wicklens gave me forty Senior Service cigarettes on the day of my birthday. I didn't smoke, so I gave them to Willou, who did. I thought how odd it was that Wed hadn't noticed I didn't smoke. But there were a lot of things Wed didn't notice, like for instance, he quite often called Patricia 'Candice'. 'If you call me Candice again, I'll kill you!' she once told him. But this threat of death didn't seem to do the trick. Half way through my eighteenth birthday meal, a huge belch rumbled up out of his stomach and he said quickly: 'Didn't hear that, did you, Candy honey?' 'Who's Candy?' asked Willou simultaneously. Patricia slammed down her knife and fork and ran out into the hot night falling. Pepino stood up. Beside my gypsy Aunt If, he looked like a little yellow duck. '*You!*' he yelled. 'You mind! You Yanki-panki!' And then he sat down again and Wed got up and wandered lazily out to Patricia.

We were eating pork ribs, for which Pepino had paid four pairs of nylons. Our fingers and chins were mucky and red from Lou's sauce of boiled tomatoes. Wed told us we should call this meal *spare*ribs and Will guffawed with derision, 'Typical American!' he said, 'call everything superfluous!' We picked the last shreds of meat from the ribs and washed these pickings down with beer. Lou had got her chocolate powder and her egg powder and on the afternoon she was told the winner of the Queen Mary Gardening Cup lived in Camberwell, she cried away her hopes into an enormous cake. She wrote (she hadn't got a fantastic imagination either) D 18 on the top with angelica she'd bought before the war. It made me uneasy. I thought, I'm glad she couldn't tattoo it onto me.

Knacky Mick never came to my birthday party, he was too ill. I saved him some cake. I thought, I've only got one friend and that's Knacky Mick and he's going to snuff it. I felt a bit like crying, but Lou and Will had their eye on me. Full of beer, they said, 'This is a new start, Dougie. This is your chance to start again.' I started to say I was perfectly content as I was, but nobody was actually listening. Will and Lou and Peppy and If had turned away from me and were lighting up the Senior Service I'd given them and talking about their chances of being rehoused, in Peppy's case in Brixton jail and in Willou's case in William Petrie Buildings, the lotteried flats with fridges and radiators. I looked round to see what was happening to Pat and Wed and I saw them kissing by the conifer hedge. I unwrapped the bobble hat Lou had knitted for my birthday present and put it on. The thought that Lou's fingers had fashioned every one of the stitches that went round and round my head made me feel very warm and happy. 'Just look at him!' she said a while later, blowing smoke at Peppy. '*Honestly!*'

On the morning of the housing lottery, Lou couldn't face cooking barracouta, so we had bread and jam for breakfast. Will turned on the Home Service to calm his wife's beating heart. I left as early as I could to walk to my park and it was a beautiful morning, still and shiny and the smell of the park in summer was as fantastic to me as the smell of the Majestic cinema was to Lou. A consignment of bedding geraniums had arrived, and I started to dig over the bed where they'd go in. I tried not to think about 879, or about Lou waiting with thousands of other women to hear the numbers called out. There were fifty-one flats in William Petrie Buildings and at least twenty times that number of applicants. Mr Dowdswell came by to look at the geraniums. 'Good work, Douglas,' he said approvingly, and then tapped my bending back and said in his confidential stammer: 'No more bla . . . no more yer bloody barley next year, thank Ga . . . thank God!' 'Hooray, Sir,' I answered.

When I got home, Lou was resting and Will was mushing up the barracouta we hadn't eaten for breakfast. 'Don't disturb your mother,' said Will.

'We didn't get one, did we?' I said.

'No,' said Will.

I went to wash my hands at the sink. Outside, the stuck-in conifers were going brown.

'869 was lucky,' said Will, 'and 849 and 859, but not 879. Shame we had the 7.'

I stared at Will and then beyond him to the bedroom where Lou was lying in the aftermath of her malaria. *Willou.* 8 and 9. Without me, they would have got lucky. I was the 7 all right. I'd made them lose.

That August Knacky Mick died and I applied for a job at the hospital where I'd visited him and where I've been now all my life. I told Willou this was my new start, and they were proud of me. But my last day at the park was one of the saddest things I can remember. They'd harvested the barley. I sat in the sunshine, staring at all the litter left among the stubble and thinking about my country.

The Garden of the Villa Mollini

Before the arrival of Antonio Mollini in 1877, the villa had been called, simply, the Villa Bianca, the White House. It came to be known as the Villa Mollini, not through the vanity of Antonio Mollini himself, but through the pride of the people of the village. They wanted to be able to say – to travellers who passed that way, to relations who journeyed there from Arezzo or Rapolano or Assisi – 'We have in our midst the great Mollini, the world's most renowned opera singer. He knows us and even remembers the names of our children.'

In fact, Antonio Mollini was seldom there. He was forty-one when he bought the villa and his voice had entered what the critics later termed its 'decade of magnificence'. His life was passed in the musical capitals of Europe – Milan, Paris, Vienna. He came to the Villa Mollini only to rest, to visit his wife and to plan his garden.

He wanted, in the design of this garden, to express a simple and optimistic philosophy. He believed that his life was a journey of discovery, revelation and surprise and that it led forward perpetually, never back. In it, there was not merely one goal, one destination, but many, each one leading forwards from the next. All were different. Repetition seldom, if ever, occurred. He would not allow it to occur. And even at life's close, he thought there would be new landscapes and new visions of hope. The garden he was going to create would thus be infinitely varied, intricate and above all beautiful.

It was fortunate, then, that the terrain on which he would realise the garden wasn't flat, but sloped gently upwards away from the house to a cypress grove, and then descended, equally gently, towards a river. On the other side of the river, there were clover fields and, beyond these, a forest. The far edge of the forest was the boundary of Mollini's land.

His head gardener, Paulo Pappavincente, was the illegitimate son of a priest. Pappavincente's mother had died at his birth and he'd been brought up by aged and devout grandparents unable to conceal their shame at his existence. Though Mollini explained his philosophy carefully to Pappavincente, using simple terms, baby language almost, the gardener was unable to see life as his master saw it. To him, it led, repetitively and inevitably, to dark and deep abysses of guilt. But he didn't want to bore Mollini or anger him with chatter about his own sufferings; he wanted to design the most beautiful garden in Tuscany, so that one day he could say to his own legitimate grandchildren, 'I made it. I made the garden of the Villa Mollini.' He did suggest, however, that a well be sunk at a certain place, not far from the house, where Mollini had thought a statue of the goddess Diana would draw the eye forward. 'I think a well also beckons, Sir,' he said. To his surprise and also to his relief, Mollini agreed. That night, as he knelt to say his prayers, Pappavincente began to feel that good fortune was stealing into his life.

The same night, Antonio Mollini's wife, Rosa, stared by candlelight at the half-completed sketches of the box aisles and the fountains, the herbarium and the rose trellises, the steps and terraces leading up to the cypress grove and down to the river, and said aloud, 'I think he must contrive a lake.'

Mollini was asleep. He lay on his back, snoring, with his legs apart. From his magnificent lungs came an unmelodious kind of squealing. Rosa pulled aside the curtains of the bed and leaned over him, holding her candle.

'Antonio,' she whispered, 'please, Antonio.'

He opened his eyes. This thin white face of Rosa's on its pale neck sometimes reminded him of a sad mask on a stick.

'What, Rosa?'

'When the river leaves our land, westwards, where does it arrive, Antonio?'

'In the village.'

'Then I expect we may have to move the village.'

Mollini stared up. He chose his mistresses for their round-
ness, for their bright colour. Rosa was his little ghostly
possession.

'We cannot move the village, Rosa.'

Tears sparkled in her eyes.

'Please, Antonio. You must make a lake.'

Pappavincente was consulted. When he heard of the plan to
dam up the river, he descended once more into his habitual
pessimism. Politely, he informed his master of the life-sustaining
properties of the village water supply. Antonio Mollini felt
ashamed. He loved the village people. He'd made a list of all
their names and the names of their children so that he wouldn't
forget them, and now, in the night, he'd allowed his wife to
suggest something that would impoverish and destroy them.
'Rosa is mad,' he said to Pappavincente, 'but forgive her. Since
the death of Pietro, her mind often wanders astray.'

The death of Pietro had occurred in the same year that
Mollini's fame was born. Consumption thus played a role in
both events. As Mollini sang Alfredo in Verdi's *La Traviata*, his
son Pietro was dying of Violetta's disease. He refused to mourn.
He looked at the little coffin. He would have more sons. He
would replace Pietro. He would christen all his sons 'Pietro', so
that if another one died, he, too, could be replaced. Rosa
accused him of callousness. 'No,' he said, 'but I will not let
death win.'

Rosa didn't conceive. She knew that loss, like starvation, can
make a woman barren. She would be barren for ever, mourning
Pietro. She longed, at that time, for a garden. She thought it
would make her feel more kindly towards the world if she could
bury seeds in the earth and see leaves emerge, bright green.
But Mollini wasn't yet rich. They lived in Milan in a narrow
house on a dark courtyard. The Villa Mollini was six years away.

In those six years, Pappavincente fathered four sons, one of
whom he christened Pietro.

Mollini fathered none. His fame grew. 'There is no adequate

epithet to describe Mollini's voice,' one French critic wrote. 'To say it is like honey, or like velvet, or like silver is merely to debase it. It is like no other voice we have ever heard.'

On its gentle hillside, the Villa Mollini, still known as the Villa Bianca and occupied by a professor of medicine, waited for the great man's arrival.

In the week following Rosa's dreadful request for a lake, Mollini left for Milan. On his forty-second birthday, the day he began rehearsals for La Scala's new production of Wagner's *Tristan und Isolde*, he met for the first time the internationally known soprano, Verena Dusa, and fell in love with her.

La Dusa was thirty-four. Her elbows were dimpled and her belly and breasts round and firm and fat. She was the mistress of the impresario, Riccardo Levi, from whose bed Mollini quickly wooed her.

Riccardo Levi demanded a duel and was refused. He threatened to ruin La Dusa's career, but his threats were ignored. La Dusa moved her dresses and her fan collection from Levi's apartment to Mollini's town house. In despair, Riccardo Levi wrote a letter to Rosa, telling Mollini's wife that she had been betrayed.

Rosa examined the letter. She held it near to her face because her eyesight was getting bad and Riccardo Levi had small, mean handwriting. As she read the word 'betrayed', she felt a pain shoot down from her knees to the soles of her feet, as if in seconds she'd become an old crone, unable to walk. She put the letter down and stood up, clinging first to the writing table, then to the wall. She went to the window. A team of surveyors had arrived. Pappavincente was describing to them an imaginary circle, the site of his well. Rosa tapped on the window, to summon Pappavincente to help her, but her tap was too feeble and he couldn't hear her. Her maid came in a while later and found her lying on the floor. She was unable to speak. Her maid called for help. Rosa was put to bed and a doctor sent for. With the arrival of the doctor, word spread to

Pappavincente and the other gardeners that the Signora was ill. Retribution, thought Pappavincente.

The doctor examined Rosa. She was in shock, he told the servants. Something must have frightened her – something she'd seen from the window, perhaps? The servants shrugged their shoulders. Rosa's maid stroked her mistress's cold white forehead. Keep her warm, said the doctor and went away. Coverlets were piled on the bed, one on top of another, so that the shape of Rosa's body disappeared completely beneath them and only her small head stuck out like a tiny sprout on a desirée potato.

She lay without speaking for a week. Her maid propped her up and spooned vermicelli broth into her narrow mouth. Outside her window, she could hear men talking and tried to turn her head to listen. 'Drains,' her maid explained gently, 'they're here to re-route the drains and lay conduits to the fountains.'

The doctor returned. His own wife quite often irritated him by succumbing to illnesses he was unable to cure except by cradling her in his arms like a baby. He looked at Rosa's blank face. He refused to cradle *her* in his arms. There were dark hairs on her top lip and creases in her eyelids. 'Where is Signor Mollini?' he snapped. 'He must be sent for.'

So the servants sent for the priest. He, too, came and stared at Rosa and placed a palm leaf cross on her coverlet mountain and then sat down, in the silence of her room, and wrote in exquisite calligraphy to Antonio Mollini, informing him that his wife appeared to be dying.

When the letter arrived in Milan, on an early morning of grey mist, Mollini's voice – that same voice that had caused thousands of Society women to weep with wonder behind their opera glasses – was whispering playful obscenities in La Dusa's ear. She squirmed and giggled and pouted and the pout of her wide lips was so delicious and irresistible that Mollini was unable to stop himself from kissing them again and murmuring through his nose, 'I love you, Verena. I love you beyond everything.'

His servant knocked at his door. He rolled over and covered La Dusa's breasts with the sheet. The servant excused himself and came forward to the bed and offered Mollini the priest's letter on a silver salver. It was written on fine parchment, like a communion wafer. Mollini snatched it up and told the servant not to disturb him again that morning. The servant bowed and retreated. Mollini glanced at the letter, tossed it onto the marble bedside cabinet and turned back to La Dusa who lay with her arms above her head, waiting for his embrace.

The letter was forgotten. He remembered it at last towards six o'clock that evening, as he was preparing to leave for the opera house. He opened it as he was gargling with blackcurrant cordial. When he read the word 'dying', he choked on the gargle and spat it all over the bathroom floor. He wiped his mouth, read the letter again and sat down on a stool. For the first time in several months, he remembered Pietro, and at once he saw, clearly and beautifully, where fate had led and where indeed it was leading. It was leading to La Dusa. Rosa was dying because she was unable to bear him more sons. It was fitting. Rosa was dried up, barren, old before her time. But here, right here in his bed, was Verena Dusa with her succulent round hips that would accommodate his future children. All he had to do was to marry her. It was gloriously simple. It was like stepping from a dark, shaded laurel walk onto a sunny terrace and finding at your feet pots of scented jasmine.

That same evening, Rosa spoke for the first time in seven days. She asked her maid to help her into the garden. When she crept out from under the coverlets, she seemed to have shrunk. Her long white nightgown was tangled round her feet. She looked like a chrysalis.

She was wrapped up in a cloak. Her hair was brushed and pinned up. She went hesitantly down the stairs, clinging to her maid's arm.

Pappavincente was standing in the garden in the twilight, looking at the well shafts. The water table was low. The construction workers had sunk the shafts almost fifty feet. He looked up and saw Rosa totter out with her maid. 'Forgive her',

Mollini had said. Pappavincente left the well and started to walk towards her. Her maid sat her down on a little stone seat. She stared about her in bewilderment. Deep trenches had been dug in the terraces. Mounds of red earth and lengths of lead piping lay all around.

'Signora,' said Pappavincente, bowing, 'for your recovery we are making all these waterworks.' But she only stared at him in bewilderment too, as if he were a lunatic, as if he were the village idiot. 'I want,' she said, looking at the devastation round her, 'my husband back.' Up above the chimneys of the house and above the garden several bats were circling. Rosa liked bats. 'Pipistrelli,' she'd call, 'pipi, pipi . . .'

Unaware that the priest had written to Mollini, Rosa that night had the lamp lit on her writing desk and sat down with her pen. She told Mollini that she had been ill and that she had imagined she was lying in a grave with Pietro. Over her body, the earth had been piled higher and higher in a colossal mound, with only her head sticking out. She could not, she said, endure such imaginings and only his love could save her from them. She would forgive him his sin of the flesh if he would just return to her. She signed the letter *Your Wife Until Death, Rosa Mollini.* Her writing, unlike the priest's hand, was cramped and ugly and her spelling not terribly good.

Rosa's letter reached Milan four days later. Mollini and La Dusa had triumphed in *Tristan und Isolde* and had been invited each night to elegant suppers by the likes of the Duke of Milan and the Count of Piedmont and had revelled together in their glory. At one of these suppers Mollini had become tottering drunk on a surfeit of champagne and pleasure and had rested his head on La Dusa's bosom and proposed marriage to her. The other guests had gasped, remembering the small, elegant wife he used to bring to evenings such as these, but La Dusa had only laughed and stroked his burning cheek and told him she was his till she died.

When he read Rosa's letter (he had a hangover when it was brought to him and his head was throbbing) he knew that he wouldn't, *couldn't* go back to her. When he thought about his life with Rosa, he was amazed he'd been able to endure it for so many years. Because it seemed full of shadow. Only at Pietro's birth had the sun shone on it and after his death it had become colourless and ghostly.

But Mollini knew also that he couldn't abandon his plans for the garden to Rosa and Pappavincente, both of whose natures were pessimistic and depressive. So he decided he would take La Dusa back with him to the Villa Mollini. He was a great man, revered in the village. He could do as he liked. He was beyond criticism. And he wouldn't hide La Dusa away. Oh, no. He would move out of the rooms he'd shared with Rosa and into other rooms which he'd share with La Dusa. When they were invited out, both women would accompany him, wife and mistress. Tuscan society would be given the chance to exclaim upon La Dusa's gorgeous beauty. And Rosa? Rosa was a religious, reserved woman. She would behave piously, with dignity, staying away from him most of the time, reading or sewing in her rooms or going to communion.

Having obtained La Dusa's willing agreement to these arrangements, Mollini wrote to tell Rosa that he was returning home, but that he was unable to live without Verena Dusa and that she would therefore be coming with him.

Five days later, they arrived at the Villa Mollini to be told by the servants that Rosa was dead. She had been found with a burned scrap of paper in her hand, which they thought might have been a letter. She had shot herself with one of Mollini's duelling pistols.

Summer was coming. The re-routing of the drains wasn't entirely successful. As Mollini and his love sat with their fingers entwined on the first of the terraces to be completed, they fancied they could smell something decidedly unsavoury.

It had been a dry spring and the river was low. Verena Dusa went down and looked at the river and said, as she strolled along with her plump little hand fondling Mollini's velvet-clad buttocks, 'You know what I would like here, my darling? A lake.'

Pappavincente was summoned. 'I am going to dam up the river,' Mollini informed him. 'Water will be taken to the village in metal containers. Every villager will have his rightful share.'

Pappavincente went down to the village, informed the people what was happening and told them to march shoulder to shoulder up to the Villa and break down the gates and threaten to kill Signor Mollini if he went ahead with his dam. 'We will!' said a few voices. 'We won't let our river be taken away!' And some of the men got out their pitchforks and their scythes. But nearly all the women of the village folded their arms and shrugged their shoulders. 'As long as we have water,' they said, 'we're really perfectly happy. Perhaps it will be less trouble to get water from the containers than from the river. And anyway, we mustn't forget how lucky we are to have Signor Mollini right here in our valley . . .'

They could see, however, that Pappavincente was in despair. They comforted him. 'You're adding to the fame of this region with your wonderful garden,' they told him, 'and a lake will make it even better. You must put swans on it, Pappavincente, and graceful boats.'

So Pappavincente walked back up to the Villa with not one villager standing with him, shoulder to shoulder. He thought he would sell his cottage and take his wife and sons and leave Mollini for ever. But then he let himself into the garden by a side gate and stood and stared at one of the new fountains and at the water lilies he'd planted at its base and thought of all the work still to be done, and he knew that, if he left the garden, he'd regret it till he died. It was his one work of art.

Mollini had understood the look of agony on Pappavincente's face. He was relieved he'd thought up the idea of taking water to the villagers in containers, because he knew that if La Dusa wanted a lake, he would have to give her a lake. He was much too afraid of losing her to deny her anything. Indeed, he begged her, begged her on his knees with his arms round her thighs to ask of him whatever she wanted, no matter how costly, no matter how perverse. All he longed to do was to give, to give.

She laughed at him. He adored her laugh, It made him tremble with delight. 'You can give me a wedding ring, Antonio!' she giggled.

He'd thought, after burying Rosa, that he would wait six months before marrying Verena. It seemed right to wait. But it was clear to him as the summer advanced that La Dusa would insist on being married before new opera commitments began for them both in September. Hardly a day went by now without her asking, 'Will it be August, Antonio?'

So he decided he wouldn't wait six months. He set a date: 17th August. He wanted the dam completed by then and a chapel built at the lake's edge, where the wedding would take place. More builders were hired. The same priest who had written to Mollini on Rosa's behalf was now given money to consecrate the ground on which the chapel was going to stand. An order was sent to Lake Trasimeno for forty-two swans. A fat ruby, encircled with diamonds, was placed on La Dusa's finger. Invitations went out to all the important people in the opera world – patrons and practitioners, both – and rooms were booked for them in every inn and hostelry for miles around.

Then in July, as the dam was finished and the river went dry and the first containers of water rolled in on carts to the village, Mollini fell ill. He started vomiting. Pain in his bowel made him curse in agony. He had a terrible fever.

The doctor came. He took off his tail coat and rolled up his shirtsleeves and gave Mollini an enema. The contents of the bowel were putrified, he noticed, greenish and foul. 'Advanced colonic infection,' he diagnosed and arranged for Mollini to be taken that night to a hospital in Siena.

La Dusa travelled in the carriage with him. His face, normally ruddy and healthy, looked grey. He was suffering. La Dusa wiped his forehead with a little lace handkerchief. She was petrified. Supposing he died before the wedding?

When they reached the hospital, Mollini appeared to be delirious, not knowing where he was. As they went in through a heavy, iron-studded door, La Dusa held her lace handkerchief to her nostrils. The stench of the place was appalling. Every

breath she breathed seemed to her to be full of poison. And
though it was night-time, it was a stupidly rowdy place. Doors
slammed, nurses marched up and down the echoing corridors
in stalwart shoes, patients cried out, gas lamps hissed, cleaning
women in filthy aprons pushed iron slop buckets forward on
the stone floors with their mops.

La Dusa felt sick. How could anyone be made well in such a
place? As Mollini was carried in, they passed a flight of stairs
leading downwards. TO THE MORGUE, said a sign. The sign
was accompanied by a drawing of a hand with a pointing finger.
La Dusa couldn't help noticing that the drawing of the hand
was very fine, like a drawing by da Vinci or Michelangelo. This
must be where their talents lie, she thought – in the direction
of death.

Mollini was put into an iron bed in the middle of a long
ward. La Dusa protested, but no one listened and they were left
quite alone. All along the row, men were groaning and sighing.
A nurse came in. She passed briskly down the line of groaning
patients, barely glancing at any of them. La Dusa stood up. She
took her handkerchief away from her nose, drew in a breath
and then let out a high F Sharp with extraordinary force.

The nurse stopped in her tracks and stared at her with a look
of utter incredulity. Several of the patients woke from sleep
and raised their heads.

La Dusa heard herself shout at the nurse, 'Do you know who
this is? This is Antonio Mollini! Why has he been put here?'

'This is the Men's Ward, Signora.'

'And why is there no surgeon? Is this what you do to your
patients – put them in a line and forget them?'

'Of course we don't forget them.'

'I want Signor Mollini moved to a quiet room and I want a
surgeon called now!'

The nurse gave La Dusa a dirty look and stomped out of the
ward. La Dusa returned to Mollini's bed and stared at him. His
eyes were closed and his breathing shallow. She was glad, in a
way, that he couldn't see the terrible ward or hear or smell the

sufferings of the other men. She stroked his hand. 'I will fight for you, my love,' she said.

After half an hour, the nurse returned. 'There is no surgeon here at the moment,' she said sourly. 'Surgeons need rest, you know. But if you can pay, we can have Signor Mollini moved to a more secluded room.'

'Pay?' said La Dusa. 'Of course we can pay!'

Mollini was lifted onto a stretcher and carried out of the ward. He was put into another iron bed in a tiny room, like a cell. A chair was brought to La Dusa and she sat down. They told her that one of the surgeons had woken up and would come and look at Mollini as soon as he had cleaned his teeth.

The door of the little cell was shut. Alone with Mollini's sufferings, La Dusa felt so frightened that she began to cry. Her tears were very bright and copious and the little lace handkerchief was soon saturated with them.

When the surgeon arrived, she was still weeping. The surgeon wore a silk cravat. He shook her hand, that was wet from holding the handkerchief. She gave him a scribbled note from Mollini's doctor. When he'd read it, he lifted up the covers and began to prod Mollini's belly.

The surgeon's hand on his bowel caused terrible pain. Mollini's eyes opened and rolled about and he choked in agony. The face of the surgeon became grave. La Dusa wiped her wet hand on her skirt and knelt by Mollini, holding him and kissing his face as the surgeon's fingers probed.

The surgeon replaced Mollini's covers and put his hands together in a kind of steeple under his chin. 'We must open him up,' he said.

He was taken away. La Dusa was told to wait in the tiny room. She lay on the bed and tried to doze, but her own anxiety and the unceasing noise of the hospital prevented sleep. The short night passed and a grey light seeped in through the tiny window.

At seven, Mollini was brought in on a stretcher and put back into the bed. He was unconscious and pale as death. The surgeon, too, looked pale and there was sweat on his top lip.

'I'm afraid,' he said, 'the decay of the large intestine was far advanced. We have done the only thing possible to save his life: we have cut the putrified section and joined the bowel together where the tissue was healthy. We believe he will survive.'

La Dusa knew that Mollini's convalescence would be long. She rented a house in a nearby street, so that she could come at any hour of the day or night to visit her love.

In the days following the operation, Mollini seemed, very slowly, to be getting well and La Dusa was full of praise for the surgeon who had saved his life. But then, on the fifth day, the wound became infected. Mollini's temperature soared and pain returned. For the first time, the nurses became attentive and La Dusa thought again of the beautiful hand pointing downwards to the morgue and became convinced that Mollini was going to die.

She had dreams of her lost wedding. In them, the forty-two swans Mollini had ordered were black. She made a decision. She would not let Mollini die before they were joined in marriage. She asked for the priest to be sent. He arrived with his candle and his holy water, thinking he was needed to administer the last rites. But no, La Dusa told him, she wanted him to marry them. The priest looked at Mollini and shook his head. He couldn't marry them if the groom was too ill to speak, he told her, and went away, giving La Dusa a strange and suspicious look.

She was in despair. She sat and watched her lover's life ebb.

But Mollini didn't die. His body's own magnificent healing powers surprised even the surgeon by fighting the infection till it was finally vanquished. He sat up. He began to eat, to laugh, to hold Verena's hand in a strong grip.

They returned to the Villa Mollini. The chapel was finished. Rain had come and the lake was brimming. In September, Verena Dusa and Antonio Mollini were married. The bride wore white satin and swans' feathers in her hair.

In the years that followed, all the original plans made by Mollini and Pappavincente for the garden were implemented.

Every statue, every shrub, every rockery and fountain was in place. 'All we can do now, Master,' said Pappavincente, 'is to wait for everything to grow.' But Mollini, whose fame and wealth had already grown to giant proportions, began to conceive the idea of buying land beyond the forest, of making pathways through the forest in order to extend his garden to the other side of it. He liked what had been achieved so far. He was especially proud of the winding maze that led down to the lake, but there were no surprises for him in the garden any more. As he turned each corner, he knew exactly what he was going to see.

The land on the other side of the wood was common land, used by the villagers as pasture for their animals. Pappavincente was told to go down to the village and inform the farmers that ten hectares of pastureland were going to be fenced off. He refused to go. He was ageing and growing stubborn as he aged. 'Very well,' said Mollini, 'I shall go myself.'

He didn't often visit the village now. He had long ago stopped making his list of the names of the villagers' children and he couldn't, in fact, remember the surnames of many of the villagers themselves. He knew, however, that the oldest man of the village, Emilio Verri, had recently died. So Mollini decided to go straight to the house of his widow, allegedly to offer his condolences.

Signora Verri was an old, old woman. 'I lost a husband, and you, Signor Mollini, you lost your beloved wife,' she said as the great man bent over her and put his hand on her bony shoulder. Mollini straightened up. He couldn't stand it when anyone mentioned Rosa's death. 'That was long ago, Signora,' he said, 'and anyway, I have some good news to cheer you up. My wife, Verena, is expecting a child.'

The old crone lifted her face.

'A child, Signor Mollini?'

'Yes. In the spring.'

Signora Verri's eyes were wet. To her, a new child was still a miracle of God.

'God bless the child, Sir.'

'Yes. He will be blessed, I'm sure. And I wanted to tell you something else. I am going to buy from the village – at a price that will keep you all in clover for many months – a little land, about twelve hectares north of my forest. And on this land, do you know what I'm going to make?'

'No, Signor.'

'A child's garden.'

'Ah. A child's garden?'

'Yes. It will be full of wonders. There will be peacocks and guinea fowl and rabbits and doves and goldfish and little houses in the trees and an aviary and a secret cave and hundreds of thousands of flowers.'

Signora Verri went to the door of her house and called her sons. There were three of them. Their handshakes were hard and their teeth yellowed from pipe tobacco. They demanded at once to know what price Mollini would pay for the land, explaining that a loss of twelve hectares would mean a reduction in livestock.

'A fair price,' said Mollini. 'What's more, I will buy all the livestock you have to slaughter and put the carcasses in my ice house till my son is born, and then there will be a huge feast and everyone in the village will be invited.'

He got away as quickly as he could. He looked back and saw the men of the village standing about in little groups, talking anxiously. But he wasn't worried. They'd get used to the idea of the loss of their pasture just as they'd got used to getting their water supply from containers and not from the river. They know, he told himself, that the only thing, apart from their children, which brings honour into their miserable lives is my fame. People of this calibre will sacrifice a lot to keep their dignity.

He was able to tell Pappavincente that the fencing of the land could begin straight away. 'No, Master,' said Pappavincente, 'the ground is much too hard. We shall have to wait till the frosts are over.'

Mollini agreed reluctantly. It was a very cold winter. Parts of the lake were frozen. Irritatingly, quite a few of the evergreens in the garden had died and the camellias were showing signs of winter damage. All of these would have to be torn out and replaced.

Mollini walked in the forest with his wife and showed her which ways the paths would go. They would zig-zag and cross each other, he explained. Then, little Pietro would be able to play games of tracking and hide-and-seek.

Although she tried not to show it, it saddened Verena that she was going to have to call her son Pietro. She liked the name Giuseppe, which was her father's name. But she was relieved to be pregnant at last. She was thirty-nine. Mollini had been nagging her for four years, ever since their first passionate year of love was over, to conceive. She'd tried very hard. She'd pampered herself with mounds of nutritious food. She'd even turned down an engagement to sing *Lucia di Lammermoor* in London, in order to follow Mollini to Vienna, so that he could make love to her at the right time of the month. She'd begun to fear that she would never conceive and she thought that if she didn't, it was possible that Mollini would leave her. My love is unquenchable, his is not, she told herself.

When her breasts began to swell and the time for her period had passed, she sent for the doctor. It was the same doctor who had given Mollini his enema and seen the slime in his bowel. He rolled up his sleeves. He inserted two icy fingers into Verena's vagina and pressed on her belly with the palm of the other hand. 'Well,' he said at last, as he disinfected his hands, 'your husband's wish has been granted.'

She decked herself in fussy, voluptuous gowns. Her bosom became gargantuan and she liked to show it off with lace frills and little cheeky ribbons. She didn't mind that she was getting ridiculously fat. She revelled in it. And Mollini too, from the moment he knew she was expecting his child, seemed to fall in love with her all over again. Even in public, he often couldn't refrain from fondling her breasts and whispering deliciously dirty suggestions in her ear. She giggled and screeched. She was delirious with happiness.

Several rooms in the Villa Mollini were being prepared for

the baby. Nurses were interviewed and two engaged for the end of April. In March, the weather grew warmer. The fencing off of the twelve hectares was completed. Nine bullocks were slaughtered and stored in the ice house. In the forest, trees were felled to make way for the paths, wire for the aviary was ordered from Florence and a million bulbs came by cart from Holland.

Then, on the night of 1st April, a cold, relentless wind began to blow from the north. This wind terrified Verena. She liked Nature to be quiet. She put her head under her coverlet and encircled her unborn baby with her hands. An hour later, her waters broke.

The midwife came stumbling through the wind, holding her shawl round her chin. In the Villa Mollini, all the lamps were lit and the servants woken from sleep. Mollini stared at the midwife scuttling about with her towels and her basins and thought of all the births that had occurred in the village since he'd built his dam. Children were alive in the village who had never seen the river.

He went, feeling anxious, and sat on his own in his music room. Upstairs, Verena was behaving like a courageous rower, pushing with the tides. The seas were stormy. The pain tore at Verena's body and the wind tore at the garden, disturbing its order.

At dawn, the baby was born. It was a boy. It weighed less than two kilogrammes. Its first cry was feeble because, despite its magnificent parentage, its lungs were not properly formed. It gasped and gasped, like a little slithery eel, for air, and died within two hours.

Verena screamed till she was sick. The wind, blowing in the direction of the village, carried her screams to the ears of the villagers as the women made coffee and the men put on their working clothes.

It was strange. A few days after the baby died, Mollini sent for Pappavincente to tell him to redesign the child's garden, and then he changed his mind. Although there was now no son to inhabit the garden, Mollini realised that he still wanted it made, exactly as he'd planned it.

'Master,' said Pappavincente, 'you will never bear to walk in it.'

'Then someone else will.'

'Who, Sir?'

'We shall see.'

Verena, huge in the bed, her breasts full of milk, announced: 'I never want to sing again. I'm going to cancel all my contracts.'

In May, Mollini left for Paris, where he was to sing Lensky in *Eugene Onegin*. Before leaving, he looked at his fat wife. She nourished herself, he decided, her own greedy flesh, not the baby's. She was still ridiculously gross and the baby, his poor little Pietro, was a tiny, sickly fish.

Verena didn't want Mollini to go to Paris. 'This world,' she said, 'this world we inhabit of roles and costumes and competition and money isn't worth a thing.' And she held Mollini so tightly to her that he felt himself suffocating. For the first time since he met her, he longed to be away from her, miles and miles away.

On the morning of his departure, Pappavincente came to see Mollini. He told him that wire for the aviary had arrived and asked him whether he should employ builders to start work on it. 'Of course,' said Mollini, 'of course.'

As the summer was coming, Mollini had decided to rent a house rather than an apartment in Paris. It wasn't far from the Bois de Boulogne. It had a pretty courtyard with a fountain.

In this house, a long way from Verena, he felt his sadness begin to ebb and his energy return. He gave a party on a warm June evening. A string quartet played Mozart. Sitting by his fountain, he saw bats circling over the city and remembered Rosa. He shuddered. He took the white wrist of his young co-star, Clara Buig, and held it to his lips. I will amuse myself, he decided, by making love to Clara.

La Buig was twenty-two. She was French. Paris thought her enchanting. Her career was at its beginning. She wasn't known outside her country yet, but to be singing Tatiana to Mollini's Lensky would soon ensure her international status.

When Mollini's party was over, La Buig stayed behind. Mollini undressed her tenderly, as he would have undressed a child. She was slim and pale. 'Do you like gardens, Clara?' he asked.

Mollini was now forty-eight. Clara Buig was young enough to be his daughter. When he touched her, her eyes watched him gravely.

The next morning, he woke alone. He sent a servant with a note inviting Clara to lunch. But Mademoiselle Buig was not at home, she was working with her voice coach. Mollini went early to the Opéra. When La Buig arrived, she was wearing a pale lemon-coloured dress. She moved very gracefully, Mollini noted, like a dancer.

After the rehearsal, he invited her to supper. They would dine in the Bois after going for a stroll under the chestnut trees. But she refused. She was very tired, she said. To sing well, she needed a lot of rest.

Mollini went back to his house and sat by his fountain. He loved Paris. No other city satisfied the eye so agreeably. I shall stay here till autumn, he decided. It's so hot in Tuscany in the summer and here, it's cool. But he knew that if he stayed till autumn, Verena would arrive, with her trunks full of dresses and jewellery and her fan collection and her maids and her boxes of sweets. The thought of this arrival dismayed him. Hastily, he sat down and wrote to his wife. He informed her that there was a typhoid epidemic in Paris. 'I implore you, do not come near the city,' he wrote. 'For my sake, my love.'

And every time he saw Clara Buig, her sweet neck, her shy smile, her expressive hands, it was as if he was seeing a corner of his garden that he'd never noticed, never expected to be there, but which, given his care and his talents, would one day be the most beautiful place of all. As the days passed, he became more and more convinced that Clara Buig could not be absent from his future.

He waited. He had to wait patiently. His invitations to supper were, night after night, refused. 'Why?' he asked eventually. 'Why, Clara?'

She took his hand, noticing as she did so that several of his nails were bitten. 'The night of your party, I was so excited,' she said, 'so flattered. I just let myself go. I couldn't help it.'

'And was that wrong, my adorable Clara?'

'Oh yes. But I won't let it happen again.'

So, only on stage did she look at him adoringly. Outside the Opéra, she refused ever to be alone with him.

Verena wrote to him almost every day. Her fortieth birthday was approaching. She was depressed. She begged Mollini to let her know the moment the typhoid epidemic was over so that she could come to Paris and be with him. She told him that the loss of their child had only deepened her love for him.

What she didn't say in her letters, because at first she didn't notice it, was that since the second week of April no rain had fallen and that the level of the lake was going down fast as the villagers pumped out more and more water for their potato crop, for their vines, for their thirsty animals.

Pappavincente was worried about all the new shrubs he'd planted in the child's garden. Water containers were driven through the new paths in the forest. He and the other gardeners spent two hours every evening going round with watering cans.

One evening, Pappavincente took a walk up the valley. He saw that the river was dangerously low and he remembered with dread the terrible drought of 1856, when all the villages along the valley began desperately trying to sink new wells and when his grandmother had wondered aloud whether Pappavincente's existence wasn't to blame for all the anxiety and suffering.

As he walked back towards the lake, he saw La Dusa standing by it, holding a parasol. He bowed to her. She was dressed in grey satin with a high lace collar and, with her feet tucked into red shoes, Pappavincente thought she looked like a fat pigeon. Her once beautiful eyes were now just two dark pleats in the flesh of her face.

'I'm so sorry, Signora,' said Pappavincente, 'about the baby...'

'Yes,' said La Dusa and waddled away up the path to the forest, carrying her weight, as she carried her sorrow, awkwardly.

The forest was cool. A hundred times, Verena had rehearsed in her mind the day when she would push the ornate baby carriage under the magnificent fans of oak and beech and watch the dappling of sunlight on her son, Giuseppe. Now, she was there alone. And it was her birthday. She stopped and folded her parasol and examined her hands for signs of age. Mollini's wedding ring was wedged so tightly onto her finger, she was unable, these days, to take it off. 'Look at these fat hands!' she said aloud and recalled with a strange kind of fascination the beautifully drawn thin hand pointing down-wards to the hospital morgue.

She'd intended to visit the child's garden. Mollini had refused to discuss with her his decision to carry on with the project and the thought of this garden being designed and planted for someone who would never see it filled her with sadness. She found, as she neared it and caught sight of the half-completed aviary that she really didn't want to go there, and anyway she was out of breath.

She returned to the house. On the first terrace she noticed that the drains were stinking again. The smell was disgusting, but she lingered near it for a moment. It reminded her of happier times.

On the opening night of *Eugene Onegin*, La Dusa arrived, uninvited, in Paris.

Mollini's house was filled with servants preparing for a party. Lanterns had been lit all round the courtyard and tables set up near the fountain.

Mollini wasn't there. La Dusa dressed herself in a white gown and put feathers in her hair. She didn't go to the Opéra, but sat in the cool garden sipping champagne and questioning the servants about the typhoid epidemic. 'What typhoid epidemic?' they inquired politely.

When Mollini returned, Clara Buig was with him, holding on to his arm. La Dusa looked at them. Mollini had grown a beard, put on weight. He looked like an English king. When he saw his wife, he bowed – just as Pappavincente had bowed to her beside the lake – and led Clara Buig forward and introduced her formally. La Dusa didn't get up. She ignored Clara's outstretched hand, but reached up and pulled Mollini towards her, so that he stumbled and fell into her lap. She bit his ear. 'If you lie to me again, Antonio, I shall kill you,' she said.

Two weeks later, they returned together to the Villa Mollini. On the journey, Mollini feigned illness, a return of the pain in his bowel. And it was true, he was suffering. He was now madly, dementedly, obsessively in love with Clara Buig. He couldn't look at his wife, let alone touch her. All he could remember was the one beautiful night when Clara had let him love her, a night he had so carefully planned to repeat by giving a party in her honour.

He couldn't close his eyes without dreaming of Clara. Thoughts of her never left his mind. By the time he arrived at the Villa, he felt so troubled he had to sit down and write to her straight away and in the letter he found that he was telling her that he loved her more than he'd ever loved anyone, that his love for La Dusa had been pale in comparison. *Pale?* As he wrote this word, he couldn't help remembering certain nights, certain delectable afternoons he'd spent with Verena, but of course these had been long ago and she'd been beautiful then. And things pass, he said to himself. We move. The horizon changes. We turn a corner and a new sight greets us. This is how it has to be.

And to reassure himself, he went out into the garden. He was shocked at what he saw. The earth was parched. The smell near the house was terrible. Everywhere, as he strolled from path to path, from terrace to terrace, there were gaps in the borders and beds where plants had withered. The fountains had been turned off. The water in the fountain pools was bright green and foul-smelling. Mollini stood still and stared up at the sky. It was a deep, relentless blue. The sun on his face was fierce and all he could hear and feel was the buzzing and shimmering of the heat.

At that moment, he remembered the nine bullock carcasses. His stomach turned. Sorrow for his little dead child compounded his sickness. He sat down on a stone seat and put his head in his hands. The salt sweat from his brow stung his eyes.

He prayed the nausea would pass. It seemed like the nausea of death, when the appetite for the world drains, leaving the mind filled with loathing.

To soothe himself, he thought of his music. 'Mollini's voice is not simply a voice,' a Paris critic had declared, 'it is an instrument. I have never before heard such an astonishing sound come out of a man.' And the sickness did, after a while, begin to pass. So Mollini stood up. Instead of returning to the house – to Verena's tears and entreaties which only repelled him and were utterly in vain – he walked on down to the lake. It was no longer blue, but brownish and full of silt. He skirted it and went up into the forest. Here, it was cool. In the shade of the big trees, nettles and sweet briars were green.

He followed one of the winding paths. He began to feel better. If only, he thought, I could stroll here with Clara, with her little hand tucked into my arm.

As he neared the child's garden, he feared that all the new bushes and hedges planted in the spring would have died, but the moment he left the forest and came out again into the sunlight, he saw that everything here was living and healthy, that already roses were climbing up the trellises and that purple and white clematis were growing strongly up the sides of the aviary.

Mollini smiled. It was a smile of gratitude and a smile of hope renewed. As he looked at the faithful work of Pappavincente and the other gardeners, he knew why he had made them go on with the child's garden: he would give it to Clara.

In August, Mollini told Pappavincente that water to the village would have to be rationed. The ration was so meagre and insufficient that the young men led nightly raiding parties to the lake, carrying buckets and churns, but the water itself was becoming soupy and brackish and the villagers and their animals developed intestinal illnesses.

Then, the widow Verri died. Mollini attended the funeral. He sensed, for the first time, that his presence among the villagers no longer filled them with pride. As he held out his hand for them to shake, they let their fingers touch his, but wouldn't hold his hand in a firm grip. To cheer them up and win back their reverence, he invited them to come and see the child's garden and to drink wine with him on the site of the summer house he was planning to build there.

So they came one morning and stood about awkwardly. The garden was beautiful, lush and healthy. They touched the flowers. The scent of them was extraordinary. They'd forgotten how superb the world could seem. They drank the dry white wine, bottle after bottle, and staggered home in mid-afternoon to dream muddled dreams. Before they left, Mollini had embraced the men and kissed the women on the lips. 'I made them happy,' he told Verena.

Verena didn't move out of her room these days. She sat up in her bed and fed her sorrow with sweet wine and chocolate. Her feet began to swell and the doctor was called. Verena burst into tears. 'I know what would cure me,' she sobbed, 'if Antonio would only take me in his arms . . .' The doctor went away, disgusted.

'My wife is suffering,' Mollini wrote to Clara, 'and I cannot help but feel sorry for her. But her suffering is nothing to my own: I'm in love with a woman I cannot marry.'

In September, Mollini left for Vienna. He was to take on his most demanding and difficult role, in Verdi's *Otello*. He had signed the contract on one condition, that the part of Desdemona be given to Clara Buig. And in Vienna at last Clara became Mollini's mistress. She had been so moved, she said, by his letters, she knew she could no longer resist.

He was in heaven. La Buig wasn't a sensual woman like La Dusa. There were moments, even, when her grave face beneath his reminded Mollini of Rosa's face, long, long ago. 'You give our love nobility and dignity,' he told Clara, 'you turn the past into the future.'

He was determined, now, that there would be a future with Clara. He wrote to Pappavincente with new designs for the summer house. It would no longer be a summer house: it would have a sumptuous bedroom and bathroom and fires in all the rooms. It would be Clara's residence.

As rumours of the love affair of Antonio Mollini and the 23-year-old Clara Buig spread in whispers round the tea-rooms and the musical salons of Vienna, it began at last to rain in Tuscany. It rained for seventeen days and nights. The villagers came out of their hovels and stuck their tongues out and let the sweet rain trickle down their throats. Verena got out of bed, threw a shawl round her shoulders and walked out in the downpour to the lake side. The water had risen by several feet. Verena walked into the water, wearing her pink satin slippers. The slippers stuck in the mud, so she waded on without them, feeling her petticoats and her skirt become heavy.

She lay on her back. She expected to sink straight away, but her large body was buoyant and she found that she was floating. She stared at the grey sky and thought how astonishingly full of colour her life had been. It took her three hours to die. On the brink of death, it seemed to La Dusa that the grey cloud moved away and that the hot sun was shining on her round face. And for a second, she imagined the autumn to come and the wonderful vibrant reds and umbers of the leaves.

By the time the winter came, Clara's house was finished. Mollini, however, didn't bother to have the fires lit.

'Clara will live with me in the Villa Mollini,' he told Pappavincente, so the shutters were closed and the place locked.

When Clara Buig at last arrived at the Villa Mollini, however, and was led by a maid to the very room La Dusa had occupied, she refused to sleep there. The house, in fact, gave her the creeps, she said. She couldn't possibly spend a night in it.

Mollini wrapped her in her velvet coat and walked with her, arm in arm, through the garden, round the lake and up into the forest. The great trees were silent. Winter had begun to bite early this year.

The pleasure Mollini took from seeing Clara's little gloved hand on his arm was acute, too precious and fleeting to mention. They walked on in silence, descending at last down the intricate paths of the child's garden to Clara's house. Golden pheasants in the aviary squawked and pecked at the wire as they passed.

Mollini opened the shutters of the house and got on his knees and lit a fire in one of the grates.

Clara walked on her own from room to room and then went outside again and walked all round the house. It was nicely set in the child's garden, surrounded by stone terraces and ornate balustrading and small cypresses. At the back of it, however, about forty yards away, Clara could see an ugly post-and-rails fence and beyond this a boring slope of empty pastureland.

'What is that?' she asked Mollini.

Mollini had followed her outside and now looked to where she was pointing.

'Common land,' said Mollini. 'The village people use it to graze their cattle.'

La Buig sniffed. Then she turned her stern child's face towards Mollini and said: 'You know what I would like to see there instead of that?'

'No, my love.'

'An English lawn. This whole garden is nothing but steps and piazzas and gazebos and mazes and borders and beds. If I'm going to live here, I really want a lawn.'

Mollini sent for Pappavincente. One of his sons arrived instead and told him that Pappavincente was ill and couldn't come.

Mollini went at once to the village, not to tell the people that he was going to take away the rest of their pasture for Clara's lawn, but to see the old man and take him some of the strong red wine he knew he liked to drink.

'We believe he's dying,' said Signora Pappavincente. She was holding a rag to her nose, and when Mollini went into the room where Pappavincente lay, it seemed to him that the odour of death was indeed very strong.

'Listen, old friend,' he whispered to Pappavincente, 'remember all that you've achieved here. Dwell on that. Feel proud of it. You've made the most beautiful garden in Tuscany, perhaps the most beautiful garden in all Italy. And it's not finished yet. It lives on. It changes and grows. It will last for ever.'

Pappavincente's head rolled on the pillow and he turned his staring, angry eyes on Mollini. 'I have sinned, Master,' he said.

He died that night. Mollini wanted him buried in the garden, but the old man's family were stubborn and wouldn't allow it.

Mollini explained to Clara that the whole village would be in mourning for a while and that it would be impossible, just at the moment, to mention the land he was going to take for her lawn.

'I understand,' said Clara, 'but you will tell them in the spring?'

'Yes. In the spring.'

'Because I want to push my baby's bassinet on the lawn. Like an English duchess. You see?'

'Your baby's bassinet, Clara?'

'Yes, Antonio. I'm going to have your child.'

Mollini took Clara's serious little face in his hands and covered it with kisses. Three weeks later, he married her. Once again, the cream of the opera world was invited to the Villa Mollini. Among the cream was an extraordinarily beautiful English soprano called Marion Shepherd. Marion Shepherd told Mollini that she thought his garden was as unbelievable as his voice and smiled such a dazzling smile that Mollini was forced to reach out and caress her mouth with his finger.

On the wedding night, Clara Buig was very restless. The baby inside her, little Pietro, as Mollini called him, kept kicking her and her head seemed to be full of strange visions and fears.

The dawn was icy cold, but as soon as the sky was light, Clara got up and dressed herself and went out into the garden. She didn't wake Mollini. He lay snoring on his back with his legs apart.

She walked towards the Villa Mollini itself, which seemed to beckon her. On the way, she came across an old stone well with delicate arching ironwork that she'd never noticed before. I expect it's just ornamental, she thought, like everything else in this garden. But she was curious about it, so she walked to the edge of it and peered in. Much to her surprise, she found that she was looking down into darkness.

Strawberry Jam

When I was fourteen, in 1957, my mother died. We buried her in the village graveyard and I wore new black shoes with high heels at her funeral. Sudden loss and the pinch of fashionable shoes were then and ever afterwards connected in my mind. I still feel my own mortality most acutely in my feet.

It was winter. My father studied recipes for hot puddings. 'Staying alive means keeping warm,' he said. Suet and sponge were it, our existence. Yet I was growing, getting tall and thin, and these limbs of mine were as cold as marble. I put the high-heeled shoes away, wrapped up in tissue paper. When I remembered my mother, I thought about my own vanity and wondered when my life would begin. Passion, I believed, might warm me up. Folded inside one of my bedsocks was a photograph of Alan Ladd.

As the spring came and the evenings got lighter, I spent a lot of time looking out of my window, as if trying to see in the familiar landscape of our neighbours' garden the arrival of the future. This garden, separated from ours only by a picket fence, was never ever dug, pruned or tended in any way and in summer puffs of seed streamed off into the wind from its thistles and willow-herb and tall grasses, sowing themselves in our lawn and in my mother's rockery. She had been a polite and timid person. Only once had she plucked up her courage and knocked on our neighbours' back door and announced with great grief in her voice: 'Your weeds are making my task very difficult, Mr Zimmerli.' Walter Zimmerli had come out and stared at his wilderness, sizing it up like a man at a heifer auction.

'The weeds?'

'Yes. They re-seed themselves all over the place.'

'And the solution?'

'Well, if you could root them out . . .'

'But look how splendid is the pink colour!'

'I know . . .'

'We like this: nature not disturbed. This is important to Jani, I'm afraid.'

The only trees in the Zimmerlis' garden were fruit trees: an old and graceful Victoria plum, a crab apple and some lichen-covered Bramleys. Every Christmas, Walter Zimmerli set up a ladder and gathered the mistletoe that sprouted near the tops of the Bramleys. In summer, out came the ladder again and the crab apples and plums were picked, but most of the Bramleys left to the wasps and the autumn gales. We didn't know why at first, till Jani Zimmerli came round with a jar of crab apple jelly for us. My mother tried to thank her. 'It is not thanks,' said Jani, 'Walter and I, we love jam.'

So in April I watched the blossom creeping out on the Zimmerlis' trees and spots creeping out on my face. The sweet puddings streamed in my blood. My father began to learn the recipes by heart.

Then, Mrs Lund arrived.

I saw her first from my window. Walter and Jani Zimmerli came out into their orchard. It was dusk. Mrs Lund followed them like a little shadow. The three stood together quietly and stared at the trees. Mrs Lund set down the suitcase she was carrying and Walter turned to her and said something in German. Mrs Lund nodded and Jani nodded and then they picked up the suitcase and went back inside the house. At supper, I told my father: 'The Zimmerlis have got a friend staying.'

'Are you sure?'

'Yes. I saw her. She's quite old.'

My father put down his knife and fork on a plate of dumplings and gravy he couldn't eat. 'I suppose you'll be keeping watch,' he said.

Watching the Zimmerlis had been an occupation of mine since the first summer of their arrival, but I used to watch the front of their house – from a window seat in our sitting room. I would wrap my face in the lace curtains and stare out at them. 'Holly!' my mother would snap. 'Leave them alone!' But I couldn't leave them alone because I was fascinated by what they were doing. Outside their door, on the grass verge, they'd set up a table, shaded on hot days by a large faded umbrella, and here they sat – sometimes both of them, sometimes Jani alone – hour after hour, waiting for people to pass. They were trying to sell jam. The jam was delicious – we were among the few who knew this – and Jani had made pretty gingham covers for the array of pots. But two things struck me as strange. First of all, our houses are on a narrow, out-of-the-way road down which almost no one travels, so that Jani and Walter could sit at their little stall for an entire afternoon without selling one single jar of jam. Secondly, whenever a car *did* stop, the Zimmerlis never seemed to be content with the small commercial transaction, but began to treat the customers like old friends, talking and laughing and invariably trying to persuade them to go into their house for a glass of sherry.

My mother didn't approve of my spying on the Zimmerlis. When I told her they invited strangers in, she didn't believe me. 'The Zimmerlis wouldn't do that,' she said, 'they keep themselves to themselves.' She died disbelieving me. She'd never heard them pleading with strangers, 'Just to keep a little company,' but I had. And I also knew something else: the jam customers were the *only* people who ever went into that house. No real friends ever arrived. We, their closest neighbours, were never invited past the kitchen door. They gave us jam. They said good evening from their perch up the ladders. But that was all. No car except theirs ever stood in the drive. Even at Christmas their house was silent and the door closed. No light ever went on in the guest room. It was as if they had no past and courted no future, only this fleeting present – a few coins in the money tin and the company of strangers.

Now, this elderly woman had arrived. For the first time ever, a light went on in the Zimmerlis' spare room and I saw Jani at the window, drawing the curtains. I imagined this shadowy person, covered with the fat Austrian feather quilt, her possessions folded and put away. I imagined Jani and Walter next door to her, talking in whispers.

And then I learned her name. I was in our garden, putting new alpines in my mother's rockery. I looked up and saw someone standing at the picket fence and it was her. I smiled.

'Very good weather,' she said.

'Yes. The winter's over, probably.'

'I think you must be Holly?'

'Yes.'

'Well. Jani and Walter have spoken of you.'

'Have they?'

'Oh yes.'

I stood up. I thought about my face wrapped in the lace curtains, a gross, gawping bride. Since my mother's death, I suffered very often from shame.

'My name is Mrs Lund,' said the woman.

'How do you do?' I said.

The weather people told us a hot summer was coming. The weeds in the Zimmerlis' patch were growing green again through last year's fallen mass. I waited for the Zimmerlis to set up the jam stall, but it didn't appear. They had company now, they had Mrs Lund. I imagined them drinking sherry with her and talking about Viennese teashops full of delicate confectionery – apricot tartlets, apple flan, damson shortcake. She was their past, come to sweeten them, and for a time I envied them, because I knew my own past – our warm, comfortable life with my mother – could only come back as a cold memory. But after a few weeks of Mrs Lund's visit, I began to notice a change in the Zimmerlis: they were losing weight.

I had never known how old they were. Walter seemed older (fatter, with wilder greying hair) than my father, who was forty-three, and Jani seemed younger (more buxom, dimpled and healthy) than my mother, who had been forty-one. Certainly, I'd always thought of them as large, not bony and big as I was, but wide and squashy as only people nearing middle age

223

become. But now they seemed reduced. Walter's belly was smaller; Jani's arms, hanging up her napkins and her table-cloths, were thinner. Even Walter's laugh, not often heard these days, seemed altered, no longer the laugh of a heavy man.

The diminution of the Zimmerlis struck me as odd. Then, one night very late (I'd taken Alan Ladd out of my bedsock and was smoothing him out on my dressing table) I heard Jani weeping. I turned my light off and went to the window. Jani was sitting on her terrace and her face was buried in her lap. After a while, Walter came out and knelt down beside her and leant his head against her shoulder. He spoke to her very softly and this was the first time that I ever thought of the German language as a comforting thing. But I also had a strong feeling – confirmed by my own sleeplessness – that something import-ant was about to happen. And it did happen. That same night, Mrs Lund disappeared.

I woke very late the next morning. It was Saturday. An unfamiliar *chock, chock* sound had woken me. When I looked out, I saw what it was: Walter Zimmerli was digging his garden! I called my father and we watched him together. A large patch of weeds had already been cleared and Walter's back was soaked with sweat. He worked on without stopping, thrusting the spade into the earth, levering with his foot, smashing the clods as he turned them over.

'Why?' I whispered.

''Bout time, anyway,' said my father.

'Yes, but why? Why now?'

'Dunno, Holly. People are often a mystery. You'll find that out.'

My father went downstairs as I stayed at the window. Then my father returned with hot muffins and milky coffee on a tray. He said I needed spoiling. Grief, he said, is very tiring. He made me get back into bed to eat the breakfast. Then I dozed. I *was* tired. And I had a dream that Walter Zimmerli had killed Mrs Lund, smashed her on the back of the neck with a marble rolling pin, and buried her in the garden. That was why – yes, of course, that was why – Jani had wept. They had murdered Mrs Lund.

Then it was mid-day and I was at the window again. On and on Walter worked, with the spring sunshine hot on his neck. Nearly half of his garden had been cleared when I heard Jani call him in. He left his spade sticking into the earth.

His subterfuge isn't bad, I thought. If he'd cleared only a very small patch, a patch only three or four times larger, say, than the spot where Mrs Lund is buried, this might have appeared odd. As it is, he pretends he's weeding his whole garden, getting rid of the willow-herb at last, answering his neighbours' complaints. But he hasn't fooled me! I saw Mrs Lund die in my dream. I saw Walter go out and begin to dig in the dead of morning. I saw Jani trying to help him, pulling with all her might at the grasses. Then I saw them go inside and wrap Mrs Lund's body in a faded rug and stagger out, one holding her shoulders, one her feet, and lay her in a shallow trough that was only just deep enough to hide her. They smashed her in. Hurriedly, Walter piled the earth on top of her and began – even though he was tired by this time and aching with fear – to turn the soil around and beyond the grave. And this is when I began to hear it, the *chock, chock* of his terrible digging . . .

I don't remember what we did that weekend. I know my father took me out somewhere, to see my cousins perhaps, who lived in a big house by a river. All I know is that Walter Zimmerli worked on and on, almost without pausing until, by dusk on Sunday, no trace of the grass or thistle or willow-herb remained and the earth was raked flat like a seed bed and in the twilight Jani made a bonfire of the weeds and I heard the Zimmerlis laughing.

During the next week, they began to plant. On their back porch were piles of wooden boxes stacked up. Each box contained twenty or thirty straggly plants and they set them in rows measured out with string about three feet apart. And I knew what they were: they were strawberries. I wanted to say to my father, 'They're planting strawberries on Mrs Lund!' But I didn't. I just stood on our side of the picket fence and stared at the Zimmerlis crouched down and at Jani's skirt in the mud, and then I offered to help. They stood up and smiled at me. 'Ah,' said Walter, 'very fortunate, eh Jani? Holly can be in charge of the straw.'

As I worked, moving down the lines very slowly with the sacks of straw, I tried to test the feel of the earth under my boots. I knew where the body was – roughly – but the soil in the right-hand corner of the garden was as flat and even as the rest. They did a good job, I thought. No one will ever know. *Except me.* Unless, of course, someone comes over from Vienna and they start to search. And I imagined how it would be then: they would find traces of Mrs Lund's visit in the house – tweed skirts, shoes of Swiss leather, a tortoiseshell hairbrush bundled out of sight in a wardrobe – and then of course they would begin to dig . . .

We finished planting the strawberries the following weekend. My father said I looked pink from all the fresh air and work, and I did find that my skinny hands and feet had been warmed up. Alan Ladd in my bedsock felt snug. And then the strangest, most unexpected thing happened: Walter Zimmerli gave me a key to his house. 'We have to go away, Holly,' he said. 'We have to go back to Vienna to sort out some papers and things and we would be so grateful if you might water our many house plants.'

'Yes,' said Jani, 'we would be grateful. But we ask you not to touch anything, any precious things, and let no one else come in. We trust you to be this little caretaker.'

I looked at the Zimmerlis: two solemn faces; two bodies, once weighty, growing thin with anxiety and guilt. 'Of course,' I said. 'I'd be happy to take care of your plants. And if the weather's very dry, I'll put our sprinkler on the strawberries.'

It was May. For my birthday, my father bought me a blue and white polka-dot skirt and a white webbing belt. He said I was getting to look like Debbie Reynolds. 'My hair's thin,' I said, 'perhaps it's our diet.' So he started to learn a new set of recipes, casseroles and hotpots and fruit fools, and we began to flourish.

Crime detection, wrote the Chief Constable of the Suffolk Police in our church news sheet, *requires faith, hope, intelligence and also physical courage.* I cut these words out and hid them in a shell box my mother had given me. The Zimmerlis left very early one morning and all the blinds and shutters in the house were closed.

'I have a feeling,' I said to my father, 'that they'll never come back.'

'Why do you think that?'

'I don't know,' I said dreamily, 'I have these peculiar thoughts.'

I made myself wait one week before going into the Zimmerlis' house. I ate well and went for long rides on my bicycle to make myself strong. Then I chose a Sunday morning. My father had gone to the pub. I took a watering-can and the door key and a wire coat-hanger. When I opened the Zimmerlis' back door, all I could see was darkness.

I was looking for two things: the murder weapon and the locked wardrobe. I flicked a light switch in the hall, but no light came on. The electricity had been turned off. I made my way in the dark to the kitchen. I set down the watering-can. Slowly, I tipped the slats of the Venetian blinds and sunlight fell in stripes onto the scrubbed table and an ornate dresser painted red and green. I opened every drawer and found all kinds of utensil – whisks and strainers, graters and slicers and scoops – but no rolling pin. *The murder weapon,* said the voice of the Chief Constable, *is seldom easily found. However, it is sometimes possible to infer guilt precisely from the* absence *of the instrument of death from its accustomed place.*

I stood and looked at the room where Jani Zimmerli had made her cauldrons of jam. Was it possible that this Austrian woman with her sweet tooth never made pastry? Never made flans or strudel or pies? I didn't think so. I imagined Walter and Jani – at least until they began to get thin – living on this kind of food, and yet nowhere in the kitchen could I find a rolling pin.

There were some fleshy plants on the window sill. I ran water into my can and doused them, pondering what to do next. No doubt my search for the rolling pin was futile. It lay, I imagined, in the mud of the river that flowed past my cousins' house. When the summer holidays came, I would announce a diving competition. Meanwhile, I had to find the locked wardrobe.

I made my way upstairs, carrying the wire hanger. I knew which side of the house the guest room was on, but I decided, first, to go into the Zimmerlis' own bedroom. Drawing the heavy curtains, I noticed that the room had a strange smell. The odour in this one room was warm and spicy, as if Jani and Walter had been in it only moments before. I looked at the bed, covered with a heavy, intricate patchwork quilt and at Jani's little dressing-table mirror draped with scarves and amber beads and a sudden, unexpected feeling of sadness came to me. It was obvious – so obvious! – that Jani and Walter had been happy here, in this room, in this house, but now, because of what they had done, their happiness was over and they would never be able to come back here. Change had come. To them. To me. Mrs Lund lay under the strawberries; my mother lay under the churchyard turf. One part of my life was gone.

I sat down on the Zimmerlis' bed. I didn't cry. I made myself think about Alan Ladd and French kissing and the future. I promised myself I would take my black high heels out of the tissue paper and try them on.

I got up and smoothed the quilt and walked, upright and purposeful, to the room where Mrs Lund had slept. I lifted the blind and looked around. There were two beds in the room, both narrow. Between them was an old washstand with a flowery jug and bowl. On the wood floor was a faded rug resembling almost perfectly the rug I'd seen in my dream. In the corner of the room, behind the door, was a mahogany wardrobe. This was so exactly like the wardrobe I'd imagined (mirror glass on the front, ornate classical carvings along the top) that I caught my breath and now hardly dared to move towards it. I looked down at the wire coat-hanger in my hand. In stories, people opened doors with coat-hangers, but would I be able to do it? I stepped forward. Only then did I notice that the key of the wardrobe was there in the lock.

Over the years, I've thought about it very many times, that moment of opening the wardrobe in Mrs Lund's room. I see myself exactly as I was then, reflected in the mirror, wearing my blue polka-dot skirt, my face solemn but full of expectation, on the brink of a momentous discovery. And then I see the inside of the wardrobe, not, as I had imagined, filled with Mrs Lund's possessions, but completely empty except for one small object, a black leatherbound notebook. These things made a kind of tableau, like a snapshot. I caught it then and I have it still in my mind, a split second of the future, waiting.

I picked up the notebook, sat down on one of the beds and opened it. On the first page, in fine italic handwriting were the words: *Tagebuch von J. B. Zimmerli* – the diary of J. B. Zimmerli. Above the first entry were written the date and place: *Wien, November 1937*. I turned the pages, understanding hardly a word of the careful handwriting, but noting dates and places. The entries ceased, with several blank pages remaining, in March 1938. As I came to the final entry, something fell out of the notebook onto the floor. I picked it up. It was a photograph of two children, a boy and a girl, aged perhaps ten and eight respectively. It was summer in the picture. The two children squinted into bright light. Behind them was the glimpse of a lake.

That night, I tried to sort it all out in my head. I'd found nothing in the Zimmerlis' house, apart from the absence of the rolling pin, that proved them guilty of Mrs Lund's murder. No possessions stowed away, no sign of her suitcase. I'd gone into every room. I'd tried to think clearly, like a proper detective, aware that clues are not always hidden, but sometimes in plain view, but the longer I searched, the more I began to doubt my first conclusion. It was possible, after all, that Mrs Lund had left very late on the night that I saw Jani crying. A taxi could have come for her, or Walter could have driven her to the station. Perhaps, even, she had left *before* Jani's weeping and it was precisely because Mrs Lund had left that Jani was so upset? And what about the digging? Well, here too, there were logical explanations: Walter's neighbours, including my mother, had been nagging him to do something about his weeds for long enough. Perhaps Mrs Lund, too, had ticked him off and even given him the idea of planting the strawberries.

I decided I would let the whole matter rest for a while. Already my brain felt tired with it and I was beginning to feel glad that I didn't work for the Suffolk Constabulary. I would go in from time to time and water the house plants and I would make sure the strawberries didn't die. And I would wait. In time, I thought, I will probably understand.

The only thing I'd taken from the house was the photograph of the children. I looked at it for a long time and the longer I looked, the more I became convinced that these were the children of Walter and Jani. Because it had always seemed strange to me that the Zimmerlis, who appeared so contented with each other, hadn't got their own family. Had something terrible happened to these children? Was it for them that Jani cried? Were the strangers, clutching their pots of jam, the only people to be told of the tragedy? Was this their *function*, to be silent, anonymous listeners? My father often said he found it easier to talk about my mother's death to strangers than to his friends. One day, he said, he told the lift-man at his office and the lift-man had been very nice to him. If this was true for my father, perhaps it was true for Walter and Jani?

As the days passed, I found I was getting very fond of the photograph. I could imagine the scenery behind the children: the huge lake, a hazy shore line, incredible mountains with snow on their peaks. It calmed me to think of a foreign place – as if part of the future might take place in it. I hid the photograph in my other bedsock, but the nights were warmer now, so the socks and the pictures lay folded under my pillow.

As the weathermen had predicted, that summer of 1957 was very hot. Through the first two weeks of June, my father and I watered the Zimmerlis' strawberries and by the third week the strawberries were ripe. There was no sign of Walter and Jani and birds had already begun to peck at the fruit. We stood by our fence and surveyed the crop.

'Terrible waste,' said my father.

'Let's pick them,' I said, 'and make jam.'

We bought a preserving pan. In our larder, we found dozens of jam jars, brown with dust, saved by my mother for this day she would never see. On the evening the jam was labelled and put back into the larder – thirteen pounds of it in twenty-one jars – Walter and Jani returned. We saw them kneeling down in the strawberry beds and lifting the leaves to search for the fruit. I called from my upstairs window: 'Don't worry! It's all safe!' And when I took the jam round to them the next day, their gratitude seemed to overflow, as if I'd brought them something of great value.

'So *kind*, Walter, isn't it?' said Jani, picking up one of the pots. 'So much work and kindness.'

'Indeed,' said Walter, 'indeed this is most thoughtful.'

'You could sell it on the road,' I suggested.

'Yes,' said Jani, 'but you must have all the money. Holly must have the profit.'

'Yes,' said Walter, 'and next year too. The plants will grow a little larger and we shall have a better crop.'

'It's kind of you,' I said, 'but you don't have to give me any money.'

'But we want to do this,' said Jani, 'maybe you can buy a polka blouse to match your skirt.'

I returned the house key to them. As I went to the door, Jani came with me and put her arm, which was still much thinner than it had once been, round my shoulders. 'Like you,' she said, 'we have had some sad times. We lost Walter's mother.'

'She died?'

'Yes. In one way so sad, yet in one way happy. Walter's father was killed by the Nazis in 1938 and, since this time, his mother was all these years in an institution, not knowing really what the days were, but thinking the time is before the war and she is a girl again, like you. In her last days, she says to the nurse, do my breasts grow?'

'I'm very sorry,' I said.

'Yes,' said Jani, 'sorrow for all. But that is why we put in the strawberries: *Mutti's* favourite fruit.'

I pieced it together then. Mrs Lund – an old friend of the family? – had been a courier. She'd not only brought the news of the death of Walter's mother, but had come to hand over the few possessions of the dead woman, the most important of which was the diary belonging to her husband, J. B. Zimmerli. It was for Walter's mother that Jani had wept, and it was their mourning that had made them thin. There was no body in the garden. The only bit of the mystery I couldn't solve was the identity of the children and I thought now that I never would.

I knew I had to find a way to return the photograph to the wardrobe in Mrs Lund's room, and I had made a plan. I would offer to help the Zimmerlis with their jam stall. On a hot afternoon, I would ask them if I could go into the kitchen for a glass of water – a request they couldn't refuse. Then, quickly and silently, I would go upstairs and return the photograph to the black notebook.

But I wanted to have one last look at it. I went up to my room and reached under my pillow to pull out my bedsocks, but they weren't there. With feelings of guilt and dread, I began to search my cupboards and drawers. Alan Ladd I could replace, but those children by the lake, that picture was perhaps all that remained of them. I looked out at the Zimmerlis' house. They'd trusted me, called me their 'caretaker' and I'd betrayed them.

And then I saw my bedsocks. They were hanging on the washing line. I ran down to the garden, past my father who was sitting in the sun. I unpegged the socks, which were still damp. 'Need them,' I said to my father and fled back up to my room.

I put my hand into each of them in turn. Alan Ladd, made of inferior paper, was scrunched into a ball no bigger than a marble. I threw him into my waste paper basket. But the photograph of the children had survived. It was only slightly creased and not faded at all.

I held it against my face, smoothing it out. And then I noticed that there *was* something different about it. Before the washing, the photograph had been backed with thick, black paper, as if it had been stuck into an album and cut out with part of the album page still glued to it. Now, the black layer of paper wasn't there. I turned the photograph over. In the bottom right-hand corner of it, a faded caption was still just decipherable. Dated 1926, it read: *Walter und Jani an der See.* And I understood.

For four years, I kept the Zimmerlis' secret. In precisely the way I had planned, I returned the photograph to the notebook and of course Jani and Walter never mentioned either the diary or the picture to me. I grew fond of them and they seemed to become fond of me, yet on certain days, for no reason at all, they would behave very coldly towards me, as if they were saying to me, 'Don't come too close. Friendship is too knowing. We prefer still, as always, to talk to the strangers, who will never find out anything and who will never come back.'

And so, hurt one day by a rebuff of Jani's – 'Holly, go home now. You talk too much, always of boyfriends, always of your future. It's boring, you know.' – I decided to tell my father. We were sitting together in the kitchen. It was 1961. My father had encouraged his thinning hair to grow long over his ears. I took a sip of the white wine we were drinking and looked at my loving, would-be hippy dad and said solemnly: 'Walter and Jani Zimmerli are brother and sister.'

He smiled and nodded. 'Don't tell the vicar,' he said.

The morning I left home for my first term at university, I knocked on the Zimmerlis' back door to say goodbye. Jani opened it, her hands and arms covered in flour. 'I'm making pastry,' she said, 'come in.'

We went into her kitchen. I put the kettle on and watched her work. Her arms were fleshy again by this time. When the dough was kneaded to her satisfaction, she began to roll it out, using a painted metal canister as a rolling pin. It reminded me of a thing my mother used to do: when she planted beans, she'd tread in the soil with her boot and roll it flat with an old tin barrel.

Tropical Fish

John Sparrow is dying.

Coming to the farm bungalow in the heat of early July, John Sparrow's old friends notice the changes. Large John has shrunk, under the candlewick cover, to sparrow. The hand he gives each of them to shake (always polite, John, always correct) is bird bone. Then in the kitchen, where his wife Mary makes tea or squash as they prefer, she shows them her new microwave oven. It tells digital time. As they stand and admire it, the blue numbers flick on. Time is passing for John Sparrow, but at least he's going rich.

His bed is near a window. He can still raise his head and see his acres, his single-minded land running flat to the sky. Harvest is coming. His wheat's the colour of buff board. John Sparrow nods at it: good land, good decisions. Once he farmed temperamental stuff, mucky stuff: soft fruit, chickens, a jersey herd. Then he sold the cows and the poultry and tore out the raspberry canes and ordered his arable seed. He made way for it. He bulldozed his hedges and cut down the ash and sycamore and filled in the clay ponds. With no obstacles in its way, his seed grew strong and straight. Yet it needed more room. John Sparrow walked the boundaries of his farm and sized up the pastures of his neighbours and sized up their struggles. Solicitors were engaged. Contracts passed to John Sparrow in buff envelopes. His seed, legitimised, marched on.

Now, he's leaving it. Mary Sparrow gets out the electric carver and slices bread for him. White bread and packet soups are what he tries to eat. Reared in a backward place, he's dying a modern death.

*

234

On this hot, dusty day, Bob Sparrow, John's only child, waits for the London train.

Bob Sparrow is the height his father once was, with his father's broad nose and the smile of his mother, furtive and sweet. At thirty, unmarried yet, Bob Sparrow's a fortnight from his twentieth harvest and days, perhaps, from his inheritance. His back is broad, his elbows fleshy, his belly in its leisurewear soft and fat. With his smart sneakers, with his briefcase full of catalogues, he looks like a rep. His nails are clean. He stands and waits and stares at the railway lines that shimmer. He fondles the change in his pocket. Easy, says his stance. Easy, says this nonchalant jingling of money.

On the train, he buys a four-pack and gets out his brochures. He spreads them around: sprayer arms, ten-row planters, water throwers, combines, bailers, tractors and ploughs. Two old farmers drinking tea stare across the aisle at the pictures. Bob Sparrow catches them staring, as if at pornography. He folds the shiny catalogues away and sits holding his paper cup, his face turned towards the fields.

He's on his way to an exhibition, *Agripower '87*. MIP is the dying John Sparrow's most cherished philosophy: Machinery is Profit. And the son, Bob Sparrow, is obedient to the mind which saw the folly of the dairy herd, the waste of the raspberry fields, the mind which altered the landscape. MIP. This year, the investment is large and the farm is a company, Sparrow Holdings Ltd. The old men drinking tea mumble in lost voices. And the Norfolk flatlands pass and vanish, minced up by the train.

Bob Sparrow leans his head against the hot window and daydreams of flying. He's never seen the Sparrow land from the air, but he can imagine its symmetry, his good ditches squaring it off on a neat grid. He'd like to own a plane. He wants to put himself above the land and look down. His mind puts up a windsock one field from the garden where the widow, Mary, will go patiently in circles with her Flymo. The sock struts tall above the tarmac runway, going east-west away from the silos. The wind hurtles in from the east. Easy. He's airborne in seconds. The oaks – the few that remain – are in seconds small. Bob Sparrow smiles and feels pleased with life's arrangement. John Sparrow walked on his patched and sculptured land and saw how it could be straightened. Soon, the old man will lie on his back, his nose pressed up to the clay, and he, the rich son, will walk above it.

Near London, Bob Sparrow finishes the beer. His belly feels bloated and his understanding diminished as the train goes slowly into the poor suburbs, Seven Kings, Ilford, Maryland, Stratford. He turns inwards from the grimy flats, turns his back on them and gets out his catalogues. 'Do the sums before you buy,' old John advises. 'Outlay versus man hours saved. Work it out.' And always Mary nods proudly, remembering a drudgery time, water saved in a butt, sheets boiled in a copper, yet one day confuses her men and surprises herself by asking: 'What are the hours saved for?'

'Sitting,' replies John.

'Flying,' Bob wants to say.

'I think you've all forgotten,' says Mary.

Bob Sparrow gets out of the train and smells the trapped air of the station. Above his head, glaziers are painstakingly repairing ancient structures. Bob only glances at this work and hurries to the underground. Stepping up into sunlight again at Earls Court, he finds himself moving with a crowd towards the exhibition centre. This crowd annoys him. The eager people. He'd expected to be part of a chequebook élite. 'Vision,' John Sparrow is fond of saying, 'needs space.'

His orders placed (orders for machinery John Sparrow will not see), Bob moves to Stand 56. The small, single-engined white plane sits on an area of plastic grass. Bob is invited by the salesmen to inspect the housing where the spray chemicals in their cylinders are clamped. The dummy cylinders are white like the plane.

He climbs, then, into the cockpit. ('Doddle to fly, Sir, these, Sir.') From the pilot's seat he feels tall at last above the milling crowds. Only the instrument panel dismays him. How many man hours lie between this moment and his vision of his airstrip? 'Easy, eh?' says the salesman, grinning above his white shirt. Teach me, Bob wants to say. 'Land in a field with these. Land anywhere, near enough,' says the salesman. And Bob nods and thinks of his mother alone and going in little circles with her mower and turning her flat face and waving up. 'Next year,' he says. 'I'll be in a position then.'

So he moves out into the hurry of five o'clock and is caught by another tide of people going from offices to trains and buses. Though he half intends staying in the herd that pushes along towards the underground station, he drops out of it and goes into a pub where he orders a pint and a pie. He takes these to a leather bench and feels, as he sits, a deep weariness with the day. Though he thinks he will telephone the bungalow, he knows he won't go home tonight.

He talks to no one. He goes once to the payphone. The payphone is broken. He orders more beer. In the bungalow, Mary will be plugging in the carver, measuring water for the soup granules. 'Will the lad be home?' John Sparrow will ask. Beer is sad stuff when John Sparrow is dying.

Bob goes back to the bar and orders whisky. The barman is Irish. 'Storm comin',' he announces. Bob nods and pays and goes back to his corner. And within a very few minutes, the sun at his back on the thick pub window goes and he hears thunder.

Not wanting to be trapped by the rain, remembering Mary sitting on her own with the telly while John snores and snarls his way into his invalid's sleep, he swallows the whisky, puts on his jacket and goes out into the street. Lights are on in Turkish take-aways, in pizza parlours: night starting in a foreign place. The huge storm moves in from the west, low over the airport.

Bob Sparrow hurries. The place he chooses has no hotel sign, only a hand-inked card, VACANCIES. The woman who opens the door is fifty and thick-waisted and she holds a small dog in her arms.

'We used,' she says as she walks up the stairs, 'to breed champions.'

'Champion dogs?' Bob asks.

'In this house,' she says, 'we used to exhibit.'

The room she shows him is carpeted and large and painted amber. 'There's this one,' says the woman, her stubby hand on the metal door handle, 'or if you find the tanks disturbing, there's another one I let out at the back, but smaller.'

'Tanks?' says Bob.

'Yes,' and she nods towards the wall facing the bed, 'the fish.'

Bob walks past her into the room. It has a musty smell that reminds him of the smell of the silos. There are three aquaria, dimly lit, arranged with stones and coral and fern. 'The thing is,' says the woman, 'they're not silent. It's the aeration.'

'Yes,' says Bob and glances from the fish tanks to the window, against which the rain begins to hurtle.

'They need to breathe,' says the woman and for the first time smiles tenderly at Bob. 'Some find it company.'

That night, John Sparrow dies in his bed.

Mary straightens the candlewick counterpane and sits with a little lamp on and tries to imagine her future, but her future seems flat. John Sparrow imagined his flat, featureless land, but he was tall in it. Where he went, Mary's eye followed.

So blind and cold in the landscape does Mary feel now that she creeps from the room and goes to the kitchen to boil milk for a hot drink. The blue digits of the oven clock flick on: 2:41. She waits and stares. 2:42. She thinks of her son.

The storm over London has moved on. Bob Sparrow wakes and stares at the ghostly light of the fish tanks and his head throbs. The bubbles rise and sigh. His tired eye becomes a swimmer and inquisitive swift visions pass into his mind. The bodies of the fish are soft, delicate as a brain. They're supple and fragile and streaming with colour and light. And Bob Sparrow remembers a day in summer when he creeps in secret in the jungle of raspberry canes and pops his eye through a dark gap in the leaves and sees a burst of red where the fruit hang. His nimble child's brain marvels and his child's hand pushes up and cups the berries and he squashes them on his tongue. And he darts on up the row, where the patterning of light and leaf is intricate and restless, always changing and

238

moving, yet always there. He runs, playing games with the shadows and the raspberry field is beautiful and his soft limbs running are the most beautiful things of all.

Bob Sparrow snaps on the bedside lamp. For an instant, all the fish are still, as if immobilised by an electric shock. He looks away from them. The lamp casts a corn-coloured glow on the unfamiliar room. He searches in his briefcase for aspirin, swallows two, then lies on his back looking at the square ceiling. He doesn't glance again at the fish and tries not to listen to the sighing of the oxygen in the water. The throbbing in his head gradually ceases, but he can't sleep. He turns out the light and covers his face with his pillow. As time passes, he sees daylight at its edges and thinks of the dawn breaking on the rim of his land and of the harvest to come. His brain gathers it. His hard brain like a safe stores it and locks it. And nothing moves.

In the morning, the fifty-year-old woman cooks sausages for him and shows him her dog trophies. Bob Sparrow is polite. He admires the ugly trophies and then, as he's leaving, asks without interest why she keeps the fish.

'Well,' she says, 'they're a feature. Tropical fish are a feature.'

'Do you know their origins?' asks Bob, and the woman shrugs.

'I don't think those ever had origins,' she says. 'Or they might have done. In fact, I think they did because they're tropical, pet. But I've forgotten. It's the kind of thing you just forget.'

On the Monday that follows Bob Sparrow's return is old John's funeral. Mary's face at the graveside is white and still.

A year or so from this date, Bob Sparrow buys a light aircraft and beneath its elegant fins sees, to his satisfaction, his land become small: a square.

La Plume de Mon Ami

On an April Thursday, Maundy Thursday in Gerald's Letts Diary, Gerald strolled in his city suit through the lunchtime crowds in Covent Garden and saw, through the window of an expensive shop, Robin buying knitwear. Until this moment – Robin, moving towards a full-length mirror with a beige and burgundy cardigan held tenderly against his shoulders, glances up, and his round blue eyes that haven't faded with time behold, through the artful display of home-knitted jerseys on wooden poles, Gerald looking in – Gerald and Robin hadn't met for twenty years. If they sometimes thought about each other, or had a dream in which the other appeared, or sent, on impulse, a Christmas card, they also knew that their friendship belonged too delicately to the past to survive the present or the future. They doubted they would ever meet again.

Gerald, at thirty-eight, was a tall, powerfully fashioned man, with a fleeting, blazing smile of touching emptiness. Robin, at forty-two, was neat-waisted, springy, very hesitantly balding, small. As they sighted each other, as if through an ancient, long-discarded pair of binoculars, both knew unerringly what the other would see: their separate mortality. Both felt, on the same instant, sweet sadness. Gerald smiled and walked into the shop. Robin, still holding to his chest the burgundy cardigan, moved neatly towards him and silently embraced him.

Because it was lunchtime and because, as Gerald neared forty, he had become an innocently gourmandising man, he prolonged this meeting with Robin by the space of a meal, during which they discussed – very gently, so as not to lay on this fugitive encounter a feeling of heaviness – the past. That

240

night, they went to their separate homes on different sides of London and began to remember it.

Gerald liked to remember things chronologically: cause and effect; beginning, middle and end. So he started by remembering the play – the Crowbourne school production of *Antony and Cleopatra*, in which he'd played an acclaimed Antony and in which at the last minute, because of the appendectomy of a dark-browed boy called Nigel Peverscombe, Robin had played a petulant Cleopatra. Hand in hand with his memories of his Crowbourne Antony went Gerald's memories of Palomina, his first woman.

Robin preferred to remember more selectively, starting with days, or even individual moments when he'd been happy or at least carefree, and only then proceeding, holding fast to the rim of his duvet in his dark and reassuring room, to those other times when he'd begun to see himself as a clown, a fool, a player in a tragedy even. He managed, however, a rueful smile. His life since that time hadn't been disagreeable. Certainly not tragic. Next term, he was taking over as Housemaster at Shelley, Crowbourne's premier house.

Gerald remembers staring, smiling as he bows, beyond the hot flood of the stage lights on their scaffolding, at the dark space above the heads of the audience, and feeling the future touch him lightly and beckon him out. School is over. He is eighteen and a man. Palomina is out there, applauding. Ahead is the summer. No child's beach holiday with his mother and father and his two baby sisters, but a journey this year, a man's adventure, two months of travel before the start of the Oxford term. He wants to applaud with the audience. Applaud his good fortune, his youthfulness, his potency. He wants to shout. 'Bravo!' cheer the Upper Sixth, sitting at the back. Gerald and Robin move forward, separating themselves from the rest of the cast. The clapping and stamping is thunderous. Gerald shivers with ecstasy and hope. He smiles his captivating smile. 'We did it,' Robin whispers. And Gerald's wellspring of optimism is turned to admiration and affection for Robin, the young teacher, his Oxford already in the past, producer of the play and, finally, its bravest star. '*You* did it, Robin,' he corrects.

He remembers nothing about the school after that night. Not the farewells, nor the packings of trunks, not even the last singing of the school song. It fell away from him and he cast it aside. It was strange for him to imagine, as he sat on the deck of the channel steamer with Robin and watched the English coast become thin and insubstantial, that Robin would be returning to Crowbourne in September. Why live through Oxford and get to know the proper world and then go back? I will never do this, he promises himself, I will never go back to Crowbourne except as the father of future Crowbournians. Robin will teach them and remember me. In his repetitious life it will be me, not my sons, who will count.

It's chilly on the boat, windy and grey. Near Dieppe, it gets rough and Gerald and Robin sit huddled up in their coats. Robin produces a hip flask of brandy. The silver mouth of the flask has a warm and bitter taste. They don't talk much.

At Dieppe, their legs unsteady after the long boat crossing, they lug their suitcases to the Paris train. This was before the days of backpacks and weightless, shiny bags. For two months, they carried those heavy cases around, re-labelling them for each new stage of the journey. They were scraped and scratched and dented and buffeted and sat on. Arriving back at Victoria, they seemed like the sad trophies of a battle. Gerald can't remember what became of his suitcase, but he remembers the look and feel of it in his cheap Paris room, opening it and laying out on the shiny coverlet a clean shirt and the kind of striped jacket that used to be called 'casual'. Men's clothes. He'd become a man. Now Robin would show him France. All the places he'd learned about he would see and touch, wearing his casual clothes. With Robin he walks out into the Paris night. Robin leads them unerringly to a noisy, whitely lit brasserie and advises Gerald, 'Have *pied de porc*. They know how to cook it here.' When the meal arrives, Gerald stares at the trotter on his plate and thinks, good, from now on I shall seek out the unfamiliar. That night, he has a dream he's snuffling for truffles.

Of course, says Robin to himself, as if in answer to a question, I remember Paris! We were in the *sixième*. The hotel proprietor wore an eyepatch. I had room No. 10. We didn't go into each other's rooms, but stood only on the thresholds. Paris was the threshold of the journey. Gerald wore clean, smart clothes that got dirtier as the summer went on. He seemed large in that French city. I was a better size for Paris. He was golden and greedy and loud. I disliked him, suddenly. He tried to make me get up early to take him to the Louvre, but I didn't want his enthusiasm for the pictures, I wanted to go on my own and spend some time with the Cézannes. I felt in need of foliage and quiet. I said, 'Go on your own, Gerald. I've seen the Louvre.' I walked in the Luxembourg Gardens where, every time I've been there, I seem to see a nun, and started writing my diary. I'd arranged to meet Gerald there and he came running at me, waving like a lunatic. I blushed for him. 'Leave me here,' I wanted to tell him, 'go on on your own.' But he sat down and began to chivvy me about – of all people – Rubens. 'I can't stand Rubens,' I told him. So he shut up and sighed and began to kick dusty pebbles like a boy. Yes, I disliked him then. Some nuns passed and he smiled at them. I started to write down 'N' in my diary for every nun I saw. I decided they were bad omens.

Another thing I didn't like about Gerald then was his piety. It was a false piety, born out of his successes at Crowbourne and his romantic love of the girl, Palomina. He displayed it, though, in all the grand churches, Notre Dame, the Sainte Chapelle, the Sacré Coeur. Of these three, only the Sainte Chapelle is quiet and the other two mill with tourists in ugly clothes, exhibiting their own brand of false piety by lighting candles for people far away. Watching them, I try to imagine the names of the people getting the candles. Over the years, the names have changed. Now, they're mainly Japanese: Kyoko, Nukki, Yami, Go. Then, twenty years ago, they were American: Candice, Wilbur, Nancy-Anne, Buck. They disgusted me.

Gerald's lighting of candles disgusted me. I was, then as now, a very unsentimental man. I saw several Ns in the three churches that day. Ns look as if they're always whispering to Jesus and I can't abide these private conversations. They could be talking to God about me.

Of our three nights in Paris, I prefer to remember the third. We are asked – a prearranged date – to dine with Monsieur and Madame de Bladis, friends of Gerald's parents. Gerald refers to these people as 'The Bladders'. Brushing our cuffs, shining our shoes with paper hankies, we take the Métro to Neuilly, where the Bladders have a *maison particulière*. 'She's rather fun,' Gerald tells me, 'she has a sense of humour.' And the thought flits into me like a bat: do riches alter the jokes you make, the things you laugh at? I feel poor on the stuffy Métro. For the first time since leaving England, I'm at peace with Gerald's size and air of wealth. I decide, on the morrow, to grow a beard. My first beard. I don't tell Gerald my decision. I'll let him notice it himself.

The de Bladis house is emphatically grand. Porcelain black-amoors hold on their turbaned heads a marble table in the hall. Madame de Bladis is chiffoned, pearled and rouged and sweeps down her cascading staircase like a dancer. She leads us to the roof, where there is a canopied garden, complete with a tiny fountain, the noise of which creates in my own bladder a perpetual yet not unexciting desire to piss. 'Gerald, Gerald,' she says in her soft French voice, 'you are getting so beautiful. Why don't we have a daughter to offer you?!' Gerald is quieter here, awed by the roof garden, very beautiful indeed. And it's to me, in his shyness of these people, that Gerald turns – for encouragement, for the right word in his hesitant A-level French, for confirmation of an idea or an opinion. I become the teacher again and the old intimacy we had for the weeks of the *Cleopatra* rehearsals and then lost as we arrived in France, returns. As Gerald's friend, I am made welcome. We are served *anguillettes* – a kind of minuscule eel I've never eaten before or since – as a first course. All along the roof, as the sky deepens, pink lanterns are lit. Above and between these, tilting back my happy head, I see the stars. 'Your friend is smiling,' says Madame de Bladis, 'I like this.'

Gerald remembers a feeling of admiration, of envy almost for Monsieur de Bladis. A bank to run, a sumptuous house to own, a pretty wife with a plump, high-sitting bosom to be deliciously unfaithful to – these earthly rewards could be worth striving for. I will, he decides, watching the plash-plash of the fountain, watching the gloved hands of the servant who brings a hot chocolate soufflé, try to make a success of things. Oxford and the Law. The route is straight. I'm on my marks. Yet there's a little time, such as now, sitting on a roof in Neuilly on a warm night, to be *savoured* before the race begins. Even Robin is allowing himself to savour this night. He's stopped feeling cross. He's started to enjoy himself. And tomorrow we go south, as far as the Loire.

'Ah,' says Robin, 'ah, yes, yes,' as we see, admirable and stately above the town, the Château de Blois. And I know that this little lisp of pleasure he lets sigh conceals his abundant knowledge of French and Italian architectural caprice, that he will guide me through the complexities of the building in the same delighted way he guided me through Shakespeare's verse. He's twenty-two. How has all this knowledge been crammed into him? I feel as empty of history as a willow bat. As Robin prances round the dark well of the François Ier staircase, he murmurs, 'Brabante, you see. Used by Il Boccadoro. Note the balustrade. Shallow relief ornamentation. Very Brabante.' And I want to mock him. 'Very Brabante, Robin? Really?' But I don't. I let him bound on, gazelle-like in his light-treading reverence for stone, and I am invaded with my longing for Palomina. I want her there and then on the staircase. Her pubic hair is lightly brown. I want to tangle my life in her little brown briar bush. I lean on the balustrade and look down into the sunshine. A couple below me seem small and I'm dizzy with my Palomina-lust. 'Gerald!' Robin calls sternly. 'Come on!'

The *pension* Robin has found near the station is poor. Outside my window is a vegetable garden where an old man works till dusk, hoeing and coughing and lighting thin cigarettes. His cough wakes me in the morning. The place has a cold, green-painted dining room where, for dinner, we're served a watery consommé followed by some lukewarm chicken. We don't dare ask for vegetables, though in the garden I've seen peas and beans and marrows, but a dish of these arrives long after we've eaten the chicken. '*Je m'excuse*,' says a thin, vacant-eyed waitress as she plonks the dish down. We eat the beans obediently and talk about money. We should economise on rooms, says Robin. All right, I say.

I've begun to worry about how, in all the weeks to come, I'll ever get my underpants washed. At school, you put out all your dirty clothes on your bed on a Friday morning and made a list of them and they were returned to you, washed and ironed, the following week. Who washed and ironed them exactly, or where, I'm not able to say. I've never washed any clothes myself ever in my life, though I've heard there's something called Tide you're supposed to use. Can one buy Tide in France, or is it called something else? '*Marée*', for instance? I sense, by the set of Robin's nostrils as he plans our next day's visit to Chambord, that he's become too unearthly for these kind of questions. But I rather love and admire his enthusiasm for buildings and feel pleased I asked him to come with me. I notice, in the cold light of the green dining room, that he's unshaven for the second day running. Is he, I wonder, going to model himself on more intrepid travellers than us? Scott, for instance? Or Alfred Russel Wallace? But I don't ask him this. We go to bed rather early, me to write to Palomina, he to write his diary.

> *Extract from Robin's Diary. 31st July 1964.*
> Ch. of Blois v. calming. Size has a tranq. effect on me. Renaiss. arch. seems so sure of itself, so sophisticatedly playful, nothing *mean* in it. Not hard to imag. my life in a turret.
>
> G's arms and face are getting quite brown from sitting about. I think there's a kind of impatience in him to get

south. I shall rein him back – he my horse, me his
chevalier!
This room is mournful.
Saw two NN at the Ch.
Chambord tomorrow, hooray.

Extract from Gerald's letter to Palomina. 31st July 1964.
My darling Palomina,
One week since I saw you. I miss you, my darling. Do
you miss me? I miss you so much. Please write Poste
Restante to Avignon or Nice.
I saw a fine Renaissance staircase today. I missed you
on it. Do you miss me on staircases?

At Chambord, Robin remembers, he was still in his carefree
time. After Blois and now here, he's becoming a François Ier
admirer. At Chambord, the great king had a river, the Cusson,
diverted to his castle's feet. Robin lies on the sunny grass,
eating bread and a carton of brawn salad, and imagines all the
everlasting things he would like to re-route towards his master's
cottage at Crowbourne: the Spanish steps, Michelangelo's
David, Cézanne's jungles, Dylan Thomas's house-high hay, the
golden vestments of Saladin. He's aware, with his face tipped
up to the blue sky, of the Loire valley as a kind of cradle where
he and the grand houses can quietly affirm their remoteness
from the modern, the discordant, the utilitarian and the
plebeian. Tiny orchids, wild as weeds, grow near his head. *Bliss.*
Order and beauty and grace. *Blissful.* He doesn't move.
Gerald gets up and struts around, taking photographs. Robin
thinks of the frail King Charles IX who would hunt in this park
for ten hours at a stretch and blow his hunting horn till his
throat bled. Gerald is daring like this with his limbs. In the
high-jump, he'd hurl his big body at the bar. 'Run, Gerald!'
Robin wants to call to him. He loves to see him run. But
he's gone off somewhere with his camera and Robin is
alone.
He's gone off, in fact, to try to buy a stamp for his letter to
Palomina. He thinks the little kiosk where they sell postcards

and slides might also sell him a stamp, or rather several stamps, because he plans to write to Palomina a lot. He's heavy with his Palomina-lust and writing to her assuages it. '*Ah non, Monsieur,*' snaps the kiosk woman, '*nous ne sommes pas un bureau de poste.*'

'*Pardonne . . .*' says Gerald, '*pardonnez-moi.*'

'*Allez!*' says the woman with a sniff. It's as if he'd asked for a French letter. He blushes.

Robin remembers the Avignon train. It's the Boulogne night train, but there are no sleepers, nor even any seats. It's crammed with Parisians going south, sitting wearily shoulder to shoulder, like in wartime. He and Gerald stand at a corridor window and as the darkness comes, they begin to sense the air getting warmer. They're lulled by the thought of a lavender sunrise in Provence. They lie down in the corridor with their heads on their suitcases and doze and all the shoulder-to-shoulder people lean and nod and pull down their blinds and a general tiredness overcomes the train.

The train stops several times, but no one seems to get on or off. Gerald seems to be sleeping soundly, enfolding his suitcase like a lover, his long legs in creased trousers heavy and still on the dirty floor. Robin takes an old cardigan he used to wear at Oxford out of his own case and covers Gerald's shoulders with this.

At six o'clock at Avignon-Fontcouverte, where the air is chilly and white with a dense mist, they stumble out, shivering, and follow the upright Parisians to a clean, new-seeming station restaurant serving croissants in their hundreds and large cups of coffee.

Now, tasting this good, hot coffee, they feel the traveller's awareness of deprivation and blessing, warmth after cold, shelter after storm. They don't talk, but each is privately happy. And they're south at last. Along the station platform, a hazy yellow sun disperses the mist and starts to glimmer on the plane trees. Gerald's hair is tousled, giving him a shaggy, unruly look that Robin finds disturbing. On his cheek is a pink blotch, where it's lain pressed against the suitcase lid.

Gerald remembers how they walked through suburbs where buildings were sparse then, past plumbers' yards and garages and a vast, empty hippodrome to the centre of the city, lugging the heavy cases. Buses passed them, taking people to work. Gerald suggested they should get on one of the buses, but Robin said no, he wanted air. So they walked till the city streets started to narrow round them and the Pope's Palace was there above them, then sat down at a pavement café and saw from the milling crowds and fluttering banners and flags that Avignon was in the middle of a festival. 'There'll be a problem with rooms,' Robin said, and in the hot sun Gerald felt tired and sleepy. Then he remembered that at the central post office there might be a letter from Palomina, and wanted to run to the letter and press the envelope against his nose, breathing in the translucent airmail sentences of his woman.

'I've got to go to the post office,' he said, getting up. 'I'll be back in half an hour.' And he darted away, leaving Robin sitting on his own with the luggage.

The room is shadowy, remembers Robin, in a kind of well of buildings which shoulder off the light. There's a double bed with a hard bolster and no pillows. The bedcoverings feel heavy and chill.

They're lucky to find the room. All the cheap places have *complet* signs up. This is the last vacant room in the last hotel . . .

On either side of the bed, back to back they lie in the early evening and try to sleep. Robin is acutely aware of Gerald's breathing. On a rusty washbasin near the bed stands an orange packet of Tide Gerald has bought. In the absence of any letter from Palomina with which to pass a secret hour before dinner, he's washed out all his underpants. They're hung on a rail at the side of the basin and drip steadily onto the lino floor. He's naked in the bed except for a short-sleeved T-shirt, and as well as his breathing Robin is aware of his firm, round buttocks very near to his own, and feels, for the first time since the night of *Cleopatra*, a fatal stab of desire. He buries his face in the bolster and forces himself to remember the dark, Italianate features of the girl Gerald loves, Palomina, four years older than him, staying *au pair* with Gerald's family, helping with the baby sisters. She's a plump girl, not beautiful, but wide-eyed and wayward-seeming, with a mane of brown frizzy hair. The antithesis of blond, handsome Gerald. Yet pious like him, probably, with an exaggerated, lying Catholic piety. Confessing after he fucks her.

The room's above a café in the tiny, hemmed-in square. At the window, Robin can hear swallows and the sound of tables being laid for dinner.

Extract from Gerald's letter to Palomina. 8th August 1964.
My dearest Palomina,

I've written to you almost every day. When we got here (to Avignon) I went straight to the PTT and God I was so miserable when there was no letter from you. It was so beastly, and I began to ask myself jealous questions: have you found another boy? Please reassure me, my darling, that you still love me. I feel like dying. This dying feeling is so horrible I think I must break my promise and visit you when you get to your parents' house on the 23rd. Please say I can. I'm in torment without your breasts.

Extract from Robin's Diary. 8th August 1964.
Prog. into Avig. is through draperies announcing a music and theatre festival. So no rooms of course. Boulevards choc-a-bloc with German youth. Thighs etc.

Tourists are teeming coarsefish. G. and I try to behave like surface feeders, Mayfly gourmets. This will be diffic. here. We're sharing a room, for reasons of econ. mainly. G. is washing his knickers in Tide.

Had a dream last night in the train corridor Aunt M. was dead. Hope she isn't. She's the only intell. woman my family produced.

Avig. teeming with NNs.

Lost count after 9. Bad sign.

NB. P. des Papes looks monolithic, just right for the Church, but wrong for me. Adieu la renaissance.

Gerald remembers waiting in Avignon for the letter that never came. Day after day, he goes to the central post office and says his name, Gerald Willoughby. *Je crois que vois avez une lettre pour moi, Gerald Willoughby.*

'Non,' they say, '*non, rien pour vous.*'

He dreads it then: *rien pour vous.* You have nothing, Gerald, *are* nothing without the embrace of Palomina.

The city is hot, choked, dusty. They follow the tourists in a line up the ramparts of the Pope's Palace. The wind brings gusts of litter. One night, they sit on planks to hear the voice of Gérard Philippe reciting Victor Hugo at a Son et Lumière performance, and the vast walls of the Palace are lit with strange violet light, behind which the sky seems violet and the bats like black musical notes, bodiless, flying to nowhere. They return penniless and sorrowful to their room. Robin's wallet has been stolen. They spend the next day telephoning Lloyds Bank and Thomas Cook and Robin's mother in Swindon and wait, with the letter that doesn't come, for money to be sent to them.

They walk out to the famous bridge, the Pont St Bénézet, and the Rhône is slow, majestic and green as the Amazon. Gerald remembers the blue of the Loire and feels the change in river colour to be one among very many confusions: Palomina's silence, the mood of sadness that seems to have settled on Robin, the feeling of heaviness this city imparts. For the first time since leaving England, he's lonely.

Robin spends hours at the Musée Calvet. He tries to perceive where, in the Daumier drawings, amid the torrent of lines, the artist has changed his mind. Unconsciously, he's seeking out the rage in the pictures, yet hoping to be calmed by them. He sits down very frequently on the hard banquettes and the image of Gerald's turned back in the bed comes unasked-for into his mind. And he looks round and sees Gerald some way off, staring at the paintings, but not *entering* them, as Robin does, just vacantly gazing, unmoved, untouched.

*

On the eighth day in Avignon replacement traveller's cheques arrive and Gerald re-packs his underpants which have dried stiff and powdery, not quite like they were in the days of the school laundry. 'I expect there's a knack to washing, is there?' he asks, as he examines the French writing on the Tide packet. Robin merely shrugs and touches his new beard, in which there seem to be little clusters of grey. It's only since the night of Son et Lumière that he's stopped answering all of Gerald's questions. Very often, the boy looks hurt.

The absence of an airmail letter from Palomina is hurting. All Gerald can think of now is getting to the central post office in Nice. He can *see* the letter in its little metal compartment. He can *see* Palomina's bunched-up continental writing. Yet the thought that Palomina has stopped loving him is giving him pains in his bowel. 'I feel strange,' he tells Robin, as they climb onto a hot, mid-afternoon train and sit down opposite two nuns, 'I feel weak.'

He leans his head against the burning glass of the train window and closes his eyes. The train's crowded with young people, German, Dutch, American. The seats opposite the nuns were the only two available. '*Milano!*' asks a big Italian with hairy thighs, as he pushes past with his rucksack. '*Non,*' says Robin.

The Italian looks distractedly up and down the train. A tin mug, strung onto a canvas loop of his haversack, almost bangs the wimple of the outer nun, who lowers her pale face and folds her arms. '*Questo treno. A Milano, non?*' the Italian asks the nuns. '*Nice!*' they whisper, in unison. '*Ah fucki shiti!*' he says, seizing a hank of springy hair, and pushes himself towards the door, arms held high, like a wader. Robin smiles, liking the horror on the faces of the Sisters. 'God!' says an American girl, 'wait till I tell Myrna I touched Gérard Philippe. She'll die!'

The train starts to move. Cool air comes in above Gerald's blond head. Gerald remembers, on this train, the feeling of becoming very ill. He remembers falling in and out of a deep and sickly sleep and dreaming of the sea. He remembers the nuns looking up at him under their pale brows. He remembers

Robin soaking his handkerchief with Evian water and giving this to him and, when it touches his head, feeling cold to his marrow. 'I'm sorry, Robin, so sorry...' he keeps repeating. And he walks past all the hot Dutch and German bodies to a foul-smelling toilet and shits his soul out into the stained pan. There's no paper in the lavatory. With shaky hands, Gerald pulls his wallet from the shorts that lie round his feet and wipes himself with two dry cleaners' tickets saying 2prs gr flannels and 1 blue blzr. His school clothes. Swilled away somewhere between Brignoles and Vidauban.

Over Nice, where they arrive towards six o'clock, rolls a gigantic thunderstorm. Outside the crowded station, the rain begins to teem and Gerald's enfeebled brain wants to cry for England and familiarity and shelter. He's forgotten the letter waiting for him at the central post office. He's incapable of Palomina-lust. He can barely walk. Sweat is running off him like the rain off the station roof. 'Stay here,' says Robin, sitting Gerald on a bench with the luggage. 'I'll go and find us a room.'

And he watches hopelessly as Robin darts out into the forecourt, where people mill and shout and wait for taxis and buses. NICE COTE D'AZUR says a white and blue sign, and Gerald remembers that they are, at last, by the sea. Yet the bench towards which his head soon falls and rests on smells of city soot. He puts a limp arm round the suitcases and longs for Robin to return.

It's dark by the time a Citroën taxi takes them into the *vieille ville*. The storm has moved inland and is hurtling far off, over the mountains. The sea's calm in the big bay, silvery in its glut of reflected light. 'What a show,' Gerald mumbles, 'Nice is.'

Their room is an attic. Robin remembers the pigeon's noisy existence on an iron window bar and the depths of quiet falling away below them into a courtyard. For most of his life, at least two or three times a year, in a dream, he's returned to this room with its view of gutters and chimney pots and balconies and washing. The hotel is called the Jean Bart. There's one lavatory every other floor. In the room below them an eighty-year-old Finnish woman struggles with the stairs. She tells Robin she's well known in her country for her translations of D. H. Lawrence. Robin feels light and happy among the roofs. Twice a day, he carries bouillon and bread up all the flights of dark steps to Gerald's bed. He and a pert maid tidy the room around their golden invalid, who is humble in his sufferings, cut down to size. For three days, Palomina isn't mentioned. At night, Robin and Gerald lie side by side in the dark and talk of going on into Italy. Robin writes a postcard to his mother in Swindon saying: Arr. Nice. Old Town v. congenial. Trust yr hip not playing up in hot weather. Blessings, Robin. Gerald sleeps. Robin unwinds the sellotape from the Tide packet and washes, with gentle attention, his patient's underwear and his own. He dries the clothes at the window where the male pigeons wear their showy tailfeathers like long kilts.

Gerald remembers his resurrection on the fourth day. He's standing in the PTT. The building has a vaulted roof like a church. It's cool and dark. An Irish girl is weeping and being comforted by a friend she addresses as Dilly. 'Oh Jesus, Dilly,' she sobs, 'oh Dilly, Dilly . . .' And a pale PTT employee snaps, '*Monsieur Willuffby?*' and slides a glass grille open and pushes towards Gerald an airmail letter.

That night, as Robin and Gerald sit on a pavement in the *vieux port* and eat red mullet and a brilliant sunset the colour of the mullet tails descends on the cloudless evening, Robin takes out his postcard to his mother and adds, in angry schoolmaster's red biro, PS. Weather here lousy. Gerald looks helplessly from Robin's card to the sky and sighs. It's intolerable, Robin, he wants to say.

The house of Palomina's parents in the hills behind Ajaccio is remembered entirely differently by Gerald and Robin, the smell of the *maquis* and of the eucalyptus trees being the one sweet, sad memory common to both. Robin remembers the unpleasant feeling of grit under his bare feet on the tiled floors. Gerald remembers gliding on these same floors like a silky ghost to Palomina's bedroom door. Robin remembers the

254

terror of finding himself, for the first time in his life, astride a horse. Gerald, on a bay mare, remembers the joy of it, and the blissful sight, not far in front of him, of Palomina's bikini-clad buttocks going up and down on her Mexican saddle. Robin remembers the feeling, in these hard hills, in the shadow of the granite mountains, of becoming soft, boneless, vulnerable, too easily crushed and bruised, the feeling of helpless flesh. Gerald remembers arranging his big body next to Palomina's in the sunshine and letting his eyes wander in the topmost pinnacles of rock, and thinking, I could climb those. With my bare hands and wearing only my football boots, I could master the Monte d'Oro.

The storms have gone north. Over all of Corsica shimmers the breathless heat that seems, in Robin's brain, to suspend time, to make every day long and blinding and purposeless, a month of empty sabbaths, everyone and everything monotonously sighing and humming and burning.

The house sits on a small hill, itself contained in a wider valley hemmed in by the mountains. Below the hill is a stream, torrential in winter, now slow but cold and clear and full of minnows. Each evening, Robin comes down here and lowers his hectic head into the water and opens his eyes and sees in the green river his own foolish lovesick feet planted on the sand. He wishes it was autumn. In the crisp beginning of the new school year, there was purpose and dignity. In his diary, which he can hardly bear to write during this futile time, he makes plans to abandon Gerald and go on into Italy on his own. His writing in the diary is so bad, the language so truncated, he has trouble, some years later, deciphering what he wrote.

Extracts from Robin's Diary. 24th August – 30th August 1964.
Miserab. arriv. G. so puffed up to see P. I cld wring his neck.

No car avail. So we're stuck in this idiotic 'ranch'. G. thinks he's Yul Brynner. Or worse.

G. gets me on a f. horse. Failure.
Lg to see some sights, even if it's only Napoleon's House.
Boredom.

P's mother, Jeanne, is an enig prd shallow persec
woman. You sense no one loves her. We lnch in Ajacc.
Then she show us the fam. tomb. Hideous. 4NN.

Alone today. G., P., and J. went riding. Allwd car. Saw
N's house. Dispp. One gd portrait by Gros. Also Chap.
Imp. Welcome brush with Renaiss. order. Coming out
into the sun again, wanted to die.

Mst get to Italy. Flor. Siena. La bella Toscana. Je souffre.
Je souffre. Dream again Aunt M. died. Buried her
behind some frescoes.

For Gerald, this valley contains like a casket the precious
possessions which are Palomina's ruby nipples, her amber arms.
His body is a slow avalanche of desire, engulfing, obliterating.
Palomina. Paradise. His blood enquires about nothing but the
act of love on Palomina's single bed at dawn, before her mother
is awake, before Robin comes sighing out of his dreams, before
the sun has fallen across the shiny rumps of the horses in their
dusty stables. He remembers a thin line of white six o'clock
light coming under the shutters. Day. Everything in this coming
day glitters with hope: the smile under the lipstick on the lips
of Palomina's mother; the sun on his knuckles as he eats his
breakfast melon; the silver of the shivery eucalyptus; the fatal,
alluring, far-off blue of the horizon. *I'm in paradise.* He wishes
that he was keeping a diary like Robin's, so that he could
record each new ecstasy.

He's sharing a room with Robin. In the room are twin beds,
covered with white Portuguese lace, a painted chest of drawers,
an oak wardrobe, a blue and yellow china lamp and a dusty bit
of rattan serving as a mat. This modest arrangement of furniture now contains the bountiful happiness of Gerald and the
silent misery of Robin. As a kind of poultice on his wound,
Robin remembers the room at the Jean Bart and the carrying

of broth and Gerald's sweet gratitude. 'I'd have died if it wasn't for you, Robin,' he said. Now, in Corsica, with these two dark, thick-browed women and Gerald's fair hair going pale as honey, Robin feels he's dying. Not precisely of love, but of his own foolishness. He can live without Gerald. What he can't seem to manage is to live with him and yet without him.

'I know,' he says one night to Gerald, 'you'd probably like to stay on here. But there's a ferry back to Nice tomorrow and I think I'll get on it and then press on to Italy like we planned.'

'On your own?'

'Yes.'

'Don't you like it here? You don't like Palomina, do you?'

'I just want to get to Italy.'

'Don't you love the mountains? You love the river, don't you?'

'They're all right.'

'You mean it's churches and paintings and things you miss? But you saw Napoleon's House, didn't you. You liked that.'

'I want to leave, Gerald.'

'But we agreed, Robin, we'd have this holiday together.'

'I know.'

'So you can't just desert me. And, listen, Palomina's father's arriving tomorrow. We'll get taken to more things. He's a big wheel. The Tomasini family are big wheels here.'

I should, said Robin to himself, twenty years later, have left the next day. Why didn't I leave? Why did I do what Gerald wanted?

Obediently, he puts on a clean shirt and trims his startling beard for the return of André Tomasini. This man, who has made a lot of money by Corsican standards, arrives in an ancient Chevrolet and is accompanied by four slender-hipped young men, wearing medallions. These men are embraced by Palomina like brothers. Tomasini is a small, cruel-faced man, whose authority seems to reside in his thin-tipped Roman nose. He greets Gerald and Robin unsmilingly ('oh, I see, my daughter invited you, did she?'), covers Palomina's face with intimate kisses and ignores his wife until she informs him that lunch is ready when he bangs her bottom like a dinner gong.

They sit down to the meal. Tomasini begins a lengthy, superstitious grace, invoking the name of '*notre ancêtre illustre, Letitzia Ramolini, mère de l'Empereur*'. What this had to do with the eating of *saucisson* and trout remains, to this day, a mystery to Gerald, part of all that he suddenly couldn't understand. Now, the house where he's lived in ecstasy is invaded with conversation and gesture and innuendo and private knowledge from which he's deliberately excluded. Outside, the light is as fierce, the crickets as noisy, the horses as elegantly restless as on all previous days, yet Gerald knows – in Tomasini's patriarchal behaviour, in the reverently lowered eyes of Palomina, in the withdrawal of Jeanne's friendly conversation – that his status is altered. No matter if Palomina works *au pair* in his family, here it's only the Corsicans who count. The strangers are inferior. Gerald looks helplessly at Robin, who is eating his trout primly, in utter silence. He refuses to catch Gerald's eye. His lowered and impassive face is, the boy supposes, still dreaming hopelessly of Florentine marble. Fleetingly, he envies Robin his detachment.

'Who,' says Tomasini, as the meal ends, 'is coming riding with me this evening? Palomina?'

'Yes, Papa.'

There are four horses. Two of the young men are invited. Gerald thinks of Palomina's bouncing bottom and her mane of brown hair and stares with dismay at his mess of trout bones. Palomina and the young men have started to giggle at some private joke. Then the afternoon unfolds: Tomasini takes his wife to bed; Palomina and the young men and Gerald go down to the river. While the others play like children and splash about, Gerald sits on his towel and feels too large, his skin too pale, his hopes too serious. Robin goes and lies down on the Portuguese lace. He can hear, on the other side of the wall, Tomasini's brief and ritualised exertions. With a kind of weariness, he tugs out his diary and writes: NNN. Negative. Null. Nothing.

The following morning, Gerald wakes as usual at dawn. In this valley, the importance of each unfolding day seems to fatten with the sunrise. He stands with his eyes narrowed to the crack in the shutters and is filled with his own longing. The house is silent. Towards midnight, the young men drove away in the Chevrolet. Robin sleeps. Gerald's tall, brown body is twenty-six paces from Palomina's bed. He wants, in the touch of Palomina's stubby hand, to be forgiven his jealousy and restored to favour. He feels old – at the very centre of his life. The boy who played Antony is far off, left behind in his silly paper armour. Antony the man is here, clenching and unclenching his man's fist. He pulls on his shorts, glances at Robin's face made gentle and sad by sleep, and goes out into the dark passage. The tiled floor is icy under his feet. He's afraid. He thought love was easy, just as Latin verse and cricket and the worship of God were easy. Until yesterday, he thought this.

He's at Palomina's door. He opens it as slowly, as silently as he can. On the other mornings, her room has been dark, darkness his ally, shaping the room softly round him as he slipped under the thin sheet. Today, light startles him. He stares, his eyes wide. Palomina sits on her bed eating a nectarine and smiles at him. Juice from the fruit wets her chin. Not far from the bed, sitting in a wicker chair, wearing a towelling robe, is André Tomasini. Gerald draws in a breath, begins to back out of the room.

'Come in, come in, Gerald!' Tomasini calls kindly.

He hesitates, his hand on the door. Palomina sucks her nectarine. 'Come in and sit down,' says Tomasini. Gerald moves into the room and looks blankly at the tableau of father and daughter. Palomina looks at him wistfully, but her eyes are hard. 'Sit down,' says Tomasini again. He perches on a hard chair, where some of Palomina's clothes are strewn, smelling of sun oil and her ripe body.

'Now,' says Tomasini, 'don't look so alarmed, Gerald. We're not barbarians here, you know, we're not *banditi* like you

259

English always suppose, but we like to get everything right for our families, you understand?'

'How do you mean, "right"?' says Gerald.

Palomina licks the nectarine stone. Tomasini lights a cigarette.

'My daughter is twenty-two,' says Tomasini. 'Do you think I want her to spend her life *au pair* in England?'

'No . . .'

'No. This is for learning a language, no more. She is twenty-two and she must have a future.'

'Of course she must . . .'

'Boys of eighteen do not marry.'

'I could – '

'No, no. Don't be silly. Boys of eighteen do not marry. Now, I think you have had some hospitality in this house from my wife, no?'

'Yes. Yes, we have . . .'

'Good. So you will tell your parents we made you welcome?'

'Yes . . .'

'Good. But this is enough. You understand?'

Gerald gapes. Palomina turns her head to the window. 'I think you understand,' says Tomasini, 'I think you're a clever boy, Gerald. I think you're going to do well at Oxford.'

'Sir, I – '

'And a boy who's going to do well at Oxford can understand what is being asked.'

'You want me to leave.'

'Of course. And your friend. You take the ferry today.'

Finding no words in him, Gerald merely nods. Palomina. Paradise. Over. She won't save him. He stares in silence at her as she puts down the nectarine stone and licks her fingers, one by one.

During the lunch in Covent Garden, Gerald said, lighting one of the cigarettes he was trying so hard to give up, 'I suppose our happiest time was after Corsica, in Italy.'

Robin, who didn't smoke, passed Gerald the ashtray. 'I've

always,' he said, 'loved Italy. I always will, I expect.' And he smiled across the table at his friend, to whom it was pointless to say, no, Italy was worse than anything. All you thought about was that stupid Palomina. Standing in front of the David, even right there, I could still see it in you, your silly longing. It marred everything we did.

'I go to Nice sometimes,' Robin said, taking a toothpick out of a white china jar. 'Once I went to look at the Jean Bart.'

'The what?'

'The Jean Bart. Our hotel.'

'Was that what it was called?'

'Yes. It's still there. Our room's still there. The room where you were ill, remember?'

'Oh that was an awful time, wasn't it! Poor you. You were so kind to me. I remember you used to have these dreams about an aunt or someone you thought had died.'

'Aunt Mabel. Yes. She had died. She died the day we arrived in Ajaccio.'

'Oh, I'm sorry, Robin.'

'Yes. She was lovely. She's buried in Tintagel.'

'Tintagel?' said Gerald, raising an arm to summon a waiter. 'Can't say I've ever been there. Time to get the bill, do you think?'

Wildtrack

Micky Stone, wearing camouflage, crouches in a Suffolk field, shielding his tape recorder from the first falling of snow. It's December. Micky Stone, who is approaching his fiftieth birthday, perfectly remembers touching his mother's fingers as she stood at the metal window of the cottage kitchen, watching snow fall. She was saying something. 'Isn't it quiet?' she was saying, but ten-year-old Micky was deaf and couldn't hear.

Now, in the field, holding the microphone just above his head, he hears the sounds it gathers: the cawing of rooks, the crackle of beech branches as the birds circle and return. He hears everything perfectly. When he looks down at the tape machine, he hears his head turning inside his anorak hood.

Seven operations there were. Mrs Stone, widowed at thirty-five, sat in the dark of the hospital nights and waited for her son to wake up and hear her say, 'It's all right.' And after the seventh operation she said, 'It's all right now, Micky,' and he heard. And sound entered his mind and astonished him. At twelve, he asked his mother: 'Who collects the sound of the trains and the sea and the traffic and the birds for the plays on the wireless?' And Mrs Stone, who loved the wireless plays and found in them a small solace in her widowhood, answered truthfully: 'I've never thought about it, Micky, but I expect someone goes out with a machine and collects them. I expect a man does.' And Micky nodded. 'I think I'll become that man,' he told her.

It was a job you travelled for. Your life was a scavenge-hunt. You had lists: abattoir, abbey, accordion, balloon ascent, barcarole, beaver and on and on through the alphabet of things living and wild and man-made that breathed or thumped or yodelled or burned or sang. It was a beautiful life, Micky thought. He pitied the millions who sat in rooms all their working days and had never heard a redshank or a bullfrog. Some people said to him, 'I bet it's a lonely life, just listening to things, Micky?' But he didn't agree and he thought it presumptuous of people to suggest this. The things he liked listening to least were words.

Yet Micky Stone had a kind of loneliness in him, a small one, growing bigger as he aged. It was connected to the feeling that there had been a better time than now, a short but perfect time, in fact, and that nothing in his life, not even his liking for his work, would ever match it. He remembers this now, as the sky above the field becomes heavy and dark with the snow yet to fall: the time of Harriet Cavanagh, he calls it, or in other words, the heyday.

Suffolk is a rich place for sound. Already, in four days, Micky Stone has collected half an hour of different winter birds. His scavenge list includes a working windmill, a small town market, a livestock auction and five minutes of sea. He's staying at a bed-and-breakfast in a small town not far from the cottage with the metal windows where he heard his first sounds. He's pleased to be near this place. Though the houses are smarter and the landscape emptier now, the familiar names on the signposts and the big openness of the sky give him a sense of things unaltered. It's not difficult, here, to remember the shy, secretive man he was at nineteen and to recreate in the narrow lanes the awesome sight of Harriet Cavanagh's ramrod back and neat beige bottom sitting on her pony. The thing he loved most about this girl was her deportment. He was a slouch, his mother often told him, a huddler. Harriet Cavanagh was as perfectly straight as a bamboo. And flying like a pennant from her head was her long, straight hair, the colour of cane. Micky Stone would crouch by the gate at the end of his mother's garden, close his eyes and wait for the first sound of the horse. It always trotted, never walked. Harriet Cavanagh was a person in a hurry, flying into her future. Then, as the clip-clop of the hooves told Micky that the vision was in sight, he'd open his eyes and lift his head and Harriet in her haste would hail him with her riding crop, 'Hi, Micky!' and pass on. She'd be out of sight very quickly, but Micky would stand and listen till the sound of the trotting pony had completely died away. When he told his mother that he was going to marry Harriet Cavanagh, she'd sniffed and said unkindly, 'Oh yes? And Princess Margaret Rose too, I dare say?' imagining that with these words she'd closed the matter. But the matter of Harriet Cavanagh didn't close. Ever. At fifty, with the winter lying silently about him, Micky Stone knows that it never will. As he packs his microphone away, the snow is falling densely and he hears himself hope that it will smother the fields and block the lanes and wall him up in its whiteness with his fabulous memories.

The next morning, as he brushes the snow from the windscreen of his car, he notices that the driver's side window has already been cleared of it – deliberately cleared, he imagines – as if someone had been peering in. Unlocking the door, he looks around at the quiet street of red Edwardian houses with white-painted gables on which the sun is now shining. It's empty of people, but the pavement is patterned with their footprints. They've passed and gone and it seems that one of them stopped and looked into Micky Stone's car.

He loads his equipment and drives out of the town. The roads are treacherous. He's looking forward to hearing the windmill when, a few miles out of the town, it occurs to Micky that this is one of the stillest days he can remember. Not so much as a breath of wind to turn the sails. He slows the car and thinks. He slows it to a stop and winds down the window and listens. The fields and hedgerows are icy, silent, glittering. On a day like this, Harriet Cavanagh once exclaimed as she passed the cottage gate, 'Gosh, it's beautiful, isn't it, Micky?' and the bit in the pony's mouth jingled as he sneezed and Micky noticed that the animal's coat was long and wondered if the winter would be hard.

Now he wonders what has become of the exact place by the

hawthorn hedge where he used to stand and wait for Harriet on her morning rides. His mother is long dead, but he suspects that the cottage will be there, the windows replaced, perhaps, the boring garden redesigned. So he decides, while waiting for an east wind, to drive to the cottage and ask its owners whether they would mind if he did a wildtrack of their lane.

It's not far. He remembers the way. Through the smart little village of Pensford Green where now, he notices, the line of brick cottages are painted loud, childish colours and only the snow on their roofs unifies them as a rural terrace, then past two fields of apple trees, and there's the lane. What he can't remember now as he approaches it is whether the lane belonged to the house. Certainly, in the time when he lived there no cars ever seemed to come up it, only the farmers sometimes and in autumn the apple pickers and Harriet Cavanagh of course, who seemed, from her lofty seat in the saddle, to own the whole county.

Micky Stone feels nervous as the lane unfolds. The little car slithers. The lane's much longer than he remembers and steeper. The car, lurching uphill, nudges the banks, slews round and stops. Micky restarts the engine, then hears the wheels spin, making deep grooves in the snow. He gets out, looking for something to put under the wheels. The snow's almost knee-deep and there are no tracks in it except those his car has made. Micky wonders if the present tenants of the cottage sense that they're marooned.

Then it occurs to him that he has the perfect excuse for visiting them: 'I took a wrong turning and my car's stuck. I wondered whether you could help me?' Then, while they fetch sacks and a shovel from the old black shed, he'll stand waiting by the gate, his feet planted on the exact spot which, thirty years ago, he thought of as hallowed ground.

So he puts on his boots and starts out on foot, deciding not to take his machine. The silence of the morning is astonishing. He passes a holly tree that he remembers. Its berries this year are abundant. His mother, tall above her slouch-back of a son, used to steal branches from this tree to lay along her Christmas mantelpiece.

The tree wasn't far from the cottage. As he rounds the next bend, Micky expects to see it: the gate, the hawthorn hedge, the graceless little house with its low door. Yet it isn't where he thought it would be. He stops and looks behind him, trying to remember how far they used to walk, carrying the holly boughs. Then he stands still and listens. Often the near presence of a house can be heard: a dog barking, the squeak of a child's swing. But there's nothing at all.

Micky walks on. On his right, soon, he sees a break in the hedge. He hurries the last paces to it and finds himself looking into an empty field. The field slopes away from the hedge, just as the garden used to slope away. Micky walks forward, sensing that there's grass, not plough under his feet and he knows that the house was here. It never belonged to them, of course. When his mother left, it returned to the farmer from whom she'd rented it for twelve years. She'd heard it was standing empty. It was before the time of the scramble for property. No one had thought of it as a thing of value.

Micky stands for a while where the gate used to be. On my mark, he thinks. Yet the altered landscape behind him robs it of familiarity. It's as if, in removing the house, someone has removed his younger self from the place where he used to stand.

No point in staying, he decides, so he walks slowly back past the holly tree to his car. He gets in, releases the handbrake and lets it slip gently backwards down its own tracks. At the bottom of the lane, he starts the engine, reverses out into the road and drives away.

In the afternoon, he goes down to the shingly beach. The sun's low and the wind coming off the sea strong enough to make the sleeves of his anorak flap. He crouches near a breakwater. He sets up his machine, tests for sound levels, then holds the microphone at the ocean. He remembers his instructions: 'With the sea recording, Micky, try to get gulls and any other seabirds.

And do plenty of selection, strong breakers close up, smaller splashing waves without much wind, and so on. Use your judgement.'

The scene his microphone is gathering is very beautiful. He wishes, for once, that he was gathering pictures as well as sound. The snow still lying high up on the beach and along the sea wall is almost violet-coloured in the descending afternoon. A film maker might wait months to capture this extraordinary light. Micky closes his eyes, forcing himself to concentrate on the sound only. When he opens them again, he sees a man standing still about thirty yards from him and staring at him.

Micky stays motionless, closes his eyes again, hears to his satisfaction gulls calling far off. When he opens his eyes once more, he sees that the man has come nearer, but is standing in the same attitude, intently watching Micky.

So Micky's thoughts return to the morning, to his discovery that someone had been peering into his car, then to his visit to the house which had gone, and he feels, not fear exactly, nor even suspicion, but a kind of troubled excitement and all the questions his mind has been asking for years about this place and the person he loved in it suddenly clamour in him for answers. He looks up at the stranger. He's a tall, straight-standing person. His hands are in the pockets of a long coat. In his stern look and in his straightness, he reminds Micky of Harriet Cavanagh's father, in the presence of whom Micky Stone felt acutely his own lack of height and the rounded disposition of his shoulders. But he tells himself that the fierce Major Cavanagh must now be an old man and this stranger is no more than forty-five, about the age Harriet herself would be.

Micky looks at his watch. He decides he will record three more minutes of sea and that then he will go over to the man and say what he now believes he's come here to do: 'I'm looking for Harriet Cavanagh. This may sound stupid. Are you in a position to help me?'

Then Micky turns away and tries to concentrate on the waves and the birds. He dreads speaking to the man because he was never any good at expressing himself. When Harriet Cavanagh said of the shiny white morning, 'Gosh, it's beautiful!' Micky was struck by her phrase like a whip and was speechless. Harriet had chosen a language that suited her: it was straight and direct and loud. Micky, huddled by his gate, knew that the dumbness of his first ten years had somehow lingered in his brain.

The three minutes seem long. The gulls circle and fight. Micky forces himself not to move a muscle. The sea breaks and is pulled back, rattling the shingle like coins, and breaks again. When Micky at last turns round, the man has gone.

On the edge of sleep, Micky hears the wind get up. Tomorrow, he will go to the windmill. He thinks, tonight I can hear my own loneliness like something inside me, turning.

Micky climbs up a broad ladder into the lower section of the mill. Its owner is a narrow-shouldered, rather frail-seeming man who seems excited and pleased to show Micky round.

'It's funny,' says the skinny man as he opens the trap door to the big working chamber, 'my Dad once thought of buying a windmill, but he wanted to chuck out all the machinery and turn the thing into a house. But I'd never do that. I think far too many of the old, useful things have vanished.'

Micky nods and they mount a shorter ladder and scramble through the trap into the ancient body of the mill. Light comes from a window below the ratchet wheel and from the pulley hatch, where the sacks of corn are wound up and the bags of milled flour lowered.

'We're only in use for part of the year,' says the owner, 'but we can lower the grinding wheel so that you can get the sound of it.'

Micky nods and walks to the window and looks down. Every few moments his view of the icy fields is slashed by the passing of one of the sails, but he likes the feeling of being high up for once, not crouching or hiding. And as he stares and the arms of the windmill pass and re-pass, he thinks, I must stand up tall now for what I want and what I have always wanted and still do not possess: the sound of Harriet Cavanagh's voice.

'All right, then?' asks the mill owner, disappointed by Micky's silence. 'I'll set the wheel, shall I?'

Micky turns, startled. 'Thank you,' he says. 'I'll set up in here. Then I'll do a few minutes outside.'

'Good,' says the mill owner, then adds, 'I like the radio plays. "The Theatre of the Mind" someone said it was called and I think that's a good description because the mind only needs sound to imagine entire places, entire situations. Isn't that right?'

'Well,' says Micky, 'yes, I think it is.'

It's dark by the time Micky gets back to his lodgings. As he goes in, he can smell the meal his landlady is preparing, but he doesn't feel hungry, he's too anxious about what he's going to do. He's going to telephone the big house where Harriet lived until she married and went to live in the West Country. Though Major Cavanagh and his wife will be old, Micky senses that people who live comfortably live long and he feels certain that when the receiver is picked up it will be one of them who answers. And he knows exactly what he will say, he's prepared it. 'You won't remember me, Major, but I'm an old friend of Harriet's and would very much like to get in touch . . .'

There's a payphone near the draughty front door af the guest house. Micky arranges 10p coins in a pile on top of it and searches in the local directory for the number. It's there as he expected. Cavanagh, Major C.N.H., High House, Matchford.

He takes a deep breath. His landlady has a television in her kitchen and music and laughter from a comedy show are blaring out. Micky presses the receiver tight to his ear and tries to shut out the noise. He dials the number. He hears it ring six times before it's picked up and a voice he remembers as Mrs Cavanagh's says graciously, 'Matchford two one five.'

'Mrs Cavanagh,' Micky begins, after pressing in the first of the coins, 'you won't remember me, but – '

'This isn't Mrs Cavanagh,' says the voice. 'Will you hold on and I'll get her.'

'Harriet?' says Micky.

There's a pause. Micky reaches out and holds on tightly to the top of the payphone box.

'Yes. Who is this?'

'Micky Stone.'

Another pause. The laughter from the landlady's TV is raucous.

'Sorry. Who?'

'Micky Stone. You probably won't remember me. I used to live with my mother in Slate Cottage.'

'Oh yes. I remember you. Micky Stone. Gosh.'

'I didn't think you'd be here, Harriet. I was going to ask where you were so that I could ring you up and talk to you.'

'Were you? Heavens. What about?'

Another burst of laughter comes out of the kitchen. Micky covers his left ear with his hand. 'I hadn't planned what about. About the old days, or something. About your pony.'

'Golly yes. I remember. You used to stand at the gate . . .'

'Wait!' says Micky. 'Can you wait a moment? Can you hang on?'

'Yes. All right. Why?'

'Hang on, please, Harriet. I'll only be a minute.' Micky feeds another 10p coin into the pay slot, then runs as fast as he can up the stairs to his room. He grabs the tape machine and the microphone and hurtles down again. His landlady opens her kitchen door and stares as he rushes past. He picks up the telephone. The recorder is on and turning, the little mike held against Micky's head.

'Harriet? Are you still there?'

A pause. Micky hears the door of the kitchen close.

'Yes.'

'So you remember me at the gate?'

'Yes . . .'

'I once helped whitewash your stables and the dairy . . .'

'Yes. Lucky.'

'What?'

'Lucky. My little horse. He was called Lucky. My children have got ponies now, but they don't awfully care about them. Not like I cared about Lucky.'

'You rode so well.'

'Did I? Yes. I loved that, the early morning rides. Getting up in the dark. It was quite a long way to your lane. I think it'd usually be light, wouldn't it, by the time I came up there? And I'd be boiling by that time, even in snowy weather. Terribly hot, but awfully happy. And I remember, if you weren't there sometimes, if you were working or having breakfast or something, I used to think it was rather a bad omen. I was so superstitious, I used to think the day would go badly or Lucky would throw me, or Mummy would be cross or something, and quite often it went like that – things did go wrong if I hadn't seen you. Isn't that stupid? I'd forgotten all that till I spoke to you, but that's exactly how it was. I suppose you could say you were my good luck charm. And actually, I've often thought about you and wondered how you'd got on. I was rather sad when they demolished Slate Cottage. Did you know they had? I remember thinking every bit of one's life has kind of *landmarks* and Slate Cottage was definitely a landmark for me and I don't like it that it's not there any more. But you knew it had gone, did you?'

'Not till today . . .'

'Oh, it went years ago. Like lots of things. Like Lucky and the morning rides. Horrid, I think. I hate it when things are over. My marriage is over. That's why I'm staying here. So sad and horrid it's all been. It just makes me think – jolly stupidly, because I know one can never bring time back – but it does make me see that those days when I was growing up and you were my lucky charm were important. What I mean is, they were good.'

Lying in bed, Micky waits till the house is quiet. Outside his window, the snow is falling again. When he switches on the recorder and listens to Harriet's voice, he realises for the first time that he forgot to put in a new tape and that most of his work at the windmill is now obliterated. About a minute of it remains, however. As Harriet Cavanagh fades to silence, her words are replaced by the sound of the big sails going round and round.

The Kite Flyer

In my captors' glossless eyes do I see
an enviousness of the lustre in mine own.

— *from the Prison Treatise of Anna of Didsmill 1643*

Very often, when Olivia Kingswell spoke encouragingly or chidingly to herself, she addressed herself as 'my dear'. 'Pick up the pieces, my dear.' 'Don't make a spectacle of yourself, my dear.'

Then, on a certain day, a Sunday in early summer, she decided to break this habit. 'You are Olivia,' she told her bulgy blue eyes in the hall mirror, 'it's as simple as that.' And she felt amazed, as she went to the kitchen to baste the Sunday joint, that she'd been so polite, so over-polite to herself for so long. 'It's ridiculous!' she sniffed.

On the same Sunday, her husband, Anthony Kingswell, as he sat and waited for his beef and potatoes, felt cold. The coal scuttle in the sitting room was empty. He took it out to the coal bunker and filled it up, fetched dry kindling from the woodshed and made a fire. It was May. The light coming in to the Kingswells' sitting room was so glaring that the colours of Anthony's fire looked feeble. He knelt over it, holding out his hands.

Olivia, her apron on, her nose pink from the hot kitchen, came in. She had the carriage of a Great Dane, Anthony thought, stately but bounding. Today, on his knees, he felt small beside his wife.

'Darling,' she said, 'what are you doing?'

273

'Trying to warm up,' he said.

'It's *May*,' said Olivia.

'I know it's May,' said Anthony.

Sunday was usually the day when Anthony Kingswell felt warmest, happiest and most close to God.

For nine years, as Vicar of the Church of St Barnabas, Didsmill, he had thought of Sunday as 'belonging' to him. This wasn't arrogance, it was simply a reaffirmation, as the Church years succeeded one another, that he had chosen the right profession. Walking, in early light, from the vicarage gate to the vestry door, smelling damp yew, touching the iron cold of the latch, he would feel God slumbering in his blood. Then, robing for Communion, as old Tom Willis tugged out with leathery hands a funereal clang from the bell, his cheeks would start to become rosy with Jesus, his fingernails pink and shiny with Jesus, and at his throat would wait the syllables of praise and thanksgiving for the knowledge that God was now wide awake in his body. Even in the depths of winter, Anthony was warm on Sundays. He could have given January sermons in his underwear. He'd look out at his meagre congregation, hunched up in overcoats and scarves and woolly hats and think, poor things, I hold up the chalice to their lips and they sip, and yet they're chilly. What a sad coldness this must be.

Now, on this Sunday in May, the second Sunday before Whitsun, here was Anthony lighting a fire and kneeling in front of it and shivering. He knew it had been growing in him for some weeks, this awful feeling of being cold. In the same way, Olivia's awareness that she had been too polite, too evasive a person had been growing in her for about the same number of weeks, though neither Olivia nor Anthony could have said for precisely how long. However, these things were happening: God was slipping out of Anthony's veins, Olivia had learned the rightness, the sternness and the beauty, even, of her Christian name.

Though she was a conscientious vicar's wife – efficient at fund-raising, gentle-voiced, an enthusiastic maker of bramble jelly –

Olivia had never been very curious about faith. She saw it as something Anthony possessed and always would, and which she didn't and never would, like a penis. It neither worried her, nor made her envious. What she had acknowledged – until recently, until she made one of the great discoveries of her life – was that her life lacked purpose. She would sit at Matins and watch her husband mount his pulpit, and know that Anthony and the Church of England were like the desert traveller and his camel, self-sufficient in the midst of emptiness, going patiently on from one small oasis to another. Olivia never yearned for her own camel. She got on with the years. One of the things she loved most about life was discovering the past. She often felt that without her local library she would have been a rather morose woman, but history made her excitable. And then, quite by chance, among the red and green and brown spines of the seventeenth century, she discovered Anna of Didsmill.

One of the questions never asked by those later involved in the 'case' of Anthony and Olivia Kingswell was 'Why did Anna of Didsmill inspire Olivia in the way she did?' The answer (or at least *part* of the answer) lay in the fact that Anna was not only a martyr to her cause and a woman of action, she was also the eldest daughter of a country schoolmaster (as was Olivia), she was born on 16th July, 1620 (exactly three hundred and fourteen years to the day before Olivia), and is known, in prison, to have asked her captors for a dish of greengages, Olivia's favourite fruit. Thus, it was immediately clear to Olivia that she shared much 'common ground' with Anna. Part of this 'common ground' was the actual earth on which they both walked – the lanes, the fields of Didsmill. As Olivia's hands turned the pages of Anna's history, they trembled.

To summarise for those who do not know of her, Anna of Didsmill was born into a moderately poor Puritan family five years before the accession of Charles I. At the age of twenty-two, shepherding her father's flock of pupils into the school yard one August morning in 1642, Anna heard the voice of her stern God coming out of the school-house weathercock. The voice told her to emulate the Maid of Orleans, to don a soldier's uniform and help bring victory to the Protestant cause against the King.

That same night, wearing her brother's clothes, she rode secretly to Fenny Stratford, where Cromwell was camped, and two months later she was fighting with his army at Edge Hill. During the battle, she fell from her horse and was captured by the Royalists. In prison, her identity as a woman was quickly revealed. She was abused by her guards, raped and tortured. She was tried for treason, found guilty and hung at Didsmill gibbet. While in prison, she wrote (and smuggled out) a treatise on the wrongs she had suffered at the hands of men, exemplifying all the evils and degradations society metes out to women. Thus, she was both a woman of action and a reformer. Yet historians had neglected her. She languished in Olivia's library in one small book. Olivia rescued her. She gave a talk to the Didsmill and Didsborn WI about her. She discovered the cottage where she'd lived and the site of the old schoolhouse (burned down in 1805) where she heard God's voice. Slowly, yet persuasively, Anna was entering Olivia's mind. And one day, Olivia walked on the downland where the gibbet had once stood. She knew there would be no trace of it. On the exact spot where Anna of Didsmill had died, there was an aircraft hangar and the land for six miles around it was a criss-cross of runways and concrete barracks. It was an American airbase. It was rumoured that missile silos were going to be built here.

Olivia put her hands up to the perimeter fence and imagined that this woman of long ago spoke to her in the sighing of the wire: 'Do what you can,' the voice said kindly.

If it was quite easy, then, to understand why Olivia Kingswell found a new direction of her life through her discovery of Anna of Didsmill, it was much more difficult to determine (and remember, these two events went on simultaneously) why Anthony Kingswell began to lose his faith.

On this May Sunday, when he lit his feeble fire, Anthony was fifty-four years old and had held his faith in a forgiving and accessible God for more than twenty years. He had entered the Church at the age of thirty-three, the age of Christ's death. (He liked the events of his life to reverberate.) He had never regretted it. He had always imagined his faith would last him out. God was tangible to Anthony. When he snuffled on his pipe, he felt God in the embers and in his saliva. When he dreamed about his boyhood, he saw God in that space of bony flesh between the hem of his flannel shorts and the turnover of his grey socks.

You might suggest that, because he was a man who felt God to be so much a part of the physical world, he was bound to feel the presence of God diminishing as his middle age advanced. Though a good preacher, he wasn't a truly spiritual man. His faith was instinctive, not cerebral. And this fact seemed, in part, to explain what was happening. For some reason, his mind, his rational self had started to question, or at least to worry about, the existence of God. Being the man he was, he sought to reassure himself by finding God in His usual places – in his pipe embers, in the dry, sweet smell of the altar rail, in the vicarage garden, and most of all in his own blood. So, when he found that he felt cold, it was natural that he also felt afraid.

The vicarage, where Anthony and Olivia had lived for nine years, was a solid, Victorian, well-ordered house. Olivia managed it well, yet inhabited it lightly, keeping a careful distance from Anthony's study, which, as visiting parishoners usually sensed, was the only 'serious' room in the house. It had never been suggested that Olivia might occupy a 'serious' room of her own. 'For what?' Anthony would have asked. 'To write the WI Newsletter in?'

But then, after Olivia had discovered Anna, she began to have a recurring dream in which she walked aimlessly through her house, topping up the flower water, polishing coasters, plumping cushions, readying each room for someone else, always for someone else, till her own presence in the house became as faded as chintz and the rooms were like lazy strangers, just sitting about, offering nothing. So she turned a guest room into her 'serious' room. She removed the bed. She bought a cheap desk, a filing cabinet and a worklamp. Bookshelves were put up. She took down the chintz at the window. She put *A Life of Anna of Didsmill*, alone as yet, in place on the new bookshelves.

Anthony came and stared at these changes and stared at Olivia and pulled his cardigan closer round his body.

'What's it all for?' he asked.

'My work,' she said lightly.

'You've got no curtains, Olivia,' was his only comment.

Her 'work' progressed faster than she'd imagined. Making constant trips to her library and inspirational demands upon the chief librarian's time, she discovered numerous references to Anna in detailed histories of the Civil War. One of these books mentioned that Anna's prison Treatise (or what remained of it) was kept in the Bodleian Library. Two days after learning this, Olivia was in Oxford, holding twenty-three yellowed and stained pages of Anna's words in her hands. She felt, as they were unlocked from a glass case and handed to her, as if she were about to faint. She sat down and ate a peppermint. A research assistant brought her a magnifying glass.

It was early June now. While Olivia was away, Anthony wrote to his friend, Canon Stapleton in Winchester, whose footsteps into the Church he'd once followed. 'I feel,' he said in the letter, 'as if the great bird that is the Trinity, its warm body and its two protecting wings have flown away and left me.' He thought that writing these words to Canon Stapleton might comfort him, but it didn't. He got up from his writing desk and walked, his face set hard, up to Olivia's study. He stood at the door. One shelf was almost filled with books now. Anthony stared and stared. His wife's endeavours filled him with dread. He wanted to scrumple up the papers that now littered the desk and hurl them out of the window into the June wind.

*

Unluckily for Anthony, this particular summer was cool. Sunlight on the garden, particularly sunlight on the grey-green poplar leaves, shivering, flashing, he imagined as 'God's currency'. He loved to sit in a comfortable chair, his eyes two thin slits just open on this glory. But, in June, there didn't seem to be many glorious days. The sky was moody. Anthony looked up at the sunless blanket and said, 'Why, oh my Redeemer, have you hidden your coinage from your servant?' Then he glanced at the window of Olivia's study, wide open. She worked on, oblivious of weather. She had a title for an article, she told Anthony: *Anna of Didsmill, A Heroine for Today*. If the article was published, she would try to gather enough material for a book. When she talked about these things her bulgy eyes were wide, like a child's eyes open on her first sight of the sea. And Anthony shuddered. How well he recognised that shining light. He had grown used to finding it, many times a week, in his own face in the mirror. '*I* used to be the one!' he wanted to say to his wife. 'I should be the one!'

It was Monday. Anthony walked in from the garden. On Monday evenings Anthony always held a 'surgery' for his parishoners. Today, the thought of the surgery appalled him. He needed to receive advice, not give it.

He poured himself a glass of sherry and sat down in the sitting room. He held his glass up to the light, and stared at the liquid. One of his most secret ways of finding God was in sherry. He lit his pipe, warming his hands on the bowl. The warm pipe, the cold, strong sherry, he calmed himself with these, filling and refilling his glass and muttering peculiar prayers as, upstairs, Olivia worked on.

Not long after this Monday (Anthony had been too ill with his sherry drinking to hold his surgery and the people who came talked to Olivia instead), Olivia declared that Anna had 'instructed' her to make a trip to Greenham Common.

Anthony stared at his wife.

'No, Olivia,' he said.

She stared back at him. Colossal she seemed. A warrior. She's becoming a man, Anthony thought.

'I'm sorry, Anthony darling,' she said, 'I'm just *telling* you that I am going to Greenham on my birthday, July 16th. I am not asking for permission.'

'I can't have it,' said Anthony, 'a vicar's wife simply must not take part in this kind of political antic.'

'It's not an antic,' said Olivia, 'and anyway, churchmen and politicians are more closely linked over the question of peace than over any other, as you yourself should be aware.'

And she strode out of the kitchen where they had been eating supper and bounded upstairs to her study. Anthony heard the key turn in the lock, got up from the table, went to the Welsh dresser which, since Olivia's mother's death in 1971, had proudly displayed a Wedgwood dinner service, took down five plates and a gravy boat and smashed them on the stone floor. Olivia did not come down. He took up two more plates and hurled them at the chimneybreast. Olivia unlocked her door, ran down the stairs and into the kitchen and hit her husband in the face. He sat down among the broken china and started to cry. Olivia stared at him, disgusted. Children! she thought scornfully. Men are *children*! But then, he reached out for her hands and held them to his face. 'Help me, Olivia,' he sobbed. 'I'm losing Jesus.'

Olivia postponed the trip to Greenham. Instead, Canon Stapleton (whose reply to Anthony's Trinity letter had been vague and dismissive) was persuaded by Olivia to come and stay with them. The weather brightened in July, and Anthony and Canon Stapleton went for long walks in the Didsmill beech-woods. 'Something,' said Stapleton to Anthony, 'has made you angry with God. That's all. You're angry with Him and through your anger you've lost Him. If you can remember *why* you're angry with Him, then you'll be able to forgive Him and beg His forgiveness and you will find him again. Tiffs with God are more normal than you imagine.'

On they walked, under the green fanlights of beech, and Anthony listened and felt hope revive. But, search as he tried, he simply couldn't remember why he was angry with God. He knew why he was angry with Olivia, but he couldn't remember why he was angry with God, or even if he was angry, and after some days, Canon Stapleton had to return to Winchester and at his departure Anthony felt invaded by despair.

That same day, Olivia's outline for her article was accepted by *History in Perspective*, a monthly history magazine. As Olivia showed Anthony the letter, her eyes were luminous with joy. He stared morosely past her, so envious of her happiness he couldn't utter. She smiled. She crowed. 'I'm determined there'll be a book,' she said.

'Beware of pride,' he muttered and handed her back the letter. A look of disbelief crossed her face. 'Anthony,' she said breathlessly, 'this quarrel of yours with God, please don't turn it into a quarrel with me!'

You might say that the events described so far represented the 'first stage' in the odd case of Anthony and Olivia Kingswell. From this point, they entered the 'second stage' or 'second act', if you like, of what some would later describe as a tragedy.

The second stage really began that night when, lying in the dark beside his wife, Anthony Kingswell stumbled on the notion that it was Olivia who was responsible for God's withdrawal from him, that it was Olivia who, by seeking to change the natural order of things with her wretched Martyr of Didsmill, was deflecting God away from him and towards herself.

This was a strangely irrational decision for Anthony to come to. No one knew better than Anthony that Olivia's faith was, at best, peripheral to her life. She'd always been happy to let him be the believer and had certainly never shown any sign of wanting to get closer to God than she already was. This, however, Anthony decided as he lay and looked at his wife's sleeping body, must have been a deliberate deception. She must have been envious of his faith for years and waited, waited for her chance to deflect it . . .

Without waking Olivia, Anthony got out of bed and went down to his study. Outside the window, he could hear the cry of a nightingale and he felt more at peace, more assuaged than he'd felt for months. He reached for his bible and turned to the *Epistle of Paul to the Ephesians*, Chapter 5, verse 24: . . . *as the Church is subject unto Christ, so let the wives be to their own husbands in every thing.*

Then, in his neat and rather beautiful writing, he wrote out these words on a card, tiptoed to the kitchen and propped the card up on the Welsh dresser in the exact place where the gravy boat used to stand. He breathed deeply. He could sense, through the Venetian blind, the approach of dawn and he knelt and prayed: 'In the coming of morning let me feel you again, my true and only God. Like a lover who runs to the shore as the sails of his beloved are glimpsed on the horizon, let me run to meet you in the sunrise and find you there.' He stayed in his attitude of prayer, with his chin on the kitchen table, till he could feel the room fill with soft, yellowy light. Olivia, in her dressing-gown, found him like this and touched his head gently. 'Come back to bed, Anthony. It's only half past five,' she said. And he opened his eyes. It seemed to him that in the split second before Olivia touched him, he had felt it near him, waiting, the Holy Spirit. In another moment, as the kitchen filled with the dawn, it would have entered him.

'You prevented it!' he cried, and turned upwards to his wife a face of stone.

Not long after this, Olivia went to Greenham.

Courage in the midst of desolation had always moved her. She had remembered all her life a story her school-master father had told her about a tribe of American Indians called the Ram Tiku, whose sacred valley had been destroyed by lumberjacks. Generations of these Indians, living now on dry, difficult earth, sent their braves in to reclaim the valley, until there were no young men left and the valley became a shrine in the mind, not a place anyone could remember. The perseverance of the Greenham women reminded Olivia of the perseverance of the Ram Tiku. The American soldiers had the tough, beefy faces of lumberjacks. The women's 'benders' were like polythene tepees. And life – such as it could be there – congregated round little fires. Drinking Bovril, Olivia told a group of young women (some of their faces were like the painted faces of braves) the story of Anna of Didsmill. They listened eagerly. 'Didsmill,' said a stern-browed woman called Josie, 'we must start thinking about Didsmill. Next year they're building silos there.'

The group round Olivia grew. Someone gave her a helping of bean stew on a plastic plate.

'You know,' said Olivia, 'if Anna had been on the side of the King, as Joan of Arc was on the side of her King, she would have become a heroine, a saint perhaps. It's what side you're on that matters. I've understood this now.'

There was rueful laughter. Olivia looked round at the squatting women spooning up their stew. 'Forgive me,' she wanted to say to them. 'Forgive me my sheltered life. It's going to change.'

'I would really like,' she said at length, looking round at the camp, with its mud and its urban litter, 'to help begin something at Didsmill. I think it's going to become an important place.'

It was a warm but windy day. On the Didsmill downland the wind was fierce as Anthony came out of the vicarage, hurled his home-made kite into the car and drove fast to the rolling hills above the Didsmill base.

Here, he got out and threw his head back and imagined, under the white bellies of the clouds, the earth turning. He felt a sudden lightness. His spirits lifted. He gathered up his kite and started to run with it, playing the string out behind him. It was an insubstantial thing and it began to lift almost at once. Anthony stopped running and held the taut line. He'd made kites since he was a boy, dragon kites, aeroplane kites, seagull kites. He knew how to handle them. And today's wind was perfect. The kite was white and he watched it turn and dance, turn and dance, then stream off higher, tearing at the string. He ran with it again. It was almost at the limit of the strong nylon line now and Anthony felt weightless, so full of the spirit of the kite he almost believed he could follow it aloft, up and up into the fathomless blue . . . And then he saw what he hoped would happen: half a mile above him, the kite began to break up. The white paper sheets were torn from the fragile frame and came flying down to earth like a scatter of leaves. Anthony watched them fall, the twenty-three white pages of Olivia's article, he watched them scatter and tear and go flying off over the curves of the hill. The kite string was limp in his hand and he was breathing hard. 'Beautiful . . .' he murmured. And he knelt.

So she returned from Greenham to find her article (of which she had made no duplicate) gone.

'Where is it, Anthony?' she said, patiently.

'On the downs,' he said from the depths of his pillows.

Returning from the kite flying, he had lain down exhausted on his bed and slept, and when he woke the exhaustion was still there and he slept again, and now he felt entombed in the bed and couldn't move. He was pale and his eyes were hectic. He's going mad, Olivia thought.

He lay and stared at his room. He thought of autumn coming and then winter and he knew that his soul was filling up with ice. But it was clear to him now: the light he saw in Olivia's eyes was *his* light. She had stolen it. It was God's light and it belonged to him. Without it, he would grow colder and colder. On the windy down, destroying her article, he had stolen some of it back. For a few moments, it had warmed him. But it hadn't lasted. And here was Olivia, strong as a stag beside his bed.

'I'll write it again, you know,' she said through hard, set lips and she turned and bounded from the room. His door slammed. She was without sympathy for him.

He didn't speak to her for two days and she didn't speak to him. He stayed in bed. She worked in her room. She fed him frozen pies and jelly on smeared trays she hadn't bothered to wipe. On the third day, he left her. Weak and grey, he put a small suitcase in the car and drove to Winchester, where Canon

Stapleton took him in. 'All I can advise,' said Canon Stapleton, 'is some time in retreat.'

So Anthony entered Muir Priory. He was given a tiny, white room with a narrow, uncurtained window. On one of the walls was an ivory crucifix.

The second draft of Olivia's article was completed in ten days and she knew it was better than the first.

September came, dry, windy and bright. Olivia typed out the article (careful, this time, to keep a copy of it) and sent it off to *History in Perspective* and waited. While waiting, she wrote to the Greenham woman, Josie, and asked if she would come and stay with her, 'to make concrete plans for something at Didsmill'.

When she thought about Anthony, she felt cross with God. He could be so spiteful, this supposedly loving Deity. It was mean of Him to have withdrawn from Anthony's spittle. But she was aware that, among these thoughts, crouched her knowledge of her own withdrawal from her husband. He had always preferred God to her and she'd always accepted this. God was, as she'd so often imagined during Matins, Anthony's camel; she was simply the mat, frayed by desert winds, on which the rider had lain. Now, she was tired of being a mat and she folded it away. The camel lay buried in an eternity of sand. The rider was hungry, lost. The nights were cold. Olivia felt wistful, yet unmoved. She tore the card on the dresser into pieces, made up her bed with clean sheets that held no trace of the smell of Anthony. Let the men heal each other, she thought.

The vicarage, without Anthony, was very quiet. Olivia filled it with bowls of greengages and with whispered conversations to Anna. 'Anna,' she said, making sandwiches for the visit of the temporary vicar, 'I am fifty-one.'

The temporary vicar was a fat, pasty man. 'I suffer from acidity,' he said as he ate Olivia's tea.

'You know,' Olivia heard herself reply, 'I don't think I'm interested in symptoms any more, only in causes.'

The vicar belched and smiled. 'Well,' he said, wiping his mouth with his napkin, 'fishpaste is one.'

When he left, Olivia knew how glad she was to be alone. She got out the Ordnance Survey map and calculated the distance from Greenham to Didsmill. It was twenty-three miles. Anna was twenty-three when she was hung. Twenty-three pages of her treatise remained. While in prison, she wrote to her mother and father twenty-three times, asking for forgiveness.

Then Josie arrived. She was very tired and dirty. Olivia, gentle as a mother, ran a deep bath for her in the big, old-fashioned bath, put her to bed and brought her supper on a clean tray.

In Muir Priory, away from his parish and its responsibilities, away from Olivia, Anthony began to feel calmer.

Dean Neville Scales, warden of the Priory, was a long-limbed man with a passion for gardening. He liked to preach about God in Nature. He made sure that the Priory gardens were colourful and neat, his pride and joy being a grove of Japanese acers, scarlet and gold and purple.

The first leaves were going from the acers as Anthony walked alone on the priory lawns. Dew on the springy grass: God's moisture everywhere except on his own tongue. He wetted and wetted his lips. Prayer came to him lightly, its syllables flowing freely into his mind. This was a benevolent sign. He walked and prayed and, though the contours of the garden were mirror-sharp, he felt on his forehead some warmth from the sun.

He liked the simple, stark routine of each day and he liked the emptiness of his room. When he thought about his home, it seemed like a place too cluttered with objects and with feeling. He saw Olivia in it everywhere – Olivia's light. I hate her, he thought.

To Dean Scales he confessed. 'I still feel loving kindness towards all things, or at least to most things, but not towards my wife.'

In the Dean's silence, he detected shock.

'God's ministers cannot harbour hatred,' he said, blowing his nose on a clean square of silk. 'Whatever your wife has done, you must try to forgive her.'

'I can't, Dean.'

'Are you telling me she's in mortal sin?'

'No, Dean.'

'Then your hatred is petty?'

Anthony sighed. He felt ashamed to say that his hate sprang from envy. The enviousness itself seemed, in the confessional, vain and silly, his idea that Olivia had 'stolen' God from him fanciful and stupid. He felt humble and sick. He longed, longed for some relief from his confusions.

'Let me stay here till I find God again, Dean.'

'We shall see how you progress.'

'I can't go back into the world.'

'And your responsibilities?'

'I can't honour them, till I find Jesus . . .'

'What makes you believe you will find Jesus here?'

Anthony sighed deeply. 'I must,' he said, 'or I shall go mad.'

Two weeks passed. The leaves on the gold acers were edged with brown. In everything, Anthony strove for obedience – from the cleaning of his supper plate (one evening, the Priory cook served up hamburgers and the raucous, treacherous world came teeming back into Anthony's head and made wounds in his fragile calm) to the hour-by-hour discomfort of kneeling. Each day was punctuated by fourteen 'stations of prayer', this punitive number echoing the fourteen Stations of the Cross. The first station was at five-thirty and the last at midnight. The time for sleep was short, but it was a grateful, dreamless sleep that Anthony slept. On the edge of it, in his curtainless room, he'd lie and look out at the stars and allow into his troubled head thoughts of heaven.

Josie Mecklin was a tanned, freckled woman with the patient smile of a teacher. During her stay in Olivia's house, she expected to instruct this middle-class vicar's wife on the true meaning of hardship and deprivation. But, to her surprise, she found she spent a lot of time listening to Olivia talking about martyrdom and belief. Olivia, it seemed, didn't need telling what had to be done. 'I think,' said this Great Dane, this stag of a woman, 'we are the "new Amazons". We're middle-aged, middle-class, pampered and ignorant. But we're *strong*. We're strong because we've understood. We'll fight to the death.'

Josie stayed three days. She spent a lot of time lying in the bath. She'd talk to Olivia through the bathroom door. A plan emerged from the clouds of steam: on the anniversary of the death of Anna of Didsmill, October 3rd, two hundred women would march from Greenham to the Didsmill base. They would take candles and brushwood torches. They would arrive at Didsmill as the sun was going down and hold a silent, night-long vigil at the main gate. At first light Olivia would read aloud passages from Anna's treatise. Then they would disperse peacefully, many of them to walk the twenty-three miles back to Greenham.

Olivia, sitting on a hard chair in the passage, felt her heart begin to race. No moment in her life now seemed as meaningful as this one – her marriage, the birth of her two sons, Anthony's ordination, none of these milestones had knocked with such strength on her ribs. She put a hand to her chest. 'Let me not die, God, before these things happen.'

Pink and shiny from her baths, Josie ate hungrily in Olivia's kitchen. Over cups of coffee, maps came out and a route from Greenham to Didsmill was decided on. It was also decided that Olivia would return to Greenham with Josie and spend a reciprocal three days there, talking to the women about Anna and enlisting volunteers for the Didsmill march. In her loft, Olivia found a sleeping bag used by one of her sons at scout camp. It smelt of mothballs and it had a damp, cold feel. But already, Olivia could imagine her body inside it, warming it up.

On the morning of Olivia's departure with Josie, a letter arrived from *History in Perspective*. 'Thank you,' it said, 'for your interesting and excellently researched article. We would like to offer you the sum of £150 and we will hope to include the article in our February issue.'

Olivia drew Josie's hard shoulders towards her and let her excitement crackle in an impulsive kiss on her new friend's cheek.

*

On October 2nd, God returned to take up temporary lodging in Anthony's body.

He was in the Priory library, searching for a book Dean Scales had recommended to him, called *Nazareth and 20th Century Man*. A young curate, a withdrawn person Anthony had never spoken to, was sitting at one of the library tables. As Anthony passed him, he noticed that the curate was reading the very book Anthony had come into the library to find. Anthony stopped. He sat down opposite the curate and stared at the man's lowered head and at the book under his white hands. He felt like a supplicant. 'I have made,' he said in prayer and with a strange confusion of metaphor, 'my willow cabin at your gate, Lord. In it, I stand and wait. I serve you, but you do not come to me.' At this point in Anthony's prayer, the curate looked up at him and smiled and handed Anthony the book. The young man then got up without a word and walked out of the library. Anthony held the book to his chest. It was warm from the other man's touch. At last, at *last* a sign had been given. Tears came to his eyes. The tears were hot. With a sob of joy, he felt God streaming down his face.

Anthony left Muir Priory with the Dean's blessing on the late afternoon of the following day.

It seemed very strange to him to be driving his car. It was raining. His hands fumbled to find the windscreen wipers. The noise of the car distressed him. The houses he passed seemed ugly beyond imagining. He began to long for the beauty of his garden and the peace of his church. He was full of anxiety. The world, he thought, opposes God's habitation in me. He drove on. In the cloudy sky, the light went early and the road in front of Anthony grew pale, its contours indistinct. But as darkness came on and blotted out the landscape around him, he felt calmer.

As he neared Didsmill, the rain ceased. Anthony stopped the car on a quiet road and got out, hoping, before the world and Olivia sprang at him again, to catch a glimpse of the same stars he'd seen from his window in the Priory. But the sky was uniform black and Anthony felt disappointment change to fear. He needed reassurance. He needed a *sign*. The stars, in place above him, would have been a sign.

He was about to get back into the car, when, far along the road in front of him, yet seeming to lie exactly in the path of the car, he saw a flickering light. It was a fluid, yellowy light, moving, beckoning. 'There it is,' Anthony whispered, 'my sign.'

And he began to walk towards it. As he neared it, he saw that the light was moving across the road, not towards him as he had believed. He squinted at it. It undulated under the trees. And now there was a faint sound accompanying the light, a shuffle of feet, and Anthony knew that, far from being alone on the road as he had thought, he was with a great shapeless, hidden gathering of people.

He could see them now: a slow procession, a long, long line of marchers holding candles and torches. He stood in the shadow of the trees, hiding. He could hear hundreds of voices, whispering, laughing. Women's voices. He turned away. The lights and the voices seemed to follow him, mocking. *You took us for a sign!* He tried to pray, but all his mind would construct were the four syllables of his wife's name: O-li-vi-a!

The threads were gathering now. The ending of the story of Anthony and Olivia Kingswell was coming . . .

All night, in the dusty, unkempt house he could barely recognise as his home, Anthony sat and waited for his wife. He grew cold. A wind got up. Anthony covered himself with a blanket. He dozed in the chair and dreamed of his future: his pulpit had been rebuilt in gold; it was higher than before. From it, he looked down on the potato faces of his parishioners. 'I,' he thundered, 'am the ploughman, and I plough you into the earth!' He woke shivering and trembling. He stared at the room, ghostly now in dawn light: dead flowers on the table, dust and crumbs on the carpet, old newspapers on the arms of chairs, boxes of leaflets piled up where a vase pedestal used to stand . . .

When she came in at last, the room was filled with sunlight

and she wasn't alone. She stared at him. The woman at her back stared at him.

'Anthony,' she said coldly, 'why didn't you let me know you were coming back?' And she crossed the room and kissed him and he could feel her hard forehead against his, bruising him.

He said nothing. She pulled away and looked at him. So thin, he is, was her thought. 'This is Josie,' she said, and the woman smiled. Anthony pushed the blanket off his body and stood up. He was freezing.

'There's a fine wind, Olivia,' he said. 'Let's go for a walk together. We can take a kite.'

Sleep, thought Olivia. I have never wanted sleep so much as I want it now. But she agreed to go with him. Later, she would sleep.

As she went out with Anthony, she heard Josie upstairs, running a bath and Olivia knew that, tired as she was, she was at last happy in her life.

But the life of Olivia Kingswell had only minutes – twenty-three minutes exactly – to last.

Anthony didn't drive to the downs. He drove to a potato field, a large field spread round a deep pond, muddy and grim in its recent harvest, with a few rotting potatoes left among the cut stalks. Here, with his nylon kite string strong as wire, he strangled Olivia and threw her body into the pond. The body didn't sink, but lay bobbing on the surface and the algae, displaced by its fall, reformed around it. Anthony felt the sour taste of this green, elemental weed on his tongue and vomited into the mud. Out of his mouth came pouring the chewed and mangled pieces of the body of Christ.

Olivia's murder, when it became known, caught the public interest for some time. 'Why?' the people asked. '*Why* did he kill her?' But after the trial, it was quite soon forgotten. Even the question *why*, never answered to counsel's satisfaction, was forgotten and Anthony started on his six-year prison sentence in the same way as he had started on his Priory retreat – with a frail kind of hope.

God, however, did seem to have left him, and the only feelings of wonder he ever experienced again were on windy days. He taught some of his prison colleagues how to make kites out of coat-hanger wire, newspaper and paste, and when the wind bellowed round the prison walls, these things could be seen dancing above the exercise yard. In the tug of their strings, Anthony could feel the pull of heaven.

The Bellows of the Fire

The two things I cared about most in the world until this morning were my dog, Whisper, and the bungalow under the viaduct.

Whisper is black and white with black blobs round her eyes and my aunt Nellie Miller says she reminds her of a panda.

Whisper is a one-person panda. The one person she loves is me. She waits for me to get home from school with her nose in the letter-box flap.

The viaduct is about a mile from our house. In winter, I can't get to it before dark, but in summer I take Whisper there every day. Trains used to go over it, but the railway line was torn up before I was born, so I've always known it like it is now, which is like a roof garden of weeds.

On rainy days, I hardly stop on the viaduct to look at the bungalow, because down there in the mist and drizzle it looks a bit sorry for itself. But in the sunshine, you see that it isn't sorry for itself at all and that the people who live there give it so much love and attention, you can't imagine they've got time for normal life.

Despite what's happened and what may happen in the future, I still feel that if that bungalow was mine, I'd be one of the happiest people in Devon. The only thing I'd add to the garden would be a wall all round it to keep Whisper in, so that she couldn't roam off to the sea when I wasn't there and drown.

The sea's second on my list of places I like, except that the sea does something to me: it makes me long for things. I sit down on the beach and stare out at invisible France, and this feeling of longing makes me dreamy as a fish. One of the things I long for is for time to pass.

It was my fourteenth birthday last week. We don't seem to celebrate my birthday in our family any more and I think this is because my mother says it only reminds her how fast her life is slipping away.

The only birthday I remember well is when I was six. My mother still considered herself young then and we had a new car and we drove to Dartmoor. The plan was, we were going to make a fire and cook sausages in it. I thought this was the best idea my parents had ever had.

But in the car, on the way to Dartmoor, my brothers bagged all the good jobs in advance. 'Bags collect the wood.' 'Bags light the fire.' 'Bags be in charge of cooking.' Only after a long time did my mother remember me and say, 'What about you, Susan? What job are you going to do, dear?' I didn't know what other jobs there were. 'She can't do anything, she's too little,' said my brothers.

We drove for ages in silence, but then my father had an idea. 'You can be the bellows of the fire, Susie. That means you have to blow on it and your breath keeps it going.' This didn't seem like a nice job to me. Blowing out cake candles was horrible enough. So I thought, I'm not going to breathe on their fire. I'm going to be absolutely quiet and hardly breathe at all. I'm going to be as silent as a stone.

Since then – or perhaps always, I don't know – I've been very quiet in my family. I notice things about them, like how they all love noise and seem to believe that happiness is *in* noise somewhere and that misery is in silence. They think that I'm a miserable person. What I think is that there are millions of things they'll never understand.

Our house is a modern house in a terrace of identical ones. Noise and mess from these houses spills out all over the puny little gardens and all over the street. If you were a visitor from France or somewhere and you thought all of Britain was like our terrace, you'd say it was the most hideous country in the world. Getting away from our house is something I think about every day of my life. My brothers are trying to get work in this town. They're trying to get jobs, so they can stay on and live in houses like these ones, or worse. And girls I know at school, that's what they want too. They want to be beauticians or hairdressers in the crappy shopping arcade. If I thought that was going to happen to me, I'd drown myself.

I took Whisper to the sea this evening. I throw things into the waves and she gets them out. She's terrific at this, much better than other dogs we see. Then we lay in the sun while her coat dried and I told her the news that came this morning.

I like secrets. I'm going to keep this one as long as I can. It'll come out eventually, though, and then my mother will say, '*Film*, Susan? What film?' And I will have to tell her the story.

It's a story about a community. It's set in a town like ours, not far from the coast. It's based on something which actually happened, on a person who actually lived, a girl called Julie who was fourteen and a fire raiser. She was a Girl Guide and her Dad worked for the town council. These things were important in the story, because the places where she started the fires were the places where new things were getting done, like a new Leisure Centre was being built and a new Bingo Palace.

Being a Girl Guide, she knew how to start fires without matches or paraffin or anything, so there was never any evidence left lying about, and this is why it took the police ages and ages to track Julie down. And also, they decided all the wrong things to start with. They decided the fires were started by a person from an ethnic minority, who resented the clubs and places where he wasn't welcome, so all they were really looking for were young Indians or West Indian youths. It took them a year before they suspected the daughter of a town councillor, and by that time, seven fires had been raised and the Bingo Palace had burned to the ground. She was caught in the end only because she set fire to the Girl Guide hut.

So, anyway, the thing is, they're making a film about her. The TV company came down here months ago. They arranged auditions in all the schools. All they said was, you had to be about fourteen and interested in acting. I haven't been in many school plays. When we did *The Insect Play*, I was only a moth with nothing to say. But I am very interested in acting, because in the last year I've realised that what I do all the time at home is *act*. I act the sort of person my family think I am, with nothing to say for herself and no opinions on anything, when inside me I'm not like that at all, I just don't let my opinions out. I'd rather save my breath. I plan, though. At school with one or two of the teachers and then on my walks with Whisper to the viaduct and the sea, I plan a proper life.

Not that many people from our school went to the auditions. They thought it was going to be too hard, and anything that seems hard to them, they let it go. But it wasn't difficult. You had five minutes to look at the script and then you had to read out a speech from near the end of the film, where they ask Julie why she started the fires, and she tells them. She tells them what she feels about communities like this one. She despises them. She thinks they've been hypnotised and corrupted. She thinks greed is all they understand.

It was quite a long, angry speech. When it came to my turn to read it, I pretended I was saying it all to my brothers and that they didn't understand a word of it and the more confused they looked, the more angrily the words came out. When I ended it, I knew I'd made an impression on the person who had asked me to read it. He was staring at me in amazement and then he said would I be able to come down to London in July for a second audition, which would be in front of a camera.

In the letter that came this morning, they told me that over two hundred girls had been seen for the part of Julie and that now there are just six of us. And us six will go to London – not all together, but each of us on a different day – and we will all pretend to be Julie, the arsonist, and other real actors will pretend to be her Mum and Dad and everyone and they'll decide at the end of all that who they're going to cast.

*

When I think about this now, I realise that although I've longed to get away from this town and longed to be the owner of the bungalow under the viaduct, I've never before longed for anything I could actually have, *now*. Getting away and living in that little house were all way-into-the-future kinds of things, but this, this part in the film is waiting for someone now, this year, now, and I've got a one-in-six chance of getting it and I want to get it so badly that it's been impossible, since this morning, to concentrate on lessons or eat a shitty school dinner because what I could feel all the time was my heart beating.

The only time I could feel calmer about it was on my walk with Whisper. What I told myself then was that I have had years of 'acting experience' at home and probably those other five girls have had none and what you see and hear of them is all there is. But me, I've been saving my breath. Saving it up for now.

When we walked back, by the time we got to the viaduct, I'd made myself believe – and I'm going to stick to this – that I am definitely the right person for this part and that the TV people are intelligent enough to recognise this and to offer it to me. And when I get it, that's going to be something.

But I still, to be on the safe side, looked for a long time at the bungalow under the viaduct and told myself that if you know how and where to look for them, there are loads of different ways you can be happy. Being an actress is one. Having a nice home in a place where there's silence is another. You just have to work at it all, slowly and carefully, like Dad made that fire catch on Dartmoor in the rain, one stick at a time.

The New People

Millicent Graves is leaving.

Today, with her friend and companion, Alison Prout, she has been for her last walk to the village and back. She has sat for a while on a wooden seat under the war memorial. The ice-cream van, playing four bars of a tune she thought was called 'The Happy Wanderer', drew up by the war memorial and obscured her view of the village green, the pub, the bank and the co-op. A few kids queued up at the van's window. Millicent Graves, who had heard on Radio 4 that some ice-cream men were also drug traders, stared at the children. They were pale and obese. Millicent Graves imagined that inside their skulls was confusion and darkness.

Upstairs now Alison Prout is packing clothes. The clothes are Millicent's. There are hats and furs, unworn for thirty years but preserved in boxes with mothballs and tissue paper. There is a black lace ballgown and a black velvet 'theatre dress'. There are white kid gloves and oyster-coloured stockings. Millicent can remember the feel of these ancient clothes against her skin. She has told Alison to pack them all – even the black lace gown and a hat with ostrich plumes – because she wants to believe that in her new life there will be the time and the climate for a little eccentricity. She can see herself in the old feathered hat, perfect for keeping the hot sun off her head. She might, she has decided, go shopping in it and enjoy watching the shopkeepers' faces as out from its ridiculous shade comes her order for half a kilo of parmesan. Or it might become a gardening hat, in which case it will be the nuns who spy her on the other side of their wall – a small but striking figure in her new landscape, going round with the watering can, placing cool stones on the clematis root. Alison Prout has had a bitter argument with Millicent on the subject of the clothes, certain as she is that Millicent's motive for taking them is detestable vanity. Millicent was, long ago, beautiful. Now, she is, simply, old. But the clothes, the foolish, expensive clothes, are a reminder – another among many reminders – of her power. And that power, Alison admits to herself as she folds and sorts her friend's possessions, is not yet completely spent.

In a week's time, Millicent and Alison, who have lived together in the cottage for nineteen years, will have left it for ever and The New People will have moved in.

It is a summer afternoon and the light on the garden is beguiling, Alison thinks, as she passes and re-passes the small bedroom window, carrying Millicent's things. Millicent is down-stairs, dusting the weasel. She has promised Alison that she will 'make a start on the books'. There are more than two thousand of these. When The New People first arrived to look round the cottage they appeared genuinely afraid at the sight of them. They'd imagined thick walls, perhaps, but not this extra insula-tion of literature. Then, as Millicent led them on into the sitting room and they noticed the stuffed weasel under its glass cloche, their fear palpably increased, as if the long-dead animal was going to dart at their ankle veins. And yet they didn't retreat. They knew the weasel would be leaving with the women; their glances said, 'We can take down all these book shelves.' As they left, they muttered, 'We shall be instructing the agents . . .'

After they'd gone, Alison had started to cry. 'They'll change it all,' she sobbed, 'I always imagined people like us would buy it.' Millicent reprimanded her. 'Change is good,' she said fiercely, 'and anyway, dear, there are no more people like us.'

But later that evening, Millicent found that she too was looking at the shape and detail of rooms and wondering how they would be altered. After supper, she'd gone out into the garden and stared at the summer night and thought, they will never see it as I see it, those New People, because even if their hands don't change it, their minds will. 'We've got ghosts now!' she announced to Alison as she went in. 'Ghosts who come before instead of after.'

Now, polishing the weasel, Millicent senses that the ghosts are with her in the sitting room. She turns round. 'What we don't understand,' they say, 'is why you're going.'

'Ah,' says Millicent.

Then she notices that Alison has crept down from sorting the old clothes and is sitting in an armchair, saying nothing.

'Is it a long story?'

'No,' says Millicent. 'I'm going because I've been replaced. I look around, in very many places where I once was and now I not only do not see myself there, I see no one who ever resembled me. It's as if I have been obliterated. And I can't, at the age of sixty-nine, accept my obliteration, so I am simply going somewhere where I shall be visible again, at least to myself.'

The New People look utterly perplexed. They want to say, 'We knew you literary folk were a bit mad, a bit touched, but we thought you tried to make sense to ordinary people. We thought this was common courtesy.'

'No,' snaps Millicent, reading their minds, 'it is not common courtesy, yet what I am saying is tediously simple.'

'Well, I'm afraid we don't understand it.'

'Of course you don't. Of course you don't . . .' Millicent mumbles.

'What you still haven't told us,' say The New People, trying to drag the conversation onto a solid foundation, 'is where you're actually going.'

Millicent looks at Alison. Alison turns her face towards the window and the afternoon sun shines on her hair, which is still reddish and only dulled a little with grey.

'Umbria,' says Millicent.

'Sorry?' say The New People.

'Yes. The house we're buying is by a convent wall. It belonged to the nuns for centuries. It was a place where important guests were put. Now, we shall be the "guests".'

At this point, The New People get up. They say they have to leave. They say they have a great friend who's mad on Italian food and who is starting a local Foodie Society. 'Tonight,' they laugh, 'is the inaugural nosebag!'

Millicent turns away from them and goes back to her polishing. When she looks round again, she finds they've gone.

'They've gone!' she calls to Alison, who is after all upstairs and not sitting silently in a chair.

'What, Millie? Who've gone?'

'Those people,' says Millicent, 'those ghosts. For the time being.'

At supper in the kitchen, Alison says: 'I think I'm going to try not to think about The New People, and if I was you, I'd try not to think about them either.'

'What a very complicated construction that is, Alison,' says Millicent, helping herself to the raspberries she picked a few moments ago in the dusk.

'Particularly tomorrow evening,' says Alison.

'Why particularly tomorrow evening?'

'While I'm out.'

'Out? Where are you going?'

'To say goodbye to Diana.'

'I see,' says Millicent. 'Well, it is going to be extremely difficult *not* to think about them, because they will be here.'

'They're only here in your mind, Millie.'

'I mean, they will actually *be here*. They're bringing a builder.'

'Tomorrow evening?'

'Yes. They're driving down from London.'

'Oh. Then I won't go out.'

'That would be considerate.'

'On the other hand, I promised Diana . . .'

'I marvel that you feel an emotional goodbye to be necessary.'

'Not "emotional".'

'In fact, why not, when we get to Italy, just send a postcard?'

'As if we were on holiday, I suppose you mean.'

Millicent sniffs. Another thing she hopes of her future life is that Alison, fifty next year, will have no more love affairs. She's never expressed this hope, except in her recent poetry, which, as once-praising, now-contemptuous critics have noted, is all about betrayal. She hadn't realised that betrayal was so unfashionable a subject nor indeed that her poems were 'all about' it. Perhaps, she decides capriciously, she will ask The New People about these things and watch their moons of faces closely to see whether or not they understand the words.

They arrive at seven. Alison has promised to be back by seven thirty. On entering the cottage, they say, God, they're sorry, but since their last visit someone has told them that she, Millicent Graves, is quite a famous poetess and it's awful to say they'd never heard of her.

'Oh, I see,' says Millicent. 'Then why did you say you thought literary people were mad?'

'I beg your pardon?' they say.

'You said you knew that literary folk were a bit touched . . .'

'We said that?'

'Or did I imagine it?'

'You imagined it. You must have done.'

They introduce the builder. He doesn't look, to Millicent Graves, like a builder, but more like a town councillor, wearing a brown suit and brogues. 'Perhaps you're a New Builder?' she asks. The man frowns and tugs out a pipe. He says he's been in the construction business half a lifetime. 'I think,' says Millicent, as she pictures Alison arriving at Diana's house and being greeted with a kiss, 'that everything's become very different and confusing.'

She leads them in. As they reach the sitting room, and the builder starts to look up at the bowed ceiling beams and to prod the springy, flaking plaster of the walls, Millicent finds she can't remember the name of The New People and wonders in fact whether she's ever known it.

'Oh, Prue and Simon,' they tell her.

Yes, she wants to say, but the surname? What was that? Something like Haydock-Park, wasn't it, or is that a Grand Prix circuit or a racecourse? She asks the New Builder his name. 'Jack Silverstone,' he announces impatiently.

'Lord!' exclaims Millicent. 'Everybody's careering about.'

The New People glance at each other. We must obliterate every trace of her, says this fearful look. And Jack Silverstone nods, as if in reassurance: It can all be changed. You won't know it's the same house. It's going to cost a bit, that's all.

'Where do you want to start?' asks Millicent.

'Oh . . .' says Prue.

'Well . . .' says Simon.

'Upstairs,' says Jack Silverstone.

So now, as Millicent gets out the sherry bottle from Alison's tidy kitchen cupboard, they're up above her head in the bathroom. Conversations, in timber-framed houses, escape as easily as heat through the floors and Millicent can hear Prue say to Jack Silverstone: 'This is the one drawback, Jack.' And it appears that Prue wants two bathrooms. Though they will only use the cottage at weekends, she feels, 'It simply isn't viable with one.'

'What about downstairs?' asks Jack Silverstone.

'Downstairs?'

'The little room next to the kitchen.'

'Her study? Convert that into a second bathroom?'

'Why not? Got no use for a study, have you?'

'Simon?'

'Good God, no. Don't plan to bring work here. Need a phone, that's all.'

They start to clatter towards the stairs. Now they'll come down and go into the study, where nothing has ever been disturbed but only moved about gently to accommodate the hoover, and start a conversation about piping.

Millicent leaves the sherry unpoured and marches quickly to the desk where all the unfashionable words on the subject of dereliction have been set down and picks up the telephone. By the time The New People have opened her door and exclaimed with barely concealed annoyance at finding her there, she has dialled Diana's number and has begun to wonder whereabouts in Diana's very beautiful house Alison may be standing or sitting or even lying down, because although it is now 7.25 by the silent study clock, Millicent is certain that Alison is still there and that unless summoned immediately she will come home very late, long after The New People have gone, leaving Millicent alone with the darkness and the ghosts.

The telephone rings and isn't answered. The New People have retreated to the kitchen where impatiently in their minds they are tearing Millicent's old cupboards off the walls.

'So tell us why you're going. Won't you?' say The New People, sipping sherry.

'Well,' says Millicent, 'I'll tell you a story, if you like.'

'A story?'

'Yes. And it's this. Men have never been particularly important to me, but one man was and that was my father. He was a scientist. All his early work was in immunology. But then he became very interested in behaviours, animal behaviour and then human behaviours. And from this time, our family life was quite changed, because he started bringing to his laboratory and then into the house all kinds of strangers. They would mostly be very unhappy people and their unhappiness and noise made it impossible for us to live as we'd once lived and everything we valued – silence, for instance, and little jokes that only we as a family understood – had disappeared for ever. And then my youngest sister, Christina, whom I loved very very much, committed suicide. So you see. Sometimes one has to act.'

Three faces, turned in expectation towards Millicent, turn away.

'Dreadful story,' mumbles Prue.

'Can we have a look at the study now?' says Jack Silverstone.

'Yes,' says Millicent. 'My study in Italy overlooks the nuns' vegetable garden. They told me they hoe in silence, but I expect from time to time one might hear them murmuring, don't you think?'

They don't know how to reply. In the study, they whisper. They've understood now how their plans can be overheard.

Millicent pours herself more sherry and notices that, as she predicted, Alison is not home and that the sun has gone down behind the laurels.

The New People emerge, beaming. Clearly, they have decided where the lavatory can go and where the bath. Millicent fills their glasses. 'The convent is, of course, crumbling,' she tells them, 'that's why the nuns have been forced to sell off the guest house – to try to repair the fabric. The Church in Italy used to hold people in their blood. Prayer was food. But it isn't like that any more. It's in decay, and all over the place there are empty churches and the old plaster saints have been replaced by plastic things.'

'There's a lot of shoddy muck about,' says Jack Silverstone, 'take my trade . . .'

'One imagines that perhaps certain African or South American Indian tribes are held to certain ways and certain places in their blood, but I think no one else is, do you? Certainly not in this country, unless it's an individual held to another individual by love. What do you think?'

'Well,' says Prue.

'Time,' says Simon.

'Time?' says Millicent.

'Yes. If you're in something like Commodities, as I am you don't have the time for any other commitments.'

'And as for the Church,' says Jack Silverstone, 'all that ever was was bloodthirsty.'

At this moment, Millicent hears the sound of Alison's car. It's eight thirty-five. The New People get up and thank Millicent for the sherry and tell her they've seen everything they needed to see.

Alison looks white. Her straight, small mouth is set into an even straighter, smaller line. Millicent decides to ignore – at least for the time being – the set of Alison's mouth and tells her friend with a smile: 'They're called the Haydock-Parks!'

'No, they are *not*, Millicent,' snaps Alison. 'Why do you always have to get names wrong?'

'What are they called, then?'

'The Hammond-Clarks.'

'Oh well, the builder is called Silverstone.'

'I very much doubt it.'

'You always doubted a great deal that was true, dear. He is called Silverstone, and I shall from now on refer to these people as the Haydock-Parks because it suits them extremely well.'

Alison goes angrily up the stairs and into her room. The door closes. Her anger, Millicent notices, has made the house throb. She wonders how many times and in what degree the timbers and the lathes have shifted, over all the years, to the violent commotions of their friendship. She ponders the origin of the phrase 'brought the house down' and wonders if it was originally applied to anger and not to laughter. How splendid if, as their removal van drove away, the house gave one final shudder of release and collapsed in a pile of sticks at The New People's feet.

She waits for a while for Alison to come down. She's hungry, but she refuses to eat supper alone.

She goes out into the garden and folds up the two deck chairs. 'Order before night' was a favourite saying of her father's, and before he started imposing a more or less perpetual state of disorder on their previously calm and prospering household, he would, each evening, observe his own strict ritual of collecting every toy scattered round the house and garden and returning it to its place in the nursery, before checking that all the downstairs windows were shut, the curtains drawn, the silver cupboard locked, the backgammon board closed, the lights extinguished and the eiderdowns in place over the bodies of his sleeping daughters. Millicent remembers that Christina once admitted to her that she would often let her eiderdown slip onto the floor on purpose and lie awake waiting for this infinitely comforting moment when it would be lifted gently from the floor and placed over her. When the strangers kept arriving, there was no time in her father's life for 'order before night'; there was, as Millicent remembers it, simply night. It descended swiftly. Patiently, the family waited for dawn, but it never came. Christina died. Millicent retreated from death by starting to write poetry.

She hadn't expected fame. It had come as suddenly and as unexpectedly as the arrival of the strangers. And it had changed her, made her bold, excited and free. Other people complained about it; Millicent Graves always found it an absorbing companion. Now, she misses it. Her frail hope is that in Italy she will miss it less. It still astonishes her that work once so highly valued can now be so utterly forgotten.

She props up the deckchairs in the porch. In the distance, she hears the church clock chime the three-quarter hour. The evening is warm. She wonders how often and for how long the convent tolls its massive bells and whether these summonses will help to structure a future which she knows she hasn't imagined fully enough. Alison has expressed anxiety about the bells, complaining that the days will seem long enough without being woken at dawn.

Resigned to an evening alone, Millicent makes a salad and eats it. She supposes that Alison is sleeping, but then when the telephone rings, it's answered upstairs. Tiptoeing to the sitting room, Millicent can hear Alison talking in halting sentences, as if she's trying not to cry. Millicent sniffs. 'I'm much too old for all this!' she says aloud.

In the night, the ghosts of The New People come into Millicent's room and tear off her wallpaper and replace her old velvet curtains with something called a festoon blind, that draws upwards into big bunches of fabric, like pairs of knickers.

'I see,' says Millicent.

They don't say anything. They're standing back and admiring the window.

'We used to wear cotton knickers like that,' Millicent tells them. 'I never saw my own, not from any provocative angle, but I used to see Elizabeth's and Christina's when we were invited to parties and they would bend down to do up their shoes, and

I used to think that the backs of girls' legs looked very strong and lovely.'

The New People are utterly silent and satisfied and fulfilled by the curtains and have drifted off into a contented sleep with the festoons falling caressingly about their heads.

'Night in this cottage,' Millicent whispers, knowing that nothing she says will wake them, 'is usually kind because it's quiet. I've found that in this quiet, I've often started to understand things which may not have been plain to me during the day.

'It was during one particular night, very, very cold, with that bitter feeling of snow to come, that I decided I couldn't endure it, the unloveliness of England, I just couldn't stand it any more, its comatose people, its ravaged landscape. Because we're in a dark age, that's what I think. But no one listens to what I think any more. Millicent Graves is out of fashion, passé, past, part of what once was, a voice we no longer hear.

'So I decided I would go. It seemed, from that night, inevitable. And you see where I've put myself? Slap up against a convent wall! But do you know why I'm able to do that? Because the wall itself, which I believed was so strong, so much more substantial than anything we have left in this brutal-minded country, the wall itself is crumbling! The money I've paid for my little house will prop it up for a bit, but I don't think it will rebuild it, and the best I can hope for is that it doesn't collapse on my head – not till I'm buried, at least.'

At this mention of burial, Millicent sees The New People open their eyes and listen and she thinks she knows why they look so startled: the thought has popped into their minds that despite all the extensive re-planning and re-decorating they're going to do, traces of Millicent's habitation may still remain in the house to disturb them. They imagine how they might be made aware of her. They're giving a dinner party, say. Friends of Simon's from the City will have driven down with their wives, and suddenly Prue or Simon will remember that even the walls of the dining-room used to be lined with books, and the flow of their conversation, which is as easy for them as the flow of money, will be halted – just for a moment – because one of them, searching for a word or phrase, understands for a second that there are thousands of words they will never use or even know and remembers that access to these words was once here, in the very room, and is now lost. The moment passes. It's all right. But Simon and Prue both separately wonder, why is it not possible never to think of her?

'Good!' says Millicent aloud. 'That's something, at least, their little discomfort.'

She has gone to sleep and is dreaming of Italy when she's woken by Alison's gentle tap on her door. This knocking on each other's doors is a courtesy neither would want to break; it allows them to share their life without any fear of trespass.

Millicent puts on her light and Alison comes in and sits down on the end of her bed. 'I couldn't sleep, Millie,' she says, 'I think we have to talk.'

'Yes, dear,' says Millicent.

Millicent decides to put on her glasses, so that she can see Alison clearly. Dishonesty must not be allowed to slip past her because dishonesty she can never forgive. She watches Alison's breasts rise as she takes a big breath and says with great sadness: 'I'm not certain that I can go to Italy with you. I think that, for the moment, it's not possible for me to go.'

Millicent blinks. Her eyes were always like a bird's eyes, hooded above and beneath.

'Diana, I suppose.'

'Partly so.'

'And the other part?'

Alison's eyes have been turned away from Millicent until now, but as she speaks, she looks up into her face.

'I can't,' she says, 'feel all the pessimism you feel. Don't think I'm being harsh, Millie, when I say that I feel that some of it comes not from the way our world has changed, but from the way *you've* changed – from being so very beautiful and praised, to being . . .'

'Old and despised.'

'That's how you choose to see it. I don't think anyone

despises you. They've just learned, over the years, to disagree with you sometimes and not praise everything you write.'

'They don't praise any of it, Alison. They want me to be quiet.'

'Well, again, that's how you've decided to see it.'

'No. They do. But that's not what you've come to discuss. I suppose it's Diana's beauty, is it? You're infatuated.'

'I may be. What I find I can't believe when I'm with her is that this country has lost all the good things it had. I know it's lost some of them, but I don't believe it's "finished", as you say it is. I just can't believe that, Millie. I can't. And I know that if I go to Italy, I'm going to miss it. I'm going to be homesick for England.'

'What for?' says Millicent indignantly. 'For riots? For waste? For greed? For turkeyburgers?'

'Of course not.'

'Then for what? For this garden, maybe. Or Diana's garden. But what are English gardens, dear? They're fragile oases, preserved by one thing and one thing only: money. And when the economy falters, as falter it undoubtedly will, all your peace of mind – that keeps you in the garden and other people outside it, suffering in those concrete estates – will vanish. Then what joy or satisfaction will you get from the garden?'

'I can't believe it will come to that.'

'It's coming, Alison. Do you know what the Haydock-Parks are going to put in before anything else? A burglar alarm.'

'I know all that. But there are so very many decent people, Millie, who want the country to survive, who want to make things better . . .'

'Decent people? Who? Name one decent person.'

'The kind of people we've always known . . .'

'Our friends? I don't think they're "decent", Alison. I think they're infinitely corruptible and infinitely weak, and when it comes to saving England, the task simply isn't going to fall to them, it's going to fall to people like the Haydock-Parks, The New People, and what kind of "salvation" do you ever imagine that's going to be?'

310

Alison is silent. When she thinks about it, she is perfectly happy to let Millicent win the argument. What she will not let her do is change her mind.

The silence endures. Alison picks at the fringe of her dressing-gown cord. Millicent takes off her glasses and rubs her eyes.

'I have never,' says Millicent after a while, 'been at all good at being quite and utterly alone. How in the world do you think I'm going to get on in that Italian house without you?'

'I really don't know, Millie,' says Alison sadly, 'I expect I shall worry about you a great deal.'

Refusing to think about Alison after she has gone back to her own room, Millicent snaps out the light and lies on her back and sees the dawn starting to frame the curtains. Just outside her window is a clump of tall hazel bushes. Pigeons have roosted in these trees for as long as Millicent can remember and she thinks now that if she's going to miss one thing, it will be the murmuring of these birds.

They lull her to sleep. She dreams her dead sister, Christina, comes and stands by her bed and puts her child's hand on Millicent's grey head. 'I am wearing,' Christina announces solemnly, 'the Haydock-Parks' curtains, just to mess them up, and in a few moments I'm going to drink this little phial of White Arsenic I've stolen from Father's lab, and it will make me die.'

'Don't die, Christina,' Millicent begs, 'dear Christina . . .'

'Oh no, I'm definitely going to die,' says Christina, 'because I think loss is the saddest thing anyone could possibly imagine. Don't you, Millie? I think losing something you once had is the most unbearable thing of all. Don't you?'

'What have you lost, Christina? I'll find it again for you. I'll get it back, whatever it was. Just as long as you don't die . . .'

'No. You can't get it back. Thank you for offering, Millie, but I know that what we once had in this house went away when the strangers arrived and even if Mother pleaded and begged and *made* Father send them away, I know that they damaged us,

311

damaged our love, and however hard we tried to get it for ourselves again, we never ever could.'

This dream is so sad that Millicent has to wake herself up, even though she knows that her old head which her fifteen-year-old sister was touching is very tired and in need of sleep.

Thoughts of Christina and of death linger with her. She feels, as she has never felt before, afraid not so much of death, but, in dying, of yielding territory to others who may desecrate and destroy the few things which have seemed precious to her and which, in the absence of any belief in God, have been part of a code by which she's tried to live.

In Italy, she promises her new hosts, the nuns, she will alter nothing in their house, nothing fundamental, and to the land around it she will behave kindly. But when she dies, what will happen to it? Who will come next? Which strangers?

'Probably,' she says aloud to the pigeons, 'it's wiser to own no territory at all and just be like that man in my Samuel Palmer print, who lies down alone in the landscape with his book.'

Next door, she hears Alison get up.

'Daybreak,' announces Millicent.

Evangelista's Fan

I

Salvatore Cavalli, the eldest son of a Piedmontese clockmaker, was celebrating his twenty-seventh birthday in the year 1815 when he learned that the King of Piedmont had decided to remove a large slice of time from the calendar.

This was disturbing news.

For several hours, Salvatore Cavalli's father, Roberto, had not been able to bring himself to pass it onto his son. He found the courage to do so only after he'd drunk several glasses of wine and eaten seventeen chestnuts soaked in brandy at the birthday dinner. Then, Roberto Cavalli wiped his mouth, put an eighteenth chestnut onto his plate, turned to his son, took a breath and said: 'Salvatore, I heard today that the King has ordered a number of years to be erased permanently from recorded time. What are we to make of that, do you think?'

Salvatore stared at his father. He wondered whether the clockmaker, a man of such precision in all his dealings, was beginning to show some inconsistency in his thinking. 'Papa,' said Salvatore, 'nobody can erase time. It's not possible. I think you must have misunderstood.'

But Roberto Cavalli had not misunderstood. With his mouth full with the eighteenth chestnut, he explained to Salvatore and to the assembled birthday guests that the King had been so horrified by the revolution in France and had suffered so miserably in his years of exile during the wars with Napoleon that he now preferred to pretend that none of these events had ever happened. His subjects were ordered to collude with this pretence and to purge their memories and their conversations of all reference to the years 1789 to 1815 inclusive. Punishments for disobeying the edict would be severe. Anyone heard uttering the word Bonaparte would be executed on the spot. The concept of *egalité* was decreed dead and had been officially interred in a dry well in the palace grounds. Worse and more difficult, nothing at all that had occurred during this time – *nothing at all* – was to be publicly recognised or discussed.

'So there it is,' said Roberto. 'The strangest decree ever to come forth, isn't it? And on this day of all days, my poor son. But there's nothing we can do about it. A decree is a decree and all we can hope is that we'll get used to it.'

That night, Salvatore refused to sleep. He stood at a window, counting stars. All twenty-six years of his life had been officially swept away. He existed only in the future – only from this moment of becoming twenty-seven – and all his past was consigned to a void, to a hole in time. He felt outraged. He came from a family whose profession it was to measure time, a family of rational, clever, mathematically minded people. He found the King's decree absurd, adolescent, unhistorical, unscientific and untenable. He refuted it utterly. His father's cowardly acceptance of it infuriated him. He spoke to the stars, as they paled in the paling of the sky. 'I shall have to leave home,' he said, 'leave home and leave Italy. Leaving is the only honourable solution left to me.'

Salvatore's proposed departure caused anguish in his family. He was already an accomplished assistant in the clockmaker's workshop. Roberto reminded him that their ancestors had started out as humble glass blowers but that for four generations they had been master craftsmen, rivalled only by the great watchmakers of France and Switzerland. 'You *may* not leave, Salvatore!' said Roberto. 'I forbid it. You are not free to abandon the family firm of Cavalli.'

'I have no other choice,' said Salvatore.

'Think of everything that has been done for you,' said Salvatore's mother, Magnifica, crying into a piece of Bavarian lace, 'the start you've had in life . . .'

Salvatore felt choked. He tried to stroke his mother's hair. 'There *was* no start, Mamma,' he said. 'I have no past. I am a day old.'

'Don't be stupid!' said Roberto. 'Don't be pedantic.'

'I'm not being pedantic, I'm following orders. The years 1789 to 1815 have been cancelled.'

'In public, in public!' whispered Roberto, as if the King might be standing on the other side of the door, listening to the conversation. 'Only in public! In private, they still exist. And this house is full of proof of their existence and yours, and these things can't be taken away: your baby curls in a box, your first prayer book, your tutor's reports, the engraving I gave you of the great Galileo Galilei, the first little clock you helped me make . . .'

'I can't live only in private, Papa,' said Salvatore, 'and anyway, I want to see something of the world.'

'Why?' asked Roberto. 'What's wrong with Piedmont?'

'Everything. A place in which time can be annulled and events denied and history rewritten is not a fit place to be and I pity you and Mamma if you're unable to see this.'

Salvatore felt pleased with this quick and pertinent response, but some days later, lying in the cabin of a ship that reeked of tar, hearing the sea boil all around him and knowing that Piedmont was lost to his sight, he heard the true harshness of his words and, for the first time, regretted them. He thought of Roberto and Magnifica alone with his absence, confused and afraid, and for a while he wished that the ship would turn round and take him back. But it sailed on.

His ultimate destination was England. Rumours had reached Piedmont during the wars that Napoleon had devised two alternative plans for the invasion of England: to fly horses and men and arms over in hot-air balloons; to dig a tunnel, like a mine, held up by wooden planks, under the Channel, through which his army would pass. But his engineers had informed him that balloons were too fragile for the English wind and the earth beneath the Channel too crumbly for a mine, and so the schemes were abandoned and England had never become part of the Emperor's conquered lands.

It was because of this that Salvatore had decided to sail there. He didn't fear the windy climate. He thought that time, in an unconquered place, would be running normally. He had heard that the English were a finicky people, who did most things by the clock, and so he was confident that his skills would be in demand and that he could make his way in London.

He became quickly acclimatised to sea travel. He let Roberto and Magnifica go from his thoughts. The motion of the ships didn't make him sick; it filled him with a strange exaltation and sense of freedom.

At Lisbon, he fell into conversation with the ship's doctor, who spoke four languages and who began to teach him some words of English – earth, soul, city, morning, river, house, heart, bosom, Putney, ironmonger, fog – and proudly recited to him a poem in English about the beauty of London seen from Westminster Bridge which contained all but the last four of these:

> Earth has not anything to show more fair:
> Dull would he be of soul who could pass by
> A sight so touching in its majesty:
> This City now doth like a garment wear
> The beauty of the morning . . .

From this poem, once the Portuguese doctor had translated it for him, Salvatore formed an image of London as a place bathed in silvery light, a domed place, with silent ships at anchor and all its citizens at rest in the early dawn, watched over by well-oiled and perfectly adjusted clocks.

'I was right to leave Piedmont,' he said to the doctor. 'With the arrival of this new decree, my family skills will no longer be valued there. This follows logically.'

'Well,' said the doctor, 'I wish you success and I *expect* you to succeed. From my understanding of the English mind, I would say it has always been curious about contrivances and devices.'

*

Salvatore found premises in Percy Street. The previous occupant had been a bookbinder who had died quietly while resting from his labours in a leather hammock. Some of his books remained on a dusty shelf above Salvatore's workbench. He removed them to his bedroom (until such time as someone arrived to collect them) and forced himself to read a little from them every night, so that the language would enter him fast, like his mother's old cures for fever and melancholy, and make him strong.

He put up no sign. He had nothing, yet, to sell. And he needed, he believed, to understand the language and to know his way around London before he could start to trade there. He painted his premises green. He hung his precious engraving of Galileo Galilei over the mantel. This was to help him engage his future customers in conversation while they looked at his clocks and watches. He would remind them that it was an Italian, the great Galileo, who, observing very carefully the swinging of a lantern in Pisa Cathedral in the year 1582, had understood that the period of swing of a pendulum is independent of its arc of swing, and so adapted the pendulum to clockmaking via his simple idea of the wheel-cog escapement. He thought this story might be new to them and that it would intrigue and impress them.

Meanwhile, he began on the wheel-work of a range of 15-carat-gold keyless pocket watches, employing the Cavalli pump-winder patented by his grandfather, Domenico, in 1800. It was March and cold in his rooms. The kind of ferocious winds considered too fierce for Napoleon's hot-air balloons screamed at his door. There was no sign of spring anywhere. The silvery light he'd imagined from the poem on the ship didn't seem to fall in London except, now and again, just before dusk, just before the lamps were lit, and then it gleamed wetly on the street for half an hour and was gone.

And nor was London a gently sleeping city. Its very air seemed to hold noise within it, so that even while you slept you breathed it in and woke startled and disturbed. More even than the fiery Piedmontese, the men here seemed enraptured by argument and brawl. In Salvatore's own street, in the grey light that passed for broad daylight, he saw a man pick up a cat from the gutter and hurl this living weapon at the head of another man. The cat's body struck a railing and fell into a basement. The second man pulled out a pistol and shot the first man in the thigh. All down the street, windows opened and people stood staring. The wounded man lay pale and shrieking on the stones, but nobody went to his aid. After a while, he was put onto a cart of potatoes by some ragged boys and taken away.

That night, Salvatore dreamed that he'd lost not only his home but one of his legs as well. He got up and dressed and touched the great Galileo's forehead for luck and walked to Westminster Bridge and stood in the middle of it and tried to see the things spoken of in the poem. And, as it happened, the morning was a fine one, the wind less rowdy than of late. Spread out under a clear sky like this, the city did indeed seem beautiful and serene and Salvatore felt tall, as if he were at the centre of a picture. Then, he realised that from this heart of London, if a person turned very slowly in a 360° circle, his eye could come to rest on no less than thirteen public clocks.

His work on the watches progressed very slowly. He had never been a fast worker. (Would his father remember this and start to find his absence satisfactory?) But now, Salvatore's hands and his ingenuity felt constrained, as if he were, in fact, afraid to complete the watches. Certainly, he preferred wheel-work to enamel face-work. His numerals never satisfied him, never had the perfection he recognised in the internal machinery or the face pointers. So this, in part, explained why the watches remained unfinished, but not entirely, because he knew that his future was in them: he was nothing and no one, in his empty green shop, until he had begun to trade with the world outside.

It took him two months to understand the cause of his fear. It grew out of his personal predicament after the King of Piedmont's decree. He'd become uneasy about the validity of his profession. What did all this mathematical monitoring of time signify and what did it *serve*, if time could be mangled by the edict of a frightened monarch? He was in a country, now, where people seemed to pay proper attention to time, yet nevertheless he felt that, even here, his profession had been dealt some kind of blow from which – in his imagination – it might never recover fully.

It was May. The daylight was brighter, kinder, and Salvatore had made a few acquaintances now and went with them to the taverns and the coffee houses and spoke English and was less alone.

He went to a signmaker and placed an order for an expensive painted sign. It was to show a clock face with its glass casing cracked and its hour hand detached from the centre pinion. Underneath the picture, in black lettering, were to be written the words:

CAVALLI, S.   REPAIRER OF TIME

II

The wording of the sign made people stop and think and look up.

In the window of the shop, Salvatore had placed his unfinished watches and a set of sandglasses made by his ancestor, Vincente Cavalli, mounted in a fine ebony casing. He turned them every so often. He watched passers-by pause and stare at the minuscule movement of the white sand.

He wrote to Roberto and Magnifica: 'I have decided to specialise in reparation, rather than fabrication. This, I believe, will be better suited to my temperament and I will no longer have to disguise my ineptitude with face-work. My first task was to mend a Viennese table clock showing solar and lunar time by means of an astrolabe and delicate moon pointers. The pointers were jammed at the first phase, yet the moon here is full and overflows into the night mists. I say prayers for your understanding and forgiveness to this big, spilling moon.'

He prayed also that his business would thrive – and it did. 'A stopped clock,' said one customer, 'is a thing no Englishman can endure,' and it soon became apparent to Salvatore that his sign put Londoners in mind of the unendurable and they hurried to him in considerable numbers with timepieces of extraordinary diversity and differing complexity. People were, on the whole, polite to him. They made emphatic reference to his countryman, Galileo, there on the green wall. They spoke slowly and corrected his faults of syntax with good-natured courtesy. They paid promptly and greeted their mended clocks with affection, as though these might have been convalescent pets. Very occasionally, they returned with gifts of appreciation: an ounce of tobacco, a box of raisins, a lump of quartz.

It began to be clear to Salvatore that his decisions had all been right. He wrote again to his parents, from whom he'd received no word at all: 'I have begun to prosper a little in my new life.' At the same time, he felt that the life he had and which he referred to as 'new' didn't yet quite belong to him. It was like a coat he wore, a borrowed garment with holes in it, which let in, not cold exactly, but something mournful, something which sighed and should not have been there.

And then, on a late summer afternoon, a young woman walked into his shop. She was dressed in pale grey and white. There were white roses in her hat. Her hair was black (like the black hair of Piedmontese women in their youth) and her eyes were brown and of startling beauty.

Salvatore got up from his work table and bowed. Since arriving in London, his mind had been on language and on commerce; he'd given women hardly any thought. But now, suddenly in the presence of this person, he remembered how the sight of a particular woman could move him and terrify him at the same time, so that he'd feel exactly as he'd felt as a boy and imagined his life as a grown-up – wanting it and not wanting it, touched by possibilities, excited yet afraid.

In his still-imperfect English, Salvatore asked the woman how he might serve her. He thought that he saw her smile, but it was difficult to be certain, because on this warm day she had brought with her a fan and she held this fan, barely moving it, very close to her mouth.

'Oh,' she said, 'well, I've come as ambassador – ambassadress would be the correct term, but I think there are no ambassadresses on earth, are there? – for my clock.'

'Ah,' said Salvatore.

'It's a Dutch bracket clock, made by Huygens. The background to the dial is red velvet, slightly faded. The dial is brass and supported by a winged and naked figure of a man I've always taken to be God, or at least a god. It stands above the fireplace in my bedroom and I'm very fond of it indeed. A velvet background is unusual, isn't it? I couldn't say why I like it so much, except that it has always been there, ever since I can remember, ever since I could *see*.'

'And your clock is broken, Signorina?' asked Salvatore. He said this with great tenderness. His fear of the young woman had left him and only his longing remained.

'Well,' she said, 'it says twenty-seven minutes past one. It's paused there. The god still holds up the dial proudly, so it's possible that either he's showing me the time of the end of the world or else he hasn't noticed that his world has stopped. What do you think?'

Salvatore found much of this difficult to understand. He recognised a way of talking somewhat different from that of many young women, a kind of self-mockery in the speech, which he found seductive and he knew that she had asked him a question, but he really hadn't the least idea how to answer it. She looked at him expectantly for a moment, then smiled and hurried on: 'Take no notice of me! My mind is like a cloud, my father says, always drifting. And I expect it's because of my drifting mind that I've done what I've done. But it has upset me so much.'

'What have you done?' asked Salvatore, moving a step nearer to the young woman and snatching at the air with his nostrils to inhale more deeply a sweet perfume, which was either the smell of her body or the smell of the roses in her hat or a mingling of the two. She lowered her eyes. 'I've lost the winder

321

key,' she said. 'I've ransacked the house for it. I've looked inside the grand piano – everywhere . . .'

Salvatore's eyes now rested on her small gloved hand holding up the fan. He wanted to take the hand and hold it against his face.

'. . . in every one of my shoes . . . in my father's pockets . . . under my bed . . .'

'But it has departed?'

'I believe it must be there, in the house, but no one can see it. There are certain things, of course, that are there and cannot be seen, but a winder key isn't usually one of them, is it? You come from Italy, I suppose?'

'Yes.'

'Italy is one of countless places that I've never seen, despite the fact that they exist and are there. But I have no doubt that Italy is more beautiful than almost anywhere on earth. Is it?'

Salvatore thought: I would like to go up into the sky with her, in a hot-air balloon, and float down on Piedmont, onto my parents' roof . . .

'I don't know,' he said, 'because I do not know the earth.'

At this moment, a church clock struck the hour of four and the young woman hurried to the door, saying that because her 'dear Dutch clock' had stopped she'd lost the race with time and was late for all her social engagements. She said she would come back the following day, with her servant to carry the clock, and Salvatore would manufacture a new key, adding before she left: 'Then all will be well again.' And after this, she was gone, adjusting her hat as she moved away down the street.

Salvatore sat down. He wiped his face with a handkerchief. He knew beyond any possible doubt – and indeed this knowledge seemed to be the only thing that was truly his since his arrival in England – that the young woman with the fan was his future. 'I shall marry her or die,' he said aloud.

She didn't return the next day as promised.

Salvatore had risen early, dressed himself with care, polished the glass of the engraving of Galileo Galilei and waited, but there was no sign of her.

After six days of waiting – during which he went out several times a day and walked up and down the street, searching among the heads of the people for the white roses of her hat – Salvatore told himself that he had misunderstood her. His grasp of English was still shaky, after all. She had not said 'tomorrow', she had said 'this time next week'. And he felt relieved and calmed.

So certain was Salvatore that she would come on this new tomorrow, that again he took extra care with his appearance, dusted the sandglasses and bought lilies from a flower seller to scent the green world of his workshop.

That same morning, he received a letter from his father. 'My dear son,' wrote Roberto Cavalli, 'by leaving the family, you have yourself tampered with time and continuity. Now, your mother and I feel cheated of our rightful futures and to console herself my beloved Magnifica is eating without ceasing and could die of this terrible habit, while I have no appetite for anything at all . . .'

Salvatore wanted to write back at once to say that, when his future arrived, when – through his new idea of a marriage – he was fully able to inhabit his new life, then he would return to Piedmont, defying the King's edict by becoming responsible for the repairing of time, a skill for which he had now discovered himself well suited. But he didn't write. He sat at his workbench, waiting.

'Today, she will come,' he told himself, as the hours suc-ceeded one another faster and faster. 'Today, she will come.'

Night came, that was all. And then another tomorrow and another.

Salvatore told himself: 'You are so stupid! Why didn't you ask for her name? Then you could find her. You could pay a respectful call, informing her that you'd come to collect the Huygens clock, to save her and her servant the trouble of the expedition. It would be perfectly proper. And then the key that you would make for her! What a key! Just to put it into the heart of the mechanism would be to experience a deep frisson of pleasure. And then to turn it! To set the escapement in motion! To know that time was beginning again . . .' Salvatore knew that his thoughts were carrying him away, but he also believed that if he could only have the clock in his possession he could win the heart of the woman he now thought of as his future beloved.

He began work on designs for keys. Their heads had different emblems: a lyre, a rose, a pair of folded wings. He neglected other work to perfect them. And then, in the middle of the rose design, a realisation arrived in his mind like a canker in the flower: *she has found the original key!*

It was so simple, so obvious. She had opened the mahogany drawer where she kept her fans and there it lay. And so she had rewound the clock, set the pointers at the right time and given the matter no further thought. She would never come into his shop again. She was lost.

Salvatore put away his designs. He felt sick and sweat began to creep over his head. He remembered his father's letter and its terrible last sentence: 'I have no appetite for anything at all . . .'

III

A feebleness of spirit overtook Salvatore from this moment. It was as if the King's edict had reached out to him, far away as he was, and annihilated him.

On the shop door, he put up a sign: *Repair suspended owing to illness.* From his bedroom window he watched the London summer glare at him and depart. He heard men rioting in the street below. They were shouting about the price of bread. Salvatore felt indifferent towards the price of anything.

In his more optimistic moments, he decided his extreme weakness was due only to exhaustion, to the difficulties he had

had to endure since his arrival in London and his struggles with language. On other days, he felt certain that this new disappointment had dealt him a fatal blow. He noticed that his hair was starting to fall out. At twenty-seven, he hadn't expected this, just as he hadn't predicted that time could be wiped from the calendar. The capriciousness of the world was too much for the individual. However hard he fought to order his life, the random and the unforeseen lay in wait for him always.

He remained in his bed and didn't move. He ate nothing. He began to be prey to visions. He saw his lost beloved come into his room, naked except for her fan, which she held in front of her private parts. Then he woke one morning to the sound of someone eating. He saw his mother, sitting at his night table, spooning veal stew into a mouth that was much more fleshy than it had been, and he saw that all her flesh had magnified itself so grossly that her body almost filled the small room. He wanted to ask her why she had let this happen to her, but before he could frame the question, she said with her mouth full: 'It's my name: Magnifica. Why aren't you quicker to understand things?'

Salvatore tried to get out of bed. He wanted to lay his head in her enormous lap and ask her to forgive him. As he struggled towards her, he fainted and woke up lying on his floor, quite alone.

After this, he tried to eat. He nibbled at biscuits, felt deafened by the sound of them being broken against his teeth.

He put some pomade on his thinning hair. His scalp felt frozen, but he found that, under this ice, new thoughts were beginning to surface in his exhausted mind. The successful man, he decided, the man capable of a happy life, defies the random by his ability to *foresee* what is going to happen. He doesn't – as I have tried to do – feebly repair the past; his mind is attuned to what will *become* necessary. He acts in advance to prevent (as far as is humanly possible) the random from occurring. Such a man would have foreseen the possibility of the rediscovery of his beloved's winder key and asked discreetly for her name and address long before that possibility became a fact. Such a man, aware of the vanity of princes, would have predicted that the King of Piedmont was likely to attempt some wanton comedy with time and schooled himself as to how best to come to terms with it, so that he didn't have to feel as if his life had been cancelled. The random will still, of course, occur, but the damage caused to a life by the unforeseen will be less severe.

If only, if only, thought Salvatore, I were descended from a line of such men – men who possessed some cunning, not merely with the moment-by-moment measurement of the present, but also with the computation of the future – then I wouldn't be lying in this room in mourning for my lost love; I would be holding in my hands a Dutch clock. I would be working every hour of the day and night to make myself worthy of the woman I've chosen as my bride and who would one day be a bridge to Piedmont and the past. I would be happy.

The clarity of these thoughts consoled Salvatore for a time and then began to torment him. For why hadn't he had them sooner? They were no use to him now. They could only tantalise him with what might have been and now never would be.

He moved his bed. He put it under the window, so that he had a view of the street. He thought it would cheer him to watch the people hurrying by, each to his or her personal labyrinth of the unforeseen. He stared at the faces, so intent upon some destination, so certain of arrival. But instead of being cheered, Salvatore felt more and more sorrowful and ill. He experienced spasms of violent hiccups that hurt and exhausted him. After one of these, he had a vision of a fiery balloon floating down on London and so enthralled by this was he (was it there? was it not there except in his mind?) that he stopped looking at the street and began the habit of watching the sky.

The sky in England, he soon realised, was the most changeful and unpredictable thing of all. In Piedmont, a day that began fair stayed fair, or, if it didn't, the clouds gathered slowly in an orderly mass like an army and then marched in line towards the sun. Here, a morning could be fine for half an hour and then the sky could darken to night and a drenching rain start to fall and the temperature drop by several degrees. The poor English, thought Salvatore, they never know what's going to happen next in the sky. No wonder they're a brawling nation. They're venting a national rage against the utterly unfaithful seasons.

He became preoccupied with the weather. It was autumn now – two months since he had found and lost his beloved – and the sky was in a state of perpetual movement. He remembered sunny October evenings in Piedmont, sitting under a mulberry tree in Magnifica's garden when not a leaf moved and the day proceeded so calmly towards the night that it disturbed no one and no one noticed it go until it was gone. Here, the October dusk came flying in like a poltergeist, setting the shop signs swinging, rustling the leaves, sending smoke billowing back down the chimney in Salvatore's room, where he still lay in an enfeebled and pitiful state, his pillow darkened by his falling hair. With his mind swinging like a pendulum between the distant past in Piedmont (a past of long duration until it was obliterated by an external hand) and the recent past of his meeting with the only woman in his life who had ever truly moved him (a past of fleeting duration and obliterated by his own inadequacy), he felt himself begin to lose hold of earthly things. It was as if the air itself were snatching at him and wouldn't rest until it had whirled him up into the sky.

Some part of him, however, resisted. It refuted insanity, rebelled at the idea. It forced him to get out of bed, to shave his face, to comb his thinning hair. It dressed him in a black coat and sent him downstairs into the shop, where the dust was thick on every surface and now clogged the workings of the unfinished watches that still sat in the window.

Salvatore stared at all this. Pushed under his door were notes from customers demanding the return of their unmended goods, the notes themselves curled and discoloured already by the passage of all the days since they'd been delivered.

Everything Salvatore could see appeared futile to him. He wanted nothing more to do with the reparation of time. His sign (he'd been so pleased with the wording on the sign, so proud of the little conceit!) now seemed to him a particularly stupid thing. He wished the wind had blown it down. Time could not be repaired. A sublime moment came and went and that was all. He was in a useless profession.

He ate a little food. He thought that to eat might help anchor him to the earth. All he had were some dried plums, but the taste of them was sweet and reviving.

To still his mind, he now fought to glimpse some small particle of his future. What in this world, he asked himself, can I do that will console me with its usefulness? What is there that is not futile?

He took his box of plums and went and sat by the mantel and looked up at Galileo. He tried to remember what the great man had done in *his* hours of adversity, in the last years of his life, when he was being overtaken by a terrible event beyond his control – his blindness. He had worked, with his son Vincenzo, on the pendulum-drive escapement. Salvatore imagined drawings discarded, half finished, covering his desk and Galileo's milky eyes so near the paper that he could use his long nose as a paperweight. He had fought his blindness to the last day and just three months before his death had been experimenting with mercury – a substance as volatile as time itself.

Salvatore ate another plum. He could feel his warm blood flowing in and out of his heart. Why mercury? What was Galileo doing – at terrible risk to himself because of his eyesight – with mercury?

The plums (a gift from a lawyer with a broken travelling clock) had some magical property. They seemed to revive in Salvatore a worm of optimism. They and Galileo's example. He sat there smiling, his mind tuned once more to answer its own questions.

He said out loud to the dusty shop: 'Galileo was working, in his mercury experiments, with Evangelista Torricelli. Three years later, Evangelista Torricelli designed the first barometer. The barometer remains one of the few scientific devices man

has perfected that tell what is *going* to happen, not what is or
what has been.'

At this point, Salvatore got up and took the engraving of
Galileo from the wall and held it against his thin chest. 'This,'
he said, 'is where a possible future might lie, then – with the
barometer.'

IV

After his eating of the plums, Salvatore decided that, as soon as
he was strong enough, he would go and talk to one of the
numerous barometer-makers, whose premises he had often
passed in his neighbourhood. Most of them had Italian names,
but, afraid perhaps to discover that he had not been uniquely
bold in coming to London, that London was in fact quite
densely populated by refugees from Napoleon's wars, he had
never visited any of them.

He eventually chose a shop in High Holborn. In the small
window hung several wheel barometers. They were well-made
pieces, but they were not the finest examples he'd seen. They
demonstrated good craftsmanship rather than artistic delicacy
and therefore mirrored Salvatore's assessment of his own skills.
The name engraved on these instruments and over the door of
the shop was FANTINO, E.

Salvatore entered the premises nervously. He hadn't worked
out quite what he was going to say and he still looked pale and
thin. He feared he would be mistaken for a student or a poet.

The interior of FANTINO, E. was dark. It smelled consolingly
of resin and was warm. Salvatore felt as if he'd arrived in a
place that he'd known long ago but had never had the words
to describe.

A small, wiry man, wearing very thick spectacles, came out of
an inner room. He stood at a tilted angle, peering at Salvatore.
He said: 'I was about to say "good morning", sir, but I realise it

may already be afternoon. When one is hard at work, one is apt to lose all sense of time.'

Salvatore nodded and gave the man an awkward smile. 'E vero, Signore,' he said. 'Si. E molto vero.'

'Ah!' said the tilted man, 'Italian! You are Italian!' And Salvatore noticed that a look of inexpressible joy passed over his small face.

'Si,' said Salvatore. 'And I have the honour, perhaps, to talk to Signor Fantino?'

'Oh no. No, I'm afraid not. I am Signor Fantino's partner in business, Mr Edwin Sydney. Signor Fantino is at present away, in Switzerland. But how may I be of assistance to you? We are always very glad to welcome your countrymen in our premises.'

The darkness and warmth of the shop, together with the friendly manner of Mr Sydney, gave Salvatore courage. He began at once to reconstruct, for the English partner of FANTINO, E., the tortuous excursions with time that had brought him to the barometer-maker's door. And the story, though long, seemed to enrapture the little Englishman. He stood with his eyes fixed on Salvatore's face, nodding, clasping his hands at intervals, as if filled with excitement. The tilt of his body became more and more profound and, at the point in Salvatore's narrative where he described the sudden entry into his memory of the name Evangelista Torricelli, Salvatore was afraid Mr Sydney was going to fall sideways onto the floor, just as the Tower of Pisa would one day.

When Salvatore reached the end of his story, with the words, 'and so, Mr Sydney, here I am,' Edwin Sydney said: 'If I were a religious man, Signor Cavalli, I would believe you had been sent to us by Divine Providence. Please step into our workroom and accept a glass of tea and I will call my cousin Mr Benedict Simpkins, who also works with me. We shall close the shop for the afternoon – it *is* afternoon, I now believe – and together we will discuss your apprenticeship to this firm.'

It was night when Salvatore returned to Percy Street. He made up a fire and sat in front of it, staring at the coals. The coals flared and burned and fell, burned and fell. And Salvatore's ability to reach a decision about his future followed a similar, repeating sequence. By morning, he was asleep in his chair, his mind still not made up.

Mr Sydney and Mr Simpkins had given him one month in which to accept or refuse their invitation. They told him that they would teach him everything they knew about the manufacture of barometers. ('Interest in weather forecasting began in prehistoric times, Signor Cavalli. Primitive man became aware of the concept of past and future and understood that his ability to ensure survival depended upon a sympathetic combination of sunshine, wind and rain.') They would house him and feed him and nurture him back to his full strength. They would provide him with wine and tobacco and good paper for his letters to Piedmont. They would send out to a Piccadilly grocer for his favourite brand of dried plums. They would explain to him the ins and outs of bills of lading and all the paraphernalia of exportation. They would employ a teacher to improve his English. They would care for him, in short, like a son. But on one condition.

It was with his exhausted mind on this condition that Salvatore fell asleep in front of his fire. When he woke, cold and with an ache in his ear, he wondered whether he'd dreamed it up, so strange and unforeseen did it appear to him.

Sydney and Simpkins wanted him to disappear.

'Only for a short time, Signore,' they said, 'for as long as it takes you to become skilled with mercury, so that you can begin to follow in the footsteps of your countryman, Evangelista Torricelli. A year, say, or possibly nine months only. That will be up to you.'

The disappearance had to be absolute. No trace must remain of Salvatore, or of his watches, his repairs or his name at Percy Street. 'Your customers,' said Edwin Sydney, 'must be informed that you have returned to Piedmont. We will pay your landlord and close the lease. You must become absolutely invisible until you are forgotten.'

And then, when he had learned his new craft, when sufficient time had elapsed, he would be allowed back into the world. But not as Cavalli, S. As Cavalli, S. he would no longer exist. He was going to become Fantino, E.

'You mustn't think us mad,' said Benedict Simpkins, who was a larger man than Edwin Sydney, but with a slight facial resemblance to him. 'Necessity has made us act as we do. We've been looking for Fantino, E. ever since we began to trade in London.'

'But,' said Salvatore, 'where is he?'

'Ah,' said Simpkins, 'he is nowhere, Signor Cavalli. He has never existed. We invented him.'

Salvatore thought his comprehension of English must be failing him. He gaped at Simpkins.

'Yes yes,' said Sydney, coming in quickly, 'we knew you would be surprised, but there you are. We made him up. We created him. And why? Because the Italians are the best barometer-makers in the world. They are *sans pareil*. That is an undisputed fact. Their reputation is paramount. So we invented the name Fantino. As you know, "fantino" is the Italian word for "jockey". And this was my first attempt at a livelihood, in the world of racing silks. You've noted my stature, no doubt? But I was always a man fond of precision and the racecourse was, in the end, too uncertain a place for me. My cousin, Mr Simpkins, was at that time apprenticed to the firm of H. Hughes in Fenchurch Street and I joined him there. But we knew that when the time came to set up on our own, we would take an Italian name. We thought a mere name would suffice. But then we realised that we would feel more certain of our future if we had the man. And there you have it. Fantino, E. is trickery. It's a device. But why not? It's men's *devices* that shape the world. Don't you agree?'

Salvatore was silent. The two cousins smiled at him, smiled and smiled. These could have been the smiles of time-tampering kings.

'If I were to accept your offer,' he said at last, 'what would be my first name? What does "E" stand for?'

'Ah,' said Mr Simpkins, 'there our imaginations faltered and so we went straight to the originator of the Torricellian Experiment of 1643. It is, of course, Evangelista.'

After his sleep in the chair, Salvatore's mind felt a little more clear. I must lay out all the arguments in plain words, he thought. I must look at everything in a logical way and then make my decision.

He made coffee. He rekindled his fire and knelt in front of it, warming his hands on his coffee bowl.

He talked to himself as if he were no longer Salvatore Cavalli, but some disinterested third party. 'First,' he said, 'if you agree to become Fantino, E., you will also have the right to Fantino, E.'s constructed past as a maker of barometers. Your name is engraved on every instrument. The name, therefore, carries with it some years of prior existence that could go some way to redressing the balance of years lost as Cavalli, S. This is perhaps the most important point in the argument and one that should incline you to accept the proposal.

'Secondly, there is the name itself: Evangelista. This takes you yet further back, to a time of Italian greatness, to a time which acknowledged the vast importance of *prediction* in human life and addressed it scientifically. There is no more perfect assumed name for you, therefore, than Evangelista. Already you can feel the attraction, like a magnet, of this name.

'But then there is this third question of the disappearance. This disappearance means relinquishing for ever and always the possibility of your beloved's reappearance in your life. And, despite all your despair and suffering, you *have*, in some corner of your being, kept this possibility alive. You have said to yourself: suppose the winder key has *not* reappeared in the fan drawer? Suppose, simply, the bewitching owner of the Huygens clock (and don't forget that it was this very Huygens who perfected Galileo's escapement!) has temporarily become reconciled to the pausing of time at twenty-seven minutes past one? And suppose the day should come when this starts to irritate her once more? What will she do then? She will put on a grey dress (a winter dress this time). She will sew some silk roses to a hat. She will set out with her servant for Percy Street.

333

And you will no longer be there. Worse, there will be no trace of you and no means whatsoever of finding you. She will take the clock to another repairer and that will be the end – the indisputable end – of any version of your future in which she is included.'

Salvatore sighed deeply. He put down his coffee bowl. He lifted his head and saw pale sunlight coming into the room. He realised that he could remember with extraordinary clarity the face, voice and gestures of the young woman he so yearned to love. She was as visible to him now as she had ever been. Nothing about her had faded or become spoiled. Her perfection remained intact, had imprinted itself indelibly on his mind. All she lacked was a name.

Thinking only of her and no longer of Fantino, E., Salvatore went to bed and slept away the morning. He dreamed he was walking arm-in-arm with his love in a field of string beans. The low bean plants touched his legs seductively. He woke in a state of frustration and fury. Come on, Salvatore, he instructed himself, you must put an end to this! Mr Sydney and Mr Simpkins have made you the most remarkable offer of your life and you must find the means to accept it. You must become Evangelista. You must make yourself relinquish love.

But how can perfection, once seen, be relinquished? It can't, Salvatore decided, it can't, because the mind will always and always return to it and all that follows will be measured by it – to the end of life.

Unless . . .

And here, Salvatore tried to remember how Sydney and Simpkins had described their creation of Fantino, E. They had called it trickery. They had said: 'It's men's *devices* that shape the world.' And this, of course, was what he needed now – a device. He had to behave not only like Sydney and Simpkins but also like the King of Piedmont: he had to invent a contrivance which, from the perfect sum of his love's whole, would take away a crucial part.

*

Some days passed.

Salvatore got out pen and paper. He stared at the paper for long hours at a time, absent-mindedly drawing designs for winder keys. Nothing in the way of any device would come into his mind.

One early morning, waking restless and confused, he put on his coat and walked through two rain showers and one deluge of hail to High Holborn and stood at the window of Fantino, E. The shop was not yet open. Salvatore remained there for several minutes staring at the instruments inscribed with his future name. Though not, as he had remarked before, as fine as many Italian pieces, the beauty of the barometers struck him more forcefully than it had at first. The face-work, done by Benedict Simpkins, was elegant, rather plain but nevertheless perfectly balanced, the word 'Fair' being particularly finely wrought. And Salvatore imagined himself returning to Piedmont at some future time with the gift of a barometer for Roberto and Magnifica. He saw the scene: Roberto would put on his spectacles and Magnifica would get up from the dinner table and they would both gather round and stare at the instrument and touch it and caress it and one of them would say at last: 'Well, son, the weaknesses you had as a clockmaker you have eradicated in this new profession of yours.'

These tender imaginings about his parents calmed Salvatore a little. If love could not make the bridge back to Piedmont, then perhaps the barometers would, in time.

He was able to set out on his return journey to Percy Street with a relatively tranquil mind. And then, on the way, something happened to him.

He passed a fan shop. Without really knowing why, he stopped in front of it and let his eye wander over the variety of fans displayed in the window. He was searching for a fan of decorated black lacquer, similar to the one his beloved had carried. There was nothing quite like it in the shop and Salvatore, beginning to muse on its singularity, suddenly understood that he had stumbled upon the device that would destroy his beloved's perfection. The device was her fan.

335

He remembered the encounter with her in every detail. And one of these details now struck him as immensely significant. Although the day had been warm, very warm, in fact, and the air muggy in his repair shop, the young woman had held the fan strangely still. One would have expected her to be fanning herself vigorously, but she was not doing so. In other words, despite the heat and humidity, *she had not used her fan like a fan.*

'And so,' said Salvatore, standing absolutely still at the fan shop window, 'she was not *using* the fan as a fan; she was using the fan as a device. It was a device of concealment, no less significant than that of Sydney and Simpkins and the invented Fantino, E. And what the fan concealed was a hole. In an otherwise ravishingly perfect oval face, there was a missing part. It was where a dimple might have been. It was a hole so deep, it had sucked in part of the cheek and all the skin at its rim was brown and puckered. It was a hole like an anus.'

Salvatore covered his eyes with his hands. A shower had come on while he had been standing at the window and he was now shivering with cold.

It took Salvatore two years (a year longer than Mr Sydney had anticipated) to re-emerge into the world as Evangelista. Mr Simpkins and Mr Sydney put this down to the young man's obsession with perfection. At first, this had exasperated them, but then they began to pay more and more attention to the quality of their own work, and the barometers made by the firm of Fantino, E. dating from the year 1818 surpassed in beauty and accuracy anything previously manufactured by them.

Their enterprise blossomed. Money was made. It was decided, in order to bind Evangelista more closely to the family, that he would marry Benedict Simpkins' daughter, Jane. She and any children born to her would take the name Fantino.

In the summer of 1820, after a protracted and happy visit to Piedmont, Evangelista was walking with his wife Jane in St James's Park when he saw, coming towards him, wearing a coral-coloured gown and a matching hat, the owner of the

Huygens clock. It was a very warm day, but she carried no fan. She held her head high, seeming to smile at the fresh green of the park and the soft blue of the sky.

Her face was as beautiful and as untroubled by any imperfection as it had once been in Evangelista's Percy Street shop, and in his mind.

Evangelista noted this fact; then he reached for his wife's hand and walked on. Under his breath, he said his old name: 'Salvatore'.

The Candle Maker

For twenty-seven years, Mercedes Dubois worked in a laundry.

The laundry stood on a west-facing precipice in the hilltop town of Leclos. It was one of the few laundries in Corsica with a view of the sea.

On fine evenings, ironing at sunset was a pleasant – almost marvellous – occupation and for twenty-seven years Mercedes Dubois considered herself fortunate in her work. To her sister, Honorine, who made paper flowers, she remarked many times over the years: 'In my work, at least, I'm a fortunate woman.' And Honorine, twisting wire, holding petals in her mouth, always muttered: 'I don't know why you have to put it like that.'

Then the laundry burned down.

The stone walls didn't burn, but everything inside them turned to black iron and black oil and ash. The cause was electrical, so the firemen said. Electricians in Leclos, they said, didn't know how to earth things properly.

The burning down of the laundry was the second tragedy in the life of Mercedes Dubois. She didn't know how to cope with it. She sat in her basement apartment and stared at her furniture. It was a cold December and Mercedes was wearing her old red anorak. She sat with her hands in her anorak pockets, wondering what she could do. She knew that in Leclos, once a thing was lost, it never returned. There had been a bicycle shop once, and a library and a lacemaker's. There had been fifty children and three teachers at the school; now, there were twenty children and one teacher. Mercedes pitied the lonely teacher, just as she pitied the mothers and fathers of all the schoolchildren who had grown up and gone away. But there was nothing to be done about any of it. Certainly nothing one woman, single all her life, could do. Better not to remember the variety there had been. And better, now, not to remember the sunset ironing or the camaraderie of the mornings, making coffee, folding sheets. Mercedes Dubois knew that the laundry would never reopen because it had never been insured. Sitting with her hands in her anorak pockets, staring at her sideboard, was all there was to be done about it.

But after a while she stood up. She went over to the sideboard and poured herself a glass of anisette. She put it on the small table where she ate her meals and sat down again and looked at it. She thought: I can drink the damned anisette. I can do that at least.

She had always considered her surname right for her. She was as hard as wood. Wood, not stone. She could be pliant. And once, long ago, a set of initials had been carved on her heart of wood. It was after the carving of these initials that she understood how wrong for her her first name was. She had been christened after a Spanish saint, Maria de las Mercedes – Mary of the Mercies – but she had been unable to show mercy. On the contrary, what had consumed her was despair and malevolence. She had lain in her iron bed and consoled herself with thoughts of murder.

Mercedes Dubois: stoical but without forgiveness; a woman who once planned to drown her lover and his new bride and instead took a job in a laundry; what could she do, now that the laundry was gone?

Of her sister, Honorine, she asked the question: 'What can anyone do in so terrible a world?'

And Honorine replied: 'I've been wondering about that, because, look at my hands. I've got the beginnings of arthritis, see? I'm losing my touch with the paper flowers.'

'There you are,' said Mercedes. 'I don't know what anyone can do except drink.'

But Honorine, who was married to a sensible man, a plasterer, shook a swollen finger at her sister and warned: 'Don't

339

go down that road. There's always something. That's what we've been taught to believe. Why don't you go and sit in the church and think about it?'

'Have *you* gone and sat in the church and thought about it?' asked Mercedes.

'Yes.'

'And?'

'I noticed all the flowers in there are plastic these days. It's more durable than paper. We're going to save up and buy the kind of machinery you need to make a plastic flower.'

Mercedes left Honorine and walked down the dark, steep street, going towards home and the anisette bottle. She was fifty-four years old. The arrival of this second catastrophe in her life had brought back her memories of the first one.

The following day, obedient to Honorine, she went into the Church of St Vida, patron saint of lemon growers, and walked all around it very slowly, wondering where best to sit and think about her life. Nowhere seemed best. To Mercedes the child, this church had smelled of satin; now it smelled of dry rot. Nobody cared for it. Like the laundry, it wasn't insured against calamity. And the stench of calamity was here. St Vida's chipped plaster nostrils could detect it. She stood in her niche, holding a lemon branch to her breast, staring pitifully down at her broken foot. Mercedes thought: poor Vida, what a wreck, and no lemon growers left in Leclos. What can either Vida or I do in so desolate a world?

She sat in a creaking pew. She shivered. She felt a simple longing, now, for something to warm her while she thought about her life. So she went to where the votive candles flickered on their iron sconces – fourteen of them on the little unsteady rack – and warmed her hands there.

There was only one space left for a new candle and Mercedes thought: this is what the people of Leclos do in answer to loss: they come to St Vida's and light a candle. When the children leave, when the bicycle shop folds, when the last lacemaker dies, they illuminate a little funnel of air. It costs a franc. Even

Honorine, saving up for her plastics machine, can afford one franc. And the candle is so much more than itself. The candle is the voice of a lover, the candle is a catch of mackerel, the candle is a drench of rain, a garden of marrows, a neon sign, a year of breath . . .

So Mercedes paid a franc and took a new candle and lit it and put it in the last vacant space on the rack. She admired it possessively: its soft colour, its resemblance to something living. But what *is* it? she asked herself. What *is* my candle? If only it could be something as simple as rain!

At this moment, the door of St Vida's opened and Mercedes heard footsteps go along the nave. She turned and recognised Madame Picaud, proprietor of the lost laundry. This woman had once been a café singer in Montparnasse. She'd worn feathers in her hair. On the long laundry afternoons, she used to sing ballads about homesickness and the darkness of bars. Now, she'd lost her second livelihood and her head was draped in a shawl.

Madame Picaud stood by the alcove of St Vida, looking up at the lemon branch and the saint's broken foot. Mercedes was about to slip away and leave the silence of the church to her former employer, when she had a thought that caused her sudden and unexpected distress: suppose poor Madame Picaud came, after saying a prayer to Vida, to light a candle and found that there was no space for it in the rack? Suppose Madame Picaud's candle was a laundry rebuilt and re-equipped with new bright windows looking out at the sea? Suppose the future of Madame Picaud – with which her own future would undoubtedly be tied – rested upon the ability of this single tongue of yellow fire to burn unhindered in the calamitous air of the Church of St Vida? And then it could not burn. It could not burn because there were too many other futures already up there flickering away on the rack.

Mercedes looked at her own candle and then at all the others. Of the fifteen, she judged that five or six had been burning for some time. And so she arrived at a decision about these: they were past futures. They had had their turn. What counted was the moment of lighting, or, if not merely the moment of lighting, then the moment of lighting and the first moments of burning. When the candles got stubby and started to burn unevenly, dripping wax into the tray, they were no longer love letters or olive harvests or cures for baldness or machines that manufactured flowers; they were simply old candles. They had to make way. No one had understood this until now. *I* understand it, said Mercedes to herself, because I know what human longing there is in Leclos. I know it because I am part of it.

She walked round to the back of the rack. She removed the seven shortest candles and blew them out. She rearranged the longer candles, including her own, until the seven spaces were all at the front, inviting seven new futures, one of which would be Madame Picaud's.

Then Mercedes walked home with the candles stuffed into the pockets of her red anorak. She laid them out on her table and looked at them.

She had never been petty or underhand.

She went to see the Curé the following morning and told him straight out that she wanted to be allowed to keep the future burning in Leclos by recycling the votive candles. She said: 'With the money you save, you could restore St Vida's foot.'

The Curé offered Mercedes a glass of wine. He had a fretful smile. He said: 'I've heard it's done elsewhere, in the great cathedrals, where they get a lot of tourists, but it's never seemed necessary in Leclos.'

Mercedes sipped her wine. She said: 'It's *more* necessary here than in Paris or Reims, because hope stays alive much longer in those places. In Leclos, everything vanishes. Everything.'

The Curé looked at her kindly. 'I was very sorry to hear about the laundry,' he said. 'What work will you do now?'

'I'm going to do this,' said Mercedes. 'I'm going to do the candles.'

342

He nodded. 'Fire, in Corsica, has always been an enemy. But I expect Madame Picaud had insurance against it?'

'No she didn't,' said Mercedes, 'only the free kind: faith and prayer.'

The Curé finished his glass of wine. He shook his head discreetly, as if he were a bidder at an auction who has decided to cease bidding.

'I expect you know,' he said after a moment, 'that the candles have to be of a uniform size and length?'

'Oh, yes.'

'And I should add that if there *are* savings of any import . . . then . . .'

'I don't want a few francs, Monsieur le Curé. I'm not interested in that. I just want to make more room for something to happen here, that's all.'

Collecting the candles and melting them down began to absorb her. She put away the anisette bottle. She went into the church at all hours. She was greedy for the candles. So she began removing even those that had burned for only a short time. She justified this to herself by deciding, once and forever, that what mattered in every individual wish or intention was the act of lighting the candle – the moment of illumination. This alone. Nothing else. And she watched what people did. They lit their candles and looked at them for no more than a minute. Then they left. They didn't keep on returning to make sure their candles were still alight. 'The point is,' Mercedes explained to Honorine, 'they continue to burn in the imagination and the value you could set on the imagination would be higher than one franc. So the actual life of the candle is of no importance.'

'How can you be sure?' asked Honorine.

'I am sure. You don't need to be a philosopher to see it.'

'And what if a person did come back to check her individual candle?'

'The candles are identical, Honorine. A field of basil is indistinguishable from an offer of marriage.'

343

She had ordered six moulds from the forge and sent off for a hundred metres of cotton wick from a maker of nightlights in Ajaccio. The smell of bubbling wax pervaded her apartment. It resembled the smell of new leather, pleasant yet suffocating.

She began to recover from her loss of the job at the laundry. Because, in a way, she thought, I've *become* a laundry; I remove the soiled hopes of the town and make them new and return them neatly to the wooden candle drawer.

The Social Security Office paid her a little sum of money each week. She wasn't really poor, not as poor as she'd feared, because her needs were few.

Sometimes, she walked out to the coast road and looked at the black remains of what had been spin-dryers and cauldrons of bleach, and then out beyond this pile of devastation to the sea, with its faithful mirroring of the sky and its indifference. She began to smell the spring on the salt winds.

News, in Leclos, travelled like fire. It leapt from threshold to balcony, from shutter to shutter.

One morning, it came down to Mercedes' door: 'Someone has returned, Mercedes. You can guess who.'

Mercedes stood in her doorway, blinking into the February sun. The bringer of the news was Honorine. Honorine turned and went away up the street leaving Mercedes standing there. The news burned in her throat. She said his name: Louis Cabrini.

She had believed he would never return to Leclos. He'd told her twenty-seven years ago that he'd grown to dislike the town, dislike the hill it sat on, dislike its name and its closed-in streets. He said: 'I've fallen in love, Mercedes – with a girl and with a place. I'm going to become a Parisian now.'

He had married his girl. She was a ballerina. Her name was Sylvie. It was by her supple, beautiful feet that the mind of Mercedes Dubois chained her to the ocean bed. For all that had been left her after Louis went away were her dreams of murder. Because she'd known, from the age of eighteen, that she, Mercedes, was going to be his wife. She had known and all

344

of Leclos had known: Louis Cabrini and Mercedes Dubois were meant for each other. There would be a big wedding at the Church of St Vida and, after that, a future . . .

Then he went to Paris, to train as an engineer. He met a troupe of dancers in a bar. He came back to Leclos just the one time, to collect his belongings and say goodbye to Mercedes. He had stood with her in the square and it had been a sunny February day – a day just like this one, on which Honorine had brought news of his return – and after he'd finished speaking, Mercedes walked away without a word. She took twelve steps and then she turned round. Louis was standing quite still, watching her. He had taken her future away and this was all he could do – stand still and stare. She said: 'I'm going to kill you, Louis. You and your bride.'

Mercedes went down into her apartment. A neat stack of thirty candles was piled up on her table, ready to be returned to St Vida's. A mirror hung above the sideboard and Mercedes walked over to it and looked at herself. She had her father's square face, his deep-set brown eyes, his wiry hair. And his name. She would stand firm in the face of Honorine's news. She would go about her daily business in Leclos as if Louis were not there. If she chanced to meet him, she would pretend she hadn't recognised him. He was older than she was. He might by now, with his indulgent Parisian life, look like an old man. His walk would be slow.

But then a new thought came: suppose he hadn't returned to Leclos alone, as she'd assumed? Suppose when she went to buy her morning loaf, she had to meet the fading beauty of the ballerina? And hear her addressed as Madame Cabrini? And see her slim feet in expensive shoes?

Mercedes put on her red anorak and walked up to Honorine's house. Honorine's husband, Jacques the plasterer, was there and the two of them were eating their midday soup in contented silence.

'You didn't tell me,' said Mercedes, 'has he come back alone?'

'Have some soup,' said Jacques, 'you look pale.'

'I'm not hungry,' said Mercedes. 'I need to know, Honorine.'

'All I've heard is rumour,' said Honorine.

'Well?'

'They say she left him. Some while back. They say he's been in poor health ever since.'

Mercedes nodded. Not really noticing what she did, she sat down at Honorine's kitchen table. Honorine and Jacques put down their spoons and looked at her. Her face was waxy.

Jacques said: 'Give her some soup, Honorine.' Then he said: 'There's too much history in Corsica. It's in the stone.'

When Mercedes left Honorine's she went straight to the church. On the way, she kept her head down and just watched her shadow moving along ahead of her as, behind her, the sun went down.

There was nobody in St Vida's. Mercedes went straight to the candle sconces. She snatched up two low-burning candles and blew them out. She stood still a moment, hesitating. Then she blew out all the remaining candles. It's wretched, wretched, she thought: all this interminable, flickering, optimistic light; wretched beyond comprehension.

After February, in Corsica, the spring comes fast. The *maquis* starts to bloom. The mimosas come into flower.

Mercedes was susceptible to the perfume of things. So much so that, this year, she didn't want even to *see* the mimosa blossom. She wanted everything to stay walled up in its own particular winter. She wanted clouds to gather and envelop the town in a dark mist.

She crept about the place like a thief. She had no conversations. She scuttled here and there, not looking, not noticing. In her apartment, she kept the shutters closed. She worked on the candles by the light of a single bulb.

Honorine came down to see her. 'You can't go on like this, Mercedes,' she said. 'You can't live this way.'

'Yes, I can,' said Mercedes.

'He looks old,' said Honorine, 'his skin's yellowy. He's not the handsome person he used to be.'

346

Mercedes said nothing. She thought, no one in this place, not even my sister, has ever understood what I feel.

'You ought to go and meet him,' said Honorine. 'Have a drink with him. It's time you forgave him.'

Mercedes busied herself with the wax she was melting in a saucepan. She turned her back towards Honorine.

'Did you hear what I said?' asked Honorine.

'Yes,' said Mercedes, 'I heard.'

After Honorine had left, Mercedes started to weep. Her tears fell into the wax and made it spit. Her cheeks were pricked with small burns. She picked up a kitchen cloth and buried her head in it. She thought, what no one understands is that this darkness isn't new. I've been in it in my mind for twenty-seven years, ever since that February morning in the square when the mimosas were coming into flower. There were moments when it lifted – when those big sunsets came in at the laundry window, for instance – but it always returned, as night follows day; always and always.

And then she thought, but Honorine is right, it is intolerable. I should have done what I dreamed of doing. I should have killed him. Why was I so cowardly? I should have cut off his future – all those days and months of his happy life in Paris that I kept seeing like a film in my head: the ballerina's hair falling on his body; her feet touching his feet under the dainty patisserie table; their two summer shadows moving over the water of the Seine. I should have ended it as I planned, and then I would have been free of him and out of the darkness and I could have had a proper life.

And now. She was in Leclos, in her own town that she'd never left, afraid to move from her flat, gliding to and from the church like a ghost, avoiding every face, sunk into a loneliness so deep and fast it resembled the grave. Was this how the remainder of her life was to be spent?

She prised the buttons of wax from her cheeks with her fingernails. She took the saucepan off the gas flame and laid it aside, without pouring its contents into the candle moulds. It was a round-bottomed pan and Mercedes could imagine the smooth, rounded shape into which the wax would set.

She ran cold water onto her face, drenching her hair, letting icy channels of water eddy down her neck and touch her breasts. Her mind had recovered from its futile weeping and had formulated a plan and she wanted to feel the chill of the plan somewhere near her heart.

She lay awake all night. She had decided at last to kill Louis Cabrini.

Not with her own hands, face to face. Not like that.

She would do it slowly. From a distance. With all the power of the misery she'd held inside her for twenty-seven years.

Morning came and she hadn't slept. She stared at the meagre strips of light coming through the shutters. In this basement apartment, it was impossible to gauge what kind of day waited above. But she knew that what waited above, today, was the plan. It was a Friday. In Mercedes' mind, the days of the week were different colours. Wednesday was red. Friday was a pallid kind of yellow.

She dressed and put on her apron. She sat at her kitchen table drinking coffee and eating bread. She heard two women go past her window, laughing. She thought: that was the other beautiful thing that happened in the laundry – laughter.

When the women had walked on by and all sound of them had drained away, Mercedes said aloud: 'Now.'

She cleared away the bread and coffee. She lit one ring of the stove and held above it the saucepan full of wax, turning it like a chef turns an omelette pan, so that the flames spread an even heat round the body of the wax. She felt it come loose from the saucepan, a solid lump. 'Good,' she said.

She set out a pastry board on the table. She touched its smooth wooden surface with her hand. Louis Cabrini had been childishly fond of pastries and cakes. In her mother's kitchen, Mercedes used to make him *tarte tatin* and *apfelstrudel*.

She turned out the lump of wax onto the pastry board. It was yellowy in colour. The more she recycled the candles the yellower they became.

Now she had a round dome of wax on which to begin work.

She went to the bookcase, which was almost empty except for a green, chewed set of the collected works of Victor Hugo and an orange edition of *Lettres de mon moulin* by Alphonse Daudet. Next to Daudet was a book Mercedes had borrowed from the library twenty-seven years ago to teach herself about sex and had never returned, knowing perhaps that the library, never very efficient with its reminders, would close in due time. It was called *Simple Anatomy of the Human Body*. It contained drawings of all the major internal organs. On page fifty-nine was a picture of the male body unclothed, at which Mercedes used to stare.

Mercedes put the book next to the pastry board, under the single light. She turned the pages until she found the drawing of the heart. The accompanying text read: 'The human heart is small, relative to its importance. It is made up of four chambers, the right and left auricle and the right and left ventricle . . .'

'All right,' said Mercedes.

Using the drawing as a guide, she began to sculpt a heart out of the wax dome. She worked with a thin filleting knife and two knitting needles of different gauges.

Her first thought as she started the sculpture was: the thing it most resembles is a fennel root and the smell of fennel resembles in its turn the smell of anisette.

The work absorbed her. She didn't feel tired any more. She proceeded carefully and delicately, striving for verisimilitude. She knew that this heart was larger than a heart is supposed to be and she thought, well, in Louis Cabrini's case, it swelled with pride – pride in his beautiful wife, pride in his successful career, pride in being a Parisian, at owning a second-floor apartment, at eating in good restaurants, at buying roses at dusk to take home to his woman. Pride in leaving Leclos behind. Pride in his ability to forget the past.

She imagined his rib-cage expanding to accommodate this swollen heart of his.

Now and again, she made errors. Then, she had to light a match and pass it over the wax to melt it – to fill too deep an abrasion or smooth too jagged an edge. And she noticed in time that this slight re-melting of the heart gave it a more liquid, living appearance. This was very satisfactory. She began to relish it. She would strike a match and watch an ooze begin, then blow it out and slowly repair the damage she'd caused.

It was becoming, just as she'd planned, her plaything. Except that she'd found more ways to wound it than she'd imagined. She had thought that, in the days to come, she would pierce it or cut it with something – scissors, knives, razor blades. But now she remembered that its very substance was unstable. She could make it bleed. She could make it disintegrate. It could empty itself out. And then, if she chose, she could rebuild it, make it whole again. She felt excited and hot. She thought: I have never had power over anything; this has been one of the uncontrovertible facts of my life.

As the day passed and darkness filled the cracks in the shutters, Mercedes began to feel tired. She moved the anatomy book aside and laid her head on the table beside the pastry board. She put her hand inside her grey shirt and squeezed and massaged her nipple, and her head filled with dreams of herself as a girl, standing in the square, smelling the sea and smelling the mimosa blossom, and she fell asleep.

She thought someone was playing a drum. She thought there was a march coming up the street.

But it was a knocking on her door.

She raised her head from the table. Her cheek was burning hot from lying directly under the light bulb. She had no idea whether it was night-time yet. She remembered the heart, almost finished, in front of her. She thought the knocking on her door could be Honorine coming to talk to her again and tell her she couldn't go on living the way she was.

She didn't want Honorine to see the heart. She got up and

draped a clean tea towel over it, as though it were a newly baked cake. All around the pastry board were crumbs of wax and used matches. Mercedes tried to sweep them into her hand and throw them in the sink. She felt dizzy after her sleep on the table. She staggered about like a drunk. She knew she'd been having beautiful dreams.

When she opened her door, she saw a man standing there. He wore a beige mackintosh and a yellow scarf. Underneath the mackintosh, his body looked bulky. He wore round glasses. He said: 'Mercedes?'

She put a hand up to her red burning cheek. She blinked at him. She moved to close the door in his face, but he anticipated this and put out a hand, trying to keep the door open.

'Don't do that,' he said. 'That's the easy thing to do.'

'Go away,' said Mercedes.

'Yes. Okay I will, I promise. But first let me in. Please. Just for ten minutes.'

Mercedes thought: if I didn't feel so dizzy, I'd be stronger. I'd be able to push him out. But all she did was hold onto the door and stare at him. Louis Cabrini. Wearing glasses. His curly hair getting sparse. His belly fat.

He came into her kitchen. The book of human anatomy was still open on the table, next to the covered heart.

He looked all around the small, badly lit room. From his mackintosh pocket, he took out a bottle of red wine and held it out to her. 'I thought we could drink some of this.'

Mercedes didn't take the bottle. 'I don't want you here,' she said. 'Why did you come back to Leclos?'

'To die,' he said. 'Now, come on. Drink a glass of wine with me. One glass.'

She turned away from him. She fetched two glasses and put them on the table. She closed the anatomy book.

'Corkscrew?' he asked.

She went to her dresser drawer and took it out. It was an old-fashioned thing. She hardly ever drank wine any more, except at Honorine's. Louis put the wine on the table. 'May I take my coat off?' he said.

Under the smart mackintosh, he was wearing comfortable clothes, baggy brown trousers, a black sweater. Mercedes laid the mackintosh and the yellow scarf over the back of a chair. 'You don't look as if you're dying,' she said, 'you've got quite fat.'

He laughed. Mercedes remembered this laugh by her side in her father's little vegetable garden. She had been hoeing onions. Louis had laughed and laughed at something she'd said about the onions.

'I'm being melodramatic,' he said. 'I'm not going to die tomorrow. I mean that my life in Paris is over. I'm in Leclos now till I peg out! I mean that this is all I've got left to do. The rest is finished.'

'Everything finishes,' said Mercedes.

'Well,' said Louis, 'I wouldn't say that. Leclos is just the same, here on its hill. Still the same cobbles and smelly gutters. Still the same view of the sea.'

'You're wrong,' said Mercedes, 'nothing lasts here in Leclos. Everything folds or moves away.'

'But not the place itself. Or you. And here we both are. Still alive.'

'If you can call it living.'

'Yes, it's living. And you've baked a cake, I see. Baking is being alive. Now here. Have a sip of wine. Let me drink a toast to *you*.'

She needed the wine to calm her, to get her brain thinking properly again. So she drank. She recognised at once that Louis had brought her expensive wine. She offered him a chair and they both sat down at the table. Under the harsh light, Mercedes could see that Louis' face looked creased and sallow.

'Honorine told me you'd been hiding from me.'

'I don't want you here in Leclos.'

'That saddens me. But perhaps you'll change your mind in time?'

'No. Why should I?'

'Because you'll get used to my being here. I'll become part

of the place, like furniture, or like poor old Vida up at the church with her broken foot.'

'You've been in the church? I've never seen you in there.'

'Of course I've been in. It was partly the church that brought me back. I've been selfish with my money for most of my life, but I thought if I came back to Leclos I would start a fund to repair that poor old church.'

'The church doesn't need you.'

'Well, it needs someone. You can smell the damp in the stone . . .'

'It needs *me*! I'm the one who's instituted the idea of economy. No one thought of it before. They simply let everything go to waste. *I'm* the one who understood about the candles. It didn't take a philosopher. It's simple once you see it.'

'What's simple?'

'I can't go into it now. Not to you. It's simple and yet not. And with you I was never good at explaining things.'

'Try,' said Louis.

'No,' said Mercedes.

They were silent. Mercedes drank her wine. She thought, this is the most beautiful wine I've ever tasted. She wanted to pour herself another glass, but she resisted.

'I'd like you to leave now,' she said.

Louis smiled. Only in his smile and in his laughter did Mercedes recognise the young man whose wife she should have been. 'I've only just arrived, Mercedes, and there's so much we could talk about . . .'

'There's nothing to talk about.'

The smile vanished. 'Show me some kindness,' he said. 'I haven't had the happy life you perhaps imagined. I made a little money, that's all. That's all I have to show. The only future I can contemplate is here, so I was hoping – '

'Don't stay in Leclos. Go somewhere else. Anywhere . . .'

'I heard about the fire.'

'What?'

'The fire at the laundry. But I think it's going to be all right.'

'Of course it's not going to be all right. You don't understand how life is in Leclos any more. You just walk back and walk in, when no one invited you . . .'

'The church "invited" me. But also Madame Picaud. She wrote and asked me what could be done when the laundry burned down. I told her I would try to help.'

'There's no insurance.'

'No.'

'How can you help, then?'

'I told you, all I have left is a little money. One of my investments will be a new laundry.'

Mercedes said nothing. After a while, Louis stood up. 'I'll go now,' he said, 'but three things brought me back, you know. St Vida, the laundry and you. I want your forgiveness. I would like us to be friends.'

'I can't forgive you,' said Mercedes. 'I never will.'

'You may. In time. You may surprise yourself. Remember your name, Mercedes: Mary of the Mercies.'

Mercedes drank the rest of the wine.

She sat very still at her table, raising the glass to her lips and sipping and sipping until it was all gone. She found herself admiring her old sticks of furniture and the shadows in the room that moved as if to music.

She got unsteadily to her feet. She had no idea what time it could be. She heard a dog bark.

She got out her candle moulds and set them in a line. She cut some lengths of wick. Then she put Louis Cabrini's waxen heart into the rounded saucepan and melted it down and turned it back into votive candles.

Two of Them

We used to be a family of three: my mother, Jane, my father, Hugh, and me, Lewis. We lived in a house in Wiltshire with a view of the downs. At the back of the house was an old grey orchard.

Then, we became a family of two-and-three-quarters. I was fourteen when this happened. The quarter we lost was my father's mind. He had been a divorce solicitor for twenty years. He said to me: 'Lewis, human life should be symmetrical, but it never is.' He said: 'The only hope for the whole bang thing lies in Space.' He said: 'I was informed definitively in a dream that on Mars there are no trinities.'

My mother searched for the missing bit of my father's mind in peculiar places. She looked for it in cereal packets, in the fridge, in the photographs of houses in *Country Life*. She became distracted with all this searching. One winter day, she cried into a bag of chestnuts. She said: 'Lewis, do you know what your father's doing now?'

She sent me out to find him. He was on our front lawn, measuring out two circles. When he saw me he said: 'Capital. You're good at geometry. Hold this tape.'

The circles were enormous – thirty feet in diameter. 'Luckily,' said my father, 'this is a damn large lawn.' He held a mallet. He marked out the circles by driving kindling sticks into the grass. When he'd finished, he said: 'All right. That's it. That's a good start.'

I was a weekly boarder at school. In the weekdays, I didn't mention the fact that my father had gone crazy. I tried to keep my mind on mathematics. At night, in the dormitory, I lay very still, not talking. My bed was beside a window. I kept my glasses on in the darkness and looked at the moon.

My mother wrote to me once a week. Before we'd lost a quarter of one third of our family, she'd only written every second week because my father wrote in the week in between. Now, he refused to write any words anywhere on anything. He said: 'Words destroy. Enough is enough.'

My mother's letters were full of abbreviations and French phrases. I think this was how she'd been taught to express herself in the days when she'd been a debutante and had to write formal notes of acceptance or refusal or thanks. 'Darling Lewis,' she'd put, 'How goes yr maths and alg? Bien, j'espère. Drove yr F. into S'bury yest. Insisted buying tin of white gloss paint and paint gear, inc roller. Pourquoi? On vera bientôt, sans doute. What a b. mess it all is. You my only hope and consol. now.'

The year was 1955. I wished that everything would go back to how it had been.

In mathematics, there is nothing that cannot be returned to where it has been.

I started to have embarrassing dreams about being a baby again – a baby with flawless eyesight, lying in a pram and watching the sky. The bit of sky that I watched was composed of particles of wartime air.

I didn't want to be someone's only hope and consolation. I thought the burden of this would probably make me go blind and I wished I had a sister, someone who could dance for my parents and do mime to their favourite songs.

When I got home one weekend, there were two painted crosses inside the circles on the lawn. They were white.

My father had taken some of the pills that were meant to give him back the missing part of his mind and he was asleep in a chair, wearing his gardening hat.

'Look at him!' said my mother. 'I simply don't know what else is to be done.'

356

My mother and I went out and stood on the white crosses. I measured them with my feet. 'They're landing pads,' said my mother, 'for the supposed spaceship from Mars.'

I said: 'They're exactly sixteen by sixteen – half the diameter of the circles.'

We sat down on them. It was a spring afternoon and the air smelled of blossom and of rain. My mother was smoking a Senior Service. She said: 'The doctors tell me it might help if we went away.'

'Where to?' I asked.

'I don't know where to. I don't suppose that matters. Just away somewhere.'

I said: 'Do you mean France?'

'No,' she said. 'I think he might be worse abroad. Don't you? And the English are better about this kind of thing; they just look the other way.'

'Where, then?'

I was thinking of all the weekends I was going to have to spend alone in the empty school. Sometimes, boys were stuck there with nothing to do for two days. A friend of mine called Pevers once told me he'd spent a total of seventeen hours throwing a tennis ball against a wall and catching it.

'What about the sea?' said my mother. 'You'd like that, wouldn't you?'

'You mean, in the summer?'

'Yes, darling,' she said. 'I couldn't manage anything like that without you.'

What I thought next was that it might be better to throw a ball against a wall for seventeen hours than to be by the sea with my father watching the horizon for Martians and my mother reminding me that I was her only hope and consolation.

I got up and measured the crosses again. I said: 'They're absolutely symmetrical. That means he can still do simple calculations.'

'What about Devon or Cornwall?' said my mother. 'They get

357

the Gulf Stream there. Something might blow in. One can never tell.'

My father woke up. The pills he was taking made his legs tremble, so he sat in his chair, calling my name: 'Lewis! Lewis! Boy!'

I went in and kissed his cheek, which was one quarter unshaved, as if the razor had a bit of itself missing. He said: 'Seen the landing sights, old chap?'

'Yes,' I said. 'They're brilliant.'

'*Two*,' he said triumphantly.

'How did you know how big to make them?'

'I didn't. I'm guessing. I think there'll be two craft with four fellas in each, making eight. So I doubled this and came up with sixteen. Seems about right. Everything with them is paired, perfectly weighted. No triangles. No discord. No argy-bargy.'

I waited. I thought my father was going to tell me how the Martians could set about saving the world after they'd landed on our front lawn, but he didn't.

'What do they eat?' I asked.

My father took off his gardening hat and stared at it. 'I don't know,' he said. 'I overlooked that.' And he began to cry.

'It won't matter,' I said. 'We can drive into Salisbury and buy masses of whatever it turns out to be. It's not as though we're poor, is it?'

'No,' he said. He put his hat back on and wiped his eyes with his shirt cuffs.

My mother found a summer holiday house for us in north Cornwall. It was out on a promontory on a wild hill of gorse. From the front of it, all you could see was the beach and the ocean and the sky, but from the back – the way my bedroom faced – you could see one other house, much larger than ours. It was made of stone, like a castle. It had seven chimneys.

On our first day, I found a narrow path that led up from our house directly to it. I climbed it. I could hear people laughing in the garden. I thought, if I were a Martian, I would land on this castle roof and not on our lawn in Wiltshire; I would go and join the laughing people; I would say, 'I see you have a badminton net suspended between two conveniently situated trees.'

My parents didn't seem to have noticed this other house. Wherever they were, they behaved as though that spot was the centre of the universe.

On our first evening, they stood at the French window, looking out at the sunset. I sat on a chair behind them, watching them and hearing the sea far below them. My mother said to my father: 'Do you like it here, Hugh?'

My father said: 'Beach is ideal. Just the place. Better than the bloody lawn.'

That night, when I was almost asleep, he came into my room and said: 'I'm counting on you, Lewis. There's work to be done in the morning.'

'What work?' I said.

'I'm counting on you,' he repeated. 'You're not going to let me down, are you?'

'No,' I said. 'I'm not going to let anybody down.'

But then I couldn't sleep. I tried throwing an imaginary tennis ball against an imaginary wall until the morning came.

We made circles in the sand. I was supposed to calculate the exact spot where the sun would go down, as though we were building Stonehenge. My father wanted the sun to set between the two circles.

My mother sat in a deck chair, wearing a cotton dress and sunglasses with white frames. My father took some of his pills and went wandering back to the house. My mother went with him, carrying the deck chair, and I was left alone with the work of the circles. They had to have sculpted walls, exactly two feet high. All that I had to work with was a child's spade.

I went swimming and then I lay down in the first half-made circle and floated into one of my dreams of previous time. I was woken by a sound I recognised: it was the sound of the castle laughter.

I opened my eyes. Two girls were standing in my circle. They wore identical blue bathing costumes and identical smiles. They had the kind of hair my mother referred to as 'difficult' – wild and frizzy. I lay there, staring up at them. They were of identical height.

'Hello,' I said.

One of them said: 'You're exhausted. We were watching you. Shall we come and help you?'

I stood up. My back and arms were coated with sand. I said: 'That's very kind of you.' Neither of them had a spade.

'What's your name?' they said in unison.

I was about to say 'Lewis'. I took my glasses off and pretended to clean them on my bathing trunks while I thought of a more castle-sounding name. 'Sebastian,' I said.

'I'm Fran,' said one of them.

'I'm Isabel,' said the other.

'We're twins,' said Fran, 'as if you hadn't guessed.' And they laughed.

They were taller than me. Their legs were brown. I put my glasses back on, to see whether they had a bust. It was difficult to tell, because their swimming costumes were ruched and lumpy all over.

'We're fourteen,' said Fran. 'We're actresses and playwrights. What are you, Sebastian?'

'Oh,' I said, 'nothing yet. I might be a mathematician later on. What are your plays about?'

'You can be in one with us, if you like,' said Isabel. 'Do you want to be in one?'

'I don't know,' I said.

'We only do it for fun,' said Fran. 'We just do them and forget them.'

'I don't expect I've got time,' I said. 'I've got to get these circles finished.'

'Why?' said Isabel. 'What are they for?'

'Oh,' I said, 'for my father. He's doing a kind of scientific experiment.'

'We've never met any scientists,' said Isabel. 'Have we, Fran?'

'We know tons of sculptors, though,' said Fran. 'Do you like sculpture?'

'I don't know,' I said. 'I've never thought about it.'

'We'll go and get our spades,' said Isabel, 'shall we?'

'Thanks,' I said. 'That's jolly kind.'

They ran off. Their difficult hair blew crazily about in the breeze. I watched them till my eyesight let them vanish. I felt out of breath – almost faint – as though I'd run with them into the distance and disappeared.

That night, my mother got drunk on Gin and It. She had never explained to me what 'It' was. She expected me to know thousands of things without ever being told them. She said: 'Listen, Lewis, the tragedy of your father is a tragedy of *imagination*. N'est-ce pas? You see what I mean, darling? If he'd just concentrated on the Consent Orders and the Decrees and so on, this would never have happened. But he didn't. He started to imagine the *feelings*. You see?'

She was scratching her thigh through her cotton dress. Some of the Gin and It had spilled onto her knee. 'So, listen,' she said. 'In your coming life as a great mathematical person, just stick to your *numbers*. Okay? Promise me? You're my only hope now, darling, my only one. I've told you that, haven't I? So don't *start*. Promise me?'

'Start what?'

'What I'm saying is, stick to your own life. *Yours*. Just stay inside that. All right? Your mathematical life. Promise?'

'Yes,' I said. 'What does "It" stand for, Mummy?'

'What does what?'

'"It". What does it stand for?'

'"It"? It's just a *name*, sweetheart. A name for a thing. And names can make Mummy so happy, or so, you know ... the other thing. Like your father, Hugh. Darling Hughie. Mostly the other thing now. All the time. So promise and that's it. Understood?'

'I promise,' I said.

*

The next day my father came to inspect the circles. Only one was finished. Just beyond the finished one was a sand sculpture of a bird. Fran and Isabel and I had stayed on the beach for hours and hours, creating it. They had made its body and wings and I had made its feet.

The bird was huge. It had a stone for an eye. My father didn't notice it. He was admiring the circle. 'Good,' he said. 'Now the other one. I'll give you a hand. Because the time's coming. I can feel it. I've been watching the sky.'

I worked with the child's spade and my father worked with his hands. The sight of his red hands scooping and moulding the sand made me feel lonely.

I waited all day for Fran and Isabel to come. At tea-time, it began to rain and I knew they'd be up in the castle, doing a play to pass the time. The rain fell on the bird and speckled it.

It rained for two days. My parents tried to remember the rules of Ludo. I walked in the rain up the path as far as the castle shrubbery, where I sat and waited. I stared at the droopy badminton net. I counted its holes. And then I walked back down the path and went into the room where my mother and father sat, and closed the door. They'd abandoned the Ludo game. They were just sitting there, waiting for me to return.

That night, I wrote a note to Isabel and Fran:

> Dear Isabel and Fran,
>   When is your next play? I would like to
> be in it, if you still want me to be.
> Yours sincerely,
>   Sebastian

I set my alarm for four o'clock and delivered the note as the sky got light and the larks in the gorse began singing.

When the good weather came back, my father and I mended the circle walls beaten down by the rain. My mother watched us from her deckchair, wearing shorts. Her legs looked very pale. Sometimes, she went to sleep behind her glasses.

My father seemed restless and excited. He said: 'It's going to be soon, Lewis. And at night. I'm going to peg down two sheets in each of the circles. I've checked the moon. Visibility should be fair.'

'Good,' I said.

'I'm as prepared as I can be, thanks to you. Bar the food question. But your mother will cope with that. And there's always fish. Fish is a universal; it must be. But there's one other important thing.'

'What?' I said.

'You've got to be there. Your mother thinks this is a lot of drivel, so she won't come. So I'm counting on you. They want to see two of us. I'm as certain of that as I can be of anything. If there's only me, they'll take off again and go back to Mars.'

'Right,' I said.

But I wasn't really listening to him. My mind was on Isabel and Fran, who had sent me an answer to my note:

> Dear Sebastian,
>   The first rehearsal for our next play
> is going to be in a tent we've pitched
> between our house and yours. Friday evening.
> Ten o'clock. Bring a glass.
> Yours faithfully,
>   Isabel and Fran

Ten o'clock was the bedtime of our family of two-and-three-quarters. When we'd been three, it had been later. Now, my parents preferred sleep to life. In a dream, you can be transported back to pre-war time and find yourself dancing at the Café Royal.

I tried to imagine saying: 'Good night, Mummy. Good night, Dad. I'm going to a play rehearsal now,' but I couldn't. If you are the hope and consolation of anyone alive, you can't go to play rehearsals without warning.

So, I knew what I would have to do. I would have to wait until the house was silent and then creep out of it without being heard and find my way to the tent in the moonlight, remembering first to go into the kitchen and steal a glass. The thought of this made me feel very hot and weak. I sat down on the sand, with my arms on my knees.

'What are you doing, boy?' said my father.

'Resting,' I said. 'Only for a moment.'

I stood at my bedroom window. There was a thin moon. Bright but thin.

It was ten eighteen by my watch.

I could hear my mother coughing. She said the cough came from the sea air.

At ten thirty exactly, I let myself out of my room and closed my door. I stood on the landing, listening. There was no coughing now, no sound of anything.

I went downstairs, holding my shoes. I tried to glide soundlessly, like film stars glide into rooms.

I got a glass from the kitchen and unlocked the back door and went out into the night. I was wearing a grey shirt and grey flannel trousers and the things I could imagine most easily were all my grey veins going into my heart.

I moved up the path. I couldn't see the tent, but I could hear laughing – castle laughter. My mind seemed to be in holes, like a badminton net.

The tent was small. I'd imagined a kind of marquee. This tent was low and tiny. It was pitched on a little clearing in the gorse.

I bent down and called softly: 'Isabel? Fran?'

The laughter stopped. I could hear them whispering. 'I've come for the rehearsal,' I said.

There was silence. Then they giggled. Then Fran stuck her frizzy head out. 'You're late,' she said.

I began to explain and apologise.

'Ssh,' said Fran, 'sound carries. Come inside.'

She opened the little flap of the tent and took hold of my hand and pulled me in.

364

It was pitch dark in the tent and very hot. I felt blind. Fran said: 'Did you bring a glass?' Isabel said: 'Can you see us, Sebastian?'

There was a familiar smell in the little bit of air left me to breathe in; it was the smell of gin.

'You like gin, don't you?' said Isabel.

'I don't know,' I said. 'My mother drinks Gin and It.'

They began giggling again. Now, I could see two soft white shapes, one either side of me. One was Fran and one was Isabel. They were wearing identical white nightdresses. Isabel handed me a glass of gin. She said: 'It's quite comfortable, don't you think? We stole masses of cushions. Try the gin.'

'And lie down,' said Fran. 'Relax.'

I took a sip of the gin. I felt it go into my veins.

I lay down, holding my glass in the air. I felt a hand on my face. I didn't know whether it was Fran's or Isabel's. The hand removed my spectacles.

'Don't,' I said.

'We've got to,' said Isabel.

'Why?' I said.

'That's the rehearsal,' said Fran.

'What do you mean?'

'Well,' said Fran, 'don't you want to rehearse?'

'You mean the play?'

'Yes. It's a kind of play, isn't it, Isabel?'

'Yes,' said Isabel.

'Except that there are two of us and only one of you and in the real future, when it's no longer a play rehearsal, it won't be like that. But it's OK, because we're so alike that in the dark you won't be able to tell which of us is which.'

'What do you mean?' I said. I let my glass tilt deliberately, splashing gin onto my face. The taste of it was beautiful.

They giggled. I felt the skirts of their nightdresses cover my legs, like feathers. Then I saw both their faces above mine and their crazy hair touched my forehead and my cheek.

'Come on, Sebastian,' they whispered. 'There's nothing difficult about it.'

*

365

I walked back to our house just as it was getting light.

From high up, I could see my parents on the little front lawn, wearing their dressing gowns and clinging together.

When they saw me, they stared at me in horror. Then my father broke away from my mother and came roaring at me. My mother followed, trying to catch him and hold him back.

'Hughie!' she screamed. 'Don't! Don't!'

But she couldn't catch him. He hit me on the jaw and I fell to earth.

I woke up in hospital, with a wire like a dog's muzzle round my face. I couldn't utter a word.

My mother was sitting by me. She looked pale and tired.

Later, she said: 'It wasn't only that we were worried, Lewis. There was the Martian business. He told me he saw them land. He saw them from his window. And he went running to find you and you weren't there, and then, as soon as he arrived on the beach, they took off again. He thought it was because there was only one of him. And then he was in despair. He felt you'd let him down and let the world down.'

I went back to school. I could move my jaw enough to say small words like 'no'. Autumn came.

My head had emptied itself of equations and filled up with the faces and bodies of Isabel and Fran.

My father went away. My mother wrote: 'They say it's just for a while, until all's well. But I know that the only *all's well* is you.'

The night after I got this letter, I had a dream. I was at home in Wiltshire, standing in the old, grey orchard.

I saw something come out of the sky and land on the lawn. It was a shadowy thing, without shape or measurable angle, and I knew what it was: it was my life and it was a thing of no hope and no consolation. I wanted to send it back into the clouds, but it stayed there, just where it was, blotting out all the further hills.

The Crossing
of Herald Montjoy

A piece of ground near Agincourt.
October 1415.

He does not have far to ride.

The distance between the two encamped armies is little more than a mile. They are so close that at night-time, in the cold stillness, each can hear the laughter of the other, and the swearing and the cries. They're like neighbouring farmers, eavesdropping in the moonlight.

The French are noisier than the English. There are far more of them, they have more liquor and they seem to know more songs.

Herald Montjoy walks out from the French camp, through the wood on the right towards Maisoncelles, and stands among the trees and listens to the English. He can hear a lot of hammering. He thinks the exhausted soldiers may be trying to make cabins out of elm. He remembers his little nephew, Roland, who has made a tree-house. He loves Roland. Having no children of his own, he's tried to describe what he is to Roland. He has told him: 'A herald is a watcher. It's important to understand this. He oversees the conduct of armies, but doesn't really belong to them. He's not a man-at-arms, but a man apart.'

Then, a morning comes, salt-white with frost, when Herald Montjoy is summoned to the Dauphin's tent. The Dauphin instructs him to ride out across the fields to the English camp and enquire whether the English King is ready to ransom himself, to save his ragged army from certain defeat. The

367

Dauphin's tent is sumptuous with blue and gold hangings. The Dauphin is doing body-building exercises all the while he is talking. As Montjoy leaves the tent, he hears him say to the Duke of Alençon: 'God, I'm fit.'

Herald Montjoy gets on his horse. The land he must cross has been ploughed and he's worried that the horse is going to stumble on the icy ridges of earth. A mist hangs on the fields, milky and dense, and the herald wishes that this, too, wasn't there. This and the hard frost give the day such strange singularity.

A piece of ground near the Manor of La Vallée.
April 1412.

He did not have far to ride.

The distance between his parents' house and the manor where Cecile lived was little more than two miles. He and his horse knew every step by heart. It was mostly downhill. And he would see the house long before he reached it. And always his thoughts flew ahead of him and landed, gentle as birds, on Cecile's head and on her shoulders and on her feet in coloured shoes.

She was so . . . *exceptional.* He tried, on these journeys to and from her house, to decide what, if anything, she resembled – in nature, or in man's inventions. He wondered whether he could compare her to a lake of water lilies where silvery fish glimmered deep down. Or was she like a sundial, unerring, yet always speaking, in her adoration of ephemeral things, of time's passing?

He decided there was nothing and no one as strangely beautiful as her. Not even the landscape through which he and his horse had to pass, with its flowering meadows, its clear stream, its silent woods and its perfumed air. Not even his dreams, in which he sometimes gave himself wings and flew up into the sky and floated above France.

No. Cecile was more to him than any of these things. She kept honey bees in tall hives in her father's orchard. Her beekeeping hat had a gossamer veil that fell to earth all round her, and whenever Herald Montjoy dreamed of flying above France, there below him walked Cecile in her bee-veil with nothing on underneath.

He knew he had to marry Cecile. He had to possess her: her body, her soul, her petticoats, her bees, her shoe cupboard. He couldn't wait much longer.

He was a handsome man, with dark soft hair and a curling lip, and he had no doubt that when he proposed to Cecile he would be accepted. He would say to her father: 'Sir, in two or three years' time, I aim to become Chief Herald of France. I do not think that is an unrealistic boast.'

Agincourt.
October 1415.

His hat is a strange confection, indigo blue with loops of velvet that fall just above his left eye and bounce up and down as the horse canters.

This bouncing of his blue hat as he advances into the icy mist makes him fret. It's as if everything is conspiring to blind him on this frozen day. He finds himself wishing it were night, with a round moon to light the field and the songs and the hammering of the English to guide him on. He feels that, under these conditions, he would see and think much more clearly; whereas, in this fog, with the forest petrified and silent close by, he feels confused and half-afraid.

He reins in his horse and turns him into the wood and dismounts. He sets down the weighty standard by an oak tree.

He ties the horse to the tree. He takes off his hat, runs a hand through his curly hair. All around him is the tracery of the night's frost, fingering every spine. He asks himself: Why afraid, Montjoy?

He is thirty years old, three years older than Henry of England.

Is everyone on this piece of earth afraid of the battle that is there and not there in every mind? Of the future battle that is coming or may never happen – there and not there, departing like a lover, returning like a fever?

The Dauphin isn't afraid. 'Afraid? Bunk!' And then he admires his leg. 'The English won't last more than half an hour. If that.'

His instructions reveal his nonchalance: 'Just tell the King to give himself up for ransom, all right, Montjoy? Then that sack of bones he calls an army can go home and litter up Southampton.'

He's been told to ride fast, to return quickly. The Dauphin's getting impatient with all the waiting. Montjoy has never disobeyed an order in his life, yet now he's in the wood, scratching his head, standing still, staring at the trees. He feels as if he can't make this crossing, but he doesn't know why.

La Vallée.
April 1412.

He felt weightless on that April morning. He felt as if he could swing himself up off his horse and into the air. He was wearing a sky-blue tunic. The sun shone on those soft curls of his.

He was riding to La Vallée to ask for Cecile's hand. His mother and father had waved and grinned as he'd set off: 'Such a *beautiful* girl, son. So striking! We wish you joy and success.'

His thoughts, as always, had already landed on Cecile. They caressed her shoulder. They lay trapped like butterflies under her lavender-coloured cloak as she put it on and walked out of the house carrying a basket.

What was she going to put in the basket? Branches of blossom?

A thought is seldom trapped for long. It can travel anywhere. It can make decisions.

Montjoy's thoughts escaped from under the cloak. They walked with Cecile through the damp grass. They hid in the shadow of her skirts, high up in the darkness between her legs. They were touched in a caressing way as she took each step.

So then he had to slow his horse, dismount, walk to a stream, try to clear his head. 'You're running too fast,' he told himself. 'You're not her bridegroom yet.'

He knelt over the stream and cupped icy spring water and splashed his face. He gasped. There were days in a life so momentous they seemed to alter the size of the world. His heart felt as colossal as a cuckoo bird. The sky above his kneeling figure expanded and expanded, wider, fatter, closer to heaven than it had ever been.

He sat down on the grass. His horse grazed and flicked his tail at the spring flies. There *are* splendid lives, he thought. There *is* bravery and there is luck. There is ingenuity. A woman's shoe can be yellow . . .

There were yellow flowers at the stream's edge. Montjoy wasn't good at the names of flowers, but he sat there for a long while, admiring these particular ones.

Agincourt.
October 1415.

In this desolate wood, Montjoy looks for something green, something that will be soft to the touch.

This fear that he can't name has seeped from his mind, down and down all through him and touched his heart like a ghost and then his sphincter, and now he's crouching down and defecating onto the dry bracken.

He can see nothing green, nothing soft to the touch to wipe his arse with. He has to scrape up handfuls of harsh bracken and fallen leaves and clean himself with these. As he pulls up his stockings, he feels like weeping.

The wood oppresses him. He'd come into the wood to find a moment's peace before he has to complete his ride to the English camp. But the wood feels dead.

Leaving his horse tied up and the standard leaning against the tree, he makes his way back towards the ploughed field under its curtain of mist.

He walks forward, his feet unsteady on the frosted ridges. He can sense, now, that the mist is going to clear and that the day may after all be fine. Already, there's more light on the field.

He looks down at the earth. He wonders who works this land, what crop he has in mind for the year to come. The loops of Montjoy's indigo hat fall over his eyes. He is standing now on the place where the very centre of the battle will be. Here, where his feet are, an English soldier will fall, his lungs pierced with a lance, blood bursting from his throat. All around him will lie his doomed compatriots, souls vanished into the air. This is the crop to come: in an ecstasy of death, this land will be seeded with the English. And it will be his task to count them – his and the English heralds' – to make an orderly tally, even if limbs or heads are severed and fall some way from the torsos. All heralds must be precise. They mustn't look away. Afterwards, he will say to his nephew, Roland: 'I saw it. It took place near the castle of Agincourt. But you couldn't call it a great battle. It was too one-sided.'

He is aware, suddenly, that a lot of time has passed since he set out. Far ahead, he can hear the English resume their pathetic hammering. And this comforts him, somehow. His fear has lessened.

He strides back into the wood and unties his horse. The horse is trembling with cold. He slaps it gently to warm it.

He mounts and takes up his standard. He faces his horse towards the light soaking through the rising mist and rides on.

La Vallée.
April 1412.

Sitting by the stream with the sun warm on his nose, Montjoy rehearsed his declaration of love and his offer of marriage.

He imagined Cecile standing with her back towards him, looking out of a window. He went down on one knee, but she hadn't noticed this. Her shoulders were very still. He said: 'Cecile, I think it must have been apparent to you for some time that I consider you to be the centre of my universe . . .'

He imagined her smiling – *so now he's going to propose to me!* – but trying to conceal the smile.

He said: 'And really so it is. Or rather, it's more than this: you have actually altered the way I see the world. Before I met you, my life seemed so small, so circumscribed. But together, you and I could become masters – or rather, I mean, master and mistress – of a fine destiny!'

He decided it was wise, or at least diplomatic, to ask Cecile at this point whether she, too, felt the earth transformed by his presence at her side. And he imagined that she turned from the window and came running to him and pulled him to his feet and said: 'Yes, Montjoy! Yes. I feel the earth transformed!' And then he kissed her.

The kiss was so heavenly that Montjoy, alone by the stream, let it last for several minutes. His eyes were fixed on some vacant spot, unseeing. Above him flew thrushes and finches. Fleets of minnows sailed by him in the water.

When the kiss was over, Montjoy looked around him. At dusk, he would ride back this way with Cecile's promise to be his wife locked inside him like money locked in a box. And always, after today, when he rode this way, he would feel that this was hallowed ground – the spongy grass, the yellow flowers, the icy stream – because it was here that his future came to meet him.

A bee buzzed by him.

He got to his feet. He and the bee were moving to the same enchanted, perfumed destination.

Agincourt.
October 1415.

One of their scavenge-parties, sent out to gather nuts and berries and firewood, sees him coming with his flying banner from far off. Two of the party stand and gape at him; two others start running back to the English camp.

They make him feel smart, these bedraggled English, carrying bundles of sticks. His blue hat no longer feels ridiculous, but slightly stylish. He bounces high in the saddle.

He is memorising the Dauphin's instructions: 'Look, Montjoy, the thing is perfectly simple. The English can't possibly win. We outnumber them five to one. If they can't understand this simple arithmetic, do a demonstration with pebbles or coins or any damn thing that happens to be at hand. They are about to be overwhelmed. What a marvellous word! *Overwhelmed.* I love it. Right?'

And now, as the mist disperses, he can begin to see the English camp. It huddles in among some thin trees. Just as he'd envisaged, the men have made themselves hovels from sticks and bracken. There are a few threadbare tents. Smoke rises from a dozen small fires. He can see soldiers grouped around them, trying to warm themselves. They turn their white faces towards him.

Montjoy has never been to England. He has been told that one corner of it lies under water, but that elsewhere there are great forests, older than time. And these men that he sees look half drowned to him, or else, with this pallor they have, appear like people who live perpetually in a wooded darkness.

He slows his horse. Like grey ghosts, English soldiers have crept out of the trees and stand staring at him. What honour for France can there possibly be in slaughtering people already half dead? What honour for the heralds to oversee such a massacre? He thinks of Roland. In the tender privacy of the boy's tree-house, Montjoy had once said to him: 'Roland, there are two things that have counted with me in my life and one of them is honour . . .'

But his thoughts are interrupted, because now he realises that a group of men-at-arms is approaching him. They have formed themselves into a square. In the middle of the square, Montjoy can glimpse something bright. It is the crown on the King's head.

Montjoy takes off his hat. He dismounts. Carrying the standard and leading his horse, he moves forward on foot. And in this moment (he can't say why) a fragment of his earlier fear lodges in his heart and he sees coming towards him, as if in a dream or a vision, not Henry of England but his beloved Cecile, wearing a garland of yellow flowers round her hair.

He falters. Then he urges himself on. He is aware, now, that hundreds of the English ghosts have come out of the trees and are gazing at him.

He bows to the King. When he looks up, he sees a squarish, bony face and a complexion less pale than those around him. The regard is soft and the voice, when he hears it, is gentle.

'Well, herald?'

'Sir,' says Montjoy, 'I've come from the Dauphin. He and all the nobles with him urge you to consider your position. They estimate that your army is outnumbered by five to one and they feel that, to save your men from certain death, the best course you can follow is to give yourself up for ransom . . .'

Montjoy sees one of the men-at-arms belch silently. He decides that two things keep these people from fleeing back to Calais: drink and the presence of their King.

'What is your name, herald?' asks the King.

'Montjoy, sir.'

The King smiles. The men-at-arms appear to stare through Montjoy at the piece of ground over which he has just travelled.

Still smiling, the King says: 'Montjoy, say this to Prince Dauphin. We would like to remind him that there are very few

375

certainties on earth. Extraordinarily few. When I was a boy, I kept a stag beetle in an ivory box. I used to speak to it. And one evening, it spoke back to me. Until that time, I'd been absolutely certain that a stag beetle was unable to talk.'

The King laughs. The men-at-arms turn their anxious eyes from the field and look at their monarch.

'So you see,' says the King, 'one never knows.'

'What did the beetle say, sir?' asks Montjoy.

'Oh, I don't remember. Just a word or two. It was the unexpectedness that struck me. So there you are, herald. Your Dauphin can believe in his certainty or not as he pleases. It makes no difference to us. We will not be ransomed.'

The ghostly faces have clustered near to the King and are trying to listen to what he's saying. They stare and blink in the sunlight so foreign to them. They scratch their bodies through their clothing.

'God go with you, Montjoy,' says the King.

Montjoy bows. The King and his men-at-arms turn round and walk away. Montjoy replaces his blue hat on his dark head.

La Vallée
April 1412.

There was the house. There were the doves, like winged thoughts, on the roof. Smoke drifted up from one of the stone chimneys.

Montjoy was still rehearsing his proposal as he dismounted and handed the reins of his horse to a servant. Then the servant informed him that Mademoiselle Cecile and her parents had gone to visit a cousin struck down by a tumbling weathercock. They were not expected back until late afternoon.

In the tableau Montjoy had seen in his mind, there had been *morning* light at the window where Cecile stood while he told her about the alteration to his world. And he liked things to proceed as he'd imagined them. So now he hesitated: should he leave or should he wait?

He decided to wait. The servant led his horse away. He sat on a stone wall and stared up at the sky. Then, he walked to the orchard where the apple blossom was in flower and stood near to Cecile's beehives. The traffic of bees to and from them absorbed his attention for a long time. He kept picturing the honeyed world inside. He decided that the thing in nature Cecile most closely resembled was a cluster of bees. She moved in ways that he couldn't fully understand and yet all the while there was purpose in her.

Cecile discovered him in the orchard. He'd fallen asleep in the sun and was dreaming of the sea. When he woke and found Cecile standing above him, he believed, for a fragment of a second, that she was a ship in sail, moving past him and on.

She was laughing. Montjoy realised how ridiculous he must look, asleep in the grass like a peasant boy. He scrambled to his feet, straightening his tunic, running a hand through his hair. Desperately, he searched for words.

Before he found any, Cecile held out her hands for him to take. He noticed then that her face was very pink and her eyes wide. She was wearing a white dress.

'My friend!' she said. 'I'm so glad to find you here! So happy! That you should be here – and sleeping like a child – is somehow perfectly right. Because I'm in such a state! You can tell just by looking at me, can't you? I'm in such a state of pure joy!'

'Are you, Cecile?'

'Yes! And you are just the person I want to share it with. You've been such a sweet friend to me and now I can tell you my wonderful news! What day is it? I'll always remember this day. Always and always. Now ask me why!'

'Why, Cecile?'

'Because Monsieur de Granvilliers proposed to me this afternoon. I'm going to be married! I'm going to have a wonderful life!'

Cecile let go of Montjoy's hands and went dancing off round

the orchard, twirling her arms above her head. Montjoy saw that the shoes she was wearing that day were also white and it occurred to him that the grass would soon stain them. The grass appeared dry, but it wasn't. He could feel its dampness on his buttocks and against his shoulder blades and all down his spine.

Agincourt.
October 1415.

Returning at a canter, Montjoy soon leaves the smells and sounds of the English camp behind. He doesn't stop to look at the field or the wood. He isn't thinking about the battle to come, but about the kind of voice a stag beetle might possess. Up in his tree-house, Roland makes up different voices for the wind and the stars. Some of the stars don't speak, only yawn.

The Dauphin is at lunch with his favourite counts and dukes. They're eating blackbirds.

'God, Montjoy,' says the Dauphin, 'you've been an age. What happened?'

Montjoy is very hot after his ride. He can feel sweat in his hair.

'I'm sorry, sir,' he says. 'I explained to the King how far he's outnumbered, but – '

'But what?'

'He refuses to be ransomed. He seems willing to fight.'

The Dauphin picks up a blackbird and bites it in half, crunching the little bones. He speaks with his mouth full. 'Did you explain it properly? Five to *one*. Did you show him?'

'There wasn't an opportunity to show him, sir. His mind is made up.'

'Well then, he's a fool,' says the Dauphin. 'A bumptious fool. It means that he's now going to die. Simple as that. Every single one of them is going to die.'

The Dauphin eats the second half of his blackbird. He spits

out a piece of bone and wipes his mouth. 'Get me the Constable of France, Montjoy,' he says. 'We'll get all this over with tomorrow. I'm tired of being here. And the food's ghastly. Off you go.'

Montjoy backs out of the Dauphin's tent. He feels tired. He feels he could lie down anywhere and sleep.

La Vallée.
April 1412.

Out of politeness, he had to pay his respects to Cecile's parents before he could leave. They told him that Monsieur de Granvilliers had hinted at his intention to marry Cecile back in January. Cecile's mother said: 'We're very flattered. This is a very good match.'

Montjoy wanted to say: I love her better than Granvilliers. She alters my earth. I'd sleep with her in my arms. I'd buy her any number of pairs of shoes.

But he kept silent and only nodded.

Then he rode back along the way he had come. The sun was going down and glinted red in the fast-running stream. He tried not to think of anything at all. When he got to the clump of yellow flowers, he looked the other way. His horse stumbled on a stone and he wished he could become that stone and feel nothing.

Montjoy's parents were eating dinner when he arrived back at the house. They looked up expectantly from their soup and put down their spoons.

Montjoy stood in the doorway and looked at them. For the first time in his life, he envied them with an aching, fathomless envy. They had lived side by side contentedly for thirty-one years. They still shared their bed.

He put a fist up to his mouth. Through the clenched fist, he said: 'Cecile's not in my life any more. So please don't mention her again. She's in the past and I don't want to speak about it. It or her. I don't want to talk about any of it. Ever.'

He turned and left the room before either his mother or his father could say a word.

Agincourt.
October 1415.

He has been summoned by the English King, three years his junior.

It's getting dark. The rain that came in the early morning has stopped and a white moon is rising. And under the white moon lie the French dead.

He and his horse have to pick their way among corpses. There's a shine on them and on the fouled earth where they lie.

For the second time in Montjoy's life, he asks himself, as he rides on into a gathering dusk: 'Why was something as terrible as this not foreseen by me?'

He remembers the Dauphin's mockery: 'They won't last half an hour!' He remembers his own imaginary words to Roland: 'You couldn't call it a great battle. It was too one-sided.'

He's a herald. Heralds ride in the vanguard of events. They announce. They watch and assess. They bring the expected after them. But not him. Despite his eminence, despite his optimistic name, the unimaginable follows him like a shadow.

He doesn't know precisely how this day was lost. He tried to follow what was occurring. He kept weaving in and out of the wood, trying to see, trying to get a picture. He heard the English arrows fly. He saw a cloud of arrows fall on the first line of cavalry, heard them clatter on helmets and backplates, like hailstones on an army kitchen. He saw some horses go down and their riders fall, helpless as saucepans in their armour, kicked or trampled by hooves.

Then he saw, as the first line rode on, the English men-at-arms fall back. They fell back in a ghostly way, just as, before, they emerged from the wood – one moment there and the next moment not there. And where they'd been standing, facing the French cavalry, on the very place where they'd been, now there was a line of stakes, newly sharpened, pointing out of the ground. There was a thick fence of them, a thousand or more, three or four deep with room in between them for only the most insubstantial men.

He knew the horses would rear, would try to turn, would do all that they could not to be thrown onto the stakes. But many of them couldn't turn because in their massed charge, flank to flank, they were coming on too fast and so they exploded onto the fence and their riders were pitched forward into the enemy's arms.

One of the other heralds had told him at dawn: 'The English are eating handfuls of earth. This means they accept their coming death and burial.' And he'd felt pity for them, as violent as love. Now, Montjoy's horse carries him awkwardly, slipping and staggering in the mud, through the field of the French dead. The dead appear fat with this white moon up, casting bulky shadows. Montjoy covers his mouth with his blue glove and tips his head back and looks for stars. There is one in the west, yawning, and he thinks again of Roland in his treehouse and then of all the souls of the French struggling to cross the chasm of the sky.

He won't give an account of the battle to Roland because then he would have to answer too many unanswerable questions. Why did the first line of French cavalry turn round and collide with the men-at-arms coming forward? Does this mean that some of the French foot soldiers died before they even reached the English line? And then, when they reached the line, what happened that so many died so quickly? Were they packed together so tightly in a mass that they couldn't fight properly? Was the mass, shouting and pushing and afraid and confused, soon walled up behind its own dead?

It had rained so hard all through the battle, the heralds' task of seeing had been impeded.

All Montjoy can hope now, as he nears the English camp and hears voices singing, is that time will bring him understanding.

He rides on. He must make a formal acknowledgement of defeat to King Henry. He hopes that his voice is going to be strong, but fears that it may sound weak and small, like the voice of a stag beetle in an ivory box.

He feels exhausted. In his exhaustion, he aches to be no longer a man apart, but a man going home to his wife with a gift of crimson shoes.

The Unoccupied Room

Marianne is walking home through the wet dusk of the city. She wears an expensive grey mackintosh with the collar turned up, but she has no umbrella and her hair is cobwebbed with rain.

Marianne is forty-eight. She's an almost-beautiful woman who doesn't look her age. She has pale skin and a gentle laugh. She's a doctor specialising in geriatrics and her career is what matters to her now. She's divorced and unattached and certainly isn't looking for a new husband. Her only child, Nico, lives in another city. He's a radio DJ. Though affectionate to her always, she's heard him being condescending to phone-in listeners and she means to question him about this sometime: 'Why be cruel, Nico, when this isn't your nature?'

She carries a smart brown leather briefcase, inside which are her conference notes. This has been the final day of an international colloquium on geriatrics entitled 'Redefining the Seventh Age' and Marianne is aware, as the city traffic whispers by her on the damp cobbles, that she is, suddenly, exhausted. There's an ache in her thighs. Her eyes feel sore. She hasn't much further to go to her apartment, but she realises that she's been walking a long time and is surprised by the decision she must have made, but doesn't remember making, not to take a taxi home from the conference centre. She could have afforded a taxi. Her ability to afford taxis now is one of the modest pleasures of her independent life. So why didn't she take one? She's walked at least a mile and her smart shoes are spoiled. Was it that she looked for a taxi and none came by? She doesn't remember looking for a taxi. All she remembers is that she was at the plenary session of the conference but said very little, or, perhaps, nothing, at it and that she is now here, three blocks or so away from her street. Her longing to be home, to make tea, to sit down, to warm her feet, has become overwhelming. She feels as though she could sleep for several days. She wants to lie down and not move and let nothing move within her sight or hearing, unless it might be a light autumn breeze at her window or the sound, far off, of the children's carousel in the park – familiar things that wouldn't disturb her peace. She sighs as she tries to hurry on. Her elderly patients have just such a longing for rest. 'I tell you, doctor,' says one old man, who sits at his window all day, counting aeroplanes, 'the best bit of the day is the night.'

She's at her street now. She turns off the well-lit boulevard and quite soon the traffic noise becomes faint and all she can hear are her own footsteps and all she can smell is the damp of the cherry trees that line the avenue. She likes this moment, this moving out of the light into the shadows of her street.

It's a street of nineteenth-century houses converted to apartments. Railings and hedges screen the ground-floor flats from the road. Only one house remains a house, containing thirteen rooms, but Marianne can't remember who lives in this grand building.

Her apartment is on the second floor. It has a large living room and three bedrooms, one of which is very small – the room Nico occupied as a child. The floors are polished wood, waxed often and scenting the whole place. It's the kind of apartment, unlike so many in the city, that you feel you can belong to.

Marianne searches in her mackintosh pocket for her keys. She hopes they're in the pocket and not in her handbag, which has so many compartments in it that things lose themselves there. Her hands are soaking. In damp and cold, her nails, which she's bitten ever since she was nine, sometimes bleed. They feel as if they're bleeding now.

The keys aren't in Marianne's pocket, so she stops a little way from her front door, puts down her briefcase and places her handbag on someone's car roof, under a street lamp, to search for the keys.

At once, the contents of her handbag appear odd. She takes out something pale, slightly unpleasant to the touch. It's a pair of surgical gloves. In her day-to-day work, she wears gloves frequently (again and again she reminds the nurses: 'There must be a sterile barrier between your hands and all internal tissue of the patient's body'), but always disposes of them at the hospital or in the homes she visits. These gloves appear soiled and Marianne has never put a pair of soiled gloves in her handbag. Never.

She lays the gloves on the car roof. It's raining very hard now. She must find the keys, go in, make tea, sit down by the electric fire ... Then, she will think about how the surgical gloves came to be in her bag.

The keys aren't where she expected them to be. They're at the very bottom of her bag. She has to take out her purse, her chequebook, her credit card wallet, her cigarettes, her tampon holder and her hairbrush before she's able to locate them. There's a label tied to them, on which is written *Keys No. 37*, but, just as Marianne has no recollection of putting the soiled gloves into her bag, so she has no memory of this label attached to her keys.

Her friend and colleague, Petra, reminded her some days ago: 'Conferences are strange things, Marianne. They're like stepping out of your life.' And now, as she returns her purse and the other items, including the gloves, to her bag, Marianne starts to wonder whether something has happened during the last three days, something she's momentarily forgotten because she feels so tired, that has damaged her.

She leans against the car, noticing that the car is dark red. A Volvo. It might belong to the family in the grand house, or it might belong to a woman on her own, gone shopping in the rain on the boulevard, a woman who found a lucky parking space here under the cherry trees. In one's own street, there are a thousand unknowable connections. Cities express the unknowable. Live your whole life in the same one and you will wind up a traveller in it, an ignoramus.

She's at the door of the building now. She pushes it and enters. The stairwell is massive, poorly lit, always cold. The stairs are stone, very wide, slightly grand. In the middle of this grandeur is an elevator no larger than a confessional, in which it has always been impossible not to feel foolish. Most often, Marianne ignores it and walks up the two flights of stone, but this evening she steps into it gratefully and lets it carry her towards her soft sofa, her fire, and the pot of China tea she's going to make.

It's dark in the apartment. Marianne switches on the overhead light and the hall seems brighter than normal. She rubs her eyes. She lets her bag and briefcase drop. She's aware, in the warmth of the apartment, that she's been enduring a headache for a long time without really noticing it.

Though she's been looking forward to the tea, she now feels too tired to make it. She goes straight to her bedroom. The bright light of the hall still feels uncomfortable, so she leaves her bedroom in darkness. She throws off her wet clothes and, wearing only a slip and a silk blouse, gets into the large bed she used to share with her husband, Paul. For fourteen years, they lay there together. On the living-room mantelpiece were stacked the invitations to conferences and poetry readings and private views and dinner parties: Paul and Marianne, Marianne and Paul.

Not that she regrets the passing of that bit of her life. Not at all. And now, as she feels a sweet sleep coming near, waiting, coming nearer, she thinks, not for the first time, I only endured it for so long for the sake of Nico.

She knows she's slept for a few minutes but no more. She's warm. The pain in her head hasn't diminished. She lies very still.

She's been woken by something she can't identify. She raises her head, just an inch or two off the pillow, and listens. She can hear the rain on the window and the distant traffic of the boulevard. They're utterly familiar sounds and yet it seems to Marianne as if she hasn't heard them in conjunction with each other for a long, long time. It's as if there's been some vacant space between her and them. In a busy life, do you stop hearing the ordinary, the everyday? Or do you hear so much, so continuously, that half of it goes unregistered?

Marianne lowers her head onto the soft pillow. And she thinks, it was the past that woke me. I was dreaming about my parents, Otto and Lucie, dreaming myself back in our old apartment that smelled of pipe tobacco and cake baking. I was in my child's room and it was the sound I could hear from my child's bed that woke me up. It was one of those noises that used to come from the unoccupied room.

Marianne's room was at the end of the corridor. It had a small window that looked out over a courtyard, where a rusty fountain splashed during heatwaves and was silent the rest of the year. Hers was the 'last' room in the flat. The lives of their neighbours began on the other side of her wall. Their names were Joseph and Joanna Stephano. You could hear them from the bathroom, which was next to their kitchen. You could hear a kettle whistling and crockery smashing on the tiles and their voices shouting. (*'Why do they quarrel so?'* says Lucie. *'It's just their nature,'* says Otto.) But in her little bedroom, Marianne hardly ever heard them. So she'd worked out that the room next to hers was empty. It may have been a guest room where no guests ever came, or a fusty dining room that was never used, or even a box room kept closed and locked. And yet it had a function. Just one. It was where Joanna Stephano came to cry.

Marianne thinks, certain sounds from the past are never forgotten. You come out of an important three-day conference and the crying of Joanna Stephano returns to you more clearly than the voices of the conference speakers. Once, it continued most of the night. You sat up and tapped on the wall, very lightly. You wished you'd learned Morse code so that you could send a message of consolation. At dawn, you heard Joseph Stephano start to call Joanna's name and, after that, you went to sleep.

But then. You heard something else. Later that same year or in the year that followed, when you would have been nine. Something that you never understood. Or did you? Was there an explanation which you once knew and have now forgotten?

It was a noise like a door creaking, a sound out of a Gothic tale. A creak, a squeak, wood against wood, wood against iron? Something opening, slowly, slowly. You heard it in the middle of the night. It woke you and you listened and you thought, what if the thing that's making this sound were to come through from the unoccupied room into my room?

Later – how much later? – Otto knelt down and held her and said: '*Try to forget it, Marianne.*' In fact, she remembers now, Otto and Lucie kept on saying this: '*Try to forget it, sweetheart. Put it out of your mind.*' But what were they talking about? Were they talking about the thing that caused the noise that night or about something else? What happened to Joseph and Joanna Stephano? Marianne is sure that in that building, somewhere in her childhood, there was another event. It took place on the stairs. Did it? On the dark stone stairs? If Otto and Lucie were alive, Marianne would call them up and they would remember, but Lucie has been dead for four years and Otto for two. Marianne is alone in her apartment. The time of families is gone.

Marianne is wide awake now. She decides she will go and make the tea, even eat something, perhaps, and then come back to bed, switch on the early evening news. She reaches out and puts on the bedside light. She sits up. The room is painted yellow. There are yellow and blue drapes at the window. On the opposite wall is an oil painting of a naked woman on a hard chair.

She looks at these things: the yellow walls, the curtains, the picture. She looks at the lamp she's just switched on. She looks at the book beside the lamp and the digital alarm clock on top of the book. She looks at the duvet, which is blue and white cotton.

This is not her room.

She remembers how her room looks. The walls are beige, the curtains white. By her bed is a photo of Nico.

This is not her apartment.

She is in bed in someone else's apartment. This is not even her city. It used to be her city, but it isn't any more.

Marianne fights her way out of the bed and snatches up her skirt. The digital clock on top of the book says 18.49. Along the boulevard, the traffic will be heavy now, bringing people home from their offices and one of these people will be the owner of this apartment. In moments, now, she will hear the elevator stop on the second floor and hear the rattle of the elevator grille.

The elevator . . .

Marianne pauses in her dressing. The elevator is hers. No. *Was once.* That feeling of foolishness. She knows the elevator like she knows her own car.

She's trying to straighten the bed. The bed is warm from her own body. Then she searches for her spoiled shoes. She's swearing under her breath to stop herself from crying. *Something has happened to send me mad. I'm as mad as a mad cow. I'm in someone else's apartment and at this very moment the owner of the apartment is parking her car under the cherry trees.*

Wait.

She knows the cherry trees. She knows the elevator. She had the keys to the apartment with a brown label attached to them.

Marianne wipes her face with her sleeve. She stares again at the room.

And then she sees it: hiding behind the yellow walls is the ghost of her old room, the bedroom she shared with Paul for fourteen years. She had walked a mile through the rain, believing she was going home. She'd become, in a few hours, just like one of her patients who believe that a hospital ward is a university or a room in a sheltered house an Italian *pensione*. So she knows it now without any doubt: something has occurred in the last twenty-four hours to cause this damage. But she has no recollection of what it is. The one and only clue to it could be the surgical gloves.

389

She puts on her mac and grabs her briefcase. She goes out of the flat and slams the door behind her. As she tries to run down the stairs, she remembers how Nico used to race the elevator. But she hadn't really liked the game. She worried that he'd fall and gash his head on the stone.

She goes into the first café on the corner of the boulevard. She chooses a quiet table and orders coffee, not tea, and bread and soup and a glass of cognac. She asks the waiter to bring her four aspirin. The cafe is busy and she sits back on the banquette and closes her sore eyes and listens to the noise of conversation and laughter. She wishes her feet were dry and that the pain in her head would go. She remembers saying one day to Petra: 'I've always sympathised with the men and women in legends and fairy tales who sell their mules and their souls for trivial things.'

She could almost sleep, here in the warm café, lulled by arrivals and departures. But her food comes and wakes her. She takes the aspirin and begins on the soup, then the bread, then the coffee. She eats and drinks it all together – soup, bread, coffee, cognac. She can't remember when her last meal was or where.

When she's eaten and drunk everything, she leans back against the leather of the banquette and lights a cigarette. Out in the shadowy past, Otto, survivor of the death camps, says: '*People never think, when they're in a warm café, about the possibility of certain things. They don't consider that there could be bodies in the river, that bread could one day be scarce. To have these realisations, they have to go out into the street again.*'

Marianne will have to go out into the street again. She can't sleep on the café banquette, but by leaning against it she's located the source of her pain. There's a lump on the crown of her head and a scab of blood in her hair. At some time between the second day and the last day of the conference, she fell and hit her head or someone hit her. This, at least, it is now possible to assume. And there is also a second assumption. She no longer lives in this city and therefore must be staying at a hotel

or with old friends. In her briefcase is her address book
containing the names and addresses of all her friends in the
world. Some are as far away as Japan and Australia, but most
are still in Europe.

A man's voice, not Otto's, interrupts and says: '*I used to get off
on Europe. You know?*'

An American voice?

And then?

A hand, broad, tanned, heavy. An expensive wristwatch with
a platinum bracelet. She takes the hand in hers? The hand
takes her hand?

The voice again: '*What are you doing, doctor? What the fuck are
you doing?*'

Has she invented or dreamed the voice and dreamed the
hand?

The food and drink and the aspirin and now the cigarette
have soothed Marianne a little. It will be possible now – will it?
– to search carefully through her bag and her briefcase, to find
out where she's staying. Then she'll go there and sleep and
hope to wake with her memory intact.

She calls out to the waiter. She's called so loudly, people in
the café turn and stare at her. She has had to call above the
angry American voice. '*Don't do this! Goddammit, don't do this to
me!*' The waiter looks startled and comes to her at once. She
orders more coffee and another cognac. She apologises for
shouting. The waiter removes her soup plate. Marianne places
her handbag on the café table.

There are eight small compartments in the bag. Marianne
searches them all. She finds three half-used books of matches,
some Irish currency, a restaurant bill dated 19 April and a train
ticket from Berlin to Brussels. There's no hotel key or key card.
Her only discovery is that there is blood on the surgical gloves,
more on the right-hand glove than on the left.

She drags her briefcase onto the seat beside her. She lights a
second cigarette and snaps the case open. There is her conference file and on top of this a map of the city, unopened. She
used to live in this city and didn't believe she'd ever need a

tourist's map. She used to park her car every night under the cherry trees.

Her coffee and cognac arrive. She opens the conference file and takes out her notepad. On the top sheet she's written, in a hand almost unrecognisable as hers: *In the US, an estimated four million people over 65 have diet-deficiency-induced abnormalities of bone matrix. Bones often fracture simply from body weight itself. People fall.* The rest of the page is blank except for some figure-of-eight doodles and two words: *cinema* and *Pieter.*

Marianne rubs her tired eyes. Pieter is one of her patients. Pieter sits on the balcony of the nursing home, painting watercolours of the sky, which he gives to her, one by one. About once a month, he begs her to sleep with him. He's ninety-one. Sometimes, he shows her his penis and tells her it is 'perfectly good'. She tells him gently that it's against the rules of the home for the doctors to sleep with the patients. She admires his sky pictures and brushes what's left of his hair.

He says: 'Being alone. You wait. You wait till you know what it is.'

'I *am* alone, Pieter,' she replies. 'It's my choice to be alone.'

'No,' he says, 'I mean really alone. You wait and see.'

Thinking about Pieter has frightened her. Not just the fact of Pieter and his life closing with these sad last requests, but something else. It has to do with the hand on hers, with the American voice. She has done something to Pieter. She's hurt or betrayed him in some way. Of this she is now certain.

She's still searching through the contents of her briefcase, but doing this absent-mindedly now. She wonders if she should call Petra. See whether Petra can explain to her what's happened, tell her what she's guilty of. '*Darling,*' says Petra softly, '*the past is always with us. At all times. It was you who taught me that.*'

Then, she finds it. A key to a hotel room. It has a number on it: 341. Marianne turns it in her hand. Modern hotel keys are plastic and operate a computerised lock. The name of the hotel is not on the key.

She struggles for an image of the hotel. A revolving door? A foyer with jewellery and scarves in a glass case? Staff in uniforms? But what comes to her is an amalgamation of all her journeys in Europe: a doorway in a Berlin street, a view onto a Paris courtyard, a Spanish room maid, the sound of a tram in Vienna. Petra seems to be with her in each of these places. '*Information,*' says Petra, '*is no longer a problem in the Western World. The sources of information are always somewhere to hand.*'

Marianne goes back to the conference file. Tucked into the conference notes is a letter of welcome from the organiser:

> Dear Conference Member,
> We are delighted to welcome you to our three-day colloquium, entitled 'Redefining the Seventh Age'. We hope that these three days will be rewarding and enlightening for all the participants.
> You will be accommodated for the duration of the conference at the Europa Hotel, which is situated two streets away from the Conference Centre (see map).

Marianne drinks her cognac. Why, she thinks, do certain drinks seem to warm your heart?

She finds a cab. Its interior is muddy, as if it were a water-taxi.

(Otto: '*There is always, on a wet night in the city, some means of getting home, but every one of these nights, in our hearts, is a rehearsal for the night when there is no means and when there is no home to go to and we are the outcasts again.*')

The driver tells Marianne that he can't take a direct route to the Europa Hotel because one of the bridges is closed. A bomb has exploded at the central Post Office and the police have thrown a cordon round it. He will have to make a 'complicated' diversion.

'Okay,' says Marianne.

He's a young man, quite eager to talk. He's worried about a letter he posted at five o'clock to his sister in Argentina. He says: 'It takes me all year to write to her. I don't know how to turn my life into words, that's my problem. And now my letter's gone up in smoke.'

393

On a different evening, in her own city, Marianne might have taken out a piece of paper from her briefcase and said to the driver: 'Let's write it again. You dictate and I'll put it down.' *Dear Maria, Don't faint. This is a letter from that marvellous correspondent, your brother. I am fine and hope you are and how are the Executive Boxing lessons going?* But tonight, she hasn't got the strength to be helpful in this way and decides, anyway, that the offer might be a patronising one.

They drive past the shuttered façade of a vast meat market, now closed while the city planners discuss new uses for it. 'I drove a film maker here,' says the driver. 'He was going to turn the meat market into an imaginary Finland. He told me he was famous, but if he was so famous why was he in my old cab?'

As they turn into a narrow, cobbled road in the oldest part of the city, the driver half turns to Marianne and smiles. 'I told you,' he says, 'a complicated route.' And Marianne sees that they're passing a row of shop fronts, lit and furnished like old-fashioned parlours and occupied by prostitutes who smile and pout and touch their breasts as the taxi goes slowly by. One of them, naked except for a red suspender belt and gold stockings, has fitted out her shop as an opulent bathroom and is sitting, legs apart, on a gold-plated lavatory. Marianne stares. The women in their little parlours amuse her, attract her, even. The girl on the throne shocks her. Yet she can't not look at her. She turns, cranes her neck, as the cab moves on.

'That one!' says the taxi driver. 'No shame, eh? They should make a law . . .'

'There's no law any more,' Marianne hears herself saying, and then, in the muddy dark of the cab, she sees, as if down a long tunnel, herself in a hotel bathroom. The suck of the extractor fan is hungry: *give me your foul air and I'll turn it into an icy breeze.* Marianne is taking off all her clothes and folding them into a neat pile. They're the clothes she's still wearing, the silk blouse, the skirt, the dark tights, the shoes now spoiled by the rain. And she's excited; sexually aroused and excited and nervous in her mind. She's going to sleep with a stranger. She, Marianne, who lives for her work with old people and for

394

her son, Nico; she, who no longer dreams about past lovers or
even about the touch of a man's hand on her hair, is going to
go to bed with the tall American she met in the hotel bar. He
has a large body. His hair is blond, but his pubic hair is dark.
He works for a chemical company. She moves from the
bathroom, holding her hands across her breasts, and sees him
standing on the opposite side of the double bed. She wants
him. She wants to lie down and be held close to his chest, to
breathe the half-forgotten smell of a man in her arms. She
knows this is a moment of weakness, but she doesn't mind. But
then. After he's undressed and she's undressed and they're
standing face to face, she shivering a bit in the air-conditioned
room, nothing proceeds as she wants it to proceed. The first
terrible thing is the kiss . . .

'How are you going to pay?'

'What?' says Marianne.

'Is this a cash job?'

'What?'

'Cash or account, please? You got an account with the cab
company?'

The taxi has stopped and the young driver is asking about
the fare. They're at the Europa Hotel. Marianne recognises the
entrance, but doesn't understand how they could have arrived
here so quickly. Only seconds ago, they were passing by the
prostitutes in their lighted windows.

'Cash,' says Marianne.

Then she pays the driver and gets out of the cab and is swept
by the rain into the hotel foyer. She stands still in the bright
circle of it. She can hear a pianist playing and realises that this
is where it began, with the music in the bar, with some old
sentimental tunes that reminded her of her life with Paul and
even of her life with Otto and Lucie in that first apartment of
all. It was the music that kept her there, ordering drinks, and
which, after what seemed like a long time, made her angry to
be so alone. And so she looked around and saw the yellow-
haired American.

He'd been watching her. He told her that when they began

395

to talk: 'I'd been watching you, but you're smart, you knew that, didn't you? I like mature women because you all know where it's at.' He had eyes that seemed gentle. 'What do you do?' he asked. 'I know you do something.'

'I'm a doctor,' she said. 'A geriatrician.'

He gave her this long, bleak look. 'My mother's old,' he said. 'Old is hell. Death is better. But I admire you. Let me raise a glass to all that you do.'

Marianne has no idea what time it is. It feels late. She finds her room key and walks to the elevator. She takes the elevator to the third floor and goes into Room 341. A switch near the door turns on an overhead light and a desk lamp. She puts down her briefcase on the desk. She looks around her. There's nothing of hers in the room: no suitcase, no books, no clock, no make-up bag, no perfume, no shoes or clothes, no photograph of Nico in its little perspex frame. The room appears unoccupied. It's the room of a guest who's already left.

Slowly, holding her arms round herself, Marianne moves towards the bathroom. She can remember now that when she got out of the bed, where she'd lain for so short a time, hurrying to her pile of clothes, the American followed her in there. '*What are you doing, doctor? What the fuck are you doing?*' She was trying to get dressed. The floor was slippery. He'd made her take a shower before he touched her. He'd showered, too. The marble floor of the bathroom was awash with water.

There are no possessions of hers in the bathroom. She knew there wouldn't be, yet she continues to search for them – behind the shower curtain, on the hook on the door, in the white pedal bin.

She was trying to get dressed and the American was yelling at her and then something happened.

In the pedal bin there is a piece of polythene packaging. Marianne looks at it. She takes it out and reads the label on it: *Yhoders Sterile Products Inc. N.Y. Gloves. One pair. Allsize.*

Marianne sits down on the cold floor of the bathroom. The fierce extractor fan seems to suck all the air upwards, out of reach of her breathing. She knows that she's probably, in the next quarter of an hour, going to be sick. She raises the lavatory lid. It feels suddenly dark in the bathroom. As in the taxi, Marianne sees herself small and far away, as though at the end of a tunnel.

It began with the kiss that was never a kiss. He said: 'In the old days, I would have kissed you, sure. But they're long gone. I don't employ my mouth any more. I'm sorry. No mouths. Okay?'

He took her hands, as if to emphasise his apology for this, but then started to examine them and immediately noticed her bitten nails, one of which had bled recently. He left her standing there, cold, not kissed, not held. She crossed to the bed and tried to get in it, while he searched in his suitcase for something. He tore open the polythene package which contained the surgical gloves. He came to the bed and held them out to her and told her to put them on. 'Don't take offence,' he said. 'You could be Dr Death. How do I know?'

She should have left then. She didn't leave.

And there was a moment, she thinks, when he held her, when they held each other and she was warm and he stroked her thigh. But then he took one of her hands encased in its glove and guided it to his sex and said: 'Okay. Make me want you.' He had no erection. 'Talk to me,' he said. 'Give me some cinema. I can't get it away in Europe any more. It's got dark here, or something. I keep trying, but no luck.'

He wanted her to talk about Pieter. She'd told him, down in the bar, drinking whisky, with the sweet music going on, that she had this old patient who kept offering himself to her and the American had laughed, had seemed to find it funny and tender and had let it go. But now he wanted her to arouse him with this, the story of Pieter: 'What does he do? Tell me what he does. God, even the dying have their brains in their pricks! Does he make you touch him? Does he masturbate in front of you?'

If she hadn't started to tell him, then there might have been something to save, despite his refusal to kiss her, despite the awful gloves, because she *wanted* it so badly after all her years

397

alone. But, half drunk as she was, she did start to talk about Pieter and the American listened and became aroused in her hand and kept saying, 'Okay, go on. Okay, go on.' And then, suddenly ashamed – disgusted by her betrayal of Pieter, disgusted by her witless departure from a self she'd spent so long trying to become – she stopped talking and took her hand away. She picked up what she thought was her room key from the bedside table and got out of bed and went to the bathroom to put on her clothes and leave. She heard him start to yell at her. She was trying to take off the hateful gloves when he arrived in the bathroom. 'Hey! What are you doing, doctor? What the fuck are you doing? I was getting hard! Look! I've been in this stinking Europe for ten stinking days and this is the first time I feel like a man and not like a corpse and you're walking out on me!'

Marianne said nothing. She gave up on the gloves. All she wanted was to be far away from here. She knelt down by her pile of clothes and tried to put on her bra. He kept shouting. '*Words, of course,*' said Otto, '*can feel like stones, as if a building has begun to fall down all around you.*'

And then a sudden darkness came on.

Marianne flushes the lavatory and closes the lid. She washes her face and hands and wipes them with a clean towel. As a child, she vomited often. Lucie was almost always with her, to comfort her, to hold her forehead and hold back her long hair.

She feels better. Almost weightless. Now she must go down to the desk and tell the receptionist she's mislaid her room key.

She returns the glove packaging to the bin and the soiled gloves with it. What else did he leave behind which the room maid saw and cleared away? Her own blood on the floor? What did her head strike when he kicked out at her? The rim of the bath or the underside of the washbasin? How long did she lie in his bathroom? She has no recollection of returning to her own room, but she knows it was there that she woke up, there that she got dressed, as if sleepwalking into her clothes, and set out for the final day of the conference. And all day she sat listening to the speakers but didn't hear them. She went to the platform to take part in the plenary session, but said nothing. All day, she'd been dreaming of going home to her beautiful apartment above the cherry trees.

She is given a key. Her room is two floors above his. The view of the city is grand and when Marianne looks down she can see the Post Office, still burning. All around it, blue lights flash.

She remembers there used to be fires in the city when she was a child. In those days, the fire engines rang bells. Lucie used to say: '*There's the fire bell, Otto,*' as the trucks passed.

There had been a chimney fire in their street the night the police came to the adjoining apartment and found the body of Joseph Stephano under the floorboards in the unoccupied room. Marianne was in her room, standing at the window watching the firemen and the crowd in the street. Then she saw the police arrive and come into the building. She thought the fire had leapt over the street and would come down into their flat. She began to cry.

Otto came and comforted her. He said a fire couldn't leap that far, it wasn't a kangaroo. He put her back into bed and told her to go to sleep, but she didn't go to sleep. She heard people go into the unoccupied room. They were men, talking in low voices. And then she heard it again, that same creaking noise, like a door that opens onto a ghost story. She went running to Otto and Lucie, drinking coffee in the kitchen that always smelled of baking, and refused to leave them.

She sat on Lucie's knee, with her face buried in Lucie's thick hair. Otto went to listen to the 'noise' in her room and when he returned he looked all around the kitchen, as though searching for something. Marianne believes now that he was searching for words.

Then they heard Joanna Stephano screaming.

'*Otto,*' says Lucie, holding Marianne tightly to her, '*shouldn't we do something?*'

'*No,*' says Otto. The screaming goes on and on.

'*We must do something!*' says Lucie. '*Go, Otto!*'

Otto opened the apartment door, which gave directly into the big kitchen where they sat. Marianne turned round and looked.

She doesn't know now – has never known – whether she saw it, or only imagined it afterwards and then kept on seeing it in her mind: the body of Joseph Stephano being carried down the stairs. She knows only that when she understood what had happened she felt the horror of it every night for years. She'd lie in the dark, biting her nails, imagining it. It had happened just a few feet from her bed. The body of Joseph Stephano had lain right there, squashed into the space between the joists, the boards nailed over him like the lid of a coffin.

Later, when Marianne was grown up and working in her profession, the three of them used to talk about it together. By then, the fear was gone.

'*He used to kick and beat her, Otto,*' says Lucie.

'*I know,*' says Otto, '*but why is the revenge of women always so final?*'

'*It has to be,*' says Lucie.

'*I'm sometimes asked to kill,*' says Marianne. '*As an act of mercy. But I tell my patients, I heard the aftermath of a murder once. I'm not the person to ask.*'

Marianne is half asleep. Her hair is washed and dry. She hears a plane go over and imagines the American far above her, flying away from what he did to her and from what he believed Europe was doing to him. Confused Europe. Confused America. She lets him go. She doesn't want revenge. All she longs for is to return to her independent life.

Her telephone is ringing.

At first, she thinks, it's not for me, someone has got the wrong room. Then, because it goes on and on ringing, she picks it up.

'Hey!' says a familiar voice. 'Got you at last. Just got back from the States this morning and I've been calling your hotel all day.'

'Who is it?' says Marianne.

'Who is it? Who *is* it? Are you serious? It's Nico. What's the matter with you, Mother? Have you forgotten you're in the old city?'

'No,' says Marianne. 'Of course not. How could I forget a thing like that?'

Ice Dancing

Let me tell you about our house first. Then I'll talk about us and the kind of people we are.

Our house is in Maryland, USA. Our local town is called Cedar, but we're nine miles from there, out on our own, facing a creek. We call the creek Our Creek and I built our house at the edge of it, with every window looking towards the water.

I'm an architect. Retired now. This was my last big challenge, to arrange this house so that wherever you are in it you get a glimmer of Our Creek. Janet, my wife, didn't believe I could do this. She said: 'Don, what about the rooms at the back?' I explained to her that there wouldn't *be* any rooms at the back. 'Sweetheart,' I said, 'think of the house as half a necklace and the water as a neck.' The only thing that's at the back of the house is the front door.

Our Creek flows towards the mighty Chesapeake Bay. On summer evenings, Janet and I stand on our jetty, hand in hand, sipping a cocktail and watching the water slide by. Sometimes, we don't talk. We just stand there watching and sipping and not talking. We've been married for thirty-seven years and now here we are in the place of our dreams. I began life as a clerk. Janet began life behind a Revlon counter.

And we've travelled the world. We started life as dumb Americans, but we didn't stay that way. We've been to England and France and Sweden. And Russia. We've got a whole heap of memories of Stockholm and Moscow. In Stockholm, we visited Strindberg's apartment. We saw his bed and his inkstand and his hairbrushes. He used these brushes to fluff out his hair because he was embarrassed about his head. Not many Americans know this, that the great playwright Strindberg had a tiny little pinhead he was ashamed of.

In Moscow, we witnessed a multiple wedding. We were standing in the snow. The doors of a gray building opened and out of them came a stream of brides, arm in arm with their bridegrooms. It was February. Ten degrees below. And the brides were wearing thin dresses of white net and carrying blood-red bouquets. Janet never got over this sight. Years later, we'd be lying in bed and she'd say: 'Remember those Soviet brides, Don? Out in the cold like that.' It upset her somehow.

And yet winter is her favourite season. The year we moved into this house Our Creek froze. We woke up one morning and there it was: all the water normally headed for the Bay was frozen stock-still. We stood together at our bedroom window, gaping. We were snug in there, on account of the triple glazing I'd had fitted. I put my arm around Janet and held her to me and her body was warm as pie. 'Don,' she whispered, 'let's go out there. Let's go out and dance on the ice.'

I said: 'What d'you mean, dance? We don't have any skates.'

'I don't mean skate,' she said. 'I mean *dance.*'

So that's what we did. We went straight out there before breakfast. We got dressed up in our Russian hats and our winter coats and our snow boots. We were sixty years old and we started singing and waltzing on the ice! We sang any old tune that came into our heads, but neither of us has got a voice and we'd forgotten most of the words, so the whole darn thing was crazy. And then, in the middle of it all, as we kept slipping and tripping and laughing, I had this vision of Strindberg. He was standing in the sky, staring down at us. And he wasn't smiling. So I quit laughing and I said to Janet: 'That's enough. Time for breakfast.'

'Oh why, Don?' she said. 'This is *fun.*'

'It's also suicidal,' I said. 'We never thought about that.'

The thing I'll tell you about next happened in Cedar.

Cedar is a smart little Maryland town with three banks and

two churches and an avenue of limes along Main Street. There isn't one single cedar tree in it.

We were on Main Street when this thing happened. I'd been to my bank and Janet had been in the hardware store, buying a hose nozzle. It was a spring morning. The limes were coming into leaf and I stood on the sidewalk looking at Janet about to cross over to me and thinking, here she comes, my Revlon girl.

She walked to the middle of the road and stopped. Then she fell down. She lay in the road. She didn't try to get up.

I ran to her. I could see a truck coming towards us. I put my arms out, waving it down. Other people came running. I knelt down and held onto Janet. Her eyes were open and her face was yellow-white.

'Honey,' I said, 'what happened?'

She held onto me. Her mouth opened and closed, opened and closed, trying to make words, but no words came out.

'Okay,' I said, 'it's okay, it's okay . . .'

I sent a boy on a skateboard to call for an ambulance. There was a whole cluster of people round us now. I had to ask them politely to step back, to give Janet some air, to give me room to lift up her head.

We got her to the hospital. The doctors were confused. They said: 'It may have been a mild epileptic seizure. We're not sure. We'll do some tests. Meanwhile, she's fine. You can go see her.'

She was pink again and sitting up in bed. She was wearing a hospital gown, tied at the back. She took my hands in hers. She said: 'I'm sorry, honey. I thought I was back in Danesville, that's all.'

Danesville, West Virginia, was Janet's old home town. Her Dad worked in a glass foundry there. Her mother had raised four children on a foundryman's wage and sent the only girl, Janet, to Beauty School.

After two days at the hospital, they sent Janet home. They told me: 'We can't pinpoint anything at the present time. It isn't epilepsy. Let us know if she has more falls.'

We went home. We had to drive through Cedar, past the exact spot where Janet had fallen down, and I knew I would never go by this place without remembering Janet lying in the road. I thought this would be the thing that would trouble me most in the weeks to come.

But the weeks to come were like no other weeks in my whole life. Boy-o-boy.

The Janet I took home from the hospital was the Janet I knew, but right from this day the Janet I knew started to slip away from me.

She went back into her past. Not all the time. Sometimes, she was right there with me and we'd play a sensible game of rummy or do the crossword or go down to the jetty together and listen and watch for signs of spring. And then, without any warning, bang, her mind got up and walked away someplace else. Mainly, it walked to Danesville. She'd say: 'Don, the temperature on the foundry floor is one hundred thirty degrees fahrenheit. Daily temperatures of this kind burn up a person's life.' Or she'd think our kitchen, with all its built-in appliances, was her mother's old kitchen and she'd complain about soot. She'd say to me, in a simpering voice like her mother's: 'Modern detergents are not designed to cope with old-fashioned problems.'

Sometimes talking to her would help and sometimes it wouldn't.

Sometimes, if I sat her down and stroked her head and said: 'Janet, you are *not* in Danesville, sweetheart. You are here in the home I built for you, all safe and sound,' she would come out of her trance and say: 'Sure, Don, I know that. You don't need to tell me.'

Then it could happen, too, that she mistook me for one of her brothers. I'd say: 'I am not Charlie, Janet. Charlie was bald, remember? I've got hair like old Strindberg, wild and fluffy.' But she'd refuse to believe me. She'd say: 'You're Charlie. You always were a prankster. And who's Strindberg?'

She got clumsy. She'd always been a meticulous woman. Now, she dropped things and spilled her food and burned her hands on the stove. I said to her one day: 'Janet, I can't stand this any more.' I left the house and went down to the jetty and got into the little canoe we keep tied up there and paddled off down the creek in the rain. I started crying like a baby. I hadn't cried since I was an office clerk.

They operated on Janet on 30th June. It was a hot morning.

Her condition is called hydrocephalus. Water builds up inside the skull and presses on the brain. If the water can't be drained off, parts of the brain atrophy. Then the person slips away – back into the past or to any place where she can't be reached. The success rate of the operation to drain off the water is variable according to age. About thirty per cent of those operated on die.

Death, to me, has always been synonymous with falling. This is how my mind sees it; a long, black, sickening fall. And Janet saw it the same. I once asked her.

Before Janet's operation, the surgeon came to see me. He said: 'Go home. Dig the yard. Mend a fence. This is a long operation. She's in our hands now. There's nothing you can do.'

I said: 'Sure. I understand.'

But I didn't leave. I sat on a chair in a Waiting Area and concentrated my mind on holding Janet up.

I held her in different ways. I carried her above my head, holding her waist and her thigh. When this got tiring, I put her on my back – her back to my back – and her legs made an arc around mine. Then I flew her above me, my hands on her tummy. I stood her on my shoulders and hung onto her feet . . .

People came into the Waiting Area. They looked at magazines. They read the words 'Ford' or 'Toyota' on their car key tags. They didn't bother me. They recognised that I was busy.

To help me, I sang songs in my mind and I whirled Janet around in time to these. I dressed her in a floaty kind of dress to make her lighter in my imaginary arms. As the hours passed, she got younger. Her hair hung down like it used to when she was a Revlon girl . . .

Then someone spoke to me. It was the surgeon. He seemed

to have learned my first name. 'Donald,' he said, 'I'm pretty sure your wife's going to make it.'

They kept her in hospital quite a long while. Then I took her home and the summer passed and then the fall and now here we are again in the winter and this morning we woke up to find Our Creek covered with ice.

Every day, I watch Janet. I watch and wait, for the least sign that she's slipping back to Danesville, but none comes.

She's in fine spirits, too, keen to do things. She says we should travel again, see more of the world before we leave it.

Today, we dress up warm and go down to the creek and Janet says: 'Come on, Don, look at this great ice! Let's dance and fool around on it like we did before.'

She's at the end of the jetty. She's all ready to climb down onto the frozen water.

But I can see that this ice is pretty thin. It's not like it was in that other winter, two foot thick; it's a different kind of ice.

So I call Janet back. I say: 'Honey, don't go down there. It's too dangerous. Enough dancing already. Right? Just stay up here with me.'

Negative Equity

On the night of his fortieth birthday, Tom Harris dreams about a flotilla of white ships.

For a while, he enjoys this dream and feels safe in it. He's admiring the ships from a distance, from a dry cliff. He's wondering, lazily, if they're taking part in a race and looks past them for a fluorescent marker buoy.

The next moment, he realises he's no longer safe. He's in the water, in among the flotilla. He's trying to swim and call out at the same time, but he knows that his head's too small to be seen in the rough water and that his voice is too feeble to be heard. He dreams that he's about to die and so he wakes himself up and still feels frightened and says to his wife Karen: 'Actually, they weren't ships. They were dishwashers and ovens. They were kitchen appliances.'

Karen is Danish. She is forty-three. Her voice is as gentle as a nocturne. She says to Tom in this soft voice of hers: 'I think it's rather peculiar that they should be floating like ships. Would they do that? Is it their hollowness?'

'I don't know,' says Tom, holding onto Karen's hand. 'Perhaps they would float for a while, like empty oil drums, if their doors were shut.'

'But I can't imagine it,' says Karen. 'Ovens bobbing around on the waves. In my mind, they would certainly go down to the bottom.'

Tom and Karen lie silent for a while, just touching. It's a May morning, but their bedroom window is small and doesn't let in much sunshine. The house where they live has always been dark. Tom's mind has now let go of the dream and is concentrated on the realisation of being forty. But he notices that the figure 4 is ship-shaped, and he wonders whether somehow, at forty, a man loses ground and has to set sail for a new place. Karen listens to the noisy summer birds and says after a while: 'I dreamed about the new house.'

'Did you?' says Tom. This house is their future. They refer to it as the Scanda-house because they're building it to a Danish design, with warm pine floors and solar heating.

Karen gets up and puts on her white dressing gown. 'I think I'm going to go and see how the builders are getting on today. Shall I?'

'Yes,' says Tom. 'Why not?'

Then they hear Rachel get up and start talking to her cat. Rachel is twelve and their only child. She has long, smooth limbs and long, smooth, bright hair, like Karen's. Tom, who is dark and small, often finds it strange that he lives his life in the company of these two tall women who are so beautiful and so fair. It's both wonderful and difficult. It's like living with two all-knowing angels.

Tom Harris is a diver. His official title is Coastwatcher. His territory is a ribbon of sea bed ten miles long and a mile wide and his task is to examine this area for signs of life and death. He knows his job is an important one. The periphery of every living thing can yield information about the health of the whole. He was told this at his interview. 'Consider the tail of the bison, Mr Harris,' they said, 'the fin of a whale and the extreme outer branches of a fir.' And Tom is happier in this job than in any he's had. His tools are those of the archaeologist – the trowel, the knife, the brush, the memory, the eye – but his site is infinitely more vast and changeful than any ruin or barrow. Anything on earth can be returned to the sea and found there.

He wonders what he will find today, the first day of his forty-first year. In Denmark, as a child, staying near Elsinore for the summer, Karen found a lapis lazuli brooch in a rock pool. She has been proud of this find, always. And in his nine years as a coastal diver Tom has found nothing as beautiful or as valuable as this. But his discoveries have a private value. Sometimes they're so odd that his mind starts work on a story to explain how they got to be there and this gives him a nervous kind of satisfaction. He used to tell the stories to Rachel, but now, for reasons he's unclear about, they have a harsher edge. And he no longer talks to Rachel at bedtime. She prefers talking to her blue-eyed cat. The cat's name is Viola. 'Viola,' says Rachel, 'quite soon we're going to live in a much more brilliant house.'

Tom drives an old Land Rover to the sea. He leaves early, while Rachel and Karen eat their muesli and talk softly together. This morning, as he drives away from the house, he thinks, suppose I never saw them again? Suppose I could never again wake up with Karen? Suppose Rachel's life were to be lived without me? He's never had any tragedy in his life. He can't imagine how certain kinds of tragedy can be borne.

He follows a similar routine each day. He meets his co-diver, Jason, and they put on their wet suits. They comb the beach for lumps of oil and plastic waste and dead things. Jason is a neat man with a lively smile and an old passion for Jane Fonda. In summer, they occasionally find the drowned body of a dune-nesting lark. Cod come into the shallow water and are stranded by the fierce ebb tide and bloat in death. Tom and Jason note the quantity of bladderwrack, the precise colour of the spume on the breakers and the presence or absence of sea birds. They breathe in the wind. Through binoculars, they examine the sea for trawlers and tugs. Sometimes, vast sections of an oil rig are pulled across the horizon, like a piece of scenery across a film location.

They return to Tom's Land Rover and make notes on their beach observation. Jason always brings a Thermos of coffee 'to keep up the body temperature'. (His idol, Jane, has taught him everything he wants to know about the body.) Then, they put on their masks and their lamps and their compressed air cylinders, strap on their instruments and walk to the water, carrying their flippers.

Crashing through the waves always troubles Tom – the

bulkiness of them, their roar. They're a barrier to where he wants to be. He's not happy until he starts to dive and then he begins to feel it: the thrill of the sudden silence, of the long, beautiful downward flight into darkness. The light closes above his feet and the world is filleted away. He feels ardent, single-minded, like a man travelling to a longed-for rendezvous. He describes this feeling to Karen as happiness and instead of being offended she's amused. 'It's so *Nordic*, Tom!' she says. 'Really and truly.'

He moves slowly across the sea bed, his meanderings guided by the compass attached to his wrist. Steer north-east and the continental shelf will eventually drop away and leave him poised above the real depths he's never entered. So he goes in a westerly way, remembering to stay quite close to Jason, the sea grass just brushing his body, his lamp like a cartoon wand creating a pathway of colour in front of him. Clusters of tiny brownfish explode into sudden stillness, like spilt wild rice, petrified by its light.

He's hoping for some discovery today, for something man-made, trailing a thread of story. He remembers the megaphone and the thurible. The stories he made up around these have taken on substance in his mind, as if they were events and not inventions.

He keeps swimming west, then, signalling to Jason, north a little, out towards the deep. He finds a rusty camera and a bicycle wheel – nothing of interest. He and Jason measure the areas where the sea grass has died.

And so the day passes. He spends quite a lot of it thinking about his two demanding angels and the Scanda-house he's building for them, so that more light can fall on their hair and on their breakfast spoons.

When Rachel has done her homework and taken Viola upstairs ('I don't want her going out at night. She chases birds'), Karen makes strawberry tea and sits at the kitchen table opposite Tom. She warms and warms her hands on the tea mug. 'Tom,' she says, 'you know I went to the mortgage people today?'

411

'Did you? I thought you were going to see the builders.'

'First the builders. Then the mortgage people about the new loan.'

'And?'

'The Scanda-house can't be finished unless we take out another loan, can it?'

'No. But there shouldn't be a problem. This house is worth far more than we've borrowed, so when we sell it – '

'It isn't, Tom. Not any more.'

'What are you talking about, Karen?'

'They sent a young man back here with me. He looked at this house. Just *looked* at it. Barely came inside. Didn't even go upstairs. He said, "Mrs Harris, there's no question of any further loan. You already have negative equity on this property."'

'Negative equity?'

'It's a term. Nowadays, there's a term for everything you can't quite believe could ever happen. I suppose the term is meant to make it real to you.'

'It's not "real" to me. What does it mean?'

'You haven't heard it? I'd heard it somewhere. Out in the air somewhere. It means the house is worth less than the sum we've borrowed on it.'

'It's not, Karen. We had three valuations.'

'But they were a while ago and now all its value is gone. I mean, like water or something. Or into the same air where all these new terms come from. It has just gone heaven knows where. And so I don't see how the Scanda-house is ever going to be completed now.'

Tears start to fall into Karen's tea. Tom feels a hollow place open inside him and bloat with misery. He reaches out and takes Karen's hand and says weakly: 'You may have been misinformed. They may be quite wrong.' He wishes this moment were in a story or a dream. 'I'll look into it, Karen,' he says. 'I'll go into it, love.'

*

He takes a day off. He talks to the builders, to the mortgage company, to the bank loans department. He is told that the gap between what his present house is worth and what he has borrowed to pay for the new one is now approximately £40,000. The only way the Scanda-house can be finished is by borrowing yet more. But nobody will lend him any more because he can't, now, repay the existing loan. His collateral is used up, suddenly, without any warning, like the compressed air in a cylinder that has no reserve valve. He can't move.

He tells Karen he will find a way. 'What way?' she says. 'Tell me what way.'

'I don't know,' he says, 'but I will.'

They say nothing to Rachel. One evening, she informs the cat: 'Our room in the Scanda-house is going to be right up in the roof, Viola, and we're going to be able to see the sea.'

Tom considers asking Karen to go back to work. She used to be an art teacher. One day, she said: 'I can't do this any more, Tom. These children are too savage for me. In Denmark, pupils are not like this.'

She got Tom's agreement. He could see that the children had no interest in the kind of knowledge that Karen could give. So Karen left the school and stayed at home and painted and now and then made a little money from drawings and watercolours. One of the things promised to her in the new house is a studio of her own. It would have a big, sliding window and a balcony made of steel. And Tom longs to see her in there, working quietly, in her own space at last. He can't ask her to return to teaching. He *can't*. She's forty-three. She wants a sunny house with a studio and her days alone with her painting. It's not unreasonable.

Back he goes, down into the deep, to think, to try to work it out. He moves more slowly than usual over the sea bed, barely noticing what appears in the beam of his lamp. He feels like the victims of his stories about the megaphone and the thurible, caught up in something they never intended, that no one intended, but which happened nevertheless. He retells the stories to himself, to see if they shed light on his predicament:

413

– One day, a Scouts decathlon is taking place on the beach. There are scarlet markers out at sea for the thousand metres freestyle. The Scoutmaster's name is Dawlish . . .

– One winter's day, a Mass is said out at sea on a trawler for a drowned fisherman. The thurifer is a boy named Marcus Grice who is prone to sea-sickness . . .

Tom stops and thinks, so much of our life is invention, so much the way we *choose* to see it. I see Karen and Rachel as my bossy angels. Karen sees the lost land of her childhood coming back to her in the guise of a house. The men I work for see this ribbon of water as the conscience of England. In both cases, I have inherited so much responsibility.

– And so. A boy named Pip (the fair-haired boy Dawlish loves single-handedly in his single bed night after night) is coming last in the thousand metres freestyle. Out at the scarlet marker, Pip starts to panic, to wave his arms, to signal that he's in trouble. Dawlish, wearing his Scoutmaster's heavy shoes, wades into the sea and calls to Pip through the megaphone . . .

– And so. At a certain moment in the Mass for the dead fisherman, with twenty-foot waves hurling the trawler about, Marcus Grice realises he is about to vomit. Forgetting everything but his own nausea, he drops the thurible and staggers to the ship's rail. Burning incense falls onto the trawler's wooden deck . . .

'Oh no,' said Karen, when Tom told her these stories, 'I see the endings. I see tragedy coming. Don't tell me. I hate tragedy, when it's so senseless.'

As Tom swims on, he realises a truth that he's never understood before: he wants, through the design of the new house, to remind Karen that England is only partly a dark place, that it can be calm, not savage, that beautiful light often falls on it. This, in his imagination, is why it matters so much. His worst fear is that Karen will leave, one day, and go back to a place where she once found lapis lazuli in the water.

Sailing yachts and kitchen appliances: he dreams of them often now. The thing which is nimble and defies the water; the thing which, superseded, might float for a while and then sinks.

Karen gets used to this dream of his. When he wakes and reaches for her hand, she just strokes it gently and says: 'That old dream, Tom. It's so rotten to you. I wish it would go.'

One morning, she says: 'I told Rachel about the Scanda-house. I explained there is nothing we can do. Just make it watertight and wait. She understands.'

And they're being so good about it now, his fair women. Hardly any tears from Karen after that first time; no sulking from Rachel. They've understood what's happened and that's that. In the mornings, when he leaves, there they are, chatting softly together, as if the future were going to arrive today. They eat their muesli. They raise their faces to his for a goodbye kiss, exactly as they always and always did.

He's the one who cries. Nobody sees him do it, not even Jason. He tries not to see himself do it. He dives down to the sea floor and switches off his lamp, so that the darkness round him is as absolute as the darkness of the grave, and lets his tears fall. His sobs, through his breathing apparatus, sound unearthly.

He does little searching for human objects any more. He prefers lying in the dark. He's tired of the stories men tell. The only thing he's started to long for is to go beyond the coastal shelf, to go to the true deep, where all the variety of the ocean lives. He's begun to believe – at least with half his mind – that only if he is brave enough, insane enough, to go down into this vast darkness will he find the solution to the problem of the house.

One evening, Tom comes home and hears Karen talking on the telephone to her mother, Eva. He can understand quite a bit of Danish. Karen is telling Eva that she's waiting for her life to change. She says: 'I'm not *living* my life any more, Mama. I'm waiting to start it again, when I've got my studio.'

He sits down dumbly and listens to this conversation. He knows that Eva has offered to lend them money, but that the money offered is nowhere near enough and, even if it were, it couldn't be accepted because it couldn't be repaid. Eva is a kind woman and she has passed this quality of kindness onto Karen.

At supper, addressing both Karen and Rachel, Tom says: 'I want to talk about our situation. I promised you I'd find a way out of it. And I still mean to. I don't want you to think I've just given up.'

'No, Tom,' says Karen, 'you're not a person who gives up.'

'It's not your fault anyway,' says Rachel.

Tom pushes away his half-finished meal and lights a cigarette. He doesn't often smoke and the cigarette tastes old. 'I thought,' he says, 'I would have a word with the insurance company.'

Karen says: 'I don't think the insurers can do anything, Tom.'

'Well,' says Tom, 'they will have some idea about the future – about when the value gap might start to close.'

Rachel is looking at Tom's face intently, as though it were a map of the world. 'Do you think it will ever?' she asks.

'Yes,' says Tom. 'Yes.'

He sees the summer pass. The insurers say that they really do not know when the value gap may start to close and they dare not guess. The temperature of the sea rises and then starts to fall again. Tom promises himself that, before the winter comes, he will do the thing he has planned.

It requires the hiring of a boat. He chooses a Saturday morning in September when the air is bright. As he manoeuvres the boat out of the harbour, he looks back and sees, half hidden by trees, his new house, waiting.

He is four or five miles out when he throws the anchor. He can see the grey smudge of a ferry going towards Harwich and wonders whether, for some of the Dutch passengers coming over from the Hook of Holland, this may be their first sighting of England. When Karen first saw England, she and her friend Else said together: 'It looks a bit like home.'

He checks his equipment carefully. He knows certain important things are being done incorrectly: he should have a reserve valve on his cylinder; he should not be diving alone.

He lets himself tip backwards into the water and goes down

slowly, barely moving his flippers, his lamp directed onto the depth gauge at his wrist. He has no idea how far he has to dive before he starts to see it, the life of the true deep. For the first hundred feet of his fall, there seems to be nothing but himself and the drifting bladderwrack and the bubbling of his own breathing.

But then they start to swim into his light: shoals of silver herring; the brown swirl of an eel; a kite-shaped ray with its dancing tail; the blue bodybags of squid; the fingers of cuttle-fish; the first red fronds of deepwater seaweed.

For a while, he hangs still, poised where he is, turning and turning his head so that his lamp beam makes an arc and every arc reveals a new picture. He opens his arms to everything he sees, like he used to open his arms to Rachel when she was a small child. With every suck of compressed air that he takes, his feeling of elation increases.

He goes lower, lower. He's no longer looking at his depth gauge. And then, just ahead of him, he sees a dark mass and feels his body pressed by an underwater current. The mass moves by him and on, and thousands of brownfish rush from its path and Tom knows that something vast is down there with him and he chooses to believe that he's found a whale.

He turns and starts to follow it. He scans it with his lamp, but he can see nothing, only the small fish darting from its path. He wants to touch it, to hold onto it, to become its passenger. He wants it to lead him down. *Only by going deeper and further can anything be solved.*

Tom doesn't know whether he can keep pace. He has to swim as fast as he can, taking in a lot of air, but he does keep pace until he feels the mass suddenly drop away beneath him. It drops and he's stranded there alone, at some mid-point, foolishly kicking his flippered feet. Then he makes the steepest dive he's ever made in his life. Briefly, he thinks of Jason's face wearing a look of terror, then of Jane Fonda wearing a striped leotard and hanging from a wallbar by her feet, and then of nothing, nothing but the beauty of the dive. It doesn't matter whether the thing that leads him down is a whale or not. It's a whale in his mind, just as the Scoutmaster and the thurifer were real people in his mind. It is something alive which, in its every moment of existence, can express its own individual purpose. He has only to follow it and he will attain perfect clarity of thought. The deeper he goes, the more euphoric he feels.

And then, without warning, he's in darkness. He remembers it from his sea-bed crying, this darkness-of-the-grave, and with a heavy arm reaches up to switch on his lamp. But no light appears. The battery of his lamp is used up.

In a mere few seconds he feels a drunken sickness come on and now he can't say if this darkness is the real, external darkness of the deep sea or only a darkness of his mind. Far, far away, weak and soft, he hears Karen's voice say: 'Oh! This darkness of us northerners, this blackness of ours . . .'

Sick as he feels, he knows that he must take control. Karen must be his light now, Karen and Rachel, there on the dry cliff, in a dry wind, with the sun on their hair.

He starts to swim up. But he's lost all sense of time. For how long has he been following the imaginary whale? And how deep is he? Without a light to shine on his depth gauge, he has no means of knowing.

So one question only remains, the question of equity: is the sum of water above him greater than the corresponding sum of compressed air left in his cylinder, or is the sum of the air greater than the sum of the water? He says it like a mantra, over and over, to calm him, to keep his sickness in check: *Which is greater? Which is greater?*

Somewhere far above him his bossy angels wait in the bright September sun and all he can keep trying to do is swim upwards to meet them.

Bubble and Star

Leota Packard had been born and raised in Georgia, not far from Jimmy Carter's home town of Plains. But when she was twenty, she left the South and never returned.

Once in her subsequent life – during the Carter presidency – she found her mind wandering like a lost child back to her mother's porch swing; and there it sat for a few minutes, rocking to and fro, watching the fields. Above the fields, it saw creatures dancing in the air – gnats and fireflies. But this wasn't its usual habit. If Carter hadn't become President, it might never have gone back. Because normally it stayed in Canada, where Leota lived after her marriage to Eugene Packard, a Canadian plastics manufacturer. It stayed in the bright and tidy house Packard built for them two miles from Niagara Falls. It was perfectly happy there and seemed to have no need or inclination to remember the past.

But then, when Leota and Packard were old, when the plastics company had made them rich, when they had lived together for fifty years, the subject of Georgia came back suddenly into Packard's head. Not into Leota's head, but into Packard's. He began saying to strangers at parties: 'Leota is old enough to remember slavery.' The mouths of the strangers would gape and their eyes turn towards Leota, but she would ignore them and look at Packard through the purple sun visor she wore in all weathers and say: 'Those people were not *slaves*, Pack.' And he would reply: 'They were not free, neither, Leota. And that's the truth.'

He was getting angry with the world.

Leota watched him through her visor and wondered when this anger had started.

She decided it had begun the day they went to the unveiling of a painting.

He said to her as they set out: 'Take off that frigging visor, Leota! You see the world through cough linctus.'

She replied: 'I like it that way, Pack.'

'Okay,' he said, 'but it's not the way it *is*!'

'How can you say what way it *is*? Everyone sees it differently.'

'Not me,' he said, 'not any more. I see it as IT IS!'

The painting was black. They sat with friends and neighbours in two rows in the town gallery and looked at it and there it was, a black square on a beige background with nothing in it but black, black. The gallery had raised $100,000 to acquire it and yet it looked completely and utterly worthless. Leota had taken off her visor, but as they all sat there in silence she put it on again so that there would be a new kind of magenta colour to the border of the black square.

The artist was introduced to the audience. His name was Pethcot and he wore round black glasses, like pebbles. He smiled and preened and was about to begin to talk about his marvellous square when Packard stood up and said: 'I guess I always knew your world was hollow. Now I get it; it isn't only hollow, it's filled with crap.'

He walked out of the gallery and Leota followed him. For all that day and most of the night, he sat on a chair with a board over his knee, playing Solitaire and mumbling: 'Cheats and liars! Don't *speak* to me . . .'

There was a side of him which had always been down on things, hard on things, including himself and the factory. Asked what the factory made, he had often replied: 'We make trash and the cans to put it in.' He knew 'plastic' wasn't a popular word; it was a word Canadians worried about. Leota reminded him: 'If you manufactured from wood, Pack, they would worry about the trees, but everything has to be made of something.'

He answered that anxiety wasn't always rational, any more than despair was rational. 'Who's talking about despair?' asked Leota. 'Everyone,' said Packard. 'Every soul alive.'

This didn't seem rational to Leota. She reminded Packard that one of the products made by the factory was an incubator housing. She said: 'The parents of those babies in your incubators may have been in despair for a while, but when they see their babies aren't going to die they're happy as birds.'

'Nah,' said Packard. 'Wrong. You don't see to the heart of things, Leota. They're happy as birds *for a while*, only until they remember how easily it was going to come.'

'How easily what was going to come?'

'Death. The whole vanishing thing.'

'Pack,' said Leota, 'stop it. You're a normal man, not a poet. Get your mind on something real. Think of the Blue Jays and the great season they're having!'

'I don't give a fly's arse for the Blue Jays,' said Pack.

'Why not? Baseball used to be your craze.'

'Well, it's not any more. I'm through with baseball.'

Leota thought: it's okay to be through with a craze if you can replace it with something else, preferably another craze, even something as trivial as TV game shows. Crazes kept people alive. If you didn't care one way or another about anything, you died. She reminded Pack that Burt Lancaster had kept birds in Alcatraz and this had helped him to go on living, day after day. But Packard only laughed: 'That dates you, Leota! You saw that film in black and white. It predates your visor.'

She didn't mind being teased. Pack was a large man. Large men were often teases. And she'd lived with him for fifty years, just the two of them, no children, no pets, and survived it all and still loved him. But she decided she did mind him getting angry with the world. She minded it for two reasons: 1. she knew that anger takes all the fun and joy out of everything, and 2. it made her feel guilty. It made her wonder whether she shouldn't start to be angry too – whether anger, when you got old, was the only appropriate emotion left. And she'd always been very accepting of the world, never analysed anything with care. Even in her dreams of Georgia, she saw fireflies, not black workers in the fields with their backs bent. It was shameful when she thought about it. And the people who were angry with everything – like Steve Cairns, the seventeen-year-old son of their neighbours, who fought with his father and stole from local stores and left vomit in the driveway – made her frightened. She couldn't help it. Steve Cairns terrified her, him and everybody like him, all the angry punks and bullies. She wanted them to leave Canada. She wanted to send them to the frozen moon.

She lay beside Packard and looked at his white hair on the pillow. She'd noticed, at the unveiling of the black square, that his hair had started to stick out crazily from his head, stiff and wild, as if electricity were fizzing through it. She supposed that fury could generate an electrical charge. Electricity could be made by unexpected things, like the left front door handle of her car, which gave her a slight shock each time she touched it. If Packard's hair got too straight and startling, it might be time to take him away somewhere, to one of the islands in the Hudson Bay, where there was nothing to feel angry about, no charlatan painters, no trash in the water, no TV news of wars and homelessness. Or, she might advise him, simply, to go to the Falls.

Pack had been raised within sight of them and had said all his life that he was 'proud to know the Niagara'. It was there that he went when something upset him. He frequently reminded Leota, when he returned from these expeditions, that 3,000 tons of water *per second* went over the lip. He said: 'Most people in the world live hundreds of miles from any astonishing thing. They don't feel wonder any more. They don't know *how* to feel wonder. And it is wonder, Leota, and that alone that keeps man in check. I'm telling you.'

He didn't need to tell her, really. She could remember watching the stars over Georgia and everyone on the porch saying they felt small and insignificant. And it wasn't as though the subject of the Falls didn't crop up when people visited them from America or England, because it did. One of Packard's favourite pastimes was to re-tell the stories of the stunters, the people who had tried to defy the Falls in barrels or other contraptions 'of their own pathetic making'. Packard despised the stunters, 'the boobies', as he called them, for trying to make profit from the Falls.

He denied that they were brave. He said: 'What's brave about trying to grab notoriety?'

The visitors always listened attentively. They seemed enthralled by the stunts. Leota assured them: 'You don't have to take Pack's view of the matter. He knows it's not the only view.'

'Nah,' he said, 'but it's the only sane view. Take that guy, Stephens, from England. You know what that booby did? To try to keep his barrel the right way up, he stuck a hundredpound anvil in the base of it and tied his feet to the anvil and his arms to the lid of the barrel . . .'

Leota always thought, at this point, that she could see the guests trying to remember what an anvil was. She thought an anvil was a hard kind of thing to picture any more. But Pack had pictured it so many times he had no difficulty and he always went straight on. 'You can see what's coming, can't you?' he said. 'That stupid guy! When the barrel went over and hit the water, the anvil dropped out the bottom, wham, in the first second. And Stephens went with it. All except his right arm! And that's the only bit of him they ever found – his damned arm!'

'Oh, no!' the guests would say, 'Oh, God! Oh, my!' And Packard would smile. 'Stephens was the arch booby,' he'd say, 'but there were others. You bet.'

Packard always referred to Steve Cairns as 'The Deli'. The nickname amused him. 'You get it, Leota? It refers both to the word "delinquent" and to the quantity of Russian salad he and his friends leave on the neighbourhood walkways.'

He'd always sympathised with Mr and Mrs Cairns, said, heavens, if kids are like that, thank God we don't have any. But now, in his new fury with so many things, he started to invite The Deli into the house for coffee and a smoke. Leota would come into the kitchen and find The Deli sitting with his feet on the table. Occasionally, she made Pack his favourite malted milk and stayed to listen to the conversations. She learned that The Deli's body was slowly being covered with tattoos; he had a woman's breast on each knee, a jewel-handled dagger going from his pubic hair to his navel and a raptor on his back. He offered to show them, but Leota said: 'That's kind of you, Steve, but no thank you, dear.'

Later, she said: 'It's pathetic, Pack. It's so juvenile.'

'Sure,' said Packard, 'but he's looked at the grown-up world and he doesn't like it enough to join it. And who can blame him?'

'That's the way young people always were,' said Leota, 'but they used to want to do something to change it. Now, they just sit around and do things with needles.'

'They see the world's not susceptible to change any more,' said Packard. 'It's too far gone. Even here in Canada. There's no decent people any more. So steal from them. Why not? Governments steal. Big Business steals. Packard Plastics steals . . .'

'Hush,' said Leota. 'Stop thinking that way. I can't endure it. We've only got a few years . . .'

'Exactly. So let's wise up. Get rid of your visor. Let's see things as they are.'

Leota stood up and put her hands on her hips the way her mother used to do when she told off the black maid. 'Packard,' she said, 'I am taking you away.'

The travel agent found her a cabin on an island in the Hudson Bay. It had its own landing stage and a sixteen-foot fibreglass boat. Firs surrounded the cabin and came down to the edge of the water. It was beaver country. The light from the north was fierce.

'Okay,' said Packard, when they arrived on a late afternoon, 'this is all right.'

Outside their bedroom, which faced south over the water, was a wooden balcony. Packard found two faded deck chairs and set them out side by side. 'Up here,' he said, 'we will really be able to see the stars. And by the way, dear, stars are silver, sometimes yellowish, sometimes quite white, but they are never purple.'

He got two blankets for them and bought a bag of donuts from the only bakery on the island and there they sat, on their second night, eating donuts and staring at the night sky. It was early spring and cold and silent. Packard tucked the blankets round their knees and Leota took off her visor.

Packard said after a while: 'I read someplace the galaxy's in the shape of two fried eggs, back to back. We're in amongst the white.'

Leota said: 'Astronomers try to simplify everything for us, but the things they ask us to imagine are still pretty darned hard.'

Packard laughed. This was a sound Leota hadn't heard for a while. Then he said: 'I like the way the stars mock us. They're more merciless than the Falls. The Falls are *there* at least, but up there . . . we think we're looking at solid worlds, but we're not, we're looking at travelling light.'

'Why does it stop travelling?' asked Leota.

'What?' said Pack.

'Why does it stop at a fixed point? Why doesn't it come on and on until it gets so close to us it blinds us?'

'It wouldn't blind you, Leota. You'd just be in among a sparkling bilberry soup!'

Pack hadn't noticed that Leota had taken off the visor, but now he did and he held out his hand, sticky with sugar, for her to hold. 'I'm sorry,' he said. 'And for the way I am now. I don't know why light stops travelling. And I don't know why I'm so darn mad about everything. I guess I'm just a booby, like all the rest.'

'No you're not,' said Leota.

'Anyway,' said Packard, 'I'll be up there in a while. The dead turn into interstellar gas, I bet they do. See that very bright, cold star – that one?'

'Yup. I see it.'

'Look there for me. It's a waterfall star, must be. I think it's called Sirius. My gas particles will be popping somewhere there.'

'Hush up, sweetheart,' said Leota, 'this is a vacation. So why not live for now?'

But he didn't live another day.

He went out in the fibreglass boat at dawn and a west wind blew in from the Northern Territories and the boat overturned. Packard's body wasn't found for seven days. It had been washed ashore on an island so small it was inhabited only by gannets and geese, who pecked at his nose and at his eyes and at his white hair. The police said to Leota: 'We don't advise you to see the face, Ma'am. Identification from the feet and hands will be sufficient.'

Leota had never known loneliness. She never could have imagined how much time it consumed. She'd sit for hours and hours, with her chin on her hands, doing nothing and *being* nothing, except lonely.

It was not only her years with Packard that she sat there remembering – the building of their house, the summer parties they used to give, their mall shopping, their trips to Europe and the States, their love of Cajun food, and all their early years of passion – but her long-ago childhood slowly gathered shape and colour in her mind, like a developing photograph. Her former self felt weightless, or else winged, like the gnats she'd seen at the time of Jimmy Carter. It floated above the landscape, but what it saw were all the ways the people round her were anchored to the earth. She saw all their endeavour. It never ceased. They struggled and laboured and fought until they died. She said to her friend, Jane: 'I may have misunderstood it, but I don't believe these people were angry with the world. I think they loved it to death. But Pack, in his last years, he was so mad at it all. So now I'm confused as well as heartbroken. I don't know which of them was right.'

Sometimes, when the nights got warmer, Leota went out into

the yard. She sat on a white tin chair and looked at the sky. She was searching for the bright waterfall star Packard had showed her. She moved her head in an arc, like a searchlight. She took off her visor. She ached for Pack to be alive again and by her side, eating donuts, and to show her the star she couldn't find.

In her solitude, she found it difficult to eat. It was as if there were interstellar gas in her stomach – Lonely Gas, she called it. And so she began to get smaller and narrower and lighter. Even her head. Jane said to her: 'It's not possible that the head of a person can shrink.' But Leota showed her the band of the visor, which she had had to alter by one notch. She said: 'If Pack can die in a boat before breakfast, anything is possible.'

She was now seventy-three years old and had no idea what to look for or how to order the world for the remainder of her life. She knew she couldn't spend it sitting at a table with her chin on her hands or out in the garden in a tin chair. But the fact remained, she was lost without Packard, literally lost. She had difficulty remembering the route to the hairdressers. Driving the car made her anxious, as if it was going to take her some place that she didn't recognise and didn't want to go. She didn't know, at any one moment, what book she was reading or whether she was enjoying it or not. She had to look up the times of the TV game shows she always used to watch. When she stared at the yard, she thought it looked peculiar, as if someone had arrived in the night and moved the shrubs around.

In her kitchen, she listened to the radio. She knew it was important to continue to be told what was going on in the outside world, not least because then she could try to make up her mind about Pack's anger with it. She learned from a radio programme that tigers were disappearing from India, killed by poachers, who sold the bones, ground to bags of dust, to the Chinese. She forgot what the Chinese used the dust for. She was informed that a growth industry in Russia was the sale of human hair. She found these things both disturbing and reassuring; people would do no matter what to stay alive, to buy another week, another day. But then she thought: it's a shame to kill a tiger or sell your hair for another day; and I have days and weeks and years already bought and I don't necessarily want them all. It would be better for those people to be given some of *my* time.

She knew her thinking was confused. In her narrowing head, her brain was probably getting smaller. Grief for a person or a thing could uncouple the logical part of your mind from the rest of it. In Moscow, there could be women who were going insane, grieving for their hair.

She sighed at all this. Her sighs had become insubstantial and sounded like the whispers of a child. She told herself that she had to make a plan, find a goal, or else her future would be completely and utterly blank and dark like the black square painting in the town gallery.

One afternoon, The Deli came round. Leota hadn't seen him since Packard's funeral, where she'd noticed that he had a new tattoo in the shape of a heart on his neck. He brought some limp flowers wrapped in paper and laid them on Leota's kitchen table.

'Thank you, Steve,' she said. 'Sit down, dear, won't you?'

It was summer now and The Deli was wearing a sleeveless T-shirt and torn shorts, exposing the breasts on his knees. Leota could smell sweat on his skinny body. She didn't want him there.

He said: 'I should have come sooner, Mrs Packard. I'm sorry I didn't.'

'Oh, no,' said Leota, 'there was no need . . .'

There was a long silence. Leota thought: Pack used to keep Cokes in the refrigerator for when he called.

'Can I get you a drink of water?' she asked.

'No thanks,' said The Deli. 'My parents told me you didn't get out much any more, so I came to say . . .'

Leota was staring at the heart on his neck. It seemed to be bordered with lace, like the paper heart of a valentine card.

'I can drive now,' he went on. 'I passed my test. So I thought, if there was any place you wanted to go . . .'

Leota looked up. She felt more surprised by what The Deli had just said than by anything she'd seen or heard since the radio programme about tiger bones.

'Why . . .' she said, falling as she sometimes did into her Georgia drawl, 'that is most kind of you dear, but – '

'I mean it. I'd like to drive you somewhere.'

'Well . . .' she said. 'Well. You know the place I haven't been in a long time is the Falls . . .'

'Okay,' said The Deli. 'Sure. The Falls. Why not?'

Later, lying in bed, Leota thought: why did I say the Falls? That was Pack's place. What will I do there except get spray on my visor and fill up with Lonely Gas? The truth was, she didn't want to go any place with Steve Cairns. He might throw up out of the car window. He might kill her with reckless driving. But she knew she'd had to accept his offer. After so long of wanting to ship him off to the moon, this was the least she could do.

So they went on a bright August day in Mrs Cairns' Toyota. The Deli drove very fast with one elbow leaning out the window, as if he'd practised driving for fifteen years. Leota examined the lacy heart on his neck and eventually said: 'Your little heart, dear; it looks very near the jugular vein to me.'

'Yup,' said The Deli, 'it is. It's called a 3.'

'A 3?'

'There are three levels of risk with a tattoo. Most of the body carries level 1 – low risk of any side effect, infection or damage to essential tissue. Level 2 would be, say, medium risk: soles of the feet, which could cause problems through inadvertent reflexology. Then there's level 3: inside of wrist, genitals and neck, just here.'

'Do you like danger?' asked Leota.

The Deli scratched his cropped head. 'I guess,' he said. 'I guess.'

When they got to the Falls, The Deli parked neatly and said: 'Shall I wait in the car, Mrs Packard? Do you want to be alone?'

'No,' said Leota, 'I certainly do not want to be alone. I never would go to the Falls alone.'

They got out of the car and Leota, who felt as frail as a bird, took The Deli's arm. The day was windy, but the roar of the cataract was still huge above the wind. Walking towards it, Leota told The Deli that Packard used to stand on the far right, where the grassy bank of the Niagara River tapers towards the precipice. She remembered that he used to lean far out over the rail and gaze at the translucent jade of the lip where, for an instant, the water still reflects the light before it foams white and is gone. She led The Deli to this exact spot and the two of them looked down. Leota let go of the boy's arm and held tightly to the rail. She thought the wind might easily snatch at her and hold her on an eddy above the spray, before letting her fall.

After only a few moments, The Deli said: 'When you get here, when you see it again, you have to admire those stunters, don't you, Mrs Packard? Imagine going over the edge in a barrel? Holy shit!'

Leota said: 'The first person to try it was a woman. Did you know that, Steve? She was called Annie Taylor and she'd been a schoolteacher.'

'Did she make it? Did she survive?'

'Yes, she did. I think it was in about 1901. She was a heroine for a while, till people just forgot about her. And that's the trouble with stunts. People's memory for them is short.'

'Well, I admire those stunters. I couldn't do it. Could you, Mrs Packard?'

Leota stared for a long time at the great spectacle that Packard had been so proud to know and which had comforted him with its grandeur. Eventually, she said: 'I don't know, but if I did I wouldn't want to be locked in a barrel in darkness. I'd want to go over in something transparent – like a giant bubble – so that I could see everything and know what was happening to me every second of the trip.'

That evening when the stars came out, Leota made herself a Martini and took it out into the yard, where she sat down on the tin chair. She'd given up looking for the waterfall star, but she chose a black space in the sky and imagined Packard as a cloud of Lonely Gas within it. The Martini tasted fine. 'Pack,' said Leota, 'you were wrong about Steve Cairns. I do believe you were – and so was I. Steve was just going through a *craze* for hating the world, as anyone could, but it's lessening.'

Leota finished the Martini. She didn't know why Martini glasses had to be so small.

She took off her visor and looked at Packard's invisible gas cloud with an unprotected eye. 'He's learned to drive,' she continued. 'That takes application and you wouldn't bother with driving lessons – that's what I think, anyway – unless you planned to go someplace and see some sights. And then, Pack, he told me he admired the stunters. He doesn't see them as boobies. Not at all. He sees them as brave people. So there you are. You thought you had an ally in Steve and I thought I had an enemy and both of us were wrong.'

As she went back into the house and made herself a second Martini, she felt defiant, as if something had at last been resolved. But when she woke up the next morning, she didn't know why she'd felt this. Nothing was resolved. She'd seen another side to The Deli's character, that was all. She was relieved of the burden of referring to him as The Deli and of wanting to send him off to the moon. But the fact of Packard's anger still remained. And now she saw, for the first time, that it may have had a dimension to it that she'd never acknowledged: in coming to despise so much in human endeavour, he must also have come to despise her. He'd seen how inadequate and false was her vision of her Southern childhood, how unenquiring her Georgia mind. He'd nagged and nagged at her to take off her visor. He'd told her a hundred times that she failed to see things *as they are, Leota.*

She felt bleak. She wanted to say to Pack: I disapprove of killing something as beautiful as a tiger, to grind its bones to some dust or other, of course I do. And a world where women have to sell their blood or their hair or their bodies to buy bread can't be a just place. Even I can see this. And I've always seen it.

No, says Pack's voice. Don't lie. Even now, when you should

see the past as it was, you see gnats and fireflies and golden light. You've insulated yourself, with the money I made from trash, with your house in a good clean neighbourhood, with the sweet shade of purple you've coloured all the seasons . . .

The word 'trash', among all the vexing words of Packard's, was the one that started to haunt Leota most. She looked round her house. It was orderly and warm and comfortable, with quite a few objects of beauty in it. And it was built on a plastics fortune. It was built on products Packard had found worthless.

Leota went into the kitchen. She stared at all the plastic appliances, each with its one and only function of saving her labour and time. And she thought: if I could just see what all the time had been saved *for*, then I would know what to do with the rest of my life.

She couldn't see. She sighed her child-like sigh and began putting her dirty washing into the machine. These mundane things had to be done, even though a person felt bewildered and lost. In a Moscow kitchen, a young woman ties a scarf round her head and puts bones into water for a soup. She does it because she has to go on.

But why go on? Why?

Leota didn't hear Steve knocking at her back door. Or perhaps she heard? Perhaps she said 'Come in, Steve'? She didn't remember. All she knew was that Steve was suddenly there in her kitchen. He was leaning against the washing machine, talking about Japanese cars. Then Leota said: 'Steve, fill the powder dispenser for me, will you, dear?'

'Sure,' he said. But he didn't fill it. He held the round plastic powder dispenser in his hand and showed it to her.

'Look,' he said.

'At what?' said Leota.

'At this,' said Steve. 'You've got the perfect blueprint here – for your Niagara bubble.'

She hardly wanted to let Steve out of her sight after that. She said: 'I know you have to attend school, dear, and smoke and play music and so forth, but you've masterminded the rest of my life and I want you to supervise the plan every step of the way.

He said: 'You're not serious, are you, Mrs Packard?'

'Call me Leota,' she said, 'from now on. And, yes, of course I'm serious.'

They sat at her kitchen table, drinking Martinis and making drawings. She said: 'We have to remember, Steve, the priority is visibility.'

'And strength,' he said.

Leota said nothing.

He was good at calculations. He said the only thing he could do at school was Math.

'What about History?' asked Leota.

'Trash,' he said. 'Isn't it?'

They measured Leota and weighed her. Her head had shrunk another notch on her visor and her weight was down to 101 pounds. She was the size, Steve said, of a twelve-year-old person.

It was autumn already – six months since Packard's death – when Leota and Steve drove in Mrs Cairns' Toyota to the plastics factory and Leota asked to see the manager, Ron Blatch.

'Ron comes on breezy,' said Leota to Steve, while they waited on imitation-leather chairs for Ron to appear, 'but his home life's a mess.'

He came in smiling and shook Leota's hand and said it was always a pleasure to see her. She introduced him to Steve and he was, as she knew he would be, courteous to him. She was glad, nevertheless, that Steve was wearing a polo neck that day and that Ron couldn't see his tattooed heart so close to the jugular.

She told Ron Blatch that she was funding a stunt, an attempt to shoot the Falls in a plastic bubble, and that she wanted the factory to make the bubble according to a preliminary design.

Steve produced the drawings that now showed a contraption five feet in diameter and built of transparent air-filled tubing, laid in a circular coil and encased in a clear plastic ball. At its

433

top was a watertight escape hatch that could be opened from both inside and out. Bolted to the ball was a harness made of plastic fibre.

Ron Blatch took out his glasses and put them on. He stared at the drawings. Then he smiled and took his glasses off again and shook his head.

'Stunting's illegal now, the whole length of the Niagara,' he said. 'It's banned absolutely.'

'We know that, Ron,' said Leota. 'We know that . . .'

Ron looked at Steve. 'So who's planning on breaking the law?'

'Well . . .' said Leota.

'No one,' said Steve. 'This is not for personal gain or glory. It's gonna be for charity and charity stunts can be allowed.'

'Ah-huh?' said Ron. 'Like which charity?'

'The aim,' said Leota firmly, 'is to do something in memory of Packard. He was a good man. He minded about the world and Packard Plastics have made life better for thousands of people.'

'Sure,' said Ron.

'But he was unquiet,' continued Leota. 'He was afraid that Canadians had lost their reverence for the natural world, for the things they can't contain and control . . .'

'The Falls are contained okay,' said Ron, smiling. 'Seventy-five per cent of their power is taken by the hydro-electric companies.'

'I know that,' said Leota, 'but still they're not quite tamed, are they? And, to Pack, they came to symbolise all the things he was afraid we'd lost.'

'I know he loved the Falls,' said Ron, 'but I can't break the law for him and you haven't mentioned which charity you're doing this for.'

Leota looked at Steve. She hoped his mathematical mind was working on a formula. After a moment's silence, he said: 'It's to help the old, Mr Blatch. The old are a despised group these days. It's to benefit them.'

Ron rubbed his eyes. He said nothing, but put his glasses on again and stared at the drawings in his hands. Leota thought that he wasn't really looking at them, but only pretending to look at them while he decided what to say and do.

'Ron,' she said, 'Pack was good to you, wasn't he? Fair to you all, wasn't he?'

'Yes.'

'So build this for him. Will you? And don't ask any more questions?'

Ron Blatch looked up. His expression was blank and dumb and Leota felt suddenly sorry for him. He might have liked to go home and talk this over with his wife and get her opinion on whether or not he was about to break the law, but his wife had run off with her fencing teacher and that was that.

'Okay,' said Ron.

Leota knew that it would take the company some time to manufacture the bubble. Special moulds would have to be made; Steve's calculations would have to be fed into the firm's computers. So she also knew that she had time to think carefully about what she was planning.

The nights were getting cold. She laid her light-boned body on the couch and listened to a little light Schubert and tried to weigh her own death against the sweetness and beauty of the music.

She decided there must be some sort of balance between wanting to live on and wanting to leave the world in a bubble. Yet what I *see* is the bubble. Only that. I don't see any future at all. The future of Leota Packard is as empty of everything as a Pethcot square. The future is a chair and me on it and my head on my hands.

She dozed and dreamed. The lighter her frame was becoming, the more she floated on sudden little currents of sleep.

One evening, she woke to find Steve in her living room. He was sitting on her Persian rug, rolling a cigarette. When she focused on him, she saw that he looked pale and anxious.

'Leota,' he said. 'Something terrible's happened.'

'All right, dear,' she said. 'Wait here.'

She went to the kitchen and made two Martinis. She came back into the room and gave one of them to Steve. She sat down opposite him and the two of them sipped the drinks in silence for a moment.

Then Steve said: 'They're sending me away.'

'Away?' said Leota. 'Who is and where?'

'My parents. To some frozen school up near Alaska. My dad says he can't stand the sight of me another day. I think it's my knees that freak him out. The tits expand when I sit down. I guess you noticed?'

'Yes, I did, dear. And your mother?'

'She doesn't say anything. She clings on to Dad's arm. He says every line that's on her face I've put there.'

'I haven't noticed many lines. She's a good-looking woman.'

'I know. But that's what Dad says.'

'When are you leaving, Steve?'

'Next week.'

'Well, I'm very, very sorry. A frozen school near Alaska sounds like an awful place. And you're very thin. I'd better give you some of Pack's old woollen sweaters to take with you.'

'Thanks,' said Steve, 'but what about the bubble?'

Leota sat very still and looked around her room and then out of the window, where a November rain was falling.

'I don't know, dear,' she said. 'I don't know. But you're the one we must worry about.'

That night, Leota couldn't sleep. She blamed herself for what was happening. For so long, she'd wanted to send Steve to an icy place outside her world and now he was going there. She'd willed it, out of fear and loathing, and now that all her fear and loathing had gone her will had started to prevail. 'Leota,' she whispered aloud, 'you see everything too late.'

Pointless to cry, she thought. Crying's for the boobies. So she decided to get up. It was two in the morning and cold in the house. She put on her peignoir and her satin slippers frayed at the heels and went out into the yard. She looked up at the sky and there, in the south, was the waterfall star. She remembered its name: Sirius.

It seemed almost blue, the coldest, bluest star in the galaxy. And it was large, as if it were nearer by hundreds of years than all the stars that surrounded it. Leota felt amazed that she could have searched for it for so long and not found it. It blinked at her – light refracted through time and the thousand imaginary cataracts of Packard's mind. And then she heard Packard's laugh exploding up there in its swirl of gas. 'Stars *move*,' he said, 'and the world moves. You've never understood how each and every damn thing in the universe is changing every second of time. So from where you stand, Leota, this is a winter star.'

'Okay, Pack,' she heard herself say, 'I see it now.'

She'd always been an impatient person. As a child, when she woke before dawn, she used to yell at the sun to come up. And once she'd decided on a thing, she wanted to make it happen straightaway.

At eight, she called Steve and asked him to come by. He arrived at nine with his roller skates round his neck. Leota made coffee.

'Steve,' she said, 'I've seen everything all wrong.'

'What do you mean, Leota?'

'Well. I don't need the bubble after all. You see? It was typical of me to think about a bubble, to think about plastic protection, just like my old visor, but I don't need it.'

'What are you going to use, then? A barrel?'

'No. I'm going to use nothing.'

'Come on . . .'

'It's what I want to do. You won't be able to put me off, so don't try. I'm a Georgia girl and stubborn. But I need one last favour from you, dear.'

'Leota . . .'

'I want you to drive me there. If I went alone, I could lose my nerve. And I want to do it tonight. It has to be night, because I don't want to petrify any Japanese or French tourist. And tonight feels good to me. So if your mother would very kindly lend you the Toyota . . .'

Steve got up. He put his roller skates on the floor and lit a cigarette. He walked to the window and smoked silently for a moment, then he turned and said: 'I want to be absolutely clear what you're telling me.'

'I'm telling you that I'm sorry,' said Leota. 'Sorry for everything. Sorry for all the things I didn't properly understand and sorry, in particular, that you're being sent away to the moon.'

'It's not the moon,' said Steve.

'Near,' said Leota.

'It's not enough,' said Steve. 'It doesn't explain it.'

'Well, it's too bad,' said Leota. 'That's all I can say. That's it.'

He arrived in a pick-up truck. He said: 'The days when I can borrow the Toyota are gone.' He told Leota that the pick-up belonged to the father of a bass guitarist.

Leota had chosen her outfit carefully: clean white underwear and white socks; blue-pants, bought at Queens Quay, Toronto; a white silk blouse and a pale-blue wool jacket with a little silver monogram on the pocket; white shoes she normally only wore in summer. She'd washed and combed her short white hair and fixed two jade earrings to her still soft ear lobes.

'You look nice,' said Steve.

'Thank you, dear,' said Leota.

When they left, towards midnight, Leota didn't look back at the house that Packard had built for her and where, she had to admit, she'd been foolishly happy. She kept her eyes straight ahead on the moonlit road and all her mind was on the tiny particle of the future that remained. She and Steve didn't speak until they turned off the main highway leading to the Falls and started down an old track that led nowhere but in amongst some trees and stopped at a barbed-wire fence. A hundred yards beyond the fence was the Niagara River. 'I know this,' said Steve, out of the darkness, 'it's a place where I've been.'

Leota didn't ask what he'd been here for. Instead, she said:

438

'It's so very kind of you, dear, to help me in this way. I hope you won't get into any kind of trouble on my account.'

'Don't think about that,' said Steve.

He stopped the car and they both got out. They were some way upstream from the Falls, but they could hear them, even *feel* their nearness in the ground underneath them. They stood very still, holding onto the truck. It was a cold, cloudy night with no stars.

Leota had been precise about the arrangements she wanted. She would walk on her own through the trees to the water's edge. She would wait there a few minutes. Meanwhile, Steve would drive back onto the highway and park up in the Falls parking lot. Then he would go and stand at the rail – exactly where they had stood on their visit – a few feet from the lip of the waterfall. He was to carry a strong flashlight. With the flashlight, he was to scan the water, looking for Leota's bobbing head, and, when he found it, he was to fix the light on her. 'Your light,' she'd said, 'will be the last thing I see and it will be like a star. You must be certain to follow me all the way, till I'm over and gone.'

They hung back by the truck, getting cold, because neither of them knew how to say goodbye. So then Leota just started to walk forwards, without a word. She was at the fence and climbing through when Steve called out: 'Wait! Leota, wait a minute!'

She was on the other side of the fence now. Steve ran towards her and, with the barbed wire between them, put his arms round her. She was much smaller than him. She reached up and put a kiss on his tattooed heart.

At the water's edge, she took off her shoes. She felt no fear at all. 'None, Pack,' she said. 'So there you are.'

She was impatient, in fact, to get into the surging green river. Her only worry was that her body was too light to fall straight down under the guillotine of water. She thought it might reach the lip and go flying outwards – as once had happened to a young boy – and arrive in the pool below still alive. But this was

439

a small risk. No one else had survived the Falls without the protection of a barrel.

She let time pass, but then she didn't know how much of it had gone. She'd heard Steve drive away in the truck, but she couldn't tell whether he would have taken up his position at the lip yet and switched on the flashlight.

She waited five more minutes, gauging the time by counting. Then, she put her white shoes side by side and got into the water.

It was so cold, it took her thoughts away. And the current was far stronger and wilder than she'd imagined. She was like flotsam in it, being whirled round like a fairground car. Waves broke over her and her mouth filled with water. She choked and spat. She tried to hold her head high, to swim properly, to grab her thoughts back. She'd believed that the green river would be easy and lead her gently to the edge, but it fought her, as if jealous of her destination, as if it wanted to claim her before she reached the fall.

With her bony hands, with her legs in blue pants, with her neck and chin, she fought its intention. Each time she surfaced, she could see, to her delight, the yellow beam of Steve's flashlight directed at her from the bank. As long as that light was there, she believed the river wouldn't take her. And when she knew at last that she was there; when, in the final second, she felt the water become calm before it slid her over and hurled her down, she found a voice to raise against the thunder. 'Hey!' she yelled. And it was to Leota as if all the world could hear her and would remember this moment of hers for years and years to come: 'Watch this! The last booby!'

John-Jin

When I was a child, the pier was a promising place.

You walked along and along and along it, with all its grey sea underneath, and at the end of it was the Pavilion.

'Now,' my father used to say, 'here we are.' He was a person who enjoyed destinations. Inside the Pier Pavilion were far more things going on than you could imagine from the outside; it was like a human mind in this one respect. You could drink tea or rum or 7-Up in there. You could play the fruit machines or buy a doll made of varnished shells. You could shoot at a line of tin hens to win a goldfish. You could talk about your life to a fortune teller or ride a ghost train. There was a section of the great glass roof from which flamenco music came down. And under the music was a Miniature Golf track.

My father and I used to play. Our two miniature golf balls followed each other over bridges and through castle gates and round little slalom arrangements until they reached their destination. This destination was a wishing well and every time we played both of us had to make a wish, no matter who won the game. My wishes changed with time, but I know now that my father's did not. I wished for a pair of wings and a trampoline and a pet reptile and flamenco dancing lessons. My father wished for John-Jin.

Then, when I was ten, the Pavilion detached itself from the pier in a storm and moved five inches out to sea.

I remember saying: 'Five inches isn't much.' My father replied: 'Don't be silly, Susan.' My mother took my hand and said: 'It's a building, pet. Imagine if this house were to move.'

They closed the whole pier. Things separated from their

destinations can become unsafe. When we went down to the beach, I used to walk to the locked pier gates, on which the word 'Danger' hung like an advertisement for an old red car, and watch the tugs and cranes dismantling the Pavilion bit by bit. They towed it all away and stacked it on a car park. Their idea was to raise all the money it would cost to bring it back and rebuild it and join it onto the pier again, but no one said when this would be.

It was the year 1971. It was the year I got my flamenco shoes and began my Spanish dancing lessons. It was the year that John-Jin arrived.

He was Chinese.

He'd been left wrapped in a football scarf in a women's toilet in Wetherby. He'd been found and taken to a hospital and christened John-Jin by the nurses there. How he came to be ours was a story nobody told me then. No one seemed to remember, either, what colour the football scarf was or if it had a team name on it. 'The details don't matter, love,' said my mother, changing John-Jin's nappy on her lap; 'what matters is that he's with us now. We've waited for him for ten years and here he is.'

'Do you mean,' I said, 'that you *knew* he was going to come?'

'Oh, yes.'

'So you had someone waiting in that toilet all that time?'

'No, no, pet! We didn't know *where* he was going to come from. We never thought of him being Chinese necessarily. We were just certain that he'd arrive one day.'

He was as beautiful as a flower. His eyes were like two little fluttering creatures that had landed on the flower. If I'd been an ogress in a story, I would have eaten John-Jin. I used to put his flat face against mine and kiss it. And I entertained him when my parents were busy. They'd put him in a baby-bouncer that hung from a door lintel and I'd get out my castanets and put on my flamenco shoes and dance for him. The first word he ever said was *olé*. When he learned to stand up, he went stamp, stamp, stamp in his red bootees.

'Don't wear him out, Susan,' said my mother. 'He's only one.'

'I'm not,' I said. 'I'm helping him get strong.'

When he was in bed sometimes, with his gnome night-light on, I'd creep into his room and tell him about the world. I told him about the building of a gigantic wall in China and about the strike of the school dinner ladies. I told him about the Miniature Golf and the wishing well. I said: 'The Pier Pavilion was there and then not. There and then not. And that happens to certain things and I don't know why.'

Making the pier safe took two years. People in our town were asked to 'sponsor a girder'. You could have your name cast in the girder and then you would be able to imagine the waves breaking against it. I liked the idea of the sea breaking against my name, but my parents decided that it was John-Jin who needed his own girder more. They said: 'You never know, Susan. Doing this might help in some way.'

We needed help now for John-Jin. Something was going wrong. He could do everything he was meant to do – talk, bounce, walk, laugh, eat and sing – except grow. He just did not grow. Nobody explained why. Our doctor said: 'Remember his origins. He's going to be a very small person, that's all.' But we thought that was a poor answer.

We kept on and on measuring him. He grew in minute little bursts and stopped again. When he was three, he could still fit into the baby-bouncer. I wanted to buy him his first pair of flamenco shoes, but his feet were too small. At his nursery school, he was seven inches shorter than the shortest girl. The little tables and chair were too high for him and the steps going up to the slide too far apart. The nursery teacher said to my mother: 'Are you seeking advice from the right quarters?' And that night, my parents sat up talking until it got light and I went down and found them both asleep in their armchairs, like old people.

The next day, we all went out in an eel boat to see John-Jin's girder bolted onto the pier. John-Jin kept trying to reach down into the eel tank to stroke the eels; he wasn't very interested in his girder. My mother and father looked exhausted. It was a bright day and they kept trying to shade their eyes with their fingers. I thought the girder was beautiful – as if it had been made in Spain. It was curved and black and John-Jin's name stood out in the sunlight. This was one of the last girders to be put in place. Our eel boat was anchored right where the pavilion used to be. And so I said to John-Jin: 'Pay attention. Look. Without your girder, they couldn't have finished mending the pier.' He blinked up at it, his straight, thick eyelashes fluttering in the bright light. Then he turned back to the eels.

'Where are they going?' he asked.

My parents took John-Jin to a specialist doctor in Manchester. Every part of his body was measured, including his penis and his ears. My mother said: 'Don't worry, Susan, he's far too young to feel embarrassed.'

A course of injections was prescribed for him. He had to go to the surgery every week to get one. I said: 'What are they injecting you *with*, John-Jin?'

'Something,' he said.

'Just a growth hormone, dear,' said my mother.

I was going to ask, what is a 'growth hormone'? Where does it come from? But a time in my life had come when I couldn't carry on a conversation of any length without my thoughts being interrupted. The person who interrupted them was my flamenco dancing partner, Barry. He was fifteen. He wore an earring and a spangled matador jacket. When I danced with Barry, I wore a scarlet flamenco skirt with black frills and a flower from Woolworths in my hair. And so, instead of asking more about John-Jin's growth hormones, I went dancing with Barry in my mind. I replaced the subject of growth hormones with the smell of Barry's underarm deodorant and the sight of his shining teeth. I knew my mind was a vast pavilion, capable of storing an unimaginable quantity of knowledge, but all that was in it – at this moment in my life – was a single item.

And then, John-Jin began growing.

444

We measured him against the kitchen door. When he got to three feet, we gave a party, to which Barry came minus his earring and danced with John-Jin on his shoulders. John-Jin had a laugh like a wind chime. Barry said when he left: 'That kid. He's so sweet. In't he?'

'Now we can stop worrying,' said my mother. 'Everything's going to be okay. He'll never be tall because his real parents almost certainly weren't tall, but he'll be much nearer a normal size. And that's all we were asking for.'

I know something important now. Don't ask for a thing unless you know precisely and absolutely what it is you're going to get and how you're going to get it. Don't ask for the old Pier Pavilion back. There's no such thing as the old Pier Pavilion. There will only be the *new* Pier Pavilion and it will be different. It will not be what you wanted in your imagination. My parents asked for something to make John-Jin grow. They didn't ask what that 'something' was and nor did I. And together we allowed in the unknown.

It took some time to show itself. It took ten years exactly.

I had become a dance student in London when I first learned about it. In a cold phone box, I heard my father say: 'We waited so long for another child. I used to wish for John-Jin at the end of every game of Miniature Golf. Remember that?'

I said: 'Yes, Dad. Except you never told me what it was you were wishing for.'

'Didn't I? Well, never mind. But . . . after all that . . . I never, Susan . . . I mean I never thought about the possibility of losing him.'

'Shall I come home?' I said.

It was near to Christmas. John-Jin was twelve years old. He lay in bed without moving. His curtains were drawn, to rest his eyes, and he had his old gnome night-light on. He said it reminded him of being happy. His speech was beginning to go, but he wanted to talk and talk, while he could still remember enough words. He said: 'Suze, I can't hardly move a toe, but I can still chat, *olé!* Tell me about the world.'

I said: 'Here's some news, then. Remember Barry?'

'Yes.'

'Well, he's in prison. I went to visit him. He stole a van. He remembers you. He sent – '

'If you don't love him any more, it doesn't matter,' said John-Jin.

'No, it doesn't,' I said, 'but he was a good dancer.'

I sat in a chair by John-Jin's bed and he stared up at me. His face-like-a-flower was smooth and creamy and undamaged. After a while, he said: 'I've had it, Suze. Did they tell you?'

I took his hand, which felt cold and heavy in mine. 'Not necessarily,' I said, but he ignored this. He knew every detail about his disease, which had been named after two German scientists called Creutzfeldt and Jacob. It was called CJD for short. It had been there in the growth hormones and had lain dormant in John-Jin for ten years.

He explained: 'The hormones come from human glands. The chief source of pituitaries used to be the mental hospitals – the cadavers no one minded about – and some of these died of CJD. Mum and Dad are going to sue, but it's much too late. Someone should have known, shouldn't they?'

'Why didn't they?'

John-Jin shook his head. He said: 'I can still move my neck, see? I can turn it and look at the room. So why don't you get a flamenco tape and dance while I can still see you. You could become a star, and I would have missed it all.'

I found the music and an old pair of castanets. I put on a black skirt and fixed a bit of tinsel to my hair. I was ready to begin when I looked down and saw that John-Jin was crying. 'Sorry, Suze,' he said. 'Get Mum to come and clean me first. I've no control over anything now. I live in a fucking toilet.'

In the dark December afternoon, I walked out along the pier on my own, along and along it to where it ended at the deep water.

I imagined John-Jin's girder underneath me. I wondered, in my rage, if you took that one piece away, would everything fall?

Trade Wind over Nashville

It was July and hot. At six in the morning, vapour rose from the tarmac parking lots.

'Know somethin', Willa?' said an Early Breakfast customer at the counter of *Mr Pie's* restaurant. 'You look so pretty in that waitress cap, it's like yore dyin' a' beauty!'

'I declare!' said Willa. 'I never heard such a thing in the world!'

The waitress cap was lace. Polyester and cotton lace. Then there was the gingham dress that Willa had to wear. With that on, you didn't see the last days of her thirtieth year passing. No, sir. What you saw were her pushed-up tits and the waist she kept trim and the sweet plumpness of her arms. And as she handed the early customer – one of her 6 a.m. regulars – his plate of egg, sausage and biscuit, he took all of her in – into his crazed head and into his belly.

She lived in a trailer in a trailer park off the airport freeway. Her lover, Vee, had painted the trailer bright staring white, to keep out the Tennessee sun. Willa had a Polaroid picture of Vee with his paint roller and bucket, wearing shorts and a singlet and his cowboy boots. She nailed it up over her bunk, just low enough to reach and touch with her stubby hand. Shoot! she sometimes thought, what kills me dead 'bout Vee is his titchy short legs! And she'd lie there smiling to herself and dealing poker hands in her mind so as to stay awake till he came home. And then, when he did, she'd whisper: 'Vee? That you, Vee, wakin' me up in here?'

'Who else?' he'd ask. 'Who else you got arrivin'?'

'Well then?'

'Well what?'

'Why ain't ya doin' it to me?'

So, on the next lot, at two in the morning, frail Mr Zwebner would wake to hear them shouting and pounding the hell out of their white walls. Zwebner had dreams of Viennese chocolate. Patisseries eaten with a little fork. And what he felt when Willa and Vee woke him was an old, unassuagable greed. 'That Willa,' he'd sigh, 'she's got it coming to her. She's got something, one day soon, gonna come along.'

At *Mr Pie's*, she poured coffee, set up a side order of donuts next to the plate of sausage. Seeing her arm reflected in the shiny counter, she said: 'Lord! Ain't that a terrible sight, the elbow of a person. Look at that, will ya?'

The customer looked up. His mouth was full of egg. He stared at Willa's arm.

'If Vee ever did see that, how wizened an' so forth it is, well, I swear he'd leave me right off. He'd jes take his gee-tar and his boots an' all his songs an' fly away.'

The man wiped his jowls with a chequered napkin. 'He sold any a' his songs yet, that Vee?'

'No. Not a one.'

'Then he ain't gonna leave ya yet.'

'What's that gotta do with him leavin' me or not?'

'Got everythin' to do with it, Willa.'

'I don't see how.'

'Only one thing'll make him quit, honey. And it ain't no piece a' your elbow. It's fame.'

Willa stared at the fat customer with her wide-apart eyes. Trouble with a place like *Mr Pie's*, she said to herself, is everyone stick their noses in your own private thoughts.

Out at Green Hills, in the actual hills that looked away from *Mr Pie's* and all the other roadside diners and all the gas stations and glassed-in malls, lived Lester and Amy Pickering.

Lester was a roofer. He'd started small and poor, working out of a garage in East Nashville. Now, he was halfway to being rich. Halfway exactly was how he thought of it, when he drove down Belle Meade Boulevard and past the Country Club and saw and understood what rich was. And at fifty-two, he'd begun to wonder whether he'd get there, or whether this was how he'd remain – stuck at the halfway point.

'Lester, you know, he's tiring,' said Amy to her friends at the Green Hills Women's Yoga Group. 'I see it plain as death. It's like he's up against a wall and he just don't have the go in him to climb it. It's like gettin' this far took all the vim he had.'

'Well, Amy,' the friends would reply, 'let him tire, honey. You got a good house an' your kids both in college. What more d'you want?'

'Ain't a question of want,' said Amy. 'It's a question of dream. 'Cos one thing you can't stop Lester doing, you can stop him doing 'most anything 'cept having these dreams a' his. He's the type he'll die dreaming. He's descended from a Viking, see? Got this conqueror still goin' round in his veins.'

On that July morning at six, as more of Willa's regular customers stumbled into *Mr Pie's* and she wiped the counter for them, taking care not to look at her elbow's reflection, Lester Pickering climbed into his pick-up and drove south toward Franklin. He'd been asked to tender for a job on a Baptist church, to replace tin with slates. 'Git out here early, Lester,' the Minister had advised, ''for the ole tin git too hot to touch.' And now he was doing sixty-five in the pick-up and his light-weight ladders were rattling like a hailstorm above his head. But his mind wasn't on his destination. He was driving fast to drive away the thoughts he was having, to jolt them out of his damn brain before they took hold and he did something stupid. Thoughts about Amy and the fruit seller. Thoughts about this guy who comes from nowhere and calls Amy up, knows her number an' all, and says meet me at such-and-such parking lot and I'll sell you raspberries from the mountains. And so she goes and she meets him and for two days she's bottling and freezing fruit and making jelly with a smile on her face.

'Who is he?' asks Lester.

'I dunno,' says Amy. 'Name of Tom. That's all I know.'

449

'An' how's he got all them berries? Where they come from?'

'From the hills.'

'What hills?'

'He said it's a secret where they precisely come from, Lester.'

'Why's it a darn secret?'

'I dunno. That's it about a secret, uhn? You often don't know why it is one.'

Lester was driving so fast, he missed the turn-off to the church. He braked and saw in the rear mirror a livestock truck come hissing up right behind him. Ready to ram me, thought Lester, because the thing of it is, people don't care any more. They don't care what they do.

While Willa worked at *Mr Pie's*, Vee slept on in the trailer. The sun got up high. Sweat ran down Vee's thighs and down his neck. He was on the verge of waking, it was so hot and airless in the trailer, but he kept himself asleep and dreaming. In his dreams, he was no longer Vee Easton, cleaner and dogsbody at Opryland; he was Vee La Rivière (he pronounced it 'Veeler Riveer'), songwriter to the stars of the whole darn world of Country Music. He was certain this future would come. He was so certain about it, he wasn't really dreaming it any more, he was thinking it up.

'What's the diffunce between dreamin' an' thinkin', Vee?' asked Willa.

'I'll tell ya, sweetheart. What the diffunce is, is between fairytales and actuality. What them things are now is actual.'

'You mean "real", doncha? You mean *re*-ality, Vee. That's the word you were meanin'.'

'If I'd've meant real, I'd've said real. What I mean is, things actually happening, or, like they say in the Bible, Coming to Pass. Vee La Rivière is gonna Come to Pass.'

And when Vee woke, around eleven, he remembered what day it was. It was the day of the night of his meeting with Herman Berry. *The* Herman Berry, known nationwide, but with his heart and his house still in Nashville and a set of his fingernail clippings in a glass case in the Country Music Hall of Fame, right slap next to Jim Reeves's shoes.

Vee thumped his leg and sat up. He got out of his bunk and snatched up a towel and dried the sweat on him, then opened wide the four windows of the trailer and the daytime world of the trailer park came in, like homely music. He put on some blue stretch swimming trunks and made coffee. He didn't give one single thought to Willa or to anything in his life except this big meeting with Herman Berry, when he would play him three songs he'd written. 'Keep it to three, boy,' Herman had said. 'Keep it to a trinity and I'll listen good. More 'an that and my mind starts walking away.'

But which three would he offer? Veritably speaking, Vee admitted to himself, as he turned the pages of his music notebook, there's only one of Herman's calibre and that's my new one.

He got his guitar and tuned it a bit. He felt suddenly chilly in his torso, so he put one of Willa's thin old counterpanes round his shoulders. Then he flipped the pages to his new song, called *Do Not Disturb*, and played the intro chords. Then he made like he was talking to Herman Berry and explaining the song to him:

'. . . them ther's just the introductory bars, Herman. Key of C minor. Little reprise here before the first verse. A moody reprise, I call it. Let every person know this is a sad song. Tragic song, in all absolute truth. Okay? So here we go with the first verse:

> I went up to my hotel room
> And got some whiskey from the mini-bar . . .

'In parenthetics, Herman, I didn't never stay in no hotel room with a mini-bar, but Willa put me straight on that detail. She said, you can't say "got some whiskey from the bar" just, 'cos what hotel rooms have now is mini-bars, okay? Means adding coupla quavers to the line, but then I keep it scanning in the fourth, like this:

> I set my pills out on the table,
>> And wondered how it all had got this far.

'You get "it all", Herm? "It all", that's his life and the way it's turning out.

'So now, another reprise of the opening chords. Still quietish. Still keeping the tragic mood. Then we're into the second verse, like this:

> I thought of you in Ole Kentucky,
>> And the singing of the sweet blue grass.
> For a year we'd been together,
>> Now you told me, Jim, all things must pass.

'We could change Jim, right? It could be Chuck or Bill, right? Or Herm. It all depends on how you want to personalise it an' make it a true Herman Berry number.

'Anyway, it's the chorus now. Modulation. Big, swoopy modulation to C major here. As we go into the big chorus that all America's gonna be singing soon:

> Believe me, girl, my heart was breaking!
> Breaking tho' I couldn't say a word,
> It was my life I was intent on taking,
> So then I hung the sign out,
> The sign that stopped them finding out,
> The little sign that said Do Not Disturb!

'That's the thing I'm pleased with – the chorus. Whatcha say, Herm? You don't think they're gonna be humming that from Louisiana to Ohio? Before I go to the third verse, tell me how you feel about that big, sad chorus. You don't gotta speak. Just stick your thumbs up.'

Amy Pickering knelt down on her Yoga mat in her living room and folded her large-boned body into a small, coiled position called the Child Position. She shut her eyes. She tried to have

452

vacant, childlike thoughts, but these didn't seem easy to come by, because what was in her mind was Lester.

Why did you lie to him, Amy Pickering? she asked herself. Why did you make out there was a secret about the raspberries? When all that guy was, was some friend of Betty Bushel's that likes to bypass retail and sell direct to housewives?

She didn't know the answer. All she knew was she had liked to do it. Lying about the raspberries had made her feel beautiful. It had. She had stood in her kitchen, smelling all that scented fruit, and feeling like Greta Garbo.

Amy lifted her head. She stretched her neck and smoothed her graying hair that she wore in a French pleat. Beyond the sunlit sills of her room, she could hear the peaceful neighbourhood sounds – lawn mowers and birds and Betty Bushel's dog yapping at shadows.

Then, in her mind, she saw Lester, years ago, wearing his old hunting jacket, standing in his father's yard with his father's dog, Jackson, sniffing at his boots. He'd built the kennel for that dog. He'd put on a neat little shingled roof and that was what got him started on the idea of roofs. 'It had a twenty-six year life, that kennel,' Amy liked to boast fondly. 'Two dogs, both named Jackson one after another, lived to thirteen in it. That's how good made it was. But then, Lester's dad, he said to me: "Dogs is heartbreak, Amy. I jes' can't stick to have another Jackson leave me for the Lord!" So I dunno what he did with that kennel then. 'Less he kept it somewhere to remind him of his son . . .'

He was still alive, the old man. The idea of him dying seemed to hurt Lester in his chest. When he thought about his father dying, he'd knead the area of his heart. And this is what he'd done when Amy had told him her lie about the raspberry seller: he'd stood looking at her and kneading his heart through his draylon shirt.

'Oh my . . .' sighed Amy. 'Oh my, my . . .'

'Git through m' shift at two, be home at three,' Willa had told Vee in the night. 'Then what I'll do, darlin', I'll press your shirt

and tie and steam out the fringes on your coat, so they fall
good. And that way, Herman Berry's not solely gonna 'preciate
your songs, he's gonna see yore an upright person.'

'Upright?' Vee had burst out. 'What's upright got to have to
do with song writing? You could be a mean, wastrelling bum,
an' still make it big in this business, honey. You could be an
orang-utan. It wouldn't matter. 'Cos no one's looking at ya.
They only listening. They only saying to theirselves, Is this
gonna catch on? If I record this *Do Not Disturb*, will it make it to
number one in Anusville, Milwaukee?'

Now, as Willa took off her lace cap and changed out of her
gingham frock, she told her friend, Ileene: 'You could be an
orang-utan an' still make it in Nashville, Ileene. 'Cos the point
is, all anyone's got is their eyes closed.'

'Oh yeh?' said Ileene. 'What about here, then? I swear some
pairs of eyes go up your ass, Willa, when yore wipin' tables.'

'Well, that,' said Willa, 'but then I ain't singin'.'

Ileene shook her head and smiled as she pulled on her lace
cap. 'Darn cap!' She grinned. 'Look like a friggin' French maid
in that, don' I?'

'I dunno,' said Willa dreamily. 'Bein' as how I never saw no
French maid in my whole existence.'

As soon as she got off her bus at the trailer park, Willa knew
that Vee wasn't there, because his car was gone.

'Drove off about half an hour ago with his guitar,' Mr
Zwebner said. On hot days, Mr Zwebner sat on a plastic chair
in the narrow band of shade made by his trailer, reading some
old, mutilated book. Willa could not imagine any mortal life so
monotonous as his.

'Thank you, Mr Zwebner,' she said. Then she added: 'Got an
appointment with Herman Berry tonight. 'Fore the Opry starts.'

'He famous, then? He someone I should know of?'

'Who? Herman Berry?'

'Yeah.'

'You never done heard of Herman Berry, Mr Zwebner?'

'No.'

'You kiddin' me?'

'No.'

'Shoot! I jes' don't believe what yore sayin'! I don't believe my eardrums, Mr Zwebner!'

'Okay. You don't believe.'

'Herman Berry? Why, he's so darn famous, he can't go anywhere without people want to touch him and git bits of him.'

'Why they want to do that, Willa?'

'*Why?* Well, 'cos that's what they wanna do. They wanna touch his fame and have it touch them.'

Mr Zwebner smiled and closed his leatherbound book.

'Have it touch them, eh? Like it's catching?'

'It *is* catchin'. Fame is. I swear. Vee had this friend he used to visit with, who somehow stole a dry-cleanin' ticket offa Dolly Parton's manager or secretary or someone. *One Pair Ladies' Pants, Silver.* Got it framed an' all in a silver frame. And then fame came to him in the form of he began his own dry-cleanin' outlet in Hollywood, an' now he's doin' shirts for Mel Gibson and so forth.'

Mr Zwebner shook his head. Old folks like him, thought Willa, they never believe one word you tell 'em. Like as if reality ended 'fore you was born. So she told him, have a nice afternoon, Mr Zwebner, and went into her trailer and stood in the dark of it, looking at the two bunks, hers and Vee's, and deciding then and there she'd like Vee in her life for ever. She sat down on his bunk that was still damp from his sleep and smoothed his pillow.

Then, in her quiet voice that had this kind of crack in it, ever since she was a kid and sang *Jesus Loves Me, This I Know* with her head lying on her grandma's lap, she began to sing Vee's new song:

> I thought of you in Ole Kentucky,
>> And the singing of the sweet blue grass.
> For a year we'd been together,
>> Now you told me, Jim, all things must pass.

At Lyleswood, Lester was up on his ladders, measuring the tin roof and the tin-capped belfry of the Baptist church. The Minister stood on the ground and stared up.

'Tin warped a bit, Lester?' he called.

'Yeh. It's warped, John.'

'Gonna look a whole lot finer in gray slate!'

'Cost y'all a whole lot more 'an the tin did, too.'

''S okay. We been fund raisin', like I tell you. Auctions. That's the way to do it. Hog auctions. Needlework auctions. Jelly auctions, we even had.'

'Little by little you did it, then?'

'You got it, Lester. Little by little.'

'Same way as I built my business up.'

He was about to smile down at the Reverend, but then and there as he said these words, Lester felt himself falter, like old age had climbed up the ladder and put its hands on his shoulders. He held on to the guttering. Little by little, small contract by small contract, he'd made it to halfway. Halfway between East Nashville and Belle Meade. Halfway to the antebellum-style house he dreamed of with white colonnades and a fruit garden in back, where he'd grow raspberries. But how in hell could he find the strength to make it through the second half? I won't, was his thought. Amy knows I won't, which is why, I guess, she keeps going with that Yoga of hers. Believing, if she can stand on her head, her hopes gonna fall out.

'You okay up there, Lester?' called the Minister.

'Yeh. Coming down now, John.'

Slowly, taking care to feel each rung of the ladder under his shoe before putting his weight on it, Lester descended. He could feel the sun burning down on his bald spot, but his belly was cold.

'Don't it scare you never, bein' up on a roof, Les?'

'No.'

'Guess up there yore nearer to God.'

'Day I'm scared, that's the day I'll quit.'

'How much it's gonna be, then, for the slate roof?'

456

'I ain't worked it out yet.'

''Proximately how much?'

'I ain't done the sums, John.'

'We got four thousand raised. Keep it near to that, an' you'll get the tender. We don't want no big firm comin' in and takin' our money. That's the people's roof, Lester. That's a roof built of crochet and jelly and pies.'

Lester nodded. 'Amy makes a lotta jelly,' he said, 'outta all the summer fruit.'

Willa sat on Vee's bunk a long time, singing. Then she lay down and pulled the damp sheet over her head and went right to sleep.

When she woke, she knew something had changed inside the trailer, so she sat up and stared around and then she got what it was: the hot sun had gone and at the open windows the little thin curtains were flapping about like crazy and the whole air was cold, not like the air of a summer storm, but like the air of winter.

Willa got up and put on one of Vee's sweaters, then closed the windows, snatching the curtains in. She took one look at the sky and swore she'd never seen anything made her more afraid, because the sky was cut in half, half hazy and bright and the other half pitch inky black, and the black half was coming nearer and nearer, like the end of the world was just sliding in over Tennessee.

She wanted to call to someone. She would have even called to Mr Zwebner, but he wasn't outside on his chair. He'd taken his chair in and locked his door, and Willa had the feeling that in the whole trailer park no one was moving.

So she turned on the radio, hoping for some bulletin telling her if the end of the world was coming or not, but all she could get clear enough to hear through the static was the Grand Ole Opry, live, and who was up there singing but Herman Berry. Hearing Herman, she thought, now, soon, I'm gonna feel less scared to my teeth, 'cos Vee's gonna drive home an' be with me.

457

She sat on her hands on Vee's bunk, listening to Herman Berry sing a Johnny Cash number and hoping Vee wasn't there, at the side of the stage where he liked to be, but in the car already, coming towards her. She didn't care one speck whether Herman Berry had liked *Do Not Disturb*; all she minded was whether Vee was going to get to her before the sky fell down on her head.

'Come on!' she called aloud. 'Come on, Vee!'

She turned the radio down and started listening for a car. But all she could hear was the wind. The wind was getting so bad, she felt the trailer move. She felt it rock, or lean or something, like there was an earth tremor under it.

'Willa,' she said to herself, 'yore thirty years old and yore about to die!' And the weirdest thing was, old Herman Berry just went on singing the song and at the end of it the audience clapped and shouted, like the Opry was far away in another state, where the sky was normal and the sun was going down in a normal way.

'Herman,' said Willa, 'the world is endin', honey. Someone go out an' take a look!'

Lester and Amy Pickering were at supper when they first heard the wind. Then the room got dark and Amy said: 'My! Whatever is happening, Lester?'

Lester had a mouthful of corn bread. Chewing, he went to the window and saw what Willa had seen – the slab of darkness moving over the sky.

'Uh-huh,' he said.

'What is it, dear?'

'Boy-o-boy . . .'

'Lester?'

'Take a look, Amy.'

Amy came and stood beside her husband and looked out. Then she took hold of his hand. 'God Almighty, Lester! What the heavens is it?'

'Low pressure. Big low front moving in.'

'Jesus Christ! Looks like a building falling down on us!'

'Severe low. Knock out the power, maybe. Better get us some candles and a flashlight.'

'Shoot! I never seen such a thing!'

'We got any candles?'

'I guess.'

'Get 'em, then, Amy.'

'*God!* I never in my life saw that.'

''S only weather.'

'Don't look like weather, do it? Look like *Apocalypse Now.*'

'Get the candles, okay?'

'Come with me, Lester.'

'Why?'

'I'm scared, that's why.'

'Told you, Amy, it's only weather.'

'Okay so it is. That don't mean I don't have to be afraid.'

'. . . afraid?' said Willa. 'That ain't the word for what I felt that night. If I live to be sixty – which I won't, now my heart's got broke – I'll never be that terrorised. Bad enough it was, I guess, for folk in houses. But for us in the trailer park, well, you couldn't imagine how it was, because that wind, it came and lifted up our homes. It lifted them plumb off the earth, and one of 'em, the trailer of my neighbour, Mr Zwebner, it lifted so high, it came down on the Interstate and how Mr Zwebner didn't die was only because he wasn't *in* his trailer; he was in mine, tryin' to stop me screamin' . . .'

The worst thing was, Vee didn't come home.

If Vee had come, Willa could have clung to him and maybe they would have sung songs or something to keep their fear from getting the better of them. But the hours passed and full night came on, and there wasn't a sign of him. No car arriving. No Vee in his cowboy boots, holding his guitar. Nothing. Just darkness and the screaming, tearing wind and the trailer creaking and moving and the sirens going and all the thin poplars that screened the park from the Interstate snapping in half, like matchwood.

What could Willa do but start screaming?

'Vee!' she screamed. 'Help me, Vee! Vee! Come help me! Vee! Where are ya? Vee! VEE! *VEE!*'

And some time after all that hollering for Vee, there'd been a thumping on her door and she thought, Sweet Jesus, he's home, and she undid the latch and the chain and went to pull him in, to take him in her arms and not let go of him till she died or the wind ceased, whichever came soonest. But it wasn't Vee. It was Mr Zwebner in his thick night clothes that smelled of onion or something, and he began hollering back at her not to scream. 'You make yourself sick with this screaming, Willa, I swear!' he shouted. And he put his smelly hand over her mouth and gripped her arm and shook her like you would shake a chicken, to wring its neck.

And after a moment of this shaking, she came out of her screaming and broke down and sobbed with her head on Mr Zwebner's chest, through which she could hear his old heart still just about beating.

'Mr Zwebner,' sobbed Willa, 'where's Vee? Don't tell me he's gone?'

And then the gust came that pitched Mr Zwebner's trailer onto its end and sent it spinning down onto the freeway.

'Woulda killed him dead,' said Willa, ''cept he was with me, helpin' me in my hour a' need.'

Though Amy had found some candles, she and Lester didn't need them, because, by some kind of miracle, the power lines in Green Hills stayed standing.

What came flying off were the roofs. On almost every house on every bit of the green hills, the wind tore in under the shingles and sent them hurtling down.

Lester heard this happen and saw it in his mind's eye – all the roofs just being blown away. And he stayed up all night, sitting in a chair, not afraid of the wind, but just thinking about it.

Near two o'clock, Amy said: 'Maybe we should go to bed. Or at least lie down for a while?'

But Lester shook his head. 'Can't lie down, Amy,' he said. 'Too much on my brain.'

So they sat on in the living room. Amy picked up photos of their grown-up children and looked at them and thought back to how, when they were little, and they had their rickety old house in East Nashville, they used to be afraid of it in a high wind, as if it planned to do them harm.

But Lester wasn't thinking about his children, or about the past. He was thinking about Belle Meade and the future. He was thinking about money.

'Amy,' he said, after some hours, 'know what?'

'What, Lester?'

'This storm ain't gonna hurt us none.'

'I sure hope not,' said Amy.

And then they were silent again. But Lester smiled as he sat there, because he saw what was coming. In a few months – if he stayed cool and cunning and didn't let the pressure get to him – he could make more money than he'd seen in years. Enough to get beyond this halfway point. Enough for the house with the fruit garden and the colonnades.

Only thing was, he wouldn't be able to do the Baptist church. There just wouldn't be any time for that. 'I sure am sorry, John,' he'd say to the Minister, 'but that night of the storm, it changed a lotta things.'

It got light.

The wind mellowed down, and the people of the trailer park stood about, looking at the ruin all around them.

Half the roof was gone from Willa's home, but it was still standing, so she said to Mr Zwebner: 'You have a nice rest, till the police an' all come, Mr Zwebner. You lie down right here, on Vee's bunk, okay, and cover yourself with the counterpane.'

'What will you do, Willa?'

'Ain't nothin' for me to do, really, 'cept go to work. Take my mind offa things. Always supposin' *Mr Pie's* ain't blown away to Kansas.'

So Willa washed her face and hands, wiped all the blotched

461

shadow from her eyelids and put on fresh, and went to wait for the 5.30 a.m. bus, which didn't arrive.

She began to walk. The sky was a kind of dead white colour and there were no shadows anywhere on anything.

As she walked, she thought, I dunno, I jes' dunno what coulda happened that Vee never got home. It's like God said: 'I'm gonna take one on them, Willa. Vee, or the trailer. I'm gonna puff one on them away.' 'Cos what life is, it's never all the way you want it. More like half. Like you can have Vee, or you can have your home be one of the lucky ones not destroyed by the wind. But you can't have both.

Soon after Willa arrived at *Mr Pie's*, while she and Ileene were still setting up the relishes and sauces, Lester Pickering came in and sat down at the counter and ordered an Early Breakfast.

He knew Willa by name, for it was a thing he loved to do, to get up early, while Amy was still sleeping, and treat himself to sausage, biscuit, grits, hash browns and egg before he went to work.

'How yo're, Willa?' he asked, with a grin. 'Survive the storm, did ya?'

'Just about, Mr Pickering. Trailer next to mine blew down. You want coffee, sir?'

'Sure. Lotsa coffee. Sat in a damn chair all night.'

'Me, my neighbour done come in to quieten me. I was screamin' so hard, I couldn't hear m'self.'

'Where was Vee, then?' asked Ileene. 'He didn't come back after his big success, then?'

'What "big success"?'

'You didn't listen to the Opry, Willa?'

'Sure. Bits of it.'

'You didn't hear Herman Berry?'

'Yeh. I heard him.'

'Singin' Vee's song?'

'He weren't singin' no songa Vee's. He was singin' a Johnny Cash number.'

'Before that, he sang Vee's song.'

'You was hearin' things, Ileene.'

'No, I wasn't. Tell you the title of the song, if you want: *Do Not Disturb*. Told the audience, "I learned this just today, in one afternoon, 'cos I liked it so much I wanted to sing for y'all tonight. An' it's written by a new songwriter, resident here in Nashville, name of Vee La Rivière."'

Willa put the coffee back on its burner. She rested her elbow on the chrome counter and gave Ileene one of the long, hard stares she was famous for in her childhood.

'You lyin' to me, Ileene?'

'No. I ain't lyin'. *Do Not Disturb*. He ain't written a song called that?'

'Yeh. That's his new one.'

'Well then. There y'are. He's famous now. Vee La Rivière.'

Willa said nothing more to Ileene. She went into the kitchen and waited there while Fat Pete cooked Lester Pickering's breakfast. Then she took the plate of sausage and grits and the side order of donuts and set them up on the counter.

'Everything okay for you here, Mr Pickering?'

'Yes, thank you, Willa.'

'You gonna be busy, I guess, with all them roofs flyin' off?'

'Yeh. Busier than I ever been.'

'What happens, then, to folk as lost their roof? Insurance pays, do they?'

'Yeh. Most everyone's got coverage.'

'That's lucky.' Then she smiled at Lester Pickering, whose mouth was stuffed with sausage. 'Shame I couldn't of had somethin' like that on Vee,' she said. 'Some insurance, like. Know what I mean? So that when his good luck blew in, I was covered. Know what I'm sayin', Mr Pickering?'

Over

Waking is the hardest thing they ask of him.

The nurse always wakes him with the word 'morning', and the word 'morning' brings a hurting into his head which he cannot control or ameliorate or do anything about. Very often, the word 'morning' interrupts his dreams. In these dreams there is a stoat somewhere. This is all he can say about them.

The nurse opens his mouth, which tastes of seed, and fills it with teeth. 'These teeth have got too big for me,' he sometimes remarks, but neither the nurse nor his wife replies to this just as neither the nurse nor his wife laughs when from some part of his ancient self he brings out a joke he did not know he could still remember. He isn't even certain they smile at his jokes because he can't see faces any longer unless they are no more and no less than two feet from his eyes. 'Aren't you even smiling?' he sometimes shouts.

'I'm smiling, sir,' says the nurse.

'Naturally, I'm smiling,' says his wife.

He's being nursed at home in his own small room that was once a dressing room. His curtains are drawn back and light floods in. To him, light is time. Until nightfall, it lies on his skin, seeping just a little into the pores yet never penetrating inside him, neither into his brain nor into his heart nor into any crevice or crease of him. Light and time, time and light, lie on him as weightless as the sheet. He is somewhere else. He is in the place where the jokes come from, where the dreams of stoats lie. He refuses ever to leave it except upon one condition.

That condition is seldom satisfied, yet every morning, after his teeth are in, he asks the nurse: 'Is my son coming today?'

464

'Not that I know of, sir,' she replies.

So then he takes no notice of the things he does. He eats his boiled egg. He pisses into a jar. He puts a kiss as thin as air on his wife's cheek. He tells the nurse the joke about the Talking Dog. He folds his arms across his chest. He dreams of being asleep.

But once in a while – once a fortnight perhaps, or once a month? – the nurse will say as she lifts him up onto his pillows: 'Your son's arrived, sir.'

Then he'll reach up and try to neaten the silk scarf he wears at his throat. He will ask for his window to be opened wider. He will sniff the room and wonder whether it doesn't smell peculiarly of waterweed.

The son is a big man, balding, with kind eyes. Always and without fail he arrives in the room with a bottle of champagne and two glasses held upside down between his first and second fingers.

'How are you?' he asks.

'That's a stupid question,' says the father.

The son sits by the bed and the father looks and looks for him with his faded eyes and they sip the drink. Neither the nurse nor the wife disturbs them.

'Stay a bit,' says the father, 'won't you?'

'I can't stay long,' says the son.

Sometimes the father weeps without knowing it. All he knows is that with his son there, time is no longer a thing that covers him, but an element in which he floats and which fills his head and his heart until he is both brimming with it and buoyant on the current of it.

When the champagne has all been drunk, the son and the nurse carry the father downstairs and put him into the son's Jaguar and cover his knees with a rug. The father and the son drive off down the Hampshire lanes. Light falls in dapples on the old man's temples and on his folded hands.

There was a period of years that arrived as the father was beginning to get old when the son went to work in the Middle

East and came home only once or twice a year, bringing presents made in Japan which the father did not trust.

It was then that the old man began his hatred of time. He couldn't bear to see anything endure. What he longed for was for things to be over. He did the *Times* crossword only to fill up the waiting spaces. He read the newspaper only to finish it and fold it and place it in the wastepaper basket. He snipped off from the rose bushes not only the dead heads but the blooms that were still living. At mealtimes, he cleared the cutlery from the table before the meal was finished. He drove out with his wife to visit friends to find that he longed, upon arrival, for the moment of departure. When he made his bed in the morning, he would put on the bedcover, then turn it down again, ready for the night.

His wife watched and suffered. She felt he was robbing her of life. She was his second wife, less beautiful and less loved than the first (the mother of his son) who had been a dancer and who had liked to spring into his arms from a sequence of three cartwheels. He sometimes dismayed the second wife by telling her about the day when the first wife did a cartwheel in the revolving doors of the Ritz. 'I've heard that story, darling,' she'd say politely, ashamed for him that he could tell it so proudly. And to her bridge friends she'd confide: 'It's as if he believes that by rushing through the *now* he'll get back to the *then*.'

He began a practice of adding things up. He would try to put a finite number on the oysters he had eaten since the war. He counted the cigarettes his wife smoked in a day and the number of times she mislaid her lighter. He tried to make a sum of the remembered cartwheels. Then when he had done these additions, he would draw a neat line through them, like the line a captive draws through each recorded clutch of days, and fold the paper in half and then in quarters and so on until it could not be folded any smaller and then place it carefully in the wastepaper basket next to the finished *Times*.

'Now we know,' his wife once heard him mutter. 'Now we know all about it.'

*

When the war ended he was still married to the dancer. His son was five years old. They lived in a manor house with an ancient tennis court and an east-facing croquet lawn. Though his head was still full of the war, he had a touching faith in the future and he usually knew, as each night descended, that he was looking forward to the day.

Very often, in the summer of 1946, he would wake when the sun came up and, leaving the dancer sleeping, would go out onto the croquet lawn wearing his dressing gown and slippers from Simpson's of Piccadilly and stare at the dew on the grass, at the shine on the croquet hoops and at the sky, turning. He had the feeling that he and the world made a handsome pair.

One morning, he saw a stoat on the lawn. The stoat was running round the croquet hoops and then in and out of them in a strange repeated pattern, as if it were taking part in a stoat gymkhana. The man did not move, but stood and watched. Then he backed off into the house and ran up the stairs to the room where his son was sleeping.

'Wake up!' he said to the little boy. 'I've got something to show you!'

He took his son's hand and led him barefoot down the stairs and out into the garden. The stoat was still running round and through the croquet hoops and now, as the man and the boy stood watching, it decided to leap over the hoops, jumping twice its height into the air and rolling over in a somersault as it landed, then flicking its tail as it turned and ran in for another leap.

The boy, still dizzy with sleep, opened his mouth and opened wide his blue eyes. He knew he must not move so he did not even look round when his father left his side and went back into the house. He shivered a little in the dewy air. He wanted to creep forward so that he could be in the sun. He tiptoed out across the gravel that hurt his feet and onto the soft, wet lawn. The stoat saw him and whipped its body to a halt, head up, tail flat, regarding the boy. The boy could see its eyes. He thought how sleek and slippery it looked and how he would like to stroke its head with his finger.

The father returned. 'Don't move!' he whispered to his son, so the boy did not turn.

The father took aim with his shotgun and fired. He hit the stoat right in the head and its body flew up into the air before it fell without a sound. The man laughed with joy at the cleanness and beauty of the shot. He laughed a loud, happy laugh and then he looked down at his son for approval. But the boy was not there. The boy had walked back inside the house, leaving his father alone in the bright morning.

Acknowledgements

Some of the stories in this collection first appeared in the following publications: 'The Colonel's Daughter', *Grand Street* (USA), Winter 1984; 'My Wife is a White Russian', *Granta*, 1983; 'Dinner for One', *Woman's Own*, 1982; 'Current Account', *Woman's Own*, 1983; 'The Stately Roller Coaster', *Encounter*, 1984; 'A Shooting Season', *Cosmopolitan*, 1984; 'Will and Lou's Boy', *Paris Review*, Summer 1985; 'The Garden of the Villa Mollini', *Critical Quarterly*, January 1987; 'Tropical Fish', *Listener*, July 1985; 'La Plume de Mon Ami', *Foreign Exchange*, ed. Julian Evans, Hamish Hamilton and Abacus, 1985; 'Wildtrack', *Winter's Tales: New Series 2*, ed. Robin Baird-Smith, Constable, 1986; 'The Kite Flyer', *The Seven Deadly Sins*, Severn House, 1984; 'The Bellows of the Fire', *Good Housekeeping*, 1987; 'The Candle Maker', *Trio*, Penguin, 1993; 'Two of Them', *Marie Claire*, August 1992; 'The Crossing of Herald Montjoy', *Independent*, December 1993; 'Ice Dancing', *Telling Stories*, Sceptre, 1993; 'John-Jin', *Observer*, December 1993; 'Trade Wind over Nashville', *Pandora's Stories IV*, Pandora, 1990; and 'Over', *Soho Square III*, Bloomsbury, 1990.